CLICK

by

Sara Marx

Bella
BOOKS

2014

Other Bella Books by Sara Marx

Before I Died
Decoded
Insight of the Seer (with Linda Andersson)
Mina Borsalino Flips Out

Dedication

Sincerest thanks (and love and praise) to my editor, Katherine V. Forrest. She has proven to be my all-knowing guide on this lovely writing journey and also, my true life super-heroine. K.V.—you are awesome. Keep on rockin'…

To all the usual suspects: My love and appreciation for you has no end. I do know how very lucky I am.

About the Author

Sara lives with her family in Southwest Florida where she writes, sips coffee, and chases dogs and kids.

CHAPTER ONE

From her place in bed she watched him move around the room, momentarily disappearing into the long closet and reemerging with cufflinks. He paused before the full-length mirror to fasten the monogrammed jewels in place and proceeded to pluck invisible lint from his white slacks. His crisp shirt and jacket were also white, as was his bowtie, and all were linen in keeping with the evening's theme. Kathleen quietly watched him perform these rituals and when he caught her studying him in the mirror, he turned to face her.

Her dry, thin lips turned upward in her shy smile, which did little to brighten her waxen complexion or improve the dark crescents beneath her eyes. He went to her and carefully perched himself on the edge of the bed they shared. As was his habit, his actions were swift, businesslike, and the rapidity of his movement caused her to flinch unnecessarily. When his hand came to a rest on her forehead, she relaxed against his gentle touch as he checked for fever. He dragged his fingers along her face and stroked her cheek. She nuzzled his palm and kissed it.

"I'm sorry about tonight," she whispered, raising wide eyes to look into his. "Are you disappointed in me?"

"My concern is for you, my love. I want you healthy."

She clasped his hand between hers, as if in appreciation or prayer, one of her many childlike mannerisms she knew he adored. His world revolved around her innocent ways, her eye for artistic detail, and admittedly, that he could take utter possession of her in the bedroom. He devoted to her a brand of attention that bordered obsessive, cultivating every aspect of their relationship with the care a gardener would in tending a prized orchid. When she was good, all was right in his world and he felt powerful and grand. It was this poise that made him New Orleans royalty and a force to be reckoned with in the art world.

She also knew all this and wondered if he could possibly survive without the confidence she'd provided him for so long. If he could personally survive, she wondered if his business would.

"How do I look?" he asked her, stiffening his posture for her appraisal.

"Very aristocratic, Mr. Fortier." She kissed his hand once more. "The women will be climbing over themselves to get at you."

He wrapped his arms around her and pulled her close, then kissed her, deeply and with a sense of familiar urgency. She wondered if his confidence required sex before he faced the masses on this night.

"They can climb over themselves if they wish, but I've got my Kathleen," he whispered, tightening his hold. "Always."

After a moment, she nudged away, but only as far as his hold would allow. "Let's not get you sick, darling."

His emotions appeared to be teetering between hurt for having been shrugged off and genuine concern for her illness. He loosened his hold and stood. Back at the mirror, he adjusted his tie, his eyes flitting between her reflection and his own. "If you're not better by tomorrow, I'm calling the doctor."

"I'll be better," she weakly promised him. She snuggled into the pillows, rubbing her bare arms. Her chest felt dreadfully tight and her head ached as she surveyed the white blankets on the white bed, in the all-white room. Richard's present white uniform nearly camouflaged him against the sterile surroundings. Were it not for his sun-kissed skin, he might have disappeared right before her eyes.

He stopped fiddling with his tie and turned to face her. His tone took on severity. "Perhaps I should stay with you."

Her heart surged against her ribs, but she made no display of emotion. Instead, she calmly nestled back into the pillows. "You could, but you love White Linen Night more than anyone. It's your night to shine."

"I can't shine knowing you're unwell." Again he was at her bedside, checking for temperature. "Not a drop of temperature. There couldn't be worse possible timing."

"It's probably a little virus," she sweetly cut him off. "A doctor would only prescribe rest for such a thing."

Wearing a conflicted expression, he glanced at his watch. "I did hire extra help for tonight's events…"

She attempted to compound the thought she knew was surely in his mind. "Are you sure you can you trust them?" She then gave him a final push. "You know how transient they can be."

He did. He bent to kiss her. He hesitated once more at the door, but at last he left.

She counted the minutes, enough to be sure he'd made every stop his obsessive routine required—the nursery, the library for his briefcase, then a sweep through the first floor to make sure the butler had done his job well—then she slipped out of bed and went to the window. The angle made it difficult to see when he'd made his precise exit, but soon enough he crossed the street to his awaiting car. The driver would ferry him through the French Quarter to the Warehouse District, then deposit him as close as possible to The Fortier Gallery.

As he did each year, he'd make the short walk, greeting patrons and artistic friends along the way, each step further enveloping him in his beloved art festival where he was a celebrity. The event drew thousands, go-drinks in one hand, paper fans wagging in the other, white as far as the eye could see. It was a grand tradition that bolstered art sales of the known and unknown, a gala unstoppable by neither weather nor politics. On this night, humidity had the city in a chokehold, a detail that wouldn't rate any more notice than Kathleen's absence from the event.

She watched until Richard's car was out of sight. The butler crossed the street seconds later for his nightly grocery run, just like clockwork. Kathleen looked at her scanty attire—a sheer nightie that barely came to her panties, the same as all her nighties, each hand-selected by Richard—then hurried to the master bath.

She filled the sink with water and dabbed her face with makeup remover until the dark circles under her eyes were gone and she was left looking like she'd cried black tears. Using toilet tissue, she dabbed the delicate area beneath her eyes then splashed water on her face until the water ran clear. When her face was pink and the dark makeup gone, she discarded the black clumps of tissue into the toilet and flushed. She started over with simple mascara, powder, and a bit of light lipstick.

In the narrow closet complex just off the master bedroom, she rummaged the racks until she found the white dress she'd worn at last year's event. Removing the dry cleaner's plastic, she shimmied into the costume, catching glances of herself in the full-length mirror. It didn't matter that it wasn't a particularly fashionable dress, but it did matter that it looked expensive. Grabbing the matching white mesh hat, she hurried back into the bathroom. There she pinned back her hair, allowing tendrils to spill away and softly frame her face. No matter her nice appearance, her stomach felt fluttery and her heartbeat loudly pounded in her head. She hoped her acting job hadn't been such a good one she'd convinced even herself. There was no time to think about it at present.

Back in the closet, she walked the length of shoe racks, counting until she came to number ten. It was the one she'd unbolted from the wall a week before, but left standing in its place. On the same day, the panel it hid had also been jimmied loose with a butter knife. Now, she pulled the heavy rack away from the wall then pounded the loose panel with the heel of her hand. At last it budged making it possible for her to grab the strap of the bag she'd put there. She heard a skittering sound and tried not to think about what else might also be hidden behind the walls. She tugged the bag from its cavern, then re-closed the wall and replaced the rack. Assessing the closet, she deemed it normal looking before hauling the bulging bag back into the main room. She quickly collected the dry cleaner's wrap she'd earlier removed from the dress and shoved it into the zipper compartment of the bag. She would leave no clues.

Kathleen slipped into low heels before softly, swiftly heading down the hallway.

There was another very integral component of her plan, one that would significantly raise the risk the operation might fail, but would ensure ultimate success if it did not. She calmed herself, employing every effort to tamp down emotions, a necessary approach in her plan. She ducked into the nursery where the child was already asleep.

She quickly realized the combined weight of the bag and sleeping toddler was more than she'd anticipated. With growing determination, she mustered her strength. So preoccupied with her internal pep talk was she, she turned around and nearly smacked into the nanny.

Cecelia had hair dyed so black it glinted blue in the nursery nightlight. Her red lips were a sharp contrast to her ghoulishly stark white skin and her eyes looked like they should rightfully belong to a cat. She moved like a cat, too.

Kathleen caught her breath. "We're going to have to put a bell around your neck, Cecelia. You startled me." She attempted to move around her, but the nanny took a sideways step to prevent her. Kathleen shot her an accusing glare. "Now, if you'll excuse me."

"You're looking much better," Cecelia practically purred. She seemed pleased at having caught the lady of the house in a misdeed yet to be determined. Eyes sparkling with both intrigue and humor, she went on. "It's like...a miracle."

Kathleen tried not to show her surprise. Normally she behaved calmly and coolly, whether at home, in his social circles, or around the gallery. The nanny was another story. Nothing seemed to rattle her. With her, Kathleen figured she could have well met her match.

"I am feeling better, thank you." Kathleen's tone wavered. She again attempted to move past the nanny, and again she was blocked.

"Richard said you were staying in for the evening." The nanny's low voice was tinged with smugness.

Cecelia's use of Richard's name was too frequent, too familiar. The minor twinge of anger it elicited from Kathleen was more about disrespect than jealousy, but it was enough to reignite her waning courage. "*Mr. Fortier* knows very well that we are joining him at the gallery."

Again Kathleen started around her, and again, Cecilia took a step to stop her.

"Certainly White Linen Night is no place for a child to be." The nanny wasn't deterred and didn't attempt to mask her condescending attitude. "I think I'll phone her father to be sure."

"You will refrain from speaking to me that way," Kathleen said, mustering her best authoritative voice. "Now, if you'll excuse me."

The nanny didn't attempt to stop her again. Kathleen held her bag and the child tightly to her, both extremely valuable, though for different reasons. Second thoughts had her thinking she didn't need to make an unnecessary enemy of the woman. After all, she could call Richard the moment Kathleen stepped out the door and the plan would be over before it had begun. She could understand why her newfound healthy glow and her appearance in the nursery only minutes after Richard's departure were suspicious.

Pausing a moment in the doorway, she again turned to face the nanny.

"Cece, we may not last the entire night with Mr. Fortier, since I have been under the weather." Kathleen shoved a hand into her bag and fumbled until she produced two one hundred-dollar bills. "But there's no need for you to hang around here, waiting. Take the rest of the evening off."

Any trepidation the nanny may have felt was wearing off as she looked at the bills. Kathleen waved the money again, silently willing her to take the money. For a moment, she considered offering more, but stopped herself. A move like that would make her look desperate, and again would surely warrant a call to Richard the moment she stepped out the door. The look on the nanny's face was hard to read, and Kathleen hoped money represented something—a tattoo, a night on the town—anything that would trump the bizarre allegiance she had for her boss. At last, Cecilia accepted it, eyeing her with more curiosity than suspicion.

"I don't think Richard allows you nearly enough time off. I hate to go against him, but I was once your age." Kathleen worked up her most convincing smile, though she sincerely doubted she'd ever had a single thing in common with this particular girl. That she'd taken the money offered her said Cecelia might be a con, and that had Kathleen rethinking her position on their commonalities. She forged ahead. "There's no need to mention the money to him."

As Cecilia pocketed the money Kathleen again started for the door, hopeful her performance had been a convincing one. On the landing outside the nursery, she made an authentic-sounding offer. "If you're headed to the Warehouse District, you're certainly welcome to ride with us."

After a moment, Cecilia gave her a forced smile. "Not my scene, thanks."

The deal was sealed. Trying to conceal her glee, Kathleen added, "Have a good night, however you spend it."

The child had roused from sleep, which made Kathleen nervous despite the emptiness of the house. She smiled and shushed the child as she carried her down the stairs of a house that was dark not because of the time of day, but because that was how Richard liked it. With the exception of the antiseptic room they shared and the colorful nursery, the house was otherwise drearily decorated with heavy woodwork, rich mahoganies, and deep purples, sparingly lit by rustic lamps. The place was as daunting and dark as the nanny, which had Kathleen wondering if the woman had been hired for nannying skills or for the sake of performance art against Richard's hand-selected décor.

Kathleen offered the child a rather unconvincing sort of assurance, speaking soothingly as she carefully took each stair step.

"Mrs. Fortier!"

Kathleen froze. She clutched the child to her body, feeling every bit of blood drain from her face. Her arms strained with the physical weight she attempted to bear and her head was heavy with worry. Her future and the money were suddenly in jeopardy. If Richard were to come home, the child would stay and no doubt she would be made to answer for her actions; without the child, the plan was off. Kathleen began mentally kissing the money goodbye…

She stared longingly at the front door only feet away then turned to see Cecelia on the landing above her. She mustered every bit of calm she had within her. "Yes, Cecelia?"

After brief hesitation, the nanny asked, "You think Mr. Fortier would mind if I stayed out for the night?"

Kathleen let out the breath she'd drawn in so tight her chest ached. She hoped it didn't show. "I think what Mr. Fortier doesn't know won't hurt him."

"Cool." The girl finally grinned then walked down the stairs and right past them, pausing only long enough to hold the door for Kathleen and the child. She watched the nanny go, then turned and headed the opposite direction.

The evening light was blinding compared to the dark interior of the mansion. The air was heavy and wet and carrying her load quickly had her weary. To her relief, a cab driver quickly spotted her and pulled curbside before she could trouble to flag him down. He hurried around and opened the door for her, perhaps because she was beautiful; more likely because he recognized her white attire, which hinted at society. She was clearly of means.

"Warehouse District, madam?"

"No," she said, breathless not from having hauled the child or bag, but from having committed multiple acts of deception in only a few short minutes. "Mandeville, please."

As the cab pulled away from the curb, she turned in her seat, looking for any sign she was being followed. She buckled the seat belt around the child, then gave the tot what she hoped was a reassuring smile.

The oversized bag was heavy on her feet and Kathleen plunged her hand through the zipper opening, gaining the smallest confidence as she ran her hand along the bound stacks of cash. It was now short two hundred dollars, but buying off the nanny was her first good move. Her next would be even better. She zipped the bag, sat up, and fastened her own seat belt.

Ten minutes later, the cab was on the causeway headed for the other shore. Only then did she consider the amazing feat she was pulling off. She had the child and she had the money. Between heartbeats, it finally began to feel real. The good life was within reach.

CHAPTER TWO

Five hours she'd driven for a hurricane: pink rum punch garnished with an orange slice, frozen or on the rocks, a tasty delight served in an hourglass-shaped souvenir glass stamped with the green Pat O'Brien logo. The bar was a definite first stop for tourists, but Shel Carson rated it stop number two.

First, there was business to attend to, an interview for a job she was certain she'd turn down, but as she'd already accepted travel money and made the trip through pouring rain in her wobbly, rusting Mustang, she figured she might as well hear the guy out.

She made her exit off I-10 and almost hydroplaned past her Toulouse turn. She slammed on the brakes hard enough to cause the balding tires to slip, and managed the turn, exhaling with enough breathy irritation to set her errant bangs fluttering. *Ten minutes*, she promised herself, *in and out*. Then she'd set about soaking up the New Orleans atmosphere along with its requisite booze.

She'd booked a room at Le Richelieu, a boutique hotel in the lower quarter, one block over from the Old Ursuline Convent. She'd selected the place. At $160 a night, it was a considerable downgrade from the Ritz, which Richard Fortier had suggested, and he was footing the bill. But Le Richelieu appealed in that it was too old, stale, and allegedly too haunted. Congruent with her mood of late.

Arriving at the hotel, she checked in, showered, and left in time to arrive on Fortier's doorstep promptly at seven p.m., per his instructions.

The measly two-block walk in the smothering post-rain humidity had her dabbing a thin line of sweat off her forehead. She took a backward step off the sidewalk and squinted behind crooked sunglasses at the three-story mansion on the corner of Royal and Governor Nicholls streets.

The mansion was a looming extravagance, slate gray, with tall, black-shuttered windows in a marked contrast to the delicate, lacy iron balconies. The palatial estate looked more like a hotel than Le Richelieu and Shel had an inkling of its historical significance. Tourists lingered on the sidewalks and streets, snapping pictures, and casting occasional curious glances in Shel's direction as she stood on the doorstep. She began to wonder if she had the right place. Could someone actually live here?

She fished around in her pants pocket to retrieve the crumpled memo, but the door opened before she could double-check the address. The sharp-featured man standing on the threshold nearly filled the doorway with his height, but certainly not his frame, which was gaunt at best. He was quite formally attired—a butler, she surmised. His narrow, ferrety eyes appeared to size her up and spit her out simultaneously. When at last he spoke, his tone was as off-putting and as stiff as his appearance.

"Ms. Carson?" She only nodded. He looked like a corpse. His frozen, blue-tinted lips barely moved when he spoke. "This way, madam." He turned with a poise that would have easily permitted him to balance a stack of books on top of his elongated skull.

Shel followed him into the foyer, her damp shoes alternately squeaking and shushing in the butler's pristine wake as she crossed the marble floor. The heavy door closed behind her, creating a powerful reverberation off narrow hallway walls. She removed her sunglasses and dropped them into her jacket pocket, a move that did little to brighten the dark quarters.

She followed the old gentleman over Persian rugs, past outlandish gold-plated banisters, and down marbled checkerboard hallways with floor-to-ceiling portraits on either side. She studied the bizarre cacophonies of hooded figures fighting mythic beasts, almost cartoonish scenarios that appeared at odds with their exquisite gold antique frames.

Shel knew her potential employer had money. His offer hinted at it. Suddenly surrounded by such opulence—and strangeness— she found herself straightening her posture and flipping her hands through the ends of her dark, still damp hair to smooth it.

The butler pushed through another towering door and stood back, an unspoken invitation for her to enter what appeared to be a library. When he wordlessly left her, she found herself expelling a breath she didn't even know she'd been holding.

She turned in a slow circle. The oversized room seemed uncharacteristic of the period architecture and she wondered if the space had once been multiple smaller rooms. Still, the physical size of the library could not challenge a smallness created by enormous furnishings and bulging bookcases, just as the elaborate lighting could not combat the darkness created by deep burgundy walls, or the long shadows cast by teetering stacks of books. The room was at war with itself.

Her curious gaze wandered along volumes of rich, leatherbound books that lined shelves ending just below the soaring handpainted ceiling. The pièce de résistance was the ornate chandelier dangling from an antique medallion, ending in an elaborate blossom of crystal tears. She craned her neck to study it.

The heavy whoosh of the door opening nearly caused her whiplash. Embarrassed that she'd been easily spooked, Shel cleared her throat, feeling her cheeks warm. She extended a hand to the broadly grinning, handsome fellow who'd just entered the room, and hoped her voice didn't rattle. "Mr. Fortier."

"Correct," he said, exposing dimples at each end of his reflexive smile. His blue eyes were engaging and he owned the firm handshake of a businessman used to getting his way.

Shel glanced down at their joined hands and noticed the stark contrast between her pale, spotted skin and ratty fingernails versus Fortier's smooth olive skin and perfect manicure. She quickly pulled out of his clutch and discreetly bit her lip. She figured he was used to such reactions from women, though she doubted from women like her.

She raised her chin slightly, resolved not to advance him the upper hand in a game she'd not yet determined. He motioned toward a wingback chair and seated himself in another chair facing her.

For the next few minutes, he made small talk about the weather while she internally took back the power her nerves had almost caused her to give up. She made a silent inventory of the man: white designer shirt cuffed at the elbows, crisp despite the humidity that had enveloped the city; pressed tan linen pants; Rolex; and shiny, cordovan shoes. With his sculpted chin, high cheekbones and enough copper-kissed blond hair to rival Redford, she concluded Richard Fortier would look patrician even without the benefit of his expensive threads.

She realized he was studying her right back.

At that moment, he concluded his introductory small talk. "Welcome to the fair city of New Orleans, Ms. Carson. What can I get you to drink?" He said "N'awlins" and his Rs sounded like *ahs*. She pegged him for a lifer.

"Nothing," she said, almost surprised by her brusque tone as she moved to advance the appointment. "What did you want to see me about, Mr. Fortier?"

His grin was crooked and slow growing. She noticed a twinkle of admiration in his bright eyes. "A woman of business. Amen."

He stood and made his way to a narrow space between the bookcases and toward a cast-iron fireplace with ribbon ornamentation and a slate top, which served as a dry bar. She watched him plunk two ice cubes into a glass tumbler and pour himself a drink. "I'm a man of business myself, but I find that a little scotch gets things off to a fine start." He replaced the stopper on the decanter and turned to face her, gently swirling the amber liquid in his glass. "Helps loosen the tongue. You sure you won't change your mind?"

She shook her head.

He lifted his glass up in a faux toast before taking a good gulp, and crossed the room to stand in front of her, studying her closely as if deciding whether she was the woman for the job. Her discomfort grew with his obvious scrutiny until his gaze at last locked with hers. He nodded, his decision apparently made, then turned and headed for the door. "Walk with me, Ms. Carson."

She followed him down the same narrow length of hallway, which afforded her a second look at the massive paintings. The odd, purplish-gray hues of the work coupled with early evening shadows had turned the general atmosphere of the mansion even darker and more foreboding, the oils boasting swirling black skies and fire among other macabre themes. She found herself slowing to study a particular painting that included a broken, bleeding body of a man. She stifled her desire to wince, but the small, involuntary movement didn't go unnoticed by her host.

"Truman Broussard," he told her.

"Beg your pardon?"

"The artist." He stopped before a particularly demonic portrait. "Very well liked in these parts."

"I'll run out and get one."

"Solid investment." He took her dig with a grin. "Mr. Broussard was commissioned a few years back to do some of the portraiture for the residence. Not by me, but by a very smart gentleman who realized the value they'd add to this property."

The ghoulish works ignited a chill within her. "Do you own this home, Mr. Fortier?" She reconsidered and quietly amended her question. "Is this place a home?"

He chuckled. "Indeed it is, and yes, I own it." They walked on. "A little further, if you will."

He led her to another room full of black leather and rich burgundy brocade furniture. In truth, she thought the décor looked every bit the part of an old-time whorehouse. The threshold marked an abrupt change from marble to dark hardwood floors. Soon, she altered her opinion from whorehouse to vampire's den.

Fortier motioned toward a pair of leather wingback chairs situated across from each other, and she wondered why they'd changed rooms in the first place. Perhaps he was showing off, but for the life of her she couldn't imagine why. "Please, make yourself comfortable," he said.

She doubted that would be possible in such a place. Her brow scrunched up at his elaborate foreplay of sorts, but she sat down anyway. She studied a picture of the St. Louis cemetery under violet skies for several minutes before giving him her attention.

"You like?" he asked.

"It's a bit morbid for my taste," she replied.

He chuckled and politely launched into a lengthy narrative about artistic influence, utilizing pretty words and a voice so soothing she nearly nodded off. Perhaps she was worn out from the rainy drive. She sat up straight, resisting an urge to yawn.

Since clearly he wanted to discuss himself and his home, she appeased him. "What is it you do, Mr. Fortier?"

"I broker art."

"Of course."

"I know what's on the market at all times. If it's available for purchase, I'll find it. If it's not, well, I can be very persuasive." He smiled.

"I'm sure."

"I also have a small gallery on Julia Street, a showcase of sorts for local artists and a few favorites."

While she listened, Shel noted the central figure in the purple painting—a demon—had eyes that seemed to follow her no matter where she leaned to avoid them. She gave up. The time for polite talk was over. She repeated her initial inquiry, "Why did you call me here?"

"A mutual acquaintance recommended your services to me," he carefully began, his tone and the conversation taking a sudden serious turn. "He believes you to be properly qualified and I have a high opinion of his word."

She couldn't possibly imagine an acquaintance they'd have in common. She didn't bother to consider the possibilities. None of them were good. "Who can I thank for the referral?" she dryly asked. "I'll send a basket."

He ignored her sarcasm and her question. "I've looked at your background. Impressive undercover work with the Shreveport police, all those service awards, commendations and the like." He took the last sip of his drink and set it aside.

On cue, the butler entered the room and took his glass. To Shel, it seemed the meeting had been choreographed down to the smallest detail.

Fortier seemed to sense her discomfort and waited for the butler to go before continuing. "Then you hit that little snag with the drug problem, which is certainly understandable. I mean, how can one so deeply submerse oneself into the culture without doing a little business to prove a point. Am I right?"

He'd poked her in her only, albeit very large, sore spot. His smugness disgusted her. She hated schmucks who pulled cheap shots to gain quick leverage. The tactic never worked on her. "Mr. Fortier, your charming southern drawl and smooth voice almost makes a person neglect to notice what a real jackass you may be." She rose from her seat, already looking for an exit, and added, "Almost."

For the first time, Fortier's cool demeanor showed very real signs of collapse. He all but sprang out of his seat in an effort to prevent her from leaving. "Ms. Carson, wait."

"It's been a pleasure," she said on her way to the door. "But not really."

"I apologize. That was low of me." His words rang with desperation. He reached out for her arm, but she whisked herself away, cleanly avoiding his touch. He lowered his hand. "Ms. Carson, please hear me out. Just give me five minutes."

She paused at the doorway and sighed, and for the sake only of saving him from a possible heart attack, she turned around. "Five minutes."

"Sit down? Please?"

She rolled her eyes, walked back to the chair, and dropped into the seat. "Do you always get your way, Mr. Fortier?"

"Only when it comes to business."

"I'm not so sure about this time," she muttered.

"This isn't business, Ms. Carson. I assure you the matter is very personal." He swallowed hard. Suddenly, his blue eyes turned milky with emotion. "As I mentioned, my friend tells me you're the one to go to for delicate issues."

True. In the years since she'd quit the Shreveport UC Division (or been fired, depending upon who gave an opinion) she'd undertaken a variety of freelance undercover work. Without ever renting an office or hanging a shingle, business seemed to just... find her. She'd run the gamut, everything from trickily served process papers for shady characters, to snapping shots of rich wives playing porn star for pool boys.

No matter what she'd pulled off for money in the past, she had a hunch—based on the pomp and circumstance of the meeting thus far—that Richard Fortier's request would top them all. She narrowed her gaze at him.

He seemed to understand that she was growing impatient with his storytelling. "I'll get to the point."

"Please do," she encouraged him, not attempting to buffer her impatience.

The butler returned with a fresh drink. Fortier took it without establishing eye contact with the man, who left the room right away. Still, Fortier lowered his voice. "My wife left me."

"Well, I can't make her come back if she doesn't want to." Shel scooted to the edge of her seat, preparing once again to leave. She added, "And before this goes to an even stranger place, I don't do hits."

"I don't want my wife dead."

"She take a big old ring with her or something?" She constantly retrieved rings from ex-wives and ex-mistresses, the gemstones usually far bigger than the brains of the men who'd purchased them.

"I'm afraid it's something more precious than that." Fortier's intense gaze effectively trapped her in place. He blinked, appeared at a loss for words. At last he mumbled, "She has taken my daughter."

CHAPTER THREE

Shel stared at Fortier for several long seconds. She quickly rolled through a gamut of emotions from relief at knowing she would quickly reject the case, to sadness for him and the obviously painful loss of his daughter, and finally to disappointment at losing what would surely be a good payday.

She softened her tone when she finally spoke. "I'm sorry for your loss, Mr. Fortier, but I don't get involved in custody cases. That's what the courtroom is for. If your wife has kidnapped your child, that's a felony. I suggest you start by calling the police."

"Ms. Carson, I believe my child is in grave danger," he quietly said. His eyes held a faraway look. "I'm very concerned."

Shel knew it was a waste of time to even get the details from him. She wasn't a victim retrieval specialist and she didn't take kid cases, period. In her view, kids were the only people not yet ruined by humans. Far be it from her to butt into somebody's innocence, possibly expediting what they would surely learn in due time—that the world could be an awful place. She hadn't liked kid cases when she was a cop, and as a freelancer, it was her right to reject them.

Despite her resolution, she found herself asking, "Why the concern?"

"My wife has some genuine problems. She has a violent streak." He looked at her. "Very violent."

"Still, it's a custody case." She felt uncomfortable at the prospect of being forced to comfort the increasingly emotional man. Compassion wasn't in her lineup. She impatiently asked, "When did they go?"

"Last month, during White Linen Night, of all the damned times."

Shel shook her head. "I'm not familiar."

"First Saturday night in August, thousands who fancy themselves art connoisseurs crowd into the Warehouse District to drink wine and talk culture. It's a very big night for us." He glanced away. "I couldn't get immediate help. The crowds were large and the police force was stretched very thin."

She boldly glanced around the opulent room and didn't bother hiding her disbelief. "Rich guy like you couldn't command some special treatment?"

"In fairness, it took me a while to realize they'd gone." He tipped his head to one side in a way that reminded her of a puppy. "You have children, Ms. Carson?"

"No."

"Very p-precious—" he sputtered, seemingly trying to keep his emotions in check. When he spoke again, his voice rasped. "I assure you my wife is quite insane. Days before she left, she killed the family dog right in front of my daughter. Throttled the poor animal with her bare hands." He clenched his fists together in a demonstration and shuddered, his expression filled with horror. "She's been very, very unstable since Harper's birth."

"Postpartum depression?"

"I don't know, but she surely did change. She'd get mean with my daughter and me. I desperately tried to get her some help to no avail. Unfortunately, I've gotten to know that side of her very well. At this point, my only concern is for my child."

His face turned a disconcerting shade of white. Although his lips moved, no words came. He shielded his eyes with his hand for several seconds, further unnerving Shel. She hoped he wasn't working himself into a stroke. After a bit, he moved his hand to reveal red-rimmed eyes and muttered an apology.

"How about we get some air, Mr. Fortier?" Shel motioned toward a bank of windows that ran the width of the room. The only brightness potential the room possessed was heavily curtained with yet more burgundy, but there were French doors at one end, and surely what was left of the daylight just beyond.

He nodded, stood, and made a wobbling path toward the doors.

She reached for the handle, but he quickly stopped her. For the first time, she noticed a thin ray of blue laser security light spanning the door's width.

Fortier pressed an intercom button and informed the butler they would take their talk to the patio. He laid his thumb against a screen on a security box and held it there until the blue beam flickered and vanished. Only then did he open the door and wave for her to exit before him.

She and Fortier stepped onto a terrace overlooking the roof of a carriage house swarming with cat's claw vines. Further below, she saw a compact lawn with borders bursting with sweet-smelling blooms. She inhaled deeply. "Plumeria?"

"And foxglove," he numbly answered. "Smells heavenly, but it is incredibly poisonous."

"Story of my life," she muttered, shooting him a look.

He returned a glance indicating that might be the only thing they had in common. Bypassing the settee, he leaned against the lacy iron railing to gaze over the courtyard paradise.

She joined him and tried to keep him talking. Talking involved breathing, and he didn't look terrific. "You've got a pretty high-tech setup here, Mr. Fortier. Must be all that art in there, huh?"

The color slowly returned to his cheeks. He nodded. "You can't be too careful."

"Right," she said, wondering if that was the case, how he'd managed to lose his only child.

Fortier's gaze settled on his colossal estate. He launched into a quiet narration. "I had all the bells and whistles installed as soon as we moved in last year. Priceless art aside, the house has a rather colorful history. Lots of curious folks come around to snap photographs."

"I noticed."

"They say damn near everything in New Orleans is haunted." He chuckled without smiling. "A few odd noises now and again don't mean it's necessarily so. But Kathleen—my wife—isn't as fond of the place as I am."

Triggered by dusk, gas lamps began to ignite around them with a soft whirring sound. Their light reflected off the water beneath the terrace. The setting was serene, lovely. "Sweet yard, too," Shel said. "Great pool."

"Never been touched. My wife abhors water."

"Why is that?"

"She lost her parents to Hurricane Katrina. Perhaps that's a part of her problem."

Shel turned to face him, letting her amusement show. No matter his state of suffering, she couldn't resist making her point. "Your emotionally unstable wife lost her parents in the flood, so you moved her into a haunted house with an enormous pool?"

He blinked several times. "I can't be sure if you're on my side or not."

She studied him a moment longer. "I can't be sure, either."

Before she and Fortier could pursue—or ignore—the matter, a faint buzz sounded behind them. She turned to see the butler ushering a guest onto the balcony. Fortier appeared relieved at the interruption. He all but ran to greet his guest, a man in a suit and tie, probably a lawyer. Shel hated lawyers.

"Peter Dubois." Looking every bit as aristocratic as her host, the gentleman extended his hand in greeting.

Shel ignored him and instead glared at Fortier.

"I asked Peter to join us," Fortier explained. "He's an old family friend."

"And your lawyer," she finished for him.

"Naturally I play my personal affairs close to the vest."

"Naturally." Her cynicism reemerged loud and clear.

Fortier waved toward the table. "Shall we sit down? Please?"

The butler disappeared and returned in moments with a bottle of scotch, glasses, and a pitcher of water, which he dutifully placed on the table before departing again.

Dubois looked familiar, leading Shel to wonder if she'd seen him in the press. Given his expensive attire and abundant confidence, she could easily imagine him behind a podium, taking kudos for whatever case he'd won on behalf of a string of high-end crooks. The expression in his eyes supported her feeling, as they held the gleam of a man who didn't operate on the up and up. It was a look she'd seen countless times in her past.

He wasted no time in getting down to business. "I trust Richard has brought you up to speed regarding his situation," he said to her.

"We were getting there," she said. She selected a glass and poured herself some water. Fortier started to top off her glass with scotch, but she quickly stopped him. "I like to keep a clear head, especially when there's a lawyer within slapping distance."

Dubois ignored her barb. "Have you discussed financials?"

Fortier meekly smiled. "We were getting there, too."

Dubois turned his attention to Shel. His voice dropped to a confidential level, as if anyone could hear them above the whirring gas lanterns, or the distant revelers and the ambient sounds of the Quarter. "This is a grave situation, Ms. Carson. We'd be much obliged if you'd take the case and help Richard and his daughter get on with their lives."

"I'm confused," Shel said, setting her glass on the wrought-iron table. She leaned on her forearms, deliberately capturing both men's attention. "Did you report the kidnapping to the police? Publicize the fact that your daughter had gone missing on TV or in the newspaper? Was there an Amber Alert—anything? C'mon, gentlemen."

Fortier and Dubois looked at each in silent conference. At last, the lawyer spoke. "Ms. Carson, it is necessary to keep this out of the news as much as possible. My client—my *friend*—maintains a high degree of confidentiality for the protection of his family and his assets. Our fear was that if someone were to discover Richard's wife and child were missing, his child could be in even greater danger."

Shel was forming some ideas, but asked anyway, "How do you figure?"

"Let's say if an unscrupulous individual found them first and held them for ransom."

Her gaze flicked between the pair. "Do you know a lot of unscrupulous folks, Mr. Fortier?"

"Sadly, Ms. Carson, the art world is full of them," Fortier answered. "For everyone's safety, I try my best to keep a low profile."

"If you'll pardon my saying, Mr. Fortier..." Shel paused, wrestling with her patience. She addressed them in the same low, hushed tones they'd used with her. "You don't move your family into a forty-four room mansion that's a primary stop on a ghost tour in the French Quarter if you're trying to keep a low profile."

Dubois looked prepared to defend his client, but Shel only gave him a tight grin and whispered, "No response necessary. The brochure about this place came with my hotel room along with a two-for-one coupon. I spotted a group on my way in, cameras high, snapping to beat hell." She straightened her posture, enjoying the growing confidence that she held the better hand in their game. "If I had the beaucoup bucks you clearly do, I'd have had my kid's face on every news channel, every hour. Please, Mr. Fortier, don't fucking waste my time. Now gentlemen, why am I really here?" She leaned back in her seat, giving the pair a chance to stew in their juices.

Fortier broke the silence. He touched Dubois's sleeve. Finally, Dubois nodded, and Fortier began to unwind his tale. "Not long ago, my wife involved herself in some unsavory business behind my back." He leaned forward and gave Shel his undivided attention. "I quashed whatever bad publicity money could manage, kept the press away from it. Still, tongues will wag. By now, there are many who know of her misdeeds and would have little sympathy for us."

"What did she do?"

"Check forgery, embezzlement…" His voice trailed off and he rubbed his forehead. "Those things I could recompense. What I could not indemnify was her adulterous, blackmailing lifestyle. Many men—and their wives—wouldn't lose sleep should she meet her demise. I notify the police or the FBI and it's public record. Frankly, someone of my social and professional standing doesn't announce his wife missing without the press having a field day. No detail would be publicly spared."

"Meaning your dirty laundry would be all over the news for the world to know." Shel nodded, leaping to her assumed conclusion. "How bad for business. That's father of the year material right there."

He forged ahead despite his obviously escalating annoyance at her cynicism. "Ms. Carson, declaring them missing could possibly endanger my wife and child. As I mentioned, Kathleen doesn't exactly have a fan club. It's entirely plausible that someone would choose to find her first and take justice into their own hands." He paused, once again scrubbing at the lines that formed on his forehead. After a lengthy sigh, he added, "At very least, such publicity might force my wife further into hiding."

"Makes a girl wonder why your wife would want away from you so badly." She leaned back in her chair, her eyes never leaving Fortier. "Or perhaps these supposed bad guys want to get back at you and not her."

"I can assure you that's not the case."

"Can you assure me?" She remained locked in his gaze. He didn't flinch. After a moment, she softened her tone. "Look, I'm trying to put myself in your place, Mr. Fortier. But if it were me, I'd do anything—bar none—to get my kid back."

"I *am* doing everything. That's why you're here." His eyes clouded once again and his voice broke when he added, "Make no mistake about it. I want my daughter back. Harper's all I've got. She's…everything to me."

Dubois seized his cue in the tag-team negotiation. He produced a manila envelope from his briefcase and pushed it across the table toward her.

She unwound the clasp and dumped the envelope's contents on the table, her eyes going immediately to a black AmEx card emblazoned with her own name. Having been on a government payroll most of her life, she'd never imagined such a thing, not even for her private amusement. Next to the card was a cell phone, and next to that, a legal-sized envelope open just enough for her to see it was bulging with cash.

She didn't let herself get used to that sight either and aimed her gaze at Fortier. "Given the parameters I've already defined for you, what is it you expect me to do?"

"Find them," he firmly answered. "No interaction required. None of that retrieval business you spoke of earlier. Simply find them and contact me with their whereabouts. Period."

"Based on your story alone? Really?" She slumped in her chair and folded her arms across her chest, looking from one man to the other.

"It's all here." Dubois produced a second envelope that he slid toward her. His expression was now fixed and cold, leading Shel to consider that he might be one of the men Fortier mentioned when speaking of his wife's illicit affairs. His tone said he had more at stake than simple representation of his client. "This is the legal paperwork that proclaims Richard to be the sole custodian of Harper, no ifs, ands, or buts."

Shel leafed through the papers.

"Are you officially divorced?"

"No," Fortier softly answered. His shoulders fell as though he'd been dreading the question. "Given her state of mind, I took every precaution for the sake of my child. I asked for, and easily received, guardianship due to the unusual circumstances."

"Unusual circumstances?" Shel raised her eyes over the top of the paper, studied him for a moment. He only nodded toward the papers, as if she held in her hands the answer to her every question. The papers appeared legal, signed by a judge, and stamped with the official Orleans Parish logo. She flipped through the other documents as well, pausing to more closely examine a particular unfamiliar one. She held it out for him to see. "What's this?"

"The circumstances I spoke of. Committal paperwork." Fortier quietly disclosed this in a manner that said it would one day be a dirty family secret. "When I do find her, I'll get Kathleen the help she badly needs. Everything is in order." He stopped and thumbed his chin, his eyes glazing over for the hundredth time. "It's the right thing to do. I am Kathleen's only living relative, and she is the mother of my child."

"How noble of you. I think I'm going to pass." Shel shoved the paperwork at them. Despite the case's lucrative potential, something didn't feel right. "All this trouble for the committal and custody assignment says this is already a matter of public record. Might as well take the extra step and contact the Feds. I'm out of here."

Once again, Fortier started to reach out to her, to keep her from rising out of her chair. Shel shot him a warning look, but silently granted him another moment of her time.

"Court documents can remain on file for years without anyone being the wiser. Once I turn this over to anyone, it's like pulling the trigger on my life—*and* my child. Everyone from the Feds to the press will be nosing around, asking questions to build a case or just get a good story. Meanwhile, where will my daughter be? That publicity is nothing more than distraction. It gives my wife too much opportunity to run and it makes them both fair game for anyone's revenge."

"Mr. Fortier, I'm sorry I can't help you." She stood and prepared to make her point by storming away before she remembered the complicated security system. She waved toward the French doors.

"Call Alfred or James, or whoever your butler is, and tell him visiting hours are over."

Again, Fortier stopped Dubois from intervening. Despite his evident disappointment, Fortier gathered the paperwork, cash, phone, and AmEx, put them back in the manila envelope, and tucked it under his arm. He also stood. "I'll see you out."

Instead of taking a direct route to the exit, he detoured her through the mansion, down another hallway lined with more similarly gory paintings. He stopped in front of a particular door and nudged it slightly open.

Shel laid eyes on the pinkest, frilliest little girl's room she'd ever seen. She couldn't hide her awe at the child-sized playhouse, table and chair set, and overflowing toy box. The centerpiece was an over the top canopy bed in the middle of a white, fuzzy rug. "Extravagant," she whispered.

"If Harper is spoiled, then I'm to blame." Fortier wore a sad smile. "There's nothing I wouldn't do for her. She's beautiful, bright...perfect. That's my baby." He nodded at a nearby dresser where a series of photographs were arranged in little pink frames.

She picked up one after another and studied the child's smiling face. "Harper's about six?"

"Four," he corrected.

She knew nothing about kids. She returned the photograph and picked up the next. A woman with aqua eyes stared at her from the frame. Long, auburn hair cascaded over the baby's fuzzy head as she nuzzled the child to her breast. "I take it this is Kathleen?"

"Yes." Fortier stood behind her. "One of my favorite pictures."

Shel set down the photograph and turned to face him. "Aren't you at all concerned that someone else could have snatched them? You seem wholly convinced your wife is the bad guy here."

"I'm convinced that she made good on her promise." He looked away and spoke slowly. "She repeatedly threatened to take Harper away from me because she knows my daughter is the only thing in the world that matters to me."

Shel took another look at the mother and baby photograph, noticing what could be described as a dubious expression on the woman's face. She realized Fortier was already tainting her feelings about a woman she'd never even met. In recent years, maintaining her objectivity hadn't been important. Getting information, serving papers—it was brain dead work. Retrieving jewelry or snapping photographs from behind a bush required more tricks than moral decision weighing. If a woman was stupid enough to cheat, a dude dumb enough to skip out on a bookie—whatever the case, they got what they deserved as far as Shel was concerned. She could perform that work on autopilot. Certainly none of it involved kids.

Shel blinked hard, trying to purge the thoughts from her head. She wasn't taking the case.

She found herself studying the paintings on the child's pink walls, sweetly warped clapboard houses with funny-faced moons hanging in blue skies. This collection was brighter, prettier—a marked departure from the art throughout the rest of the mansion. "Nice," she absently remarked in an effort to change the subject and preempt any chance of igniting Fortier's waterworks.

"Kathleen painted those. She's always dabbled in kitschy little watercolors." He tipped his head to one side, studying the one directly in front of them. "I suppose they have a certain charm."

Shel stepped closer and studied the quaint paintings, noting the "Kathleen" signature with its curling K buried near the bottom right corner of each canvas. She nodded. "Her interest in art must have been helpful for the family business."

"Kathleen was never interested in anything dealing with family." His tone turned suddenly cold as did his eyes when he angrily whispered, "She's ruined everything for us."

Shel quickly worked right back the subject. She nodded toward the paintings. "She self-taught?"

He softened, appearing too tired to work up anger. "Kathleen originally studied at Tulane. More recently, she took a few classes at Loyola." He captured her gaze and took a closer step. In moments, Shel felt the envelope against her open palm. He went on, "Please, find my child, Ms. Carson."

Without removing her gaze from his, she felt the envelope and the bulge of what had to be an outrageous sum of cash. Her resolution wavered. It wasn't like he'd asked her to kidnap the child herself…

"Think it over," he said, as if he read her mind. "Sleep on it. Take the money and the card. Find her and there will be more to follow. Your terms."

She looked down at the envelope he pressed into her hand.

He continued, "This is a jumping off point. I'll give you ten times this amount if you find my daughter."

She stared at him a moment longer. "And if I decide not to take the job?"

"You keep the down payment and I cancel the card and the phone," Fortier informed her. He shook his head and looked around his daughter's room. He reeked of abject despair as he concluded his plea. "If you decide against helping me, we'll never see each other again."

"I still need more than your word and a few pieces of paper."

"What do you want? Name it and you'll have it," he said, clearly trying not to show too much optimism, and already Shel was regretting having provided him even a glimmer of hope. "What can I do to convince you to do this?"

Shel stared at him. "I'll need the names of those people she fucked over—all of them—don't hold back a single one."

"Done."

"I'll also want any paperwork in connection to those monies you settled with them. I need to know the price and conditions of their silence. You're a businessman, I know you kept track and I'm sure every bit of it's in writing."

"That's confidential…" He'd started to offer an excuse, but upon seeing her shake her head, Fortier heartily nodded. "I'll see what I can do."

"Don't see about it, do it."

He nodded again. Shel took a deep breath. At last, she clasped the heavy envelope and shoved it inside her jacket. Feeling almost lightheaded, she turned and fled the pink and frilly room, along with the saddest man she'd ever met.

For reasons wholly unknown to her, she was breathing hard when she paused on the front doorstep of the house. She addressed him without as much as a last look. "I'll be in touch, maybe. This is just me thinking about it."

Shel heard him call his thanks, but didn't dare turn around or otherwise acknowledge his words. She easily disappeared into a group of tourists on Governor Nicholls Street. Their ringleader, carrying a scepter and wearing a stovepipe hat and cape, had clearly captured the imagination of his eager flock. They were so enthralled by his every word, they didn't seem to notice as she pushed through to the back of the group and hurried down the street.

It was a block to Bourbon Street and about a quarter mile to party central. Instead she went two blocks in the opposite direction, turned on Decatur Street, and strolled past the darkened French Market and the Mint. It had been at least a dozen years since she'd last visited New Orleans, but she was rapidly orienting herself to her surroundings with each block. She weaved through throngs of partiers headed toward the Moonwalk for a better look at the lunar spectacle cradled in a band of clouds hanging low over the black Mississippi. She craved anonymity and familiarity at the same time. She cut right onto St. Philip Street to see if O'Boyle's bar was still in business post-Katrina. To her relief, it was open. She passed through one of the arched entryways that were always wide open.

The smell of blackened crawfish hung thick in the air, having wafted over from the next-door restaurant, and regulars sharpened their pool cues and swigged beers between shots on a warped pool table. Despite the crumbling appearance of the brick building, she was pleased to discover the offbeat atmosphere remained solidly intact. She sidled up to the bar and double-checked her jacket, nervous about carrying around such a large amount of cash, especially in a place like this. The bartender approached her.

"Double vodka tonic." So much for notions of pink hurricanes.

She accepted the drink, dropped a ten on the bar top, and began her pursuit of a reasonable buzz. She didn't want to think, and she certainly didn't want to think about a missing kid. She planned to forget all about it until tomorrow, whereupon she would awaken with a fuzzy head and leave a regretful sounding voice mail declining Fortier's job offer. Yet no matter how she tried to avoid it, she pondered her strange, brief encounter with Richard Fortier. How pained he'd looked surrounded by the sea of pink frou-frou in his beloved daughter's bedroom.

Something nudged her knee, startling her. Shel looked down at a huge brown bulldog staring at her expectantly. He drooled around the sides of a pool ball he had clamped in his enormous jaws as if it were a measly squeaky toy. In total, he was an unnerving sight on three sturdy legs. His obvious handicap caused her to relax some. Even with her bad back she could probably outrun him. Maybe.

He dropped the heavy ball and picked it up several times, apparently hinting she should either play or at very least pet him. She reached down and scrubbed him between the ears for a few seconds before leaning back against the bar. She ignored him until he moved on.

She watched him steadily move around the bar, easily interacting with patrons who were probably regulars judging by their greetings for the enormous dog. Shel couldn't help but admire the animal's confidence and how he seemed to bring the softer side out of even the toughest-looking characters. There was something pure about animals. Animals and kids…

Her thoughts immediately went to Fortier's tale about his wife killing their family pet. It wasn't something any child should see. Shel wondered if the kid was already ruined beyond repair, not that it would make her less worth rescuing. Not that Shel was the one to perform such a rescue, not that Fortier was asking her to do as much. Find her, period, he'd said. Shel thought about the delicate-appearing woman in the photograph. It was hard to imagine her killing a dog. A psychotic beauty, perhaps? The beautiful part, for sure…

Shel tossed back her last sip, passed her empty glass to the edge of the bar and tapped it. The drink was promptly replaced with another. She slid a twenty across to the bartender. "That's good for the next one, too."

The bristly butterball of a bartender placed an empty shot glass on top of the cash to secure it against the gusts blowing from the old metal fans clanging away in every corner of the joint.

She studied the other patrons in the bar, an unseemly bunch who seemed to possess an even ratio of tattoos to toothlessness.

On occasion, what she assumed to be a curious tourist poked his or her head through the tumbledown French doors and promptly pulled it right back out again. She supposed they craved a wilder, louder, brighter locale. An adventurous visitor might stop for a single Abita just to say they'd had a drink with locals, but for the most part, O'Boyle's lacked the flash to properly welcome the average tourist. The bar's biggest draws were strong drink, an outdated jukebox with equally outdated music, and a few clanging arcade slots. There wasn't a string of plastic iridescent beads in sight.

It had been her intention to throw down at least another twenty in drinks, but when her modest starter tab was gone, she headed for the door, surprising herself with a little stumble-step down St. Philip. Apparently she required more than one little package of gas station doughnuts in her stomach to properly absorb three double vodka tonics, or she was getting old, which could be a real possibility.

She took the first right onto Chartres and headed back toward Le Richelieu, coming to Fortier's mansion on the way and stopping in front for a moment. The darkened windows added to the already ominous atmosphere. She could feel the spooky ambiance from across the street. "Fucking creepy," she muttered.

Moving on, Shel took the last block and pushed through the front door of Le Richelieu and gave a courteous nod to a front desk girl wearing a black leather dress that fit her like a second skin. The night people of New Orleans were markedly different from the day people. Shel paused long enough to fully appreciate the ample cleavage spilling out of her V-neck.

The girl noticed her gaze and clearly received it as complimentary. She looked coy, her ponytails bobbing. When she grinned, she flashed fangs where her eyeteeth should have been.

Surprised, Shel politely returned the girl's smile before hurriedly stepping aboard the elevator. She pressed the number four a dozen times and refrained from rolling her eyes until she was safely behind the closed steel door.

The archaic carriage lurched to a stop and the doors parted. She followed the threadbare hallway runner to room 404, digging her key out along the way. She shoved the key into the lock, gave it a jiggle as she'd been instructed, pushed the door open, and hit the light switch inside the door. Nothing. Instantly on her guard, she stepped inside, allowing the door to fall quietly shut behind her.

Her back pressed against the wall, she inched further into the room, stopping when she heard rustling coming from the general location of the bed. She patted her belt and silently unsnapped the gun holster concealed by her shirt hem.

Before she could draw her gun, she was blindsided by a heavy mass crashing into the center of her chest, nearly knocking her off her feet.

CHAPTER FOUR

Shel pushed the weight off and proceeded to crawl in the general direction of the nightstand, huffing and cursing all the way. She blindly knocked everything off the small table until she found the lamp switch and flicked it on.

She stood on wobbly legs, caught her breath, and gave her attacker—a twenty-five pound cat—an admonishing look. Her voice came out in a low rasp. "Jesus Christ, Newton—you're going to send me to an early grave, you know that?"

The fat black and white cat only pressed his face against her pant leg, purring as if he had no clue what could have possibly gone wrong with his welcome back surprise.

She took a backward step away from the tomcat. "Hell no—I'm mad now. I almost shot your fluffy ass."

Shel headed toward the bathroom, reprimanding Newton as she went. "I go and sneak you into a perfectly questionable hotel and that's how you repay me? You should be happy you even have a roof over your head in the first place."

Newton—short for Wayne Newton—was her single win following the big breakup nearly eight years ago. She'd never wanted the animal in the first place and had to dose herself nightly with Benadryl to make their cohabitation possible. But apparently hubby—yes, her ever-loving ex-girlfriend had switched teams—was even more allergic to cats.

Shel considered it as she squeezed a line of toothpaste on her brush. She'd no more had a vote in the matter of adopting a cat than anything else in that relationship. After dumping the cat on her, her newly betrothed ex had immediately left the state, relocating to Las Vegas, no less, where the pair could go gaga over the real Wayne Newton live and in person to their heart's content. Though she never considered herself butch—she never considered herself *any* label—Shel believed herself to be decidedly more masculine than her ex's new husband. Shel wondered if he, himself, might switch teams one day.

"Oh, the irony," she muttered through a mouthful of foamy toothpaste. "Cat, I would have at least picked a respectable name for you." She spat and rinsed. Out of the corner of her eye, she saw the animal watching her every move from the doorway.

"We should have figured her out sooner," she told Newton, referring to her ex-girlfriend as she often did when speaking to the cat, though she was well over the failed relationship. She dabbed her lips on a towel and dropped it on the countertop. "What self-respecting lesbian goes ape-shit over Wayne Newton, anyway?"

Back in the room, she spied her jacket and picked it up, draping it over the back of the desk chair. Richard Fortier's envelope fell on the floor. She stared at it for a moment. All thoughts of her ex flew out of her head. She picked up the envelope, gave it a good squeeze, and at last had the nerve to count the money inside. Ten thousand dollars. She replaced the bills in the envelope and made a low whistle.

I'll give you ten times this much if you find my daughter.

She blinked Fortier's words away and set the envelope on the desk.

Since the big split, she'd lived out of a total of five motels, each one a real dive. She had lived hand to mouth off the proceeds of whatever jobs found her. She had no credit, no savings, and no opportunity to save for a bigger place. Not that she'd want a place in Shreveport anyway. No love, no job, nothing left to keep her there, unless she counted the cat and often she didn't.

The result of living as a nomad meant life with a hotplate and without refrigeration. Also, she'd developed a routine of thoroughly checking the mattress each week, hunting for signs of bedbugs more than anything else. She did the same at this hotel out of habit, which was ridiculous. La Richelieu was old, but it was neat and clean. Still, old habits die hard. When she felt satisfied with her findings—or lack thereof—she slipped between the sheets and turned out the light.

After several seconds she patted the space beside her. "Come on, Newton, you nincompoop."

The cat promptly leapt on the bed and went about purring, circling, and clawing the comforter, as he did every night. At last he settled down and curled into her side.

"Spooning with the cat," she muttered, stroking Newton between his ears. "Oh, the depravity."

Shel closed her eyes, but held only a dim hope of rest and proceeded to employ every sleep position known to humankind. By two a.m., the cat sat up and glared at her, disdain evident in his gleaming yellow eyes.

She sighed and confessed, "Newton, I'm in a pickle."

She reached out and scrubbed the cat under his chin, prompting him to settle in and at least give the appearance that he was listening to her—more than she usually got from humans. She launched into a pros and cons narrative.

"A hundred grand would easily get us clear out of Shreveport. Hell—that would get us clear out of Louisiana. We could start over for real, not just live in fleabag motels."

The cat loudly purred as if in agreement.

"But it's a kid and I don't take kid cases," she countered. She had to admit that Fortier's generous down payment had her firm policy on the matter feeling flimsier by the moment. "Then again, he is the kid's father and he's got the paperwork. Jesus Christ, I'd probably be doing the cops and courts a favor, right?"

And now she was grasping.

Clearly bored with her ramblings, Newton had fallen asleep and was actually snoring.

"Good talk," she mumbled.

The case was eating at her in unexpected ways. She wondered if kids would always remind her of her own sordid past: a shit-life in a dilapidated government apartment with parents who were drunks and druggies.

In the end, her mother had died too young, the result of a drug and alcohol binge, and her father had split. At barely eight years old, Shel was entered into the system for a life of shoddy care by a series of nameless, faceless adults.

It was her own rotten childhood that had her jumping at the chance to work undercover Narco. The prospect of never again dealing with children seemed glorious. How wrong she'd been…

Shel closed her eyes and concentrated on relaxing every muscle, starting with her toes, a trick that worked for her as a kid. When she finished, despite her efforts, she felt more restless than relaxed.

She wondered if her own childhood was a strike against Fortier or a point in his favor. She knew her time undercover and the fatal error that caused her departure was certainly a strike against. Despite it, she tried to keep an open mind. She sighed loudly.

Newton stopped snoring, an indication that his owner was again annoying him.

"I can't take a kid case." And like that, it was decided. "I'll tell him first thing in the morning and give him back his shit."

She didn't feel the genuine relief she thought she'd experience at having made such a decision. She searched herself a moment to find out the reason. It was a no-brainer. "But I will keep his down payment."

Newton raised his chin and aimed his yellow eyes at her. They looked particularly eerie in the darkness.

Shel stroked the cat's chin. "Christ, Newton—he won't even miss that little bit of change."

The cat rested his head against her leg. She took it to mean he understood, not that she valued the cat's opinion. Much.

She realized that, without intending to, she'd already started thinking about a new life for herself. Perhaps it was the kid's room that had ignited the change in viewpoint; maybe she was wondering what she'd been missing out on all those years, not that she'd ever desired to parent. Perhaps it was sitting at the table with men who weren't overt thugs and crooks; men with bona fide legal paperwork in hand, and the prospect of doing something right and money to be made that exceeded her normal two or three digit commissions.

She drifted to sleep pondering how far away from Louisiana she could get on ten grand.

* * *

Shortly after nine a.m., she punched Fortier's number into the cell phone he'd given her, but didn't call him right away. She hung the Do Not Disturb sign on the room door, lest anyone discover she'd smuggled in a cat, and walked a block to the already lively French Market where she ordered a Bloody Mary crammed full of pickled green beans, okra and an enormous olive. She figured that even with the booze, the cocktail was more nutritious than her usual morning diet.

She sipped the Bloody Mary as she ambled toward old Jackson Square to catch a cab to take her the rest of the way to the Warehouse District. Within minutes, she stood in front of the Fortier Gallery on Julia Street.

She peered through the window of the still-closed shop. Inside, a man with thinning hair and a bespectacled beak of a nose tried not to notice her while he skittered about the place. She rapped a knuckle on the glass. With obvious disdain at being interrupted, he directed his beady eyes her way and quickly sized her up. She knew what he saw: jeans, T-shirt, no makeup, and most importantly, no designer purse bulging with credit cards. He easily dismissed her. It was only when she slapped a badge against the plate glass window that he came to the door, his contempt abundantly evident.

She grinned at him and quickly pocketed the badge before he could ask for a closer look, which would reveal the thing to be nothing more than a cheap souvenir. Her authentic police badge had gone the way of her authentic police job years ago. But having a badge, legitimate or not, certainly gave her better access, and hardly anyone ever asked to inspect it. People were scarily dumb.

"How can I be of assistance to New Orleans' finest?"

He reminded her of Fortier's butler, had the butler been shorter and gayer.

She gave him credit for having the irritated tone down pat. "Shreveport, actually," she incorrectly corrected him. "I'm looking for Mrs. Fortier."

"Well, she's not here." He returned inside, practically letting the door slam in Shel's face. She caught it and followed him into the shop, watching as he plucked a feather duster from a nearby bin and began to wave it over a row of easels. After a moment, he noticed her still watching him. "I could give her a message, if you like."

"Yeah." Shel played along, smiling. "Ask her why she's in touch with you and not her husband, and then tell her to get her ass home. How's that?"

He lowered the feather duster and glared at her through his tiny round spectacles. "If you know she's not here, why did you ask after her?"

"If you know she's gone, why'd you offer to take a message?" She arched an eyebrow. He didn't budge. She continued, "I'm doing some investigative work for her husband, Richard Fortier." Hearing those words come out of her mouth made it closer to official. She wasn't sure she liked the way it sounded. She mentally admonished herself. This was only a very preliminary fact-finding mission. "I'm sure somebody's already talked to you about her, but just humor me."

He blinked. "Why would they?"

It struck her as odd, but she didn't show it. Shel pulled a small leather notebook out of her pocket. "You have a name?"

"Bernard," he said in his nasal voice.

She wondered if he'd been questioned before about Mrs. Fortier. "You got a last name, Bernie? Or are you like Madonna or Cher?"

"Smith."

She looked at him, gauging his truthfulness concerning the generic last name. He didn't flinch. She nodded. "Bernie—"

"Bernard," he firmly corrected her.

"So what kind of relationship do the Fortiers have?" She wandered a bit, looking at some of the pictures in the window showcase.

"How should I know? Mr. Fortier rarely darkens the door. He's off brokering high-dollar deals. Not like this gallery."

She examined a price tag on the back of one of the pictures and made a low whistle. "This seems pretty pricey to me."

"I'm sure it does," he snootily said. "Generally, Mr. Fortier arrives for show openings and special events, and to collect the deposits, naturally."

"Naturally." Shel returned to his side. "So, he's just here for the glory."

"I didn't say that," Bernard said, his dry tone implying that it was exactly what he meant. "I've certainly never had occasion or desire to discuss his personal life."

"You never saw him with his wife?"

"Rarely. Not so much I could describe the condition of their marriage."

"You're kidding, right? A sharp guy like you?" She tossed a look toward the storefront. "You had me figured at the window for dirt poor. What's your take on the wife?"

Bernard shrugged. "I never saw her alone, and when I did see her, we never exchanged words. As for my take on her, she was an uppity little thing. Holier than thou." He lowered his voice to an exaggerated whisper, despite the fact they were the only ones in the shop. "Too good to speak to the commoners, if you know what I mean."

Shel gave him the once-over, considered the irony and shot him a grin. "Yeah, I do."

"Anyway, she was always dressed to kill, a little on the racy side, if you ask me. I can tell she's one of those women who bats their lashes and gets anything they want. I have a feeling she has her husband wrapped tightly around her little finger," he smugly reported. "Big cow eyes, hair down to here, and—" he made a motion to indicate the woman's bosom "—out to there."

"Stacked, huh?" Shel made a note.

"Voluptuous. Bought and paid for, I'm sure."

She read what she'd written on the page so far: *Bernard Smith, clueless, gossipy queen.* Still, it was good to appear official. She folded the book shut, crammed it into her back pocket, and flashed him a forced smile. "Mind if I take a look around, Bernie?"

"Oh, please do."

Shel thought his attitude suggested he'd rather eat dust than entertain her inquiry for another minute.

She began browsing the back of the gallery, noticing much of the same vampiric art she'd seen in the Fortier mansion. Even in a brightly lit shop in daytime, the paintings gave her the willies. "Hey Bernie—you sell much of this stuff?" She waved her hand at the dark oil work.

He momentarily stilled his frittering duster. "That very one you're admiring is already sold."

"I wasn't admiring it." Under her breath, but deliberately loud enough for him to hear, she added, "Stuff's uglier than a bag of assholes."

A significantly kinder, brighter work caught her eye, a drastic departure from the wretched oils. She recognized the style and asked, "This the missus's work?"

Bernard nodded. "Mr. Fortier wanted to incorporate some local flavor."

"Well, that and she's fucking him, right?" She grinned. Bernard shrugged. She went on, "It's kind of nice."

"A little undergrad for my taste."

Shel performed a quick appraisal of his off-brand shirt, shoes that had been polished too many times, and a Timex instead of a Rolex. "My guess is, Bernie, you can no more afford a painting, even in this shop, than you can afford a year's rent, electricity, and your cable subscription to LOGO. Am I right?"

He glared at her, but his mention of undergrad triggered a memory of something Fortier had told her. Since there was so little to go on at this point, she wondered if she might learn a thing or two from her alma mater. She continued to smile brightly. "I'm not familiar with Loyola University. Can I get to the art department by streetcar from here?"

Obviously delighted at the prospect of the "cop" vacating the premises, he grabbed a pen and a piece of shop stationery, and eagerly began to sketch a map.

She watched his hands move with practiced precision and nodded approvingly. "Are you an artist, Bernie, or are you just that anxious to get rid of me? I mean, you drew me everything but landscaping there."

"Mr. Fortier has a strict policy about only employing degreed artists."

Shel accepted the map and gave it a quick look. "Hey look, there's a hedge." She felt his glare on her back as she left the shop and continued on her way.

When she arrived shortly after ten a.m., Collins C. Diboll Art Gallery at Loyola was abuzz with activity. Students were unpacking crates and setting up an extensive display. She stopped a guy who'd caught her attention primarily because his hair was purple.

"Excuse me, is there a big sale or something?" she asked.

"This is for a visiting artist, not an actual sale," he politely informed her. He adjusted the thick glasses on his youthful, pockmarked face. "Of course, if you ask the dean, everything has a price, right?"

She admired his sweetly crooked grin and gave him one of her own. "Right. Will I be in the way if I take a look around?"

"Not at all. Knock yourself out. Student and faculty work is around the perimeter of the room."

"Is there someone in charge if I have any questions?" Figuring a financial transaction would speak louder than a general inquiry, she added, "Someone who takes cash?"

"And American Express and Visa," he assured her. "Any faculty you see wandering around. Or you can hit them up at the main office down the hallway."

"Thanks. I appreciate it."

"Good luck finding the next Van Gogh."

She continued inside, watching a woman directing student traffic as they assembled a display. She found it surprisingly easy to zone in on Mrs. Fortier's works. She took that as a good sign.

"Quaint, aren't they?"

Shel turned to see that the traffic director had come to stand behind her—an attractive woman with a personality far more welcoming than Bernard Smith's. "I was just thinking the same thing," she replied. "What would one of these set me back?"

"Ten grand."

Shel made a low whistle. "A little too rich for my blood, I'm afraid."

"They've been quite popular. Very gentle and sweet, painted by a former student." Apparently realizing she'd failed to introduce herself, the woman smiled and extended her hand. "I'm Jane Artello, Professor of Art Studies. Most of these people are my students, but I can't take credit for their skills."

"Mad skills." Shel glanced at the displays of pottery and mixed media arts before her gaze returned to the paintings of funny-shaped New Orleans-style homes. "You have Kathleen Fortier in class?"

Artello nodded, her short blond hair bobbing. "Quiet woman."

"Secretive?"

Artello regarded her a moment. "Gossip is a dangerous game for the tenured professor."

"I suppose so." Shel quietly flashed her fake badge.

Seemingly eager not to draw attention to the fact she'd been entertaining a cop, Artello didn't ask to inspect the badge, a disappointment as the professor was an otherwise smart-looking package.

Shel tucked the badge into her jacket pocket. "I'm investigating Mrs. Fortier's disappearance."

"I didn't know she'd gone missing," Artello said, making a poor attempt at a surprised expression. The façade didn't last long. She looked down at her feet almost shamefully and revised her statement. "I'd heard as much. I hoped it was a rumor."

"Anything you remember about her that might mean something to me or her husband?"

"Kathleen aced my class. In fact, she tested out of it the first week. Mine is a level one requirement and she was way beyond that." Artello wore a pensive look. "I believe she was all around quite intelligent."

"Happy?"

"Pardon?"

"Did she appear happy to you?"

Artello shrugged. "We never talked. She seemed quite reserved."

"Anyone who knew her better than you did?"

Artello stared at Kathleen Fortier's work, a watercolor clapboard house next to a body of water. "You might ask Coach Sawyer. He is a fan of her work."

Shel pulled out her notebook and jotted down the name. "Now, when you say fan, do you mean—"

"Gossip is dangerous territory for the tenured professor," Artello repeated.

"Gotcha." Shel put the notebook away. "Where can I find him?"

Artello provided her with the details. She rocked back on her heels and looked at Kathleen's painting, the admiration in her eyes tinged with sadness. "I've already had to inform her fans that our supply is devastatingly low. These are our last two."

"Fans?" Shel's interest was piqued. "They local?"

"Some. She also has a decent regional fan base, mostly southern cities." Artello directed her attention at the misshapen pink house with spirals emerging from the smokestack under a silvery sliver of a moon and folk-art style waves in the background. She shook her head. "I hope she is found safe."

"Me, too." Shel started to go, but doubled back when she thought of something else. "Professor, where do you send her commission checks when her works sell?"

"These particular works are donated by the students. All proceeds from sales benefit the fine arts department, naturally."

"Well, then, what the hell," Shel muttered, pulling the freshly minted black AmEx card out of her wallet. "He can write it off."

Artello looked confused. "I'm sorry?"

"Means I'll take it," Shel said, feeling surprisingly liberated to be able to make such a spontaneous purchase of anything at all—if only artwork to hang on a wall in a house she didn't have—she handed over the new credit card. "I like the one on the left—that pink house. Can you have it wrapped by the time I get back?"

The professor brightened significantly. "Certainly."

It took Shel fifteen minutes to find the University Sports Complex and track down Frank Sawyer. He seemed less than eager to speak about Kathleen Fortier. It was only after her clear announcement in front of his training staff that she was investigating anyone with a possible connection to the woman's disappearance that he squired her back to his office.

Behind closed doors, Sawyer took a seat at his desk, motioning for her to sit down in a chair opposite. Having come into the air-conditioned office from the humid outdoors, she wondered why he appeared suddenly flush and uncomfortable. His gaze helplessly flashed toward the side of his desk. There on the floor, propped against the wall, were six familiar, whimsical paintings featuring shotgun houses with daisies floating out of bricked chimneys, and silvery moons hanging overhead.

"What's this about?" Sawyer asked.

"You tell me. Do assistant coaches normally make enough money to snatch up a private collection like this or do you have an inheritance?"

He didn't even blink. "Just tell me what you want from me, Detective. I'm cooperating."

"Let's start with the art. Those Kathleen Fortier originals go for around ten thou a pop. Like I asked, you got family money or something?"

"Did you find Kathleen?"

"On a first name basis with her," she remarked, delighted to gain some ground. The coach's expressive face also pleased her. It could be that the case of the missing wife might be solved before it began. Perhaps this would be the quickest money she'd ever earned. She shook her head. "No, we haven't found Mrs. Fortier."

He was visibly relieved—not a point in his favor.

Shel wondered if knew Kathleen Fortier's location, or worse, the location of her body. Years on the force had caused her to think the worst up front, especially when someone was missing more than twenty-four hours.

Sawyer sat back in his seat and folded his hands in front of him on his desk blotter. "The paintings are for my house. It's being renovated at the moment, so I didn't rush to get them home."

"You're telling me you bought them?" She shook her head. "Forget it. I'm really looking for the kid."

His eyebrows plunged. "How should I know where she is?"

"Yet I believe you do know, since you knew the 'kid' in question is indeed a she." Shel hooked air quotes with her fingers. She stood and casually walked down the short row of artwork leaning against the wall. "You must be in the mood to bring a shit-storm scandal on the entire athletics department. You involved with Kathleen Fortier?"

"I resent your implication that I would have anything to do with a missing woman or her child," he curtly informed her. His shoulders heaved. He appeared to be restraining his building anger. She wondered how bad his temper could get. His voice lowered. "As far as Kathleen goes, I'm married."

"So that makes you a bona fide saint." She rolled her eyes. "Look at it from where I stand, Coach. It seems to me the biggest concentration of Kathleen Fortier's pricey art is in your possession. Given that you're only one of many athletic assistants, and judging by the size of this closet-shaped office, no way can you afford these luxuries. Either you stole the paintings, which is doubtful, or Kathleen gave them to you. Why would she do that? You tell me."

Sawyer lowered his voice further and appeared to soften. "I met Kathleen when I pitched in to help set up an art show. I told her I was in the process of adopting a baby girl, and that's how she came to tell me she has a little girl herself. I asked her about some of her pictures for the baby's room. I'm not even a big fan of artsy-fartsy— it surprised the hell out of me to find out how much the stuff would set me back. She gave me a gift."

"A gift of—" Shel made rough tally. "What? Sixty grand in art just for helping her shuffle a few paintings." She made it sound less like a question and more like an insinuation. She hiked an eyebrow and asked, "You sure that was the only thing you got from her?"

"She gave me just the one." He sounded earnest. "Then I heard she disappeared. Then a few days ago these pictures show up at my office. I figured I'd heard wrong about her going missing."

"Did you tell anyone about this mysterious donation?" She didn't drop her intense gaze.

"No."

"And you figured Kathleen was at home with her husband."

"Where else would she be?"

"Did you send her a thank-you note?"

He looked caught off guard by her rapid-fire questions. "No."

"Why not?" She smiled, her point practically making itself.

"I didn't think to."

"You didn't think to send a card or flowers or anything to someone who gifted you this much art?" She leaned forward and went quiet. "I think the reason you didn't send anything to her house was because you knew she wouldn't be there to get it. And had you sent something, the cops would be all over your ass following up on it."

He blinked. "Looks like you are."

"Looks like it," she confirmed. She stood to go, but stopped at the door and tried one last bluff. "You want to make any changes to that story before I get a warrant to haul you in? Seeing as you're one of the last ones she had contact with."

He swung into a defensive, businesslike mode. "Haul me in. I've got a lawyer." He sat back again. For such a meaty fellow, he primly folded his arms across his Wolfpack T-shirt. "Until then, we're finished here."

"A coach with his own attorney. You gotta love that." She chuckled as she turned the doorknob. "We'll be in touch."

CHAPTER FIVE

O'Boyle's was becoming Shel's headquarters of late. Seated at the bar, she reviewed her scanty notes.

Coach, possible lover. Wife, possible skank. Her mini-interrogation of Sawyer hadn't earned her much to go on.

She finished her drink and ordered another. In moments, the bartender—a woman with springy, dyed-blond hair with two inches of black roots showing—set the glass in front of her. When she offered a couple of bills, the woman refused to take her cash.

Puzzled, Shel looked at her money on the bar top. "Am I still in New Orleans?"

"You look like you could use it," the woman said. "I'm Jess."

"Shel," she introduced herself and raised her glass. "Thanks, Jess. Salute." She downed half the glass in one gulp and wiped her damp lips on the back of her hand.

Jess didn't go away. She aimed striking green eyes at the open notebook. "What you working on there?"

"Notes. I'm looking into a runaway case."

"Of course you are." Jess laughed, leaned on the bar, and clasped her hands together. The blond curls bounced right along with her personality. "Everybody's running from something, right?"

"Yeah?" Shel asked, amused. She decided she was happy for the distraction and closed her notebook. "Tell me about it."

Jess tapped Shel's hand and pointed down the bar at a haggard-looking woman hunched over a drink. She quietly said, "That one's running from the law." Her gaze went to a burly, bald biker with a thick, gray beard. "The wife." She nodded at the only other bartender, a nerdy-looking fellow with twitching eyes, and whispered, "The State of Georgia—all of it, from what he says."

Shel shared a chuckle with Jess and asked, "You?"

Jess shrugged. "Future in-laws who act more like outlaws." She pretended to wipe sweat off her forehead. "Dodged that bullet."

"Where you from?"

"Minnesota. I'm a cold-weather girl. I can hardly take the heat down here."

"Okay, Minnesota," Shel said, pronouncing the end like *soda*, just as Jess had. "Then why'd you come so far south?"

"I figure in this heat, it's the last place they'd expect to find me. Still, New Orleans reminds me of my nutty hometown. Lake, river—it's all water. No matter how far you go, you crave your creature comforts." Jess shot her a wink and patted the scarred bar top. "Let me know if you need another."

Shel waited for Jess to leave and once again looked over her sparse notes. Moments later, she tucked the book into the pocket of her oversized plaid shirt, and assessed what she knew so far.

Coach Sawyer might know something about Kathleen, but she figured she wouldn't get it out of the man without hauling him into a more official arena, something she couldn't do even if she wanted to. Guys like him, dumb or not, weren't easily intimidated by a fake badge or her smart mouth.

Mr. Fortier believed his wife had left of her own accord. But where would Kathleen go? She had no relatives and her parents were dead.

Shel tapped her pen on the bar top. Somebody put Better Than Ezra on the jukebox. Drink number two had been a bit stronger, and she was beginning to feel comfortably anonymous, a mood only slightly interrupted when her glance absently went to Jess. The woman smiled at her from across the bar. She smiled back. A breath of fresh air like that woman wouldn't last long in this dark place.

I figure it's the last place they'd expect to find me.

Jess's words rolled through her brain on the tail end of a thought that included Richard Fortier telling her his wife abhorred water.

Shel stood, stretched, and headed for the bathroom. A yellowed and peeling map of the United States was posted in the narrow hallway between the bathroom doors. She examined dozens of colorful pins that dotted it, hardly believing anyone would bother to leave an indication of their origin.

Jess's presumption that most of the bar's patrons were actually on the lam probably wasn't far from the truth. She studied the map and wondered about Kathleen Fortier. Did she want to be found, like some kind of game? Did she plan to extort money from her husband in exchange for the child? Did she just want people to leave her alone? Shel certainly understood the last one, but sadly figured there probably was a money angle at play. Had she not been kidnapped, where would a woman like that go to simply lay low?

She squinted at the map in the dim light cast by a bare overhead yellow bulb, swaying in the fan breeze. Within seconds, she found herself ruling out Mississippi and Alabama, states that weren't far enough away from Louisiana to qualify as actually running away unless you had money limitations. Having seen the Fortier mansion and given Kathleen's alleged penchant for scamming others, Shel figured it was safe to assume the woman had dough. Her eyes went to the coastal states, Virginia, the Carolinas, Georgia and Florida, for starters. She figured real Southern girls tended not to venture north of Virginia. The Midwest was landlocked, and the West Coast and its new age trappings also seemed out of the question. If Kathleen were the pampered, uppity woman Fortier portrayed, she'd need familiarity, a southern brand of comfort. Judging by her very nice lifestyle, she'd want a place where people threw around a lot of money. It made sense she'd need a place where she could make a nice living selling her art. It was still a factor to consider. If the woman didn't have a baby blackmail plan, whatever money she'd squirreled from Fortier or her alleged scam victims wouldn't last forever. Shel had to consider all possibilities.

Kathleen Fortier was a lifelong resident of New Orleans. If Shel knew only one thing about this particular city it was that once it got in someone's blood, nothing short of a transfusion would take it out. Though no city could be a doppelganger for the Big Easy, Shel squinted and tried to focus in on other southern cities that might be good candidates. Her slight buzz and the dim light weren't helping her eyesight any, and after a moment she gave up and pushed through the grungy restroom door.

The same song had restarted when she returned to her barstool to find a fresh drink was waiting for her. She looked around and nodded her thanks to Jess, grateful that this round was in a plastic cup. She waited until Jess's attention was elsewhere—a man with an eye patch trying to get a rise out of her, and Jess was equally busy fending him off—then scooted off the stool and slipped out the door. She felt a minor twinge of guilt for making the escape, especially leaving young Jess in the questionable hands of a pirate.

Safely on the sidewalk, she juggled her drink while she fished Fortier's cell phone out of her jeans pocket and made a brief, cryptic call.

In minutes, and just barely in front of another ghost tour, she stood on the mansion's doorstep. With a few drinks under her belt and a head full of fresh notions concerning Mrs. Fortier's whereabouts, she impatiently pressed the doorbell on the outer iron gate half a dozen times. Finally Richard Fortier himself answered the door, looking puzzled. He quickly let her inside and paraded her through the mansion until they arrived at a locked door on the third floor, between the child's nursery and what she could assume was the master bedroom.

"Kathleen's things have been packed and stored in here," he explained in response to her phone call as he unlocked the door. It swung open to reveal a tiny room that had been converted to a temporary closet, crammed to capacity with neatly stacked plastic boxes. Shel felt instantly annoyed. "Your wife's been gone only a month. Isn't there some appropriate mourning period before you pack her off for good? Just saying."

He stared at her, unwavering. "My wife and I have known where we stood with each other for many years. Taking Harper away from me was the last straw. If you had children, Ms. Carson, you would understand that nobody comes between a parent and his child."

She rolled her eyes at his dramatic statement. "Yeah, okay. Let's say you clear out of here and let me earn some of your dough, huh?" He'd started out of the room when she added, "Have your man-maid bring me a drink, would you? Not scotch."

"What's your preference?" he inquired. "I have a full bar with pretty much anything."

"Anything…" Basically desiring only to send him on a wild goose chase to ensure her privacy, she said, "You know, make it absinthe. I've always been curious."

Fortier winced, presumably at her cheap taste.

"And get me those names we talked about," she added before he could leave the room. When he looked momentarily befuddled, she impatiently clarified her request. "The jilted lovers, their contact info—all that jazz."

He left her alone.

Within minutes, the same stodgy butler as before delivered to her a bucket of ice, a bottle of green-tinted liquor, several sugar cubes, and a glass tumbler. The speed of the delivery, and that the bottle looked like an antique, told her he'd not been sent on an errand to purchase her request. So much for enjoying a peaceful search. She skipped the ice, poured a few fingers of the green liquor into a glass, and prepared to down the drink right in front of him in a move designed to disgust.

Proving he wasn't as slow as he was old, the butler swiped out his hand, grabbed her forearm, and stopped her. The green liquid lopped over the edge of the glass and dripped on the Persian rug.

"Absinthe, madam," he sternly warned her, emphasizing "madam" as though he were repulsed about having no other choice of title for her. He forcibly took the glass out of her grip, and added two sugar cubes, a bit of ice, and a liberal dose of tonic water. He glared at her when he returned the drink. "I doubt even those helps will make this drink palatable."

He turned on his heel and made a hasty exit from the small room.

Happy for the solitude, Shel downed the diluted absinthe with much aplomb, actually disappointed at her lack of audience. She grimaced, almost dropped the glass, put one hand to her burning throat, and clutched her sickly stomach with the other.

"Jesus, Mary, and Joseph," she muttered with an exaggerated rasp. She quickly picked up the decanter and held it toward the light, giving it a gentle swirl. It was bitter and god-awful—the worst thing she'd ever tried. Potent, too. Looking at the green bottle, she wondered how much of her shitty life she could forget with a few more shots. She shivered, her head still spinning, and whispered an exasperated, "Fuck me."

Feeling dangerous, she utilized caution and mimicked the butler's scientific preparation—sugar, ice, a drop of liquor, and tonic water. She sniffed the drink, but set it aside and dove into her task at hand.

An hour later, she'd destroyed the room. What began as a careful sifting through stacks of boxes had turned into a fully-fledged rampage that quite possibly coincided with her increasing level of intoxication. She'd take a little sip of absinthe, turn another carton on its side, and open another storage container. She figured the butler would play hell putting the room back together, but didn't concern herself. After a while, she'd unearthed enough photographic memorabilia to form a loose composite of Kathleen.

As a young person, Kathleen Fortier had probably been spoiled to beat all, judging from photographs of teenage Kathleen socializing with fancily dressed blue bloods at highfalutin galas. Shel found only a scattered handful of other photos, primarily a twenty-something Kathleen as a Tulane grad, and no more than a measly six pictures of the woman standing next to her husband while wearing an expression that seemed nothing short of dour.

"Pleasant little thing, this one," she said under her breath. But in truth, no matter what scowl or other unsmiling expressions Kathleen wore, not even her most unflattering photographs made her appear anything short of stunning.

Shel figured this boxed collection were photographs Mr. Fortier had selected for his wife to keep, and of course they would be the gloomy ones. She remembered getting a single crate from her ex filled to the brim with leftovers of their life together. Shel had promptly tossed it into the garbage. The memory of it had her mumbling, "Probably kept the good shit for himself. That's an ex for you."

Out of the corner of her eye she noticed a glimmer. It was a bracelet bearing two charms: a well-worn pewter palm tree and a tiny framed picture of a child. She recognized that mistrustful look; it was Harper Fortier.

"Kids don't deserve to be that wary," she whispered.

Shel sighed as she stood and made a slow circle in the center of the room, surveying the destruction she'd created. She'd significantly shortened the stacks of boxes lining the perimeter. For the first time, she was able to get a good look at the actual walls.

Framed cases containing war relics adorned nearly every square inch of vertical space. She stepped high over piles and toward a particular hanging case for a closer look: a display of two Bowie knives that, according to the bronze plaques in the encasement, were authentic weapons dating back to the early 1800s. Other framed boxes boasted a variety of revolvers and shotguns. She supposed each was equally old and valuable. The room held a veritable cache of antiques. She wondered if the collection was for art's sake, sentimental value, or a purely juvenile interest in weapons.

Past an adjoining set of fancy wooden folding doors, a narrow closet had been constructed from what appeared to have once been a hallway. A door probably led to the master, and she didn't bother with it. Clearly, the man had packed his estranged wife's things to rid his room of the memories.

The hallway-style closet ran deep enough that she couldn't see the far wall. A search for a light switch yielded nothing. Using only the bit of light cast from the adjoining room, she rummaged through the closest end of the closet. Hundreds of pieces of clothing were wedged so tightly together it was a chore to pull out a single one without taking several other pieces along with it. She pinched the shoulder of a particular sheath dress and attempted to tug it out for a better look. She whistled.

"Hello, Versace—even I'd recognize you," she said. For a split second, she envisioned Kathleen Fortier wearing it and figured she'd proven the dress to be well worth what was surely a big price tag. Shel crammed the dress back into the solid, long line of clothing.

A rustling sound from the farthest, darkest end of the narrow closet caused her to cease all movement. She stood there, still and quiet, before softly calling, "Hello?"

A shifting sound came from the far end. Shel touched her shirttail and felt her gun belt beneath. She flicked the leather strap back in a practiced move, and prepared to draw her weapon. Nothing.

She turned to go when she heard the rustling again. She spun around to see two orbs—no, eyes—too red to be human. When the eyes began to move toward her, Shel lunged backward and felt the wall a second time, hoping to find the elusive light switch. She waved her hand above her head on the chance there might be a bulb there, but came up empty. Her mouth went dry as sand. She drew her gun and backed toward the lighted room.

The eyes smoothly continued toward her. Then she stumbled over her own feet and crashed into the wall. With booze-addled reflexes and an extreme case of nerves she reached the doorway.

"What in God's name are you doing?"

Fortier, wearing a horrified expression, was standing in the middle of the small room.

Disheveled, freaked out, and now sweating, she hurriedly re-entered the larger room, nearly tripping over the very low threshold in the process. She glanced back in the direction of the closet, and realized with some embarrassment that she was still holding her gun out before her. She quickly lowered and holstered it.

"There's something in that closet."

"It's probably a rat. The Quarter's full of them." Fortier never altered his look of disbelief. His expression and tone both clearly hinted his worry that the woman he'd hired to find his child might possibly be trigger happy, if not slightly unstable. He blinked, shook his head. "Were you going to open fire on the creature? In my house?"

"No, no. Of course not." She blotted her damp face on her shirt sleeve, and quickly moved far away from the closet.

"What in hell has gone on here?" Fortier's focus had turned to the mess she'd created. "This place is chaos."

Shel brushed a hand through her hair, scooting more than a handful into her eyes for protection.

The look on his face said he wasn't listening to her. He shook his head, clearly disgusted by the room's condition. "I do hope you've found something…useful."

She felt a pain in the palm of her hand. She looked down and saw she still clutched the bracelet with the picture of the sad-looking little girl. The pointy tree charm had sharply imprinted itself in her flesh as if to drive home a literal point. She crammed it into her pocket realizing at once that she would find the child. Perhaps doing so would help her put old ghosts to rest. And then there was the money, the very good money…

He turned to face her, and his forehead wrinkled with the return of his cynical tone. "Or perhaps you're going to tell me the rat did all this…?"

"No," Shel quickly said, stepping toward him. She glanced at the bottle of absinthe still situated on the table, quietly cursing it and simultaneously swearing off it for all eternity. Attempting to shirk her foolish feeling, she shifted the subject back to his wife and child, utilizing a voice she hoped sounded more confident than she truly felt. "Is that the list?"

He nodded, and numbly handed her an envelope. She quickly unwound the clasp and briefly examined the printed sheets.

"So here are my rules," she said, tucking the envelope into her jacket. She met his eyes. "You don't contact me, I contact you. And nobody knows about our deal, understand?"

"My lawyer—"

"What you do with your lawyer is your problem. I don't want to deal with him, period."

"I have some rules, too," Fortier told her, his voice gaining strength. "I'll honor your request to not hound you for the details, but you keep me in the loop. I want to hear from you, often."

Shel appeared to consider his request for a few moments. At last she nodded.

"Also, you work alone, understand?" He held her gaze. "No subcontracting, no bringing anyone else on board, and above all, you mustn't contact the authorities."

"That's an odd stipulation," she said, shooting him a look of mistrust.

"If it comes to that, I'll do it myself." His tone made it very clear. "Do we understand each other?"

"We do," she said at last.

He extended his hand for a handshake to seal the deal, a move she pretended to not notice. Instead, she zipped her jacket and looked toward the door, performing all the obvious prerequisites for her departure.

"Where will you look for Kathleen and Harper?" Fortier asked, bringing her back to the subject on his mind. "Do you have enough to go on?"

"Only what you've shared with me." She motioned toward the piles of Kathleen's belongings that surrounded them. "Naturally, I have no way of knowing what is missing from all this. Do you know what she took with her?"

"This is only a fraction of everything I've given her." His voice held a hint of ownership that didn't sit well with Shel. "As far as anything missing, I can't account for her sizeable wardrobe and jewelry collection."

"And what about your daughter's belongings? Any favorite dolls missing?"

"No." He first shook his head, and then looked puzzled. "I don't know."

"Let's talk about the money she may have had." Shel waited several seconds for him to answer. "Does your wife have access to banking? Did she have her own lines of credit?"

"Not that I'm aware of."

"Which part? The banking or credit cards?"

Richard Fortier looked at her blankly. "Why would she need any of that? I've always given her everything she wanted."

"So, no cash?"

"None from me, but she may have cash," he slowly stated, his expression turning grim. In a low tone, he added, "Understand that she duped dozens of men. She could have access to funds I don't even know about."

She'd already considered the point. No matter what cash she had on hand, considering her wealthy lifestyle, Shel doubted Kathleen would be comfortable without the means to which she'd become accustomed. In Shel's previous work, she'd learned that people with expensive habits often made desperate bids to maintain such a lifestyle. But Kathleen was different from other marks she'd tracked before; she had a talent that could generate a decent income if any baby-blackmail plan failed her. She was an artist. Professor Artello had said Kathleen's fan base came from all over the South. So many possibilities, *if* Kathleen were alive…

"Well?" Fortier sounded somewhat impatient, jarring her from her strange reverie.

"I have some ideas." Shel nodded, her confidence building as she stepped high over the carnage she'd created.

By the time she hit the hallway, her spirits had improved significantly, and why not? A grand payday was just around the corner. She bit her lip to keep from smiling, which would be inappropriate as hell.

Appearing stunned at the mess—and perhaps his entire life of late—Fortier followed her as she trekked down the extensive staircase, then the hallway that led to the front door of the house. He hurried to keep pace with her. "When can I expect to hear from you?"

"Soon." She pushed open the front door and then the wrought-iron gate, and stepped outside.

He reached out for her arm. Not keen on being touched, she stared at his grip on her forearm for a moment and raised her gaze to meet his.

"Do you think you can honestly find my little girl?" His eyes were suddenly glassy. He swallowed hard, his Adam's apple wildly bobbing. Another round of nosy tourists emerged from a darkened street, headed toward the mansion. He ignored them. "Can you bring my Harper home?" he asked, his voice cracking. He held her arm firmly. His sadness seemed to surge through his touch.

At last, she nodded. "I'm going to try."

"Try real hard, Ms. Carson." He released his hold on her.

Shel stepped backward off the curb, relieved to be leaving the morbid home, its accompanying darkness, and its owner, the heartbroken father who practically bled sadness. Each step she took away from Fortier's depressing aura seemed to give her strength, even hope. An undercurrent of quiet wickedness spread through her, possibly at the prospect of earning so much money for such an easy job. She turned away from him, a small smile twitching her lips.

"I will." The timbre of her voice reflected her rising confidence and a cheerfulness not suited to the bleak atmosphere. She called to him as she started across the street, "Don't get too far away from your checkbook, Fortier."

CHAPTER SIX

The Internet connection in her hotel room was sketchy at best. After three complaint calls to the front desk, Shel trundled into the downstairs lobby wearing pajama pants, a tank shirt, and slippers, her laptop tucked under one arm. Disregarding stares from the desk attendant and a few partiers stumbling in at two a.m., she dropped into a plush lounge chair and fired up her computer. Satisfied with the improved signal, she settled in and went to work. By five o'clock, she'd narrowed her list to a few solid prospects. At seven, with a squirming duffel bag in tow, she checked out of the hotel and hailed a cab.

"Louis Armstrong," she told the driver as she slid into the backseat.

She turned around and gazed wistfully at her old car still parked in the hotel's side lot. When the car stalled out for the last time that morning, she'd stripped off the license plates and the VIN panel and left it for dead. Such an improper goodbye for the only thing she'd ever truly owned, but these final sentimental feelings lasted only a moment before she moved on. She'd already given up her studio apartment in Shreveport. Having abandoned the car, there was nothing to stop her from collecting her fee from Fortier and starting over without so much as a backward glance.

The cab driver didn't budge, only stared at her in the rearview mirror. At last, he asked, "What's the deal, lady?"

"Car died," she said, assuming he'd noticed her waxing poetic gaze at the old clunker. "Fought the good fight, but it's sincerely a piece of shit." When the driver kept staring, she continued, "Look, it's not worth the price to spring it from the parking lot, but if you want it, it's yours."

Clearly brimming with impatience, he asked, "I meant what's with the bag, lady?"

She looked down at her curiously bulging duffel. Newton's muffled howls told her he was staging an active protest for release from his stuffy confines. She grinned. "Yeah. You think you could swing by a pet store on the way to the airport?"

The plastic pet taxi she purchased at the store was only a moderate upgrade from the duffel bag, or so Newton expressed his opinion of it. He glared at her when she placed the carrier on the airport counter.

A clerk quickly approached her. "Welcome to AirGold, where every day is golden! How can I help you?"

Shel felt compelled to shield her body from the rays of customer service sunshine beaming through every pore of the perky blond woman. She squinted and forced a polite smile. "What have you got going to Florida real soon? I'm thinking Sarasota or the Keys."

"Only charters to both Sarasota and the Keys. I can find you a flight into the state and you could arrange flights or a car from there."

"Okay," Shel said, mentally doing the geography. "What have you got?"

"All sorts of flights." The chipper chick beamed a smile worthy of a toothpaste commercial. She clacked away on the keyboard, continuing in her Louisiana drawl, "The next flight goes to Orlando."

"Ooh." With dread, Shel envisioned a jumbo jet chock-full of noisy, frolicking children on their way to meet the world's most famous mouse. "What's next soonest?"

"Let's see…we've got Orlando, Orlando, Pensacola, another Orlando, Fort Myers—"

"Hey, Fort Myers—we've got a winner."

The woman's happy expression turned to one of concern when she noticed the pet taxi. Her downturned voice delivered the news inside a bizarre brand of baby talk directed at the cat. "Hey, little one. Your mommy's going to have to buy two seats. The airline just won't permit animals to travel cargo. You'll get banged around down there."

"What if I sign a release?" Shel asked.

As if on cue, Newton howled. The clerk's eyes went wide.

Shel didn't bother to excuse her poorly received joke. "That's fine. Two seats."

"Let's see what we've got." Again, the clerk clacked away at the keyboard. "Coach is pretty full."

A new thought crossed Shel's mind, one that she'd never considered in her entire life. "You got anything first class? And I don't want to make a bunch of stops."

"There's a nonstop flight departing in a few hours. The first-class rate is eighteen hundred dollars." The clerk paused before adding, "Each."

"Eighteen hundred?" Shel whistled. "I don't suppose the cat could fly coach."

"The airline won't permit that."

Another joke had fallen flat. Shel quickly got over it and pulled Fortier's envelope out of her pack. After a few moments of blindly fishing, she presented the woman with her shiny new AmEx. "So what do you get for that price?"

"Ample leg room, deluxe seats, premium snacks, cocktails—"

"Catnip?" Shel nodded toward the carrier, but could almost hear stereo crickets in the background. The girl looked utterly blank.

Shel muttered, "Tough crowd."

Onboard, she quickly warmed up to the perks of first class, downing two mimosas before the plane taxied off the runway. Not that her career—or budget—generally allowed for it, but she'd never been too big a fan of flying. She hoped the drinks would take the edge off. Newton, strapped into the seat next to her, still glared at her from his plastic cat jail. So far, he'd mewed his disapproval of everything.

"No whining in first class," she quietly told him.

When Newton issued another, louder protest, she draped her jacket over his carrier to muffle the sound.

Shel settled back in her oversized leather seat with extra legroom that Fortier had paid a handsome sum for. She figured he was probably used to such airline bills and probably wouldn't give it a single thought. Staring out the window at the clouds, she contemplated her mission that had begun with a simple question: how had Kathleen Fortier chosen what to paint?

Shel rubbed her tired eyes. Getting inside the head of this artsy, cultural, snooty woman would be trickier than tracking down some simpleton at a strip club to settle his casino debt. Shel would be the first to admit that going off similar architecture in waterfront towns with an ample supply of art galleries was shaky methodology at best. But how else could she get to know Kathleen Fortier apart from her husband's horrid description? It was really all she had to go on.

Shel had studied the funny, charming paintings and tried to get over her difficulty imagining an uncaring wife and mother painting such lovelies. Despite her presumed ills, Kathleen appeared to have painted for the love of the work. An artist like that could stray as far as she wished from home, but could never get too far away from a paintbrush.

In her own way, Shel understood this better than most. It was her love for cop work that kept her in the game, albeit a cheap version of her former career, with looser ethics and a far shadier clientele. It was, in fact, the barest semblance of her former life. Still, there was semblance. Doing something you knew how to do—something you were good at—was important. She seemed to be remembering that only over these past few days.

Also, Shel considered the bracelet she'd pocketed at the mansion, mainly the picture of the child. Shel had other pictures of the kid that Fortier had included in his package, but the trinket nicely fit inside her jacket or jeans pocket, which was better than lugging the larger photographs around. Shel thumbed the charms for the hundredth time before taking another look at the tiny, silver-framed photo and the child with the sweet face and pensive expression, much like the photographs of her mother.

Before she'd found the bracelet, or it found her, she'd pegged Savannah and Charleston as her best choices. The artsy cities boasted a similar feel to that of New Orleans and oozed a similar brand of Southern hospitality. Searches of both cities revealed strong interest in Kathleen's art. Again, she was thinking of the woman's livelihood, unless, of course, she was holding out for big money à la baby blackmail, as Richard Fortier seemed to strongly think. Shel tried not to be distracted by Kathleen's motivation for disappearing with the child, but it would certainly help to be able to gauge the woman's need to make money versus her desire to blackmail her husband.

Time and time again, a simple fact bothered Shel: anyone trying to lay low would not go where they would be recognized, if only by a tiny scrawled name in the corner of a painting. It was this worry that had Shel punching holes in the only theories she had about where she'd find Kathleen. It seemed evident that Kathleen wasn't stupid. The woman had vanished well enough for her husband to contact a private investigator, and that said something.

Shel didn't feel a need to factor in what Fortier had told her about his wife despising water; Kathleen wouldn't be the first person to try and throw someone off her trail by laying false groundwork. It was the stuff mystery books and Lifetime Television flicks were made of.

Thanks to the palm tree charm, her primary focus had turned to Florida. She'd spent a good part of last night on the Internet exploring galleries and finding big interest in work similar to Kathleen's in places like Siesta Key, Biscayne Bay, and Key West. Tourist towns meant transient populations, which meant Kathleen could live for months without being discovered. The lead felt as promising as anything else she'd considered.

Shel had never been to Florida. In fact, she hadn't been out of Louisiana for the past dozen years. It was her habit to find folks or track down property inside of twenty-four hours for a quick payday. The lure of big money for this particular job had her constantly fantasizing about a fresh start. The money alone wouldn't change her life, but the idea of it had inspired a bout of optimism, something she hadn't experienced in years. Also her focus felt sharp. She was determined to do this one right, whether or not her exit plan ultimately included a pocketful of Fortier funds, though it would surely be nice if it did. Given that she presently had some money, she had the luxury of time and careful consideration.

It crossed her mind that Kathleen might share a similar desire to start anew, at all costs, also with or without money. Closely trailing that thought was another, stronger, more practical one, which was that she would be wise to quit attempting to think like Fortier's wife. It was imperative that she not identify with the woman on even the remotest level if she hoped to remain objective and in Fortier's employ. He was the man with the cash and Kathleen had kidnapped their daughter. Shel couldn't help but bristle at that part. She'd known some plenty hateful people in her life, but none so hateful they'd steal a child just to spite their spouse. Shel's head felt tired. There was much to consider.

Just find her, she reminded herself.

Her head grew fuzzy with mimosas. In the event she exhausted her supply of uppity, beachy, artsy cities in Florida, she'd move on and give Fortier's AmEx a workout in South Carolina and Georgia. The mission was on autopilot for now. She downed the rest of her drink, set the glass next to Newton's carrier, and closed her eyes to rest.

On her arrival in Fort Myers her operation immediately hit a snag. No cab driver seemed in the mood to trek all the way to Siesta Key. Tamping down a slight buzz from the drinks on the plane, Shel caught a hotel shuttle to nearby Naples. According to the map she'd picked up, Siesta Key was two hours north, and the Keys four to the south. Perfect. Of course, so was Fort Myers, but the beach city would be crowded with leather-skinned twenty-somethings on spring breaks gone months into overtime.

There was something to be said for keeping a low profile while on a job. If Fortier was tracking her every move via his credit card or phone—which she suspected he was—she'd preserve her mystery by choosing a quiet, middle-of-nowhere town for her headquarters. Mystery aside, she had no real clue about Fortier's veracity. A lesser man might cop out of his agreement with her, leap ahead to the location, and find his own wife, hence screwing her over and keeping the big balance of cash owed to her. Shel never credited anyone with being too nice—or heartsick, desperate, or earnest—to screw her over. That was a fool's mistake.

With that in mind, she'd easily found and promptly deleted a GPS tracking app on the phone he'd provided her. That didn't mean he was sneaky. He may simply be cautious. She vowed to keep an open mind concerning his intentions.

The luxury shuttle took Shel to the best beach hotel Fortier's money could buy. Naples Seaside Resort was a sprawling white sandcastle in the historic part of town, situated directly on the whitest sands on the shore of the Gulf of Mexico, or so boasted the recording on loop during the shuttle ride to town. Looking at the swankily dressed travelers also taking the brief ride, she stood out like a darkly dressed pauper.

The power of her fancy black card meant she was checked in and had her luggage and cat settled in an outrageous suite within minutes. She peeled out of her jacket and slipped outside to check out the beach and judge its whiteness for herself.

She ambled along the swaying sea oats and the blue gulf just beyond. She spent a while watching the waves roll in, softly lapping the spongy white shoreline before rolling out again. In the distance, she spotted a thatched tiki-type beach bar like a mirage on the horizon. She made her way toward it.

The place was manned by a shirtless bartender wearing a "Rob" badge clipped to his uniform, which was, apparently, swim trunks. He approached her with a smile as big as his opening line. "Hey gorgeous, what'll you have?"

Shel shoved unkempt bangs off her face to let him fully appreciate her exaggerated eye roll. "Cut the shit, Rob."

"Seriously," he said, still smiling. He squinted dramatically. "Do we know each other?"

"No. Any other fiction you want to sling my way before you get me a drink?"

It was like her words didn't register with him. "Jesus, you look just like my old girlfriend in college sixteen years ago."

"Sixteen years ago, Rob, you were still pissing your pants." She slid onto the well-worn wooden stool and eyeballed the multicolored chalkboard drinks menu. "But nice try. What do you recommend?"

"Rob's World Famous Specialty." He grinned and quietly admitted, "It's just a margarita, but they're damned good."

"Sold," she said.

He slid a bowl of unshelled peanuts toward her. She cracked one open, popped the nut into her mouth, and dropped the shell on the bar's sandy floor. She looked past Rob, back to the beach and the long waves washing gently ashore. Not far from the bar, cabana boys rushed cold drinks and fluffy towels to old women wearing gold and tan Gucci swimsuits, leathering their oily bodies in the Florida sunshine. Because he seemed intent on engaging her, she humored him with small talk. "So Rob, what's so great about Naples?"

"Fantastic beaches, beautiful bodies everywhere—" He cast a glance over his shoulder and slightly grimaced at a passing woman at least a hundred pounds too heavy for her frame, not a day under seventy, and with enough wrinkles to have spent half her life under the sun. His voice dropped to a whisper. "Almost everywhere."

"No wonder you were trying to get action out of me," Shel said, chuckling. "So, how's it work—they pick you up or vice versa?"

"Wealthy dames come here while hubby's on the links." He pantomimed a golf swing, then leaned closer and quietly added, "Or off with the mistresses…"

"I see."

"The ladies want a little company, and of course I'm happy to oblige." He scooped some ice into the blender pitcher, added a squirt of sweet and sour.

Just to keep the conversation alive, she asked, "Any of them ever want to take you home?"

"Well, I am a tasty little morsel, but alas, I'm merely a temporary amusement." He added a shot of tequila, started to put the bottle away, but added another shot for good measure.

"Is that profitable?"

"I'm insulted," he said in a forced squeaky voice. His faux aghast expression faded and he comically wriggled his eyebrows before firing up the blender. He continued, yelling over the ruckus, "Nah, I didn't really figure I was your type, but you're the first person I've seen in twenty-four hours under age forty."

"You don't stop, do you?" She caught a glimpse of her forty-three-year-old face in the mirror across the bar. She supposed she could pass for younger. As it was, her shaggy bangs hid most signs of her wrinkles.

Rob killed the noise and held up a frosted green pitcher for her approval.

"Looks swell," she said. "Make it happen." She watched as he poured the slushy concoction into a glass, and utilizing great theatrics, he presented it to her. The margarita tasted fantastic. And strong. "I don't know, Rob. A few more of these and you pouring on all that bullshit, and you might become my type."

He lit up a little too much. She dropped a twenty on the bar top and started to leave. "But don't get your hopes up."

"Ah, don't go away, I'm just shitting you." His appeal seemed genuine.

Shel sat back down.

Rob leaned on the wooden bar top; his sandy blond hair tickled the tops of his bronzed, broad shoulders and lightly flapped in the breeze. "So what are you doing here in our little burg?"

"I'm looking for someone who fell off the grid." Shel stirred the icy drink with her straw.

"Lover? Friend?" he inquired.

She lowered her gaze, appeared to level with him. "I'm a… detective."

"A cop? Great." His shiny demeanor suddenly showed evidence of wear. After a quick glance over his shoulder, he whispered, "You could have been a little more forthcoming."

"Relax, Rob. I'm on my own time here and I've got no jurisdiction." Seeing how easily he'd been flustered, she added for the sake of her own amusement, "Well, almost none."

His chest visibly heaved with the breath he expelled.

She smugly leaned back on her stool and clasped her hands over the knee of her jeans. She smiled. "Now, you were saying? Friend to friend?"

"You're not my usual type of friend," he warily confessed. "And besides, I don't even remember now."

"We were talking about people in Naples."

Slowly he showed signs of coming around. His tone was low, confidential. "I was saying, you go to the Keys to fall off the grid. You come to this place to throw around a little green and be treated like a queen. Or if you're looking to put yourself in the path of your next sugar daddy or boy toy, which of course, I'd know nothing about."

"Of course."

"We're in Old Naples here." His narrative held a scandalous ring. He slumped slightly, which did nothing to detract from his washboard abs. "Old traditions, old money."

"How do you fit in?"

"Old chicks." He shrugged and rubbed his fingertips together. "I tell you they dig me. All strictly aboveboard."

"Of course," she repeated.

Another wrinkled woman wearing a floppy hat and a muumuu emerged from the beach side of the tiki bar. Shel seized her cue and pushed her nearly empty glass toward him. He probably did better work without a "cop" stinking up the joint. "Exquisite drink, Rob. See you around."

"Sure, I guess." By the time he'd turned around to face the woman, his mood had also performed a one-eighty. With the same flirtatious style in which he'd greeted her, he approached his next victim, the woman in the muumuu. Judging by her giggle, she would be a highly receptive audience. As she walked away, she heard him fire off his best first line about looking like his college girlfriend.

She smirked as she tiptoed through the sand to avoid powdering the insides of her sneakers. Reaching the hotel she left a sandy trail as she cut through the lavish lobby. Shortly behind her, a young man was sweeping it into his dustbin.

"Sorry about that," she sheepishly told him when she noticed he was shadowing her.

He politely smiled. "I do this five hundred times a shift, ma'am. No worries."

It crossed her mind she should tip him—that seemed to be the name of the game around this place—but he was gone as quickly and quietly as he'd appeared. She spotted the concierge's desk and made a beeline. The gentleman there greeted her brightly.

"Can I get a cash advance on my credit card and book a flight?" she asked.

"Certainly, ma'am," he answered with a confidence that suggested he made these things happen all the time.

Shel was alarmed at the ease with which she was able to get another ten grand off Fortier's AmEx. She stuffed the bills in her pocket and watched while the concierge performed his next trick: a small charter plane bound for Key West in the morning.

She remembered one last, annoying detail. "I'll need somebody to keep an eye on my cat. Can you arrange that?"

"Certainly, ma'am," he repeated.

Within minutes, the matter was settled. Shel returned to her suite, itinerary in hand. Once there, she dialed room service and ordered a sandwich and a beer. She hung up and addressed the still peeved cat. "Newton, whoever said money can't buy happiness didn't have a Black AmEx."

CHAPTER SEVEN

She wasted two days poking around Key West, stalking upscale galleries, flashing her fake badge at anyone who'd give her the time of day. Even a cop had fallen for it. In hindsight, she considered he might have been an impersonator too. Given it was Key West perhaps he was one of the Village People.

Duval Street was a sanitized Bourbon Street. By Friday, she'd succeeded only in marinating her liver in beer at the Green Parrot, a local fisherman's hangout standing only one block from, yet a dozen commercialized miles off the famous main drag. Come Saturday morning, the only thing she had to show for her efforts was a splitting headache. She dosed herself with Tylenol before renting a car and embarking on the slow, two-lane exit from the Keys. She paid a quick, fruitless visit to two galleries in Key Biscayne before zipping across Alligator Alley back to Naples.

At the hotel, she swiped her key card and entered her suite, nearly dropping her bag at the sight that greeted her. Newton's fur had been fluffed to maximum capacity. At the moment, he appeared to be enjoying a pedicure.

The young woman administering the service had hair as pale as the Gulf sand, and wide eyes like blue marbles. Dressed in white, her lips as red as overly-ripened berries, the woman could easily have been mistaken for a Naughty Nurse. Notions of naughty quickly dissipated when the young woman saw Shel standing in the doorway. She clapped her hands with childlike glee and greeted the cat's wandering owner.

Newton, on the other hand, looked nothing short of thoroughly disappointed that she'd returned, and as the introductions took place, he yawned as if to prove his point.

"I'm Holli with an I, the hotel's pet concierge." The introduction was made in a sweet, squeaky tone. Holli extended a smallish, perfectly manicured hand for a shake. The touch was brief. Holli soon whirled around the room, collecting her things and chucking them into a rolling trunk of cat beauty products. "Mr. Newton has had a bubble bath, a rinse, and a brush out, then a nice little massage. Didn't you, Newty?" She stopped to tickle the cat under his chin.

Newton purred loudly.

Shel rolled her eyes to no one.

With the trunk packed, the smiling young woman stood directly in front of her. It dawned on her that Holli was waiting for her tip. She fished out a wad of twenties and passed one over, then another, but Holli remained standing there, smiling.

Four twenties later, Holli flitted toward the door, calling over her shoulder, "See you again soon, Mr. Newton!"

When the door closed, Shel dropped her carry-on bag and studied the thoroughly fluffed animal that impudently stared at her. "At eighty bucks for tip alone—don't count on seeing much more of Holli with an I, Newty." She saw something shimmering in the light and moved in for a closer inspection. "Christ, are your claws pink?"

The cat slowly blinked.

She sank into a richly upholstered chair and kicked off her shoes. "On second thought, the bubble bath alone was worth the money. I'd loved to have witnessed that." She glanced around at the luxurious room with its whitewashed clapboard walls, plantation shutters, and palmy upholstered island furniture. "Don't get used to these trappings. We're out of here first thing in the morning."

She rubbed her throbbing temple and pondered her next move. She'd hit Siesta Key before checking out her second-place choices, starting with Savannah. She felt disappointed that perhaps her best lead, the palm tree charm, might have meant nothing at all.

On the drive into town, she'd made a stop at an office supply store where she'd fired off a dozen fax inquiries to galleries in and around Savannah. Before she could finish the job, she'd received two negative replies. In the morning there were bound to be more. Suddenly, her mission didn't feel as simple as when she'd started out.

The cat, apparently bored with her, retreated to the window where he curled into a ball for a nap in the late afternoon sun.

"That's right. Let me do the heavy lifting," Shel quietly scolded him. She felt drained, downright sleepy, and the chair felt cozy enough to fall asleep. Soothed by the soft hum of the central air unit, she nodded off.

She was in a slummy efficiency apartment, temporary headquarters for this latest assignment. A woman, Zoey, leaned against the door, her eyes wide with fear at the commotion taking place in the hallway. Shel didn't know how she'd gotten here; she didn't understand why this was happening to her again, but she knew what would happen next.

She frantically ushered Zoey and her young daughter to the window, but it had been painted shut for years. Shel grabbed a pillow and attempted to cushion her fist as she busted out the glass. With one miss, blood gushed everywhere. The sound of gunfire erupted and the flimsy hotel door exploded into confetti of splinters. The dank mildew scent was joined by the distinct smell of heat and sulfur. Zoey and her child were on the floor. She could taste her own blood...

It was the sound of her own strained gasp that awakened her. Her eyes scanned the hotel room as she searched for her bearings then she dropped her head against the lounger headrest and tightly shut her eyes. The comingled smell of sulfur, sweat and mildew of that night seemed permanently stuck in her nostrils. She breathed deeply until her head was full of the hotel smells that now surrounded her: lemon polish with an underlying hint of bleach. Her chest heaved as she willed her hammering heart to calm down.

When she again opened her eyes, she blinked against the sunlight already streaming into the bright, cottage-style room. Sunday morning had arrived early and weirdly. She rarely remembered her dreams and had no recollection of the night's disturbing ones. She sat up, slowly arching her back and moving her tired legs, cramped from having slept upright in the chair no matter how comfortable its design. She stood, stretched, and blotted her sweat-damp forehead before heading to the bathroom to shower. She cruised past Newton who seemed to have slept quite comfortably alone in the center of the king-sized Serta.

The cool streams of water pounded her body for a while until she at last felt the smallest sense of renewal.

She left the hotel and, on foot, began the ten-block trek to Fifth Avenue. Far from an exercise fanatic, she felt good stretching her legs after having spent so much time in the car of late. With some dread, she considered the upcoming days and the likelihood of multiple car and plane rides. She hoped a positive lead could be gleaned from the faxes she'd already sent out. Even an inkling of hope would be nice…

For the second time in twenty-four hours, she went to the office supply store in the quaint downtown area. She tried the door, but it didn't budge. Only then did she notice a handwritten sign in the window indicating the shop wouldn't open until noon.

She turned a slow half circle, surveying the increasing activity around her. Workers ferried white canvas tents up and down the police-barricaded street, aligning them in perfect long chains, preparing for some small-town festival.

An enormous, antique cup of coffee was perched on the rooftop of a corner shop, emitting fake puffs of steam for its advertisement. The mere suggestion perked up Shel immediately. She didn't stop until she reached the shop, aptly named the Coffee Cup, where she ordered the tallest, strongest latte listed on the chalkboard menu. Despite the coffee's heat, she downed most of the cup before leaving the counter.

The little café was perfunctorily furnished. The plain walls held just a few paintings and local photographs hanging much too high. Operated by older ladies wearing rags on their heads and crisp, coffee-stained aprons, the shop was a jewel of a find in the middle of such pristine, high-dollar commercial real estate. Probably its unpretentiousness added to its charm.

A few men wearing pony shirts, the standard weekend uniform, sat alone at two-seater tables, their noses buried in newspapers or fixed on their iPads, likely reading golf magazines or checking their stocks, and getting ready for whatever their day held.

The place was quiet. She liked it.

She snagged a copy of *The Daily* on her way to a corner table. Safely behind the shield of the unfolded newspaper, she was sure she looked like a dressed down version of the other patrons. She hid out, waiting for the coffee to perform its caffeinated magic. She also considered the day ahead.

She'd check for the faxes, and if nothing looked promising, she'd turn in her rental car and hop another plane, this time to Savannah. The investigation was taking too long. She didn't like it. Maybe she was growing more impatient with age.

She felt funny being so antsy about work, given that her former life as an undercover narcotics cop required ultimate patience, which she'd been good at. She had the pain in her back to prove it, a not so subtle reminder of a night long ago when she'd been forced to lay still for an hour, playing dead with a bullet lodged in her lower back. She remembered the sensation and horror of her blood pooling around her…

Something she noticed hanging on the wall before her snapped her out of her reverie with such urgency, she sprang to her feet. In her hurry, the flimsy metal chair screeched loudly across the floor and her tiny table wobbled a dangerous circle. She reached out a hand to steady it, but her coffee cup jumped off the ride and crashed to pieces near her feet.

The place went quiet. Only faint canned music could be heard coming from the swinging metal doors leading to the kitchen. All eyes were on her, but she ignored the curious gazes and remained focused on the painting hanging above the very table where she'd been seated. How she hadn't noticed it before now was beyond her. The painting depicted a row of tiny pastel houses, different from those oversized New Orleans mansions, but with the distinctive sunshiny windows and silvery moon hanging in the sky. She took a step closer to examine the picture, blinking several times as if each new look might have her changing her mind about what she felt she was seeing. No signature, no curling K, but those colors and that moon…

Shel heard an admonishing tongue click behind her. She realized she needed to say something. She spun around, her shoulders hunching slightly, and hurried to the counter. All hope for a confidential question-and-answer session was out the door since the silence she'd created would permit everyone in the shop to hear every word.

"Hey, I'm sorry about that." She shot an apologetic and somewhat shy smile at the gaping counter clerks. She motioned in the direction of the painting. "That piece caught my eye. Can you tell me where you got it?"

The counter ladies' glances seemed to move in unison, slowly and warily shifting from her to the mess she'd created to the painting, then returning to her again.

"That one's not for sale. It's one of the owner's favorites." The older of the two women pointed a hygienic, plastic-gloved finger at some other paintings hanging on an adjacent wall. These were composed of boxier subjects, paralyzingly intense color, and poor scale. "Now, those ones over there are for sale. They're painted by the owner's son, if you want me to get you a price."

Shel desperately tried to tamp down her excitement. Her chest surged with a hopefulness she hardly recognized and dreadfully missed. She found her cell phone and hurriedly snapped two pictures of the painting, aware that the counter ladies—in fact, everyone in the shop—were still observing her curious behavior. She again stepped closer, examining the painting's clean, nice borders and colors that blended with subtlety. There wasn't a signature in sight, which seemed peculiar, but she'd bet her entire wad of cash and a black AmEx the work had been painted by Fortier's wife.

Shel looked back at the counter ladies. "Is that a Kathleen Fortier?" Clearly clueless, the ladies shrugged simultaneously. They'd obviously worked together far too long. Even their bored expressions were the same. "Do you know if the owner ordered that one or bought it around here?"

"That one's fairly new. Owner only buys local. He hires local and buys from local bakers and growers—everything." The older woman broke from her bored expression and issued Shel a thin smile. She nodded toward the mess she'd left behind her on the floor. "That twelve dollar mug you broke was also made local."

"Gotcha." Shel felt herself shrink under the woman's subtle chastisement. She quickly collected the remnants of her cup and saucer, and set the pieces on the counter. She peeled a twenty off the top of her wad and shoved it into the tip jar she'd earlier ignored. "Thank you, ladies."

"You're welcome." The woman's grin was wide and looked quite genuine. She was obviously pleased with the effectiveness of her ill-disguised tip solicitation. "Come again soon, now."

Shel left the shop.

With orange and white striped barricades effectively sealing off Fifth Avenue from car traffic, the place had been transformed into a pedestrian paradise. Vendors busily carted their wares toward endless rows of uniform-sized white tents. The day was coming alive to the sounds of clinking pottery, the ring of delicate wind chimes, and the four-piece bands warming up their instruments, getting ready to perform for tips. The smells of funnel cakes and deep fried seafood hung thickly in the humid air, completing a carnival-like atmosphere, except here the crowd wore Ralph Lauren, white Capri pants, Coach handbags carelessly drooping from their forearms.

She headed for the first tent. Judging from the watercolor houses depicted in tiny frames, she had a dim hope she'd already struck pay dirt. On closer inspection, she realized the differences—darker colors, kitschier subjects, exaggerated waves, and not a shotgun house or sunshiny window in sight. She approached various individuals manning the tents and showed the picture she'd snapped in the coffee shop, but nobody seemed to be familiar with the woman's work. Time and again she was disappointed. No one seemed to have ever heard of Kathleen Fortier.

The central art themes seemed to be of watercolor beach cottages or large pink castles, glasses of vino, jazz instruments, and then there was beach photography... She continually consulted the photo on her phone, worried she'd forget what she felt certain she was looking for. Somewhere around the tenth tent of similar paintings, she figured she had her work cut out for her. She was almost relieved when she came to the tents containing wind chimes, stepping stones, and abstract bronze figures just to have an excuse to walk past them.

The balance of Sunday afternoon was spent analyzing painting after painting in a never-ending chain of tents. As the day became hotter, she grew frustrated with her task, tempted to flash her badge and simply start showing a picture of Kathleen herself, rather than that of her painting, but worried that doing so might send the elusive woman further into hiding—if the woman was in Naples to begin with.

By four o'clock, bands were breaking down and vendors packing up, preparing to cart their works back to wherever they'd come from. Shel bought a tall cup of sweet tea and sat on the curb in a bit of shade to formulate her next move.

Apparently, the office supply store kept only a three-hour day on Sundays, and she'd missed that by a few hours. So much for the entire reason she'd come to Fifth Avenue in the first place. She was ready to give up and more than ready for something stronger than iced tea. A twinge in her back told her it was time to call it a day.

She pushed off the curb and caught sight of an older couple headed across the street, toting a large painting as if it were a prized find. Zeroing in for a better look, she was struck by an exposed section not covered by paper—a silver moon in a swirl of sky. Forgetting her aching back, she rushed over to the pair.

"Excuse me, ma'am, sir," she said, interrupting their playful conversation about who made a better fettuccini—Rosso Italia or Bella Café. They halted in their tracks and eyed her with an appropriate level of suspicion. Given her dark clothes in an otherwise pastel beach town, she was clearly an outsider. Add to that her wind-mussed hair, and to them, she probably looked homeless. Her suspicion was confirmed when the gentleman's free hand went for his pocket, perhaps with the intention to either giving her a buck or to mace her. She picked up the pace of her inquiry. "I'm sorry to bother you. I wanted to ask about your painting."

His brow furrowed and his hand came out of his pocket. He edged the painting slightly back and out of her reach, and his wife touched his elbow. Shel wondered if the seventy-year-old pair thought they could fend her off so easily. Another twinge in her low back quickly deflated her momentarily inflated ego. Their combined haughtiness was off-putting, but Shel could afford to waste no time being offended. She softened her stance, smoothed her hair, and forced as warm a smile as she could manage.

"Oh, I'm sorry—I dirty down a bit when I'm shopping for my boss. Between us, he's a bigwig in town, but a legendary tightwad. I find I get a better price for him this way." She broke into a grin and added in an exaggerated whisper, "And when the boss is happy… well, I'm pretty damned happy."

To add credibility to her presentation, she briefly fished the wad of money out of her jeans pocket and gave it a little squeeze before putting it away again. The performance, though seemingly over the top, seemed to work on the pair. They looked relieved. Perhaps the wad of money made them feel right at home, or perhaps they were simply grateful she had her own cash and didn't want theirs.

"Well, now, that's just plain smart," the man said, his attitude toward her visibly improving. Strands of white, downy hair encircled his semi-sunburned head. He had a spectacularly easy smile and clearly liked to show it off. "You must be quite a businesswoman yourself."

"Yes," the wide-eyed wife dutifully agreed. "Clever indeed."

"Thank you," Shel said, treading waist high in the lie. She turned her attention to the painting that had inspired her ruse in the first place. "Anyway, that looks like a Kathleen Fortier. Is she showing here?"

"Fortier?" The gentleman shook his head. "I'm afraid you're mistaken. This is a local artist, but she's actually quite good."

"My bad," Shel said, both confused and hopeful. "Could I have a look?"

"Be my guest." The man pulled off the rest of the flimsy paper covering and held the painting out for her inspection.

She studied its folksy aqua and peach hues and perfect light, its swirling skies, waves, and silver sliver of a smiling moon. A quaint, rustic cottage stood where a shotgun house would have in an older version. She'd bet her life that it was Kathleen's work, despite the missing shotgun and signature with the curling K. She paced her words to avoid sounding too hopeful. "My mistake. In any case, I think the boss will like this artist. He's always looking for the next big deal."

"As are we," the wife excitedly told her. "And we've gotten very lucky at these art fairs over the years."

"Splendid to know," Shel said. She looked past the couple at the workers wrapping their wares. Her pulse quickened. "Do you think you could point me in the right direction?"

"There are a few tents scattered in the park. You'll find her work under the striped canopy south of the band shell."

"Wonderful. I'd better get a move on since they're closing up shop." She started away and doubled back briefly, offering one last improvisation. "By the way, Rosso Italia has top-shelf gnocchi."

They thanked her, obviously surprised they had one more thing in common.

Shel hurried across the street. She shrugged off the latest lies as easily as she had the others. She quickly formulated a new rule: lies told for the sake of finding the child would not count heavily against her. Her reemerging, single-minded determination made her quite a competent command performance liar and smiler. Holding tight to a particularly sore spot low on her back, she jogged past a bricked courtyard and down a narrow alley in the direction the man had indicated. Indeed, there was a park on the other side of a large public restroom, none of which she'd realized existed before now. She chastised herself for having missed hours of opportunity to better scour the place. Volunteers were now rushing to close the festival down. She quickly spotted the band shell and beyond that, a green and white striped canopy.

Jackpot.

She broke into a light jog toward the canopy where a good concentration of volunteers was gathered, already at work packing and carting away the work. She scanned a row of remaining paintings, noting their funny, brightly painted guest houses with sunshine in the window and perfect light.

She glanced around the area for Kathleen Fortier while considering the fact the woman could possibly be wearing her hair back or hiding behind plate-sized sunglasses. In photographs, the woman wore a snooty smile, and she was beautiful enough to warrant any feelings of conceit; therefore Shel doubted Kathleen Fortier would alter her appearance beyond anything superficial. She'd barely bothered to alter her pictures, for heaven's sakes—*if* these paintings belonged to Kathleen…

An African-American woman was giving directions to volunteers and transferring money from a cash register to a canvas zipper bag. She was tall with an athletic build, her perfectly long braids pulled into a thick, lovely ponytail. Shel was struck with a case of nerves when the woman smiled brightly and cordially greeted her, not only because the woman could easily have been a model, but also because she was clearly not Kathleen.

She forged ahead. "Lovely stuff. Are you the artist?"

"No. I'm a friend to the artist, but I'll pass along the compliment. Thank you."

"Pity." Hope resurged within her. "I was hoping to pick up a thing or two on my boss's behalf."

Proceeding with the lie she'd forged on Fifth Avenue, Shel reached into her pocket and barely flashed the wad of dough. She'd gotten more mileage out of that money than she had her fake badge of late and figured she should have made a roll of cash part of her routine long ago.

"He's putting together a sort of kid's space, and he's looking for something appropriate to hang on the walls. Anyway, thanks." She tucked the cash back into her pocket and started to leave, counting silently to herself.

The woman stopped her before she could hit number two. "The artist has some nice work that you may find to be quite child friendly. You should have a look."

Shel expressed doubt. "I can see you're trying to get out of here. I don't want to keep you."

"No problem." The woman was already motioning for the volunteers to cease movement in the background. "No problem at all. Have a look around. Take your time."

Shel nodded and noticed a few men had unwrapped the very items they'd been preparing to haul off moments earlier. She moseyed along row upon row of unmarked watercolors. "The artist really has a nice eye. Who is he?"

"She," the woman corrected.

Shel burst into a grin and said under her breath so she wouldn't be overheard, "It's really you, isn't it? Why so modest? They're amazing."

"I'm Silvia Frances. Addison James is responsible for the work," the woman said. "I give her a hand now and then in sales, but I'm no artist."

Addison James? Shel's glimmer of hope threatened to dim. She glanced around her, certain the paintings were Kathleen's work. "I see." She was tempted to produce a picture of Kathleen and simply cut through multiple needless charades. She resisted and pushed on. "She from Naples?"

"Not originally, but then, not many people are," Silvia answered, her tone indicating she'd rather sell art than make conversation about the artist. Her next sentence solidified that notion. "Is there a particular size or price range you're looking for, Miss…?"

Well behind Silvia, Shel saw a sign pointing toward the Morris Park Storage facility. "Morris. Cindy Morris."

"Ms. Morris," Silvia politely echoed the made-up name. "Can I show you anything in particular?"

"No, I think I've seen enough." She pulled the wad of cash out a second time and peeled off a few bills. She nodded at the closest painting, since they were all beginning to look alike to her. "How much for this one?"

"Five hundred," Silvia quickly answered. "Firm."

"I wasn't planning to dicker over price," Shel said, chuckling. She handed her the cash. "I'm sure my boss will like this painting. Do you have a card in case he would like a few more?"

"Who is your boss?" Silvia's brows plunged. She suddenly seemed suspicious.

"Truthfully?"

"Yes, please."

Out came another unrehearsed lie wrapped inside a confidential tone. "It's for the children's wing of the hospital. Usually when people learn that, they want more money. I don't know why people are under the impression that nonprofits actually profit."

"I understand. I do a bit of nonprofit work myself." Silvia's stance softened. She was obviously more at ease. "I suppose perhaps bad press about exaggerated corporate costs makes people cynical that way. A pity. A few bad seeds ruin things for the good guys."

"I suppose so. Anyway, we do like to give credit where credit is due. You know, hang a little bronze plaque below the work. It's sort of a tribute to the artist and generally a good advertisement for them as well." Shel shrugged and casually added, "That's why I had so many questions about your artist. But I can understand if she is a recluse or something. No big deal."

"Addison is a very private woman."

Behind them, volunteers began wrapping the painting in yards of bubble wrap.

"Okay." Shel jammed the remainder of the cash back into her pocket, playfully wriggled her eyebrows, and leaned in closer. "Not much of a looker, huh? Maybe she has a big old hairy mole or something?"

Silvia laughed, but quickly recovered. In her best serious voice, she said, "I assure you, Ms. James doesn't have a…" She gestured at her face and burst into giggles that seemed uncharacteristic of such a seemingly cultured lady.

"Well, I have a pretty nutty imagination." Shel smiled, enjoying her flirting with Silvia. Straight or not, the woman obviously enjoyed it. "Tell the mole-less Ms. James that her work will be on display in the children's wing of the hospital, if she cares to stop by sometime and take a look."

The volunteer in charge of packing handed her the large painting that had been generously wrapped.

"Wow, a watercolor burrito," she said, earning another laugh from Silvia. "If I drop this thing, it'll bounce."

When she recovered from another round of laughter, Silvia shook her hand. "Thank you for stopping by. Contact me personally if your boss would like to see something else."

When Shel drew her hand back, there was a business card in her palm. Without a word, she tucked it into her jeans pocket and hurried away.

Back on Fifth Avenue, police officers were removing barricades and reopening the street to traffic. She leaned against the brick wall of a closed shop and eagerly dug the card out of her pocket for a better look.

Thomas Taylor, Artist, City Dock Shoppes.

She squinted at the card. Not exactly the key to the universe, but at least Kathleen—or Addison—had an outlet from which to sell her art. She turned over the card, saw a scribbled telephone number, and wondered if the lovely Silvia Frances was such a pristine straight girl after all. She shrugged off the wishful thought and chucked the card into her jeans pocket.

She hiked the rest of the way back to the hotel, toting the awkwardly wrapped painting and contemplating its cost. In New Orleans, a Kathleen Fortier work would have easily gone for ten grand, yet she'd just picked up an incredibly similar piece for a measly five hundred bucks. She would spend hours that night comparing the painting she'd bought at Loyola to the one she'd picked up that day. Not that she was an expert, but the brushstrokes looked to be the same, and the colors matched identically. It made sense, Shel reasoned, that an artist would have her favorites. Obviously the subjects would have to change, or else Kathleen would risk immediate exposure. But certainly some things wouldn't change, like technique and style. Also particular colors or subjects would be a devastatingly hard artistic habit to deviate from.

Still, the obvious differences glared at Shel; the houses were different types and the signature was altogether missing. It felt like she was trying to talk herself out of believing it was Mrs. Fortier's work. It was worth hanging around Naples a few days to try and argue the point with herself.

* * *

First thing in the morning, Shel was at City Dock on Naples Bay in front of the gallery listed on the business card Silvia had given her, a relatively quiet part of town compared to noisier tourist sections. Having only been in Naples a few days, she was quickly getting acquainted with its neighborhoods. A few blocks from the City Dock was the Third Street South District, a livelier area boasting expensive eateries serving seafood, craft beers and fancy drinks created by a "mixologist," rather than a bartender. Patrons sufficiently dosed with Marga-tinis and Key Lime infused cocktails could be found toddling down the famous Naples Pier for the best view of sunset on the Gulf shore. A few blocks in the opposite direction was Fifth Avenue, a sort of West Coast Rodeo Drive for the over sixty set who loved a good pinot, prime steak and valet parking. Sandwiched between the competitive shopping districts was an authentic glimpse of old Florida, the rustic City Dock. Naples was indeed an interesting town, bigger and better versus older and quainter, proving the seaside town had a real case of architectural schizophrenia.

The street leading up to City Dock was lined with a few hotels, a handful of nautically themed shops, a pizza joint, and two art galleries, the latter few housed in what appeared to be revitalized fishing shanties. The Thomas Taylor Gallery was one of these, a smallish shop bulging with Floridian paintings. There were beaches, beach shacks, docks and piers, and enough parrots and margaritas to keep Jimmy Buffett safely in paradise for the rest of his days. Front and center in the main window stood one of those sweet pastels Shel was becoming an expert at recognizing.

The front door was propped open, and Shel quietly slipped inside and browsed the tiny shop. The limited space was utilized to capacity with paintings hanging from floor level all the way up to the very high ceiling. Multiple bins placed around the room contained an assortment of plastic encased prints that one could flip through like a filofax. As rough count, Shel figured about a quarter of all the work contained within the shop was Kathleen Fortier's. She was craning to see the topmost paintings when she heard a man's voice behind her.

"Looking for something special today?"

Shel spun to see an older gentleman with white hair, and enough fat on his frame to make him appear downright jolly. He further sealed the deal when he smiled, revealing apple cheeks and dimples. He reminded her of a postcard she'd once see of Santa vacationing on an island during the off-season. He extended a hand her way, "Thomas Taylor, I own this little hodgepodge of a place."

She shook his hand firmly. "Nice to meet you. Your shop is lovely."

"Thank you. Can I answer any questions?"

"No, but binoculars might be helpful," she said, indicating the highest row of paintings hanging almost a full story above them. They chuckled. "You've got nice stuff here, Mr. Taylor."

"Thank you. I've been painting my whole life and a good life it's been."

Shel's smile was genuine. He emanated a contented peacefulness that felt utterly foreign to her. She forged ahead. "Is everything here your work?"

"Gentle visitor, I've been fortunate to create and sell a lot of work in my life." He lazily strolled along the wall, pausing to study an occasional painting now and then. "Nowadays, I'm semi-retired. I'm painting less, drinking more wine, having some laughs, and enjoying the gifts of new artists."

Shel took a step closer to the wall, nodded toward one of the funny guesthouse paintings. "I like this one."

"That work belongs to a new discovery, a young woman who has a great eye for whimsy." He glanced back at Shel, who nodded. His eyes returned to the painting and he slightly tipped his head as he continued his analysis. "Before she blessed us with her talents, this shop was mostly sand and seascapes. It's different from our usual fare, but different is good."

"She local?" Shel tried not to sound too hopeful. "Looks like you have a lot of her work."

"She is local, and if there's something you fancy, I am happy to pass along your requests, thoughts, or ideas to Ms. James."

"Ms. James," Shel repeated. She sheepishly grinned. "I must confess, I saw some of her art in the park yesterday afternoon. That's what drew me to your shop."

He appeared happy to hear this. "She'll be pleased to receive the compliment."

Shel's heartbeat accelerated in sync with her hopefulness. "Is she around, by chance? Ms. James?"

Thomas Taylor neither blinked nor stammered. His answer was simple and frank. "I happily honor her request to remain in the background. I respect every aspect of the creative process."

"I see," Shel slowly answered. "I guess some people are better with people and others are better with a paintbrush." She gave a nod toward the house painting, reaffirmed, "Clearly she's good with a paintbrush."

"I see you also respect the process," he said, seemingly pleased that further explanation was not required. "I always recognize a good spirit when I encounter one."

With that assessment, he quietly returned to the same comfy chair where he'd been sitting upon her arrival. The Santa Buddha, Shel mentally dubbed him, but certainly he was not as wise as he believed himself to be. No one had ever used the word *good* to describe her, not even when she was a child.

Shel pushed the depressing thought out of her head and milled through the bins of paintings for several minutes and generally nosed around the shop. When it was clear that Kathleen either wasn't in the shop, or wouldn't be making an appearance, Shel thanked the kindly Summer Santa and made her exit.

She set up temporary headquarters at a bistro table outside the next-door self-service pizza joint where she sipped iced tea, and for a few hours pretended to consult a map. She was hanging out on the off chance that Kathleen Fortier might show herself. At noon, she ordered a slice of pizza. At three o'clock, she ordered another along with a lager of beer. By five, she was ignoring the glares of the bistro workers who surely wanted her to free up a table for the steady influx of customers. Meanwhile, her patience for the project had completely evaporated.

Thomas Taylor's words rolled through her mind about Addison James remaining in the background, which had given her a morsel of hope that Kathleen was actually on the physical premises. But the longer she waited, the more foolish the notion seemed, and Shel had to face the possibility that Kathleen might never see the inside of the gallery. For all that, she might never even visit Naples, despite what he said about the woman being local. It could be a ruse to sell paintings to tourists.

Finally she was forced to remind herself that it might not even be Kathleen Fortier's work. There could actually exist a woman named Addison James, a socially phobic, talented artist who, by some coincidence, had a knack for designing similar funny-shaped, pastel houses. Weirder things had happened. It was Shel's gut feeling that had her waiting around. The very fact that she'd managed to rouse her long-dormant instincts was even stranger than the possibility of finding Kathleen Fortier in Naples.

She hoped asking the shop owner about the artist's Naples residency wouldn't prove detrimental to her case. No way would she want to risk scaring the woman further into hiding with so much money at stake. Shel realized she was often thinking about the woman in terms of being scared and not wanting to be found, and she wasn't sure why she kept ending up there in her mind. She hoped it wasn't that instinct because she could use the money. Shel's stomach churned every time she thought about it. All this talk of change had her wanting to employ other changes, too, like trying her hand at a life with a semblance of honor.

Either way, until Shel knew the score, it was vital that Kathleen not know anyone was looking for her. If the woman was biding her time, holding the kid for money and Shel's clumsy search inadvertently caused a sudden spike in that ransom, her bottom line was sure to go down. She'd be starting a new life, all right, but without money it could feel much like her old very quickly.

Shel pushed her bangs aside and wiped the sweat off her forehead. Naples was every bit as humid as Louisiana, but with the addition of real heat, and she seemed to be suffering the climate change more than she'd suspected she would. She was thinking about this when a tiny Volvo station wagon pulled curbside. Silvia, the woman from the art sale, emerged from the car wearing a large, stylish bag slung over her shoulder.

Taken aback, Shel reacted by raising a plastic menu to shield her face. She watched Silvia practically disappear into the backseat and reemerge with a brunette, curly-haired child on her hip.

Shel's heart felt like it turned a somersault. What happened next made the entire wait worthwhile: a woman came from inside the shop to greet them on the front stoop.

It would have been hard to recognize her had Shel not permanently etched the missing woman's delicate features in her mind. Gone were the long, dark tresses, replaced by a bleached blond pixie haircut. In place of the expensive designer clothing, she now wore a funny bohemian skirt presently covered by a paint-speckled apron. None of the getup did much to flatter her smaller than life, boyishly thin frame. Without makeup, jewels, or any other sign that she was the wife of a wealthy millionaire, Kathleen Fortier looked like the girl next door, a semi-believable disguise. But all the wardrobe and hair colors in the world would do nothing to mask those haunted eyes.

The woman swept the little girl into a quick embrace before ushering the child into the shop.

Shel watched as lovely, smiling Silvia followed them to the doorstep and exchanged parting remarks with mother and daughter. Then quickly she returned to her car and drove away. Shel viewed the entire scene from behind the safety of the plastic menu. After a few minutes, she lowered it, only to snap it right back up again when Kathleen reappeared, rolling a beach bike alongside her. The blond woman strapped her helmeted daughter into the back child seat and away they rode.

Shel all but hurdled over a flowerbed to get to her rental car, figuring anyone who noticed the strange action would take her for a stalker. She could live with that. She easily caught up to them and continued to tail them at a safe distance while Kathleen coasted the bike through the connecting neighborhood.

Shel's mind was alive with the fact that the hair, the makeup and clothes—all of it—were long gone. At first blush, it didn't look like the woman was in a hurry to return to New Orleans, Richard Fortier, or the life of prestige she'd once led, and that had Shel curious. No matter how conniving and no matter how good an actress the woman may be, Shel couldn't imagine why Kathleen would go through the trouble of such an elaborate change in location, income and appearance.

Despite her lack of understanding, Shel's skin prickled with excitement at the prospect that things were finally getting good.

Kathleen turned down Third Avenue North. As she drove, everything Richard Fortier said about his wife echoed in her head—Kathleen was a dreadful, dangerous mother; she was a scammer to the nth degree.

Tempted as she was to place a phone call, collect her money and scram, the vow she'd made to herself in New Orleans now had her firmly in its grip. The desire to lead a better, more upstanding life both teased and tortured her. She didn't want to go forth, money in pocket, having thrown a sheep to the wolf. Only who was the sheep? The wolf…? Damn her sudden case of conscience.

Shel rolled down the car windows letting the hot breeze blast her face, the scent of every tropical flower assaulting her senses. She coasted far behind the bike, watching the woman's gypsy skirt bob with her pedaling, flowing behind her like a ribbon. The little girl, thoroughly masked by the large helmet, waved tiny hands, as if she were attempting to physically catch the gentle wind as they zipped silently along the increasingly quiet neighborhood.

Hypnotized by the breeze and the flowing, ribbony skirt, Shel felt other senses being gradually tickled awake. A feeling of something that resembled righteousness washed through her, only it didn't feel as good as she thought it should. It felt like heartburn and headache.

As they rode deeper into the neighborhood, Shel slowed her pace even more, widening the already lengthy gap between the bike and car. The colorful skirt snapped and flapped in the breeze as they rode farther away from her. Try as she may to resist the notion, Shel couldn't help but feel it was symbolism. It looked like the promise of her colossal payoff was waving goodbye.

CHAPTER EIGHT

Shel figured a smarter woman would have turned Kathleen over to her husband, collected the cash, and begun the process of putting it all behind her. It occurred to her at least once a minute throughout her sleepless night. By morning, she could have been back on Richard Fortier's doorstep with pictures of Kathleen, the kid, and the tiny cottage where they lived. He'd said simply call with her location, but Shel had never been one to take a person at his word, nor did she trust such a large amount of cash to a wiring service. She didn't even have a bank account where he safely could plunk a hearty deposit. Bank accounts were on the record and the payments she'd collected in recent years were not. To this point, mistrust seemed to be the central theme of her existence. Perhaps with enough money and distance from Shreveport, she could overcome that, too.

She'd finally succumbed to a bit of sleep around five, only to have it tainted with another horrific flashback to her last night undercover on the Narco unit. This time she saw the bodies with remarkable clarity, could remember how she'd crawled through glass toward the smallest, touched the pale skin, felt the warmth of life slipping away…

Shel awoke in a cold sweat, marking the beginning of another bleary-eyed day. She'd showered and dressed before making the short drive downtown.

Shel checked her watch and glanced around at the sparse metal tables, the handful of seated patrons, and the Florida-centric art cluttering the walls of the Coffee Cup. Since discovering Kathleen's work there, she considered the place her lucky charm. The workers had greeted her with wide smiles that morning—her previous fiasco seemingly long forgotten, particularly in light of another twenty-dollar bill she'd stuffed into the jar without concern that the tip was four times the amount of her bill.

As she waited for her appointment, she again ruminated about turning the pair's location over to Fortier. The man could have collected his child and Shel's only concern would be which barstool to wear a groove in and on which island. It could still happen, she told herself, although her already wavering conviction about such had taken an even greater hit upon confirming the identity of the woman with the newly shorn, blond locks.

The bell jingled for the tenth or so time, and her head swiveled toward the door yet again. She rose out of her seat—with care—and greeted her appointment. Thanks to a real estate brochure, she immediately recognized the sixty-something platinum blond with too much Botox and lip filler and overly tanned skin. A frozen, pink-painted grin greeted her, as per a standard she was quickly getting used to, and Mrs. Junie D'Amico, Realtor Extraordinaire, gave her the outsider's considered once-over.

"Ms. Carson?" Junie looked very much like she hoped the answer was no. When Shel nodded, the Givenchy-clad woman rearranged her long, flowery scarf and motioned toward the counter. "I'll grab coffee and we'll get right to it."

Shel waited by the door, reflecting upon the previous night's mini stakeout of Kathleen's house, which turned out to be in the middle of a three block stretch of Third Avenue. Her watch hadn't yielded much. Nobody entered or exited the premises, and the lights had gone out promptly at nine. Shel had hung around until ten before returning to the hotel.

Her uneventful stakeout had given her plenty of time to study the neighborhood. Most of the houses had hurricane shutters in place, battened down good, considering there wasn't so much as a storm in the distant forecast at present. She'd asked Rob the bartender about it upon her return to the hotel. He explained that most residents of the town were seasonal. For six months of the year, a substantial percentage of lavish homes were left in the hands of a house staff, a league of lawn maintenance people, and whatever environmental elements the season dished out. She wondered who on earth could afford to call a Naples beach castle a simple "winter home." It seemed to her a waste.

On Third Avenue, only two houses had yet to incur complete renovation. Both appeared to be relics from the seventies—tiny, brightly painted ranch-style homes with more sand than grass for lawns. The outdated quintessential beach houses were probably no larger than eight hundred square feet each, and were, ironically, situated directly across the street from each other. The structures practically screamed investment, with owners probably waiting for the market to rise then pounce on a good price. One day in their place there would also be salmon colored McMansions. Meanwhile, they were shacks. One was Kathleen's tiny yellow, well-kept cottage. The other was a lime-green eyesore with a crooked For Rent sign in its sandy front yard.

For reasons she couldn't quite explain even to herself, Shel had taken down the phone number and looked up the realtor online when she'd returned to her hotel room. She'd placed an early morning call to Ms. Junie D'Amico and requested they meet at the Coffee Cup as soon as possible to discuss the property.

Shel's initial thought centered solely around getting a better look at Kathleen's home in broad daylight. From the vantage point across the street, she figured she'd formulate her next move, though her gut already told her what that would be. She tried to ignore the sensation, willing things to unfold around her as they were meant to do instead of rushing them. Patience wasn't her greatest strength.

Junie D'Amico returned with coffee in hand, unknowingly rescuing Shel from her internal prattle. The older woman looked revived upon her first few sips of the brew. She grinned, revealing a tiny bit of pink lipstick on her teeth. "So is it Shelly or Michelle?"

"Just Shel." She held the café door open for the woman.

"Will your husband be joining us, dear—" Junie stopped herself, glanced at Shel, and appeared to quickly come to terms with reality, either having pegged her for a lesbian or a woman too rough around the edges to attract a husband. "Never mind that."

Shel smiled, as it was clear the well-coiffed woman was desperate to connect with her on any level, if only to satisfy the visions of dollar signs in her head.

Junie nodded toward a gleaming white Escalade. "You think you can keep up with me?"

"I'll surely try."

Within minutes, Junie's boat-sized SUV docked at the small, gravel, U-shaped driveway in front of the listed rental. Shel parked behind her and waited as Junie leaped from the driver's side, smoothed her slacks, and tucked an errant white hair behind her bejeweled ear. She aimed the key remote at the car until it chirped, and glanced down.

Shel guessed the troubled expression on Junie's face indicated she was initiating her Manolos to the only gravel they'd probably ever touched. Junie tiptoed her way to the front door of the ranch-style house. Cautiously guarding long fingernails lacquered as pink as her lipstick, she punched a code into the lockbox on the lime-green house.

A wall of hot, stagnant air hit Shel when the door opened. The place smelled like damp socks.

From Junie's wrinkled nose, she also detected the odor. "This is a two-bedroom home, and if I could convince the old gentleman to sell it, people would jump on it. Of course it would be a total tear down," Junie candidly said. She seemed to realize that all the sweet talk in the world couldn't mask the eyesore of a home.

Though Shel hadn't had the least bit of interest in truly renting the place, she admired Junie's frankness. "He doesn't want to sell, huh?"

"He doesn't even want to rent." Junie raised her hands and dramatically dropped them to her sides. "He's been my most difficult project to date. But he's in a senior home, he's crotchety, and nobody's going to convince the old fool that he's not going to walk right back through that door tomorrow."

"Then why try?" Shel asked, looking around the dusty, drab quarters.

"The gentleman still has a mortgage. A peculiar insurance-based clause in his bank paperwork says that all properties under financing must be occupied." Junie glanced at Shel and rolled her heavily blue-lined eyes. "Needless to say, it's not going over well with the old man. He acts like I'm the villain in this movie."

Junie continued her rant, but Shel ignored her spiel and instead stared across a roomful of sheet-covered furniture and out the window at Kathleen's little cottage. "What about the house across the street?" she casually asked.

Junie looked surprised at the interruption. She followed Shel's line of sight out the window. "Not on the market."

"Is it a rental?" When Junie shook her head, she asked. "Any chance you know who owns it?"

"I could find out easily enough. Right off the top, I can tell you the deed hasn't changed hands in the fourteen years I've been in this area. A good realtor knows these things."

"I'm sure you do." Shel leaned against the couch positioned before the front window. She softened her tone, lest she appear overly interested. She wondered if Kathleen had purchased the home. She turned toward Junie. "Just curious—what would one of these little houses go for around here?"

Without hesitation, Junie answered, "Million-five."

"Dollars?" Shel's eyebrows hiked. At Junie's nod, she added, "Wow."

"But nothing's for sale on this street right now." Junie leaned closer to her and whispered, "Unless the guy who owns this one kicks it, which could happen any minute. I can find out if anyone else is attached to it, if you're interested."

Shel looked out the window to study the yellow house. "One point five, huh?"

Junie confirmed the price before launching back into her speech. "So this place was built in 1973, all original plumbing and wiring, which could spell trouble later, if not sooner. Surprisingly, the utilities are included in the rent, but the owner is not allowing any wiggle room in the budget to replace the decrepit appliances. Plus he demands the roof be fixed—apparently it's leaking somewhere and that's going to be expensive. Also, there's no lawn service. The whole thing's a bust, really." She turned around, her hands firmly on her dainty hips. "Honey, why don't you let me show you something else? Something newer and better that you don't have to re-roof. Something that doesn't smell like…frog farts."

Hearing "frog farts" out of the expensive mouth of Junie D'Amico earned Shel's attention. She quickly turned away from the window to gauge the woman's expression. They shared a genuine chuckle.

"I appreciate that, Junie," she said, "but I like this one. Frog farts and all."

Junie turned serious again. "I suppose it is a grand location, the beach being just a few blocks down."

"Oh, it's certainly the location I desire," Shel said, not thinking about the beach at all.

She heard the door slam shut across the street and turned to see Fortier's tiny daughter running full steam toward the road. The little girl's sudden appearance combined with the tyke's amazing speed caused her to draw in a sharp breath and listen for cars. Almost involuntarily, Shel edged toward the door, finding it hard to believe she was ready to run to the street and stop the child. She chalked it up to protecting her investment since she was convinced she lacked even a single maternal instinct.

Still, her voice hiked up a notch when she asked, "Junie, is there a lot of traffic on these streets?"

"Hardly any. Plus, there's a hospital at the end of the block and a grocery store one block over from there. Naturally a few blocks away you've got the convenience of Fifth Avenue…"

Junie's voice melted into the background as Shel watched Kathleen Fortier zip out the front door and run across the lawn after the child.

"How much is the rent?" she absently asked, still watching Kathleen, hot on the trail of her daughter, who was fast approaching the street.

"Five thousand."

Kathleen caught up with the child just short of the curb.

A car, though slow moving, blocked Shel's view for a heart-stopping moment. "Jesus Christ," she gasped.

"Tell me about it," Junie said, obviously assuming she was aghast at the dollar amount. Junie was probably used to delivering news like this every day, Shel thought, but probably not when associated with such a dive. "Not worth a penny more than three grand in this condition, but sadly, I must honor the owner's wishes."

Kathleen had done an about-face, the child in her arms, and stormed back to the house. The door loudly slammed shut once again. Shel rubbed her eyes, wondering if she'd misjudged the entire situation. Maybe yesterday's moment of softness was just that: a moment. Perhaps Kathleen Fortier had no control whatsoever over her own child. Perhaps she was a monster…

"Maybe I was wrong," Shel mumbled.

"Pardon, dear?" Junie looked slightly bewildered.

Shel returned her gaze to the window. Kathleen's house was quiet. The place seemed as mysterious as its inhabitants. She wondered how Kathleen Fortier, selling an occasional painting for five hundred bucks, could possibly afford to live in a house with that kind of rent attached to it. It gave legitimacy to Richard Fortier's claims of embezzlement or blackmail. Her heartbeat accelerated in sync with her improving mood. It seemed wrong that Kathleen being an unfit mother would be profitable to Shel, but make no mistake, were it proven true, Shel planned to be the one to profit.

She heard herself say, "I'll take it."

Junie's jaw went slack and her eyes nearly bulged out of their nipped and tucked sockets. "Look, honey, I'm happy to do my job, but this place has no air-conditioning. Furthermore, the old gentleman is also not kicking in for pool services, and he insists that the pool be cleaned and filled at the renter's expense."

"This place has a pool?" Shel muttered. She shook her head. "Never mind. How much did you say again?"

"Five grand, month to month." Junie shuffled through her paperwork, reading as she went. "Furniture stays, listed as all original, which means musty and rickety, and he is refusing to sign a full-term lease. I don't know how I'm supposed to work like this. Honestly."

Shel knew a lease didn't matter. It was Fortier's money and she'd be out of there within a few weeks anyway, possibly with a hundred grand lining her pocket. "Doesn't matter. I'll take it."

It was the first time she'd managed to silence Junie. The woman nodded, as if waiting for her voice to catch up with her, and finally said, "Let me get the papers."

A little while later, before Junie's Manolos could make their final teeter across the driveway, Shel yanked sheets off old couches and overstuffed chairs. Dust particles danced across beams of sunlight pouring through the newly opened windows, sending her into a full-fledged sneezing fit. Junie had been right about the furniture. In fact, she'd been right about everything. Shel would have to dust the place top to bottom to make it slightly habitable, no matter how short a time she planned to stay.

She brushed her hands on her jeans and moved into the bedroom. It was a small room made smaller by the king-sized bed.

Surprisingly, the mattress was relatively new and, thankfully, passed her bedbug examination. If she could properly rid the mattress of its musty smell, it would probably make for a good night's sleep.

The old man's personal effects had long ago been sent to storage, she assumed, so a closet almost the size of the bedroom was available to her, but it would, along with a small dresser, remain empty. Close to everything she owned fit inside a suitcase and a duffel bag, which she planned to quickly deposit on the closet floor—forget unpacking.

The bathroom was completely tiled in jadite, circa Holiday Inn 1973, and the galley kitchen was fine for as much as she'd use it, which would be never. Still, the smell…

A few hours, a box of Comet, and gallon of bleach later, her lungs were thoroughly seared, but the rooms were clean. The smells of bleach and cleanser beat the pants off must and mildew any day.

She returned to the hotel, gathered her things and the cat, and brought them to the new temporary headquarters. Newton sniffed the bleach-filled air and made a haughty assessment of the place. She could tell the cat disapproved of the quarters, probably having gotten used to the swank atmosphere of the fancy hotel. She ignored him, gathered her cleaning supplies, and hauled everything to the rear of the house. She stopped short when she spotted a doorway just beyond the kitchen.

"Almost forgot," she said to herself. The door was swollen shut with damp weather, but a few hard tugs did the trick. She grinned at the cat who'd been curiously trailing her. "Newton, you've got your own room."

As if he realized exactly what she'd said, Newton moseyed past her and jumped on top of the single bed in the room. He clawed a circle, pulling up and making a nest of the old chenille bedspread covering the mattress before finally settling in. It appeared Newton had reconsidered, perhaps valuing the upgrade in privacy over the downgrade in quarters.

Shel parked the damp mop against the wall near the doorway and told Newton, "The one who doesn't pay rent gets to sleep with the mop."

As Junie had indicated, she easily found tiny Guin's Market a few blocks away. There she stocked up on scant provisions: beer, toilet paper, bread, peanut butter, coffee, and cat food, and as she had a stove at the moment, she even sprang for some refrigerated ready-made pasta.

At four o'clock, she made herself a quick sandwich and drank a beer chilled in the old refrigerator. She perched on the couch and waited impatiently until five thirty. As she had the day before, Kathleen pedaled up the driveway of the house across the street and parked the bike on the cement slab front porch. She then removed the child's helmet and lifted her down from the seat. Then, without so much as a word to the kid or a glance around her, she led Harper around to a side gate, and presumably they went into the house from a back entrance. She wondered why they didn't use the front door.

"Friendly little cuss," Shel muttered.

She studied the quiet yellow house for the rest of the afternoon. By seven o'clock, she was thoroughly bored. She showered, grabbed another beer, and retreated to her own tiny cement slab of a front porch and plopped into the single plastic lawn chair. Either the old owner hadn't had much company or hadn't wanted any. It suited her perfectly.

She resituated the chair to face Kathleen's house and settled in. Using the hem of her shirt for a grip, she twisted the lid off her bottle of beer, shook out a newspaper, and alternately read and spied on her neighbor until it was too dark to look legitimate.

A light came on in Kathleen's front window. At nine o'clock, the light turned off. Shel assumed they'd gone to bed. It didn't seem like a bad idea.

Inside her own place, she checked the door locks, and climbed into the comfortable bed. But no matter how tired she felt, her thoughts wouldn't turn off.

She figured she should soon drive somewhere—maybe Fort Myers—to get cash off Fortier's AmEx. With rent and deposit, she'd nearly exhausted his cash advance, and she didn't want to put more local purchases on the credit card, thereby giving away her precise location. She'd come painfully close to blowing her cover already just using the card at the hotel. But that was long before she'd considered Naples a viable candidate in her search. Her head still spun with the coincidence. Shel knew there was more to be learned about Kathleen before she could simply turn her over to Fortier.

She remembered her old police academy days, training alongside officers whose jobs would ultimately be to employ the law in a rather black and white capacity. Early on, Shel had been selected to go undercover, and while the laws still applied, there existed a gray area in which to operate. For example, it was sometimes necessary to let a lesser offender slip by to get at his boss, the bigger takedown, for the greater good.

But there were other gray areas Shel had encountered, which required independent thought for a different kind of greater good. She'd never been a bleeding heart, but she'd come across a few practicing thugs in her time who were, in reality, only slightly off the path of an otherwise potentially decent life.

She was forced to remember the young mother who'd made a delivery to Shel's phony shit apartment. She'd marveled at the stupidity of the woman who was toting the goods in her diaper bag, no less. The woman's eyes were clear, atypical for the junkies who usually made these deliveries. The only thing showing in her eyes was real fear. This truly wasn't her scene. She'd confirmed Shel's suspicion when she'd quickly volunteered that she was a "temp" for the usual guy, just trying to earn a little much-needed money.

As she was compelled to discover the truth, Shel offered to do a line with her, an action that had the woman looking at her as though Shel were nothing more than a low-life scum. It was Shel's desired response and the point at which she "accidentally" disconnected her wire that could have had the woman in custody within minutes. The law did not distinguish between felonious acts. Once their linkage was down, she told the young mother this and more.

Zoey was her name, and within minutes she'd come clean with a story that Shel had heard half a dozen times before. Zoey had fallen in love with a boy who'd promised her a good life, but was anything but. Now, she had a baby and was desperate to make enough money so that she and her baby could go back home to her family.

Shel asked her how much she had saved up, but it wasn't enough for a cab ride, forget about flights. The boyfriend kept a close watch on money, so Zoey had made the tragic decision to moonlight in the delivery biz.

Shel knew the sting money in her possession was marked, so she instead dumped her own wallet onto the bed. It was lucky timing for the young mother as Shel would have paid rent that day. She handed over almost five hundred bucks and made the girl promise to take her baby and leave for the airport as soon as she left the seedy hotel. Zoey stared at her, mistrust now in those wide, fearful eyes.

That was a case of gray area that Shel could decipher, but the law would not. Given the sizeable delivery she'd had on her, even a good defense and brief jail time would have taken her child away from her for years. Shel figured she'd made the best decision given the grim circumstances. It had almost worked.

She blinked away the ugly memory and focused on Kathleen Fortier. She and her child may also be residing in a gray area. Shel felt in her gut that something was amiss. Given the new parameters she had set for herself, she figured it was worth a try exploring the odd feeling.

Yes, she was now freely admitting to herself that she was embarking on a new life. It was a journey begun the moment she'd accepted Richard Fortier's down payment. The deal was further sealed when she'd abandoned her car. Now, there was nothing left for her in Louisiana, excepting a possible pile of cash should she deem Kathleen unfit after all and turn over her location to Fortier. Since making the decision, Zoey had been at the front of her brain. It wasn't just the young mother thing or the bad place thing, but now, just as Zoey had been, Shel was also desperate for a clean break from her former life.

This assignment was an operation that required patience, not that she was blessed with an abundance of such, but she'd already decided this would be her last case. She'd vowed to turn over a new leaf, with or without money, though she knew her preference.

She thought about the gallery and its owner and his misconception about Shel being a "good spirit." She didn't aspire to be a great person, just a better one. But that wasn't what was bothering her. What kept her awake was another notion that tickled the deep recesses of Shel's thoughts, that Kathleen Fortier, in her paint-spattered apron, with her mussed up, butchered hair, was undoubtedly one of the most attractive women she had ever laid eyes on. Admittedly, it made being patient more tolerable.

She had always been a sucker for a damsel in distress, especially a pretty one. She quietly hoped that wasn't what was driving her desire to do the right thing or there would be no evidence of real change at all.

She squeezed her eyes tightly closed and put Kathleen's sweet face, aqua-hued eyes, and exquisite, petite body out of her thoughts. She tried not to worry about her fascination with the beautiful woman or about a child who, in a few weeks, could possibly be without her mother.

Shel drifted to sleep and from one erotic dream to another until an ear-splitting scream tore through the otherwise silent night.

CHAPTER NINE

With feet thoroughly entangled in sheets, Shel sprang from the bed then promptly went sprawling on the floor. She cursed and crawled free, bumping around the darkness of the unfamiliar house until she arrived at the front door.

She bolted for the street, running hard toward the source of the shriek. The fact that she had no shoes and no gun occurred to her with each waking moment, along with all the horrible possibilities about what she might discover when she reached the yellow house.

Light softly glowed from behind the front window blinds. Shel's heart slammed wildly against her ribs, further fueling her adrenaline rush. She hoped the kid was okay. She hoped she hadn't screwed things up by not calling Fortier as soon as she knew his wife's exact location. After all, he'd warned her that Kathleen was violently insane. Had she done as she was instructed, Fortier would have his daughter back and Shel would be on an island somewhere, relieving any possible guilt with expensive, therapeutic cocktails.

She tamped down rising fears along with the guilt of knowing that by protecting her paycheck, she'd possibly brought harm to the child. She'd drawn things out, milked the advance, and for what? Her own morbid curiosity?

Shel came in for a landing on the doorstep beneath an ancient, yellow striped canopy and hammered her fist against the front door. Instantly, the light in the house's main room switched off.

"Yeah, that'll work," she sarcastically muttered. She pounded more vigorously on the door and yelled, "I know you're there—I live across the street!"

The house remained dark and silent, igniting fury within her. It was absurd that Kathleen could pretend a devastating scream had not just originated from her house, or that the front windows weren't just lighted. Shel pounded until her fist was sore. "I'm not leaving, so you might as well come to the door!"

She considered going around back, but heard a series of locks unlatching. Then the front door barely opened. Mrs. Richard Fortier stared at her through a three-inch gap protected by a chain guard.

After a week of seeing those haunting eyes in her dreams, here they were, up close and personal. Kathleen's distress was so devastatingly powerful Shel felt the impact from the front stoop.

"Everything's fine," Kathleen mumbled. "Thanks for your concern."

She started to shut the door, but Shel stopped it with the heel of her hand. "So, what's with the racket, then?"

"It was nothing, really."

A slight breeze made Shel suddenly very aware that she stood there in nothing more than her customary night attire. She looked down at long legs that looked preposterously gangly in boxer shorts, and her tank shirt was so thin, why bother at all? Struck by a twinge of unexpected self-consciousness, she tugged the hem of her shirt lower, and awkwardly shielded her chest with an arm. "I'm staying across the street, I heard you scream."

"I appreciate your concern, but it was nothing. Thank you for checking."

Regardless of her attire—in fact, maybe because of it—Shel quickly grew impatient. "Lady, dogs are barking for a three-mile radius. Don't tell me it was nothing."

"I said I apologize. Now, it's late." Kathleen started to close the door once more, but Shel wedged a solid fist between the frame and the door. Obviously startled, Kathleen stared. Finally showing evidence of a temper, she spat, "I'll call the police."

"Be my guest. I was about to call them myself." Shel removed her hand, folded both arms over her chest and waited to see what impact her bold statement would have.

Kathleen's glare turned harder and colder, causing notions of pets with snapped necks to swirl around Shel's brain. She remained resolute.

When Kathleen's shoulders pitched slightly forward, Shel knew the police would not be summoned. She hoped her relief wasn't abundantly evident. Though surrender hung between them, she and Kathleen remained frozen in their quiet standoff.

Finally, Kathleen whispered, "Please just go. It won't happen again."

A three-inch look into Kathleen's world was all she'd get unless she acted quickly and she very much wanted to see that the little girl was okay. Taking advantage of her first successful bluff, she pressed her luck. Leaning her head against the doorframe, she said, "There could be some weirdo in there holding you hostage, okay? Let me in to see for myself and I'll go home and go to bed. Otherwise, I'm calling the police. Your choice."

The door closed.

For a moment, Shel considered the impossibility that she'd failed. Then she heard the chain sliding and in seconds the door opened and Kathleen stood on the doorstep wearing a terse expression and a simple bathrobe, her arms folded across her chest.

Up close, she was able to confirm her initial suspicion that Kathleen Fortier was quite small. Not that Shel had her pegged for a giant, but certainly she hadn't looked this delicate in photographs, or even from the other side of the street. Her pixie hair hardly shielded her wide, worried eyes and she looked regretful about that at the moment.

"Whatever it takes to get you to leave," the woman angrily whispered.

Shel waited for Kathleen to move before stepping past the threshold into the cottage. "Thank you." She wished she had her badge, though flashing a badge might have sent the woman right over the edge, thereby possibly putting the child in even greater danger. A child who was, at present, nowhere in sight.

She forged ahead and extended her hand in a businesslike move. "I'm Shel Carson. I just moved in across the street." No sense in lying at this point since Kathleen would probably know her identity before it was all over anyway. She chalked it up as another step in the direction of honest living.

Kathleen remained still, ignoring Shel's hand. "Could you just get this over with?" She dropped the whisper, and only then did Shel notice her odd dialect. Kathleen Fortier pronounced every letter of every word. The woman was becoming more of a mystery with each passing moment.

A soft-sounding hiccup drew their attention to the hallway. Wearing a pink Minnie Mouse nightgown, Harper stood clutching a well-worn stuffed rabbit. The child's shoulders twitched with hiccups and the funny little sniff-squeaks toddlers made when they were coming down from a good cry.

Having thoroughly memorized a showcase of photographs taken at every age, Shel could easily confirm this was Richard Fortier's child. More than ever, she was acutely aware of her own near nakedness. She smiled at the little girl and squeezed her arms more tightly around herself in an effort to hide whatever she could.

Harper Fortier stared at her. She wondered if the brand of leeriness in the child's eyes had been inherited from her mother. Harper looked too young to have already developed such an obvious mistrust for adults.

Kathleen spun around. "Go back to bed, now." When the little girl didn't move, her mother issued another sterner warning. "Go on. I'll bring you a drink as soon as our company leaves." She turned to face Shel, making her point crystal clear. "Which will be in only a second."

When Kathleen said "drink," her accent made itself known. The word sounded more like "drank." It was clear to Shel that the woman was attempting to iron out her New Orleans vernacular. Shel marveled at the ridiculously botched ruse.

From where she stood, she scanned the child, inventorying for bruises or other evidence of harm that could possibly jeopardize her payday, thereby necessitating immediate intervention. The child flinched with each hiccupped sob and looked petrified, but appeared to Shel to be in otherwise good physical health.

Kathleen hurriedly ushered the child down the hallway and returned in moments. Standing solidly in front of Shel, she rasped, "Are you satisfied now?"

"Cute kid." Shel's bare feet took a few steps in one direction, then the other, while she viewed what she could of the home's interior. She casually asked, "Who was screaming and why?"

"My daughter saw a bug."

Shel was dumbstruck. "Kid gets pretty upset over a bug."

"They...they're monsters here," Kathleen stammered.

Shel knew firsthand the insects in Louisiana were big enough to saddle. The whole conversation was preposterous. "Yeah? Where you from?"

The question went unanswered. She glanced around, making mental notes. The house was done simply in tasteful neutral tones accented by natural objects like seashells and pinecones. The décor was unpretentious, and in fact hardly even qualified as décor, the polar opposite of what she'd expected to find in a millionaire's wife's home.

A rag doll lay in a crumpled heap on an off-white couch. A snapshot of mother and daughter leaned against a lamp on a plain wooden end table. The furnishings were all very basic and impersonal.

She gave the conversation a little push. "You two live here alone?"

"Do you want to check for yourself?" Kathleen asked, resurrecting her cold, stiff tone.

Shel wanted to take her up on the offer, but instead turned to face her unwilling host. She studied Kathleen a moment. "No."

"Are we done?"

The fearful scream replayed itself in Shel's brain, igniting a flurry of what-if scenarios. She took a step closer, leaned very near Kathleen's ear, and whispered, "Is there anyone in your house right now who shouldn't be here?"

"Yes," Kathleen said in an equally low voice. She, too, leaned slightly forward, mimicking Shel's stance. "You."

"Okay." Standing so close to Kathleen, Shel detected the faint scent of baby powder and fresh laundry. Just like that, harsh images of the woman mistreating her child were quickly replaced with softer ones, like Kathleen stepping out of the shower, blotting herself dry with a fluffy towel, sprinkling baby powder on all the parts presently covered by a very thin robe with a pink collar...

She felt a twinge in her groin and hurriedly stepped out of Kathleen's personal space and its accompanying delicious scent. "Very good."

"Are you leaving now?"

Shel blinked, surprised at Kathleen's defensive attitude. "Look, don't get wise with me. Somebody over here starts screaming bloody murder in the middle of the night. Excuse me for getting neighborly, making sure there's not some weirdo in your house."

Kathleen rocked back on her bare heels and made a show of taking in a full-length view of Shel in her basic underwear. "Nobody's saying there's not."

Shel nodded and smiled. "Good one, Miss…?"She waited for Kathleen to supply the last name.

Kathleen said nothing.

"Okay, Miss Whatever—at least we're on a first-name basis. It was nice to meet you." Shel pushed through the door, stepped onto the porch, and turned to say goodbye in time to see the door slam. To nobody but the pitch-black night, she added, "Sort of."

She shook her head, struggling to process the house and its odd occupants. Careful of her bare feet, she hiked to the edge of the yard and started to cross the street. A rare approaching car flashed red strobes effectively stopping her in her tracks dead center of the roadway. She sighed and bowed her head in defeat, an action that again forced her to note her skimpy wardrobe.

"Great," she muttered, giving a forced friendly wave to the police officer she couldn't yet see. She squinted into the bright, bobbing flashlight beam aimed right in her face.

"What gives, lady?" a tough-sounding woman asked her.

The light abruptly switched off and Shel was left blinking away residual spots. When she could finally see, she tried not to chuckle at the fact that the woman behind the gravelly voice and big flashlight wasn't a hair over five feet tall, and about half again as wide. The officer's hair resembled a red Brillo pad spilling out from beneath her official cap. The officer held out a hand and made a gimme motion.

"Come on, hotshot. I'm going to need to see some ID."

"Well, I don't carry it in these," Shel said angrily, looking down at her boxers. She'd finally arrived at the complete end of her patience.

"Why are you running around the neighborhood in your skivvies, anyway?"

"Just visiting a neighbor."

The squatty officer glanced at her wristwatch and arched an eyebrow. "At two a.m.? What kind of visit you call that? Booty call?"

Shel glanced at the little yellow cottage, fury burning hot inside her. First, an already restless night's sleep had been rudely interrupted by a scream that had her running around the neighborhood in her "skivvies," as the officer had kindly pointed out. Second, knowing full well that she'd only had good intentions, Kathleen Fortier had the nerve not only to ignore the drama now unfolding in the street, but she was callous enough to turn off every light in her house, and apparently go to bed.

"Christ," she mumbled. Her gaze went to the bossy uniformed dame. She realized the officer was not going away until she'd seen ID. She motioned toward the little green ranch house. "Follow me inside so I can get it."

The officer glanced at the house and looked back at her with a funny expression. "You a renter?"

"Well, I'm not a squatter," Shel coldly answered, having already anticipated the next question.

The officer got back into her patrol car and veered it to the side of the road. Having properly parked, she got out again and followed Shel inside.

In moments, Shel emerged from her bedroom wearing jeans and a black T-shirt, her driver's license in hand. In the dim lamplight, she looked at the officer's name badge: K. Milford. She handed over the ID. "Here you are, Officer Milford."

"You're from Louisiana."

"That's what it says."

"You're not winning a lot of points with me," Milford said in her flinty voice. She lowered the license and glared at Shel. "You some kind of smartass or something?"

Shel rolled her eyes, but asked herself how many idiots she'd dealt with when she was working street patrol, first step in her cop career. Twenty years ago suddenly felt like yesterday. It was especially tricky being a woman. Everybody gave you attitude. Plus, this woman was no spring chick; God only knew how long she'd been at this racket. All things considered, Shel calmed down. "I heard a noise, jumped out of bed, and ran outside to see what it was. New neighborhood makes me a little nervous."

Milford cockily tilted her head to the side and grinned. "What you got to be nervous about?"

Shel plopped heavily on the couch, ignoring the puff of dust that rose up around her. "I'm a former cop, all right? I hear a noise and I react. That's what I do."

"Former?" Milford didn't cut her any slack. "You're a young one."

"Injured in the line of duty. They retired me out." It wasn't exactly the truth, but who was Officer Milford going to check with at two o'clock in the morning? Besides, in a few days, one way or the other, the uppity seaside town, its high-dollar residents, and its nosy red-headed cop would be forever in her rearview mirror. Just because she was turning over a new leaf didn't mean she had to provide a thorough explanation to every single person she encountered. There was something to be said for preserving anonymity.

Milford seemed to soften her tone and stance. "So when did you get here?"

"Today." Shel squinted at her watch and amended her statement. "Yesterday. Welcome to Naples, right?"

"Not much of a welcome, but probably all you're going to get around this place." Milford dropped the driver's license on Shel's lap and started for the door, her corpulent bottom swaying wide. She paused before making her exit. "You're different—an outsider if ever there was one, so you better learn to fit in."

Shel avoided sighing, lest she should again appear disrespectful, hence prolonging the Welcome-to-Naples lecture. She scruffed her hands through her hair and dropped them in her lap to pick up her license. "I don't plan to be here long."

"Ooh, Naples townsfolk don't like to hear that." Milford exaggerated her shudder. "If you're gonna spend any time around this place, at least make a decent effort."

"I'll take that under advisement," Shel said, as eager to rid her house of company as Kathleen had been. "Anything else, Officer?"

"Yeah, get some real clothes, would you? Just so you don't look more transient than you already claim to be."

Shel glanced down at her clothes.

"And stop springing outta bed and running around the neighborhood half naked."

Shel finally succumbed to an eye roll. "I get it."

"You got some serious wealth in these parts," Milford continued. "Townsfolk don't like to mess around with the riffraff. On this street alone, you've got Ray Townsend, owner of a whole chain of hospitals. Then there's some Vander-something-or-other on the other side of Old Ray, and a cousin to a cousin of a Kennedy on the other side of him. See? You never know who you're gonna bump into in these parts."

"Maybe I should hold an open house to get to know everyone. Serve up some pigs in a blanket and Schlitz."

Milford didn't even blink. "People around here won't care much for that attitude. Here, you either have money or you fawn all over the people who do have it. There's nothing in between." She opened the door and lingered a moment. "You better pick a side. Don't look like it's going to be the money one."

"Thank you again, Officer," Shel mumbled.

Milford grinned, touched the brim of her hat, and answered with a hint of cynicism. "All part of my civic duty." She spun a slow half-circle and seemed to be considering something. "Do they still actually make Schlitz?"

"No idea." Shel dropped her hand on the backside of the couch, eliciting another smaller dust cloud. She coughed a little and waved it away.

"Get yourself a Dustbuster."

Shel heard the door swing shut and got off the couch. She locked the door and leaned against it. "Dustbuster my ass," she muttered on the way to the bedroom. "For this place, I'd need an industrial lawn vac."

She flicked off the light, unsnapped her jeans in the dark, and let them fall to the floor. She shimmied out of her T-shirt, got into bed, dropped her head on the pillows, and landed squarely on the cat.

"Damn it!" Shel roughly scooted the cat off the bed and lay down flat this time.

From the floor, Newton made a feral-sounding howl.

"Shut up. You could scream your brains out in this neighborhood and nobody's going to come see what's going on. I'm the only one stupid enough to do that."

She sighed loudly, flipped over on her belly, and covered her head with a pillow to muffle any other cat complaints.

CHAPTER TEN

Kathleen Fortier was in the wind.

She'd vanished on White Linen Night, right out from under the nose of her husband, which was, in itself, quite an accomplishment. Richard Fortier wasn't careless with his money or his property, and calling his behavior toward his wife protective would be the understatement of the century. If he was protective, he was assiduously, *ridiculously* so. To Bucky, this was the first clue that finding the missing woman would be no picnic. Otherwise, Richard would have her back by now.

Bucky considered this as he gently pried loose his black bow tie and popped the top button of his crisp dress shirt. He dropped his silver Cartier cufflinks in the valet dish, then plucked an Alexander McQueen handkerchief from his pocket and laid it across the dresser. Both accessories were one hundred percent counterfeit, which tickled him. All night he'd been around people wearing the real deal at their uppity gala, and not one of them had been any the wiser.

He leaned slightly closer to the mirror, dipped his chin and grinned at his handsome reflection. He easily popped out green contact lenses that overlaid his natural dark brown eyes then proceeded to study his smooth, tanned skin and bit of fashionable scruff of a beard. Probably the only good thing his mother had ever given him was his Italian ancestry. He'd given himself the accompanying bulky muscles, a fine plastic surgeon had given him his angular cheekbones and chiseled chin, and the sparkle in his eye came from always being a step ahead of the game.

"You know what they say about fools and money."

His conversational tone was directed at his reflection. In fact, he knew a lot about fools and their money, especially how to cause them to part company. It wasn't easy on his ego that he himself had recently suffered an unexpected financial loss. He'd been more stunned than angry, although he had plenty of anger. An income he'd dearly earned was suddenly gone. Once it was recovered—and it certainly would be recovered—he'd make it a point to ensure no tired cliché about fools and money could ever be said about him again. Not that anyone would be brave enough to actually say it, but surely anyone in the know was thinking it.

He'd find Kathleen and his money. Nobody pulled a fast one on him and got away with it.

Bucky draped his shirt over the chair of the dressing table and glanced at his bed, duvet already drawn back, mint lying center of one of a half dozen inviting-looking pillows. He loved his life, and nobody would take it away from him. Not again. He snatched the mint, twisted off and discarded the wrapper and popped the candy into his mouth. He dropped onto the bed and stared at the ceiling.

Richard Fortier had publicly bragged that he knew his wife all too well. Bucky knew that Fortier had attempted to find her himself, even refused to contact the law about her disappearance. That was fortunate for Bucky; once the law got a whiff of that kind of cash, it would be forever out of his grasp. What good would it do him to see the woman sitting behind bars or locked up? He wasn't interested in seeing justice done; he was interested in recovery and dealing personal punishment.

He knew Fortier disliked all manner of tradition, rules and government. The man harbored an unnatural amount of hate for all things authority to the degree that Bucky suspected that if given the chance, Fortier would challenge God Himself. The rest of the odd man's hatred was reserved for anyone who'd give his wife a second look. He'd paid handsomely for her last round of shenanigans, actions that included buying off the law he so despised. He'd probably pay dearly again once he managed to locate the conniving wench.

Bucky had also had some firsthand experience dealing with Kathleen's brand of nuttiness, but nothing like this latest trick of hers. Richard must be feeling similarly exasperated, as he'd never known the man to bring on private help to track her down.

Bucky chuckled despite his own monetary losses. "Methinks the lady vanished herself real good this time."

In fact, it was Bucky who'd put Fortier in touch with a half-assed investigator named Shel Carson. Carson definitely fit Fortier's preferred type of employee; the guy liked working with near-transients, and the more flawed the past, the better. He felt most comfortable among the dregs of society. Fortier was the kind of guy who'd make you feel like a million bucks if you were playing ball on his roster, by his rules. Failure to do so would result in political or social ruination. Not that Bucky thought Carson had much to lose in either area, but simply enough, if she failed to produce Fortier's adoring wife, Fortier would find what made her tick, her secret longings, any career fires she might be privately stoking—every bit of it—and he'd make her life unbearable. *Period.*

Bucky smiled as he considered it. He fired up his iPad and checked his email. Again, there was no news.

The upside to Richard Fortier bringing Carson into the loop was that she might actually find the little imp. That was why he was keeping a very close eye on Fortier's new hire. Though he knew Carson had initially rejected Fortier's offer of employment, she'd also abandoned her shitty car and boarded a plane to Florida—first class, no less. She was quickly warming to the perks of his employ. No matter how much Fortier annoyed Bucky, the man was not without talent.

Bucky had other talented friends. A good one was Freddy, a professional much like himself, whose history on paper and in cyber had been expunged by glorious, cleansing Hurricane Katrina. These days, both were living as upstanding citizens and dear old Freddy was high on the ladder at a major credit company. It was handy. Each time Fortier's AmEx surfaced, Freddy knew, hence Bucky knew.

He set his iPad on the nightstand and turned out the lamp. He nestled into the pillow and as he so often did, he thought about Kathleen Fortier. He pictured the fragile appearing, pale-skinned dame with something mysterious brewing behind those wild, wide eyes. He wondered if she'd have the same effect on Carson as she did most men. It gave Bucky pause, made him even more curious about the missus. Not only did she appear to thoroughly dislike her own husband, she'd also spurned Bucky's advances. Imagine— Bucky, positively teeming with testosterone to the point that people felt him before they even saw him—her rejecting Bucky? Rejection wasn't even in his vocabulary.

Yes, Kathleen Fortier might enjoy Carson's attention. Why the notion hadn't occurred to Bucky before now was beyond him, and a relief to him at the same time. He laughed out loud.

No matter. The beautiful crazies were always the most fun to watch fall apart. In the end, Bucky would teach the lovely Mrs. Fortier a lesson. It would be strictly a bonus that he'd be getting back at Carson, a long-owed debt he'd wanted to settle for years. Even if the woman didn't recognize him, he would never forget her face. And he'd get his money back. Oh, lovely karma.

He rose up just enough to peel out of his undershirt and tossed it toward the dresser. He nestled back into his stack of pillows and settled in, congratulating himself for being so damned brilliant. Perhaps Kathleen Fortier thought she had enemies, but he could guarantee he was her worst. She'd learn that when he found her.

CHAPTER ELEVEN

Kathleen followed an unbending routine, from the time the woman left the house on her bike at eight a.m. until she returned home at five thirty.

She'd first drop Harper at a church a few blocks away at what Shel presumed to be a daycare or preschool. Then it was off to the art gallery for Kathleen. At five sharp, Silvia delivered the tot to her mother's workplace. Shel considered Silvia's role and wondered if Kathleen Fortier had hired the woman to be her assistant. If so, her job description covered a hodgepodge of areas from periodic art sales to child taxi. As Silvia's pitch-perfect wardrobe looked quite expensive—especially when compared to Kathleen's secondhand T-shirts and bohemian skirts. Simple enough, Silvia didn't appear to be the type who'd need to take odd jobs like nannying and taxiing.

From a local shop Shel picked up a secondhand bike she intended to employ as a stealthier means of following Kathleen. It seemed better than merely watching her comings and goings from behind a fake newspaper on her front porch. While it was possible that copying her mode of transportation might help Shel gain insights into Addison's perception, in truth Shel thought it looked…freeing. She wanted to see what that felt like.

The only used bike available was a beach cruiser complete with a wicker basket that couldn't be removed. At least the bike was black; the color, she hoped, would offset the frivolity of the basket. It crossed her mind that having the basket would be convenient for picking up groceries. On the tail end of that thought came a warning to herself against her many recent odd feelings of domesticity. She blamed it on the fact that for the first time, she was residing in a bona fide house and wisely reminded herself that every bit of it, bike included, was temporary.

Her first day tailing the woman had Shel wondering what the hell she'd gotten herself into. She'd barely ridden a bike as a kid, and wondered why she thought her talents at present would be improved over those of her eight-year-old self. Thankfully, the neighborhood was all but deserted when she made her maiden voyage down the slightly sloping driveway. She'd coasted, wildly weaving in hopes of attaining some semblance of balance, zipping on and off the concrete several times. When she inevitably crashed, she was grateful that for once the odds worked in her favor, as the bike launched her roughly onto the sandy yard as opposed to the unforgiving concrete driveway.

After a few more attempts she eventually made it to the street where she proceeded to wobble-coast to the first stop sign. Her feet winding the pedals backward in an airless manner, her heart pounding nearly out of her chest, she realized there were no brakes. In her panic, she grabbed the handlebars roughly, which activated hand brakes she'd not even known existed, again nearly vaulting her right off the thing.

Breathing hard, she mentally recounted the required routine and started again.

Three blocks later, there was a negligible improvement in her steering and balance, but by then, her mark was blocks ahead of her. The only thing gained from the first morning's tail had been enjoying the nice view of Kathleen's sweetly swaying bottom as it disappeared off into the distance.

Shel gracelessly pulled off the road, into the parking lot of the neighborhood library, where she ultimately came to a stop halfway into a dense hedge. Operation bike tail had been a total bust. Shel cursed her lungs, back, knees, and every other part of her anatomy screaming internal protest at her spontaneous exercise. After she caught her breath, she turned the bike around and very slowly pedaled home.

At the lime-green cottage, she pushed the bike around back and leaned it against the railing of the tiny porch that was designed to overlook the even tinier pool. As she clutched the small of her back, Shel wondered if she'd ever feel compelled to touch the torturous mechanism again. Her muscles felt as though she'd resurrected them from the dead. At the moment, it was impossible to believe she'd ever been fit. In fact, she'd been in damned good shape before her old boss had put her in an undercover narcotics gig and she'd managed to get her ass shot and left for dead.

She blinked the thought away, pondering how angry she still felt after all these years. No wonder she couldn't manage a simple bike ride. These days, with her pale skin and scrawny physique, she more resembled the druggies from her undercover life than she did a real human being. Officer Milford had been right about the fact that she clearly looked like an outsider in this wealthy, suntanned town.

Her gaze wandered over a blue custom tarp that was stretched across the narrow inground backyard pool. Though she'd planned to thoroughly ignore the clause in her rental agreement about maintaining the pool, she found herself giving it a good look. She'd always enjoyed swimming at the YMCA when she was younger. Years later, after the shooting, her physical therapist had instructed her to use the gym pool to speed up her recovery. A little sun might help her look like she belonged, add to her cover…

She ambled toward the pool on rubbery legs and reached down and unfastened the bungee cords that secured the cover. She peeled it back and grimaced as the rancid odor hit her, nearly knocking her backward. Making a low whistle, she covered her nose and mouth with the stretchy sweatshirt collar.

"And they say the French Quarter smells bad," she muttered, staring down at the pool shell. Shallow, murky green water filled the deep end, which was precisely where the drain was located and dammed up, by the looks of it.

Shel sat down on the cement lip of the pool, muttered a few complaints before utilizing every bit of upper body strength to slowly lower her body into the pool. When she was close, she did a little free fall to the bottom. Her shoes were now drenched, but no way would she take bare feet into the black, pasty water. Cringing, she waded deeper, trying not to think about what could be living down there. When she was thigh deep, she reached down, blindly wagging her hand through the blackness until she at last found the drain. She swished it free of sticks and leaves, plunking several handfuls of the disgusting muck onto the cement rim before racing back toward the shallow end and the ladder. She climbed out of the pool, gagging, trying not to smell herself.

Tall, unkempt hedges bordering the yard gave her added security as she stripped off her disgusting jeans and freely walked toward the house for a clean pair. Twenty minutes later, she was in the backyard with a rented pump and hose, chemicals and instructions from a local pool guy named Kenny.

She dropped the length of hose into the deepest end and hit the switch. The machine roared to life and she leaned against the porch, watching as the green sludge was pumped out of the pool and onto the grass.

"Smells delicious!"

Shel spun toward the nails-on-chalkboard voice that was screaming to be heard over the equally obnoxious sound of the pump. She tried to stabilize her pounding heart and put on her best bored tone.

"Officer Milford. To what do I owe the pleasure?"

"In the neighborhood. Thought I'd drop by." The short cop tugged off her hat. The wild shock of red corkscrews. Shel almost thought her late night memory had exaggerated. It hadn't. She grinned, leaned against the same porch railing as Shel. "Home improvements?"

"I suppose."

"Stinks to high heaven," Milford hollered, gazing out over the pool. "You planning to fill it back up or plant flowers in it?"

"Flowers?" Shel called, puzzled.

"Sure. I know in some parts of Louisiana they'll put flowers in anything—bathtub, toilet…Put it on display in the front yard in front of God 'n everyone."

Shel ignored her remark, nodding toward the porch and the variety of large chemical containers now parked there. "Filling it back up with water, Officer."

The machinery got louder and Milford's eyebrows practically hit her hairline. She cupped her ears and continued to yell over the noise. "That's a whole mess of chemicals. Hope you know what you're doing."

"Me, too."

"Folks around here don't usually do their own pools. They—"

"I know—they employ scantily clad pool boys to do the work."

"There's that attitude again," Milford told her. "I was going to say they don't do it themselves because it's too easy to ruin the pool."

"Oh yeah?" Milford had Shel's reluctant attention. She put on a tone that was intended to come off as nonchalant, which was hard to achieve over the ruckus. "How so?"

"You drain this thing too low without running that there hose out to the sewage ditch, you'll cause a water buildup. Whole pool insert will pop out and float like a boat." They both lurched unexpectedly when the pump hit fever pitch. Milford simply raised her own volume even higher. "You'll crack all that nice tile up on top. Wreck the whole thing!"

Shel shut off the pump and stared at her. The machinery sounded like it was dying as it wound down. She realized her ears were ringing. They both stood there wagging fingers in their ear canals.

Milford nodded toward the bit of green water still at the pool's bottom. "That's low enough anyhow. Just clean the insert, refill the pool and shock it good."

"Then why did he rent me this pump?" she asked herself more than the cop.

"Kenny, right?" She was referring to the only pool supply store in town, a mom-and-pop operation that reeked of chlorine and cigarette smoke. Shel nodded. Milford shrugged. "Probably for a quick hundred bucks. And why not, right? You don't look like you know any better, being an outsider and all."

"So you told me." Disgusted, Shel unplugged the pump and dragged the heavy contraption back out of the water. She surveyed the splattered, green mess as she wound up the hose. "Now what?"

"Now you're going to have to clean that tile, but be sure and clean your filter or all your work's for nothing."

"I don't have time for this crap," Shel muttered.

"Suit yourself." Milford leaned forward and stretched, looked prepared to go. She took a step, but dropped back, snapped her fingers. "One more thing. That retirement story of yours didn't really check out."

Caught off guard, Shel glared at her.

"Here's what I know—you come around here, looking all kinds of different—" Milford gestured toward Shel's clothing, hair, and any other point she could reference—"prancing around the neighborhood in the middle of the night in your undies, telling the local cop stories about how you got honorably discharged from public services. Doesn't bode well with folks."

"Well, Officer Milford, to be honest, I didn't do anything wrong. Therefore I don't really give a shit what the folks think."

"It doesn't bode well with *me*," the cop said, lowering her gaze along with her voice. "I don't take kindly to being lied to, especially from my brethren, former or what have you."

Shel could tell that Milford's friendly lean was really anything but. The woman wanted answers, and rightly so, Shel supposed. It was her town, after all.

Shel dropped the coil of hose she'd gathered and returned to the porch. She leaned against the railing and bowed her head, nearly chinning her clavicle. After a bit, she spoke. "I got fired for drugs, which by now you already know." Shel fixed a steely stare on her visitor. "But I shouldn't have."

"Well, that's an old story, hon. Every junkie says they shouldn't have got fired for drugs, arrested for drugs—that they didn't kill anyone for—"

"I know. I'm a cop, remember?" Shel glared at her then softened her tone a bit. "*Was* a cop."

"What are you really doing here in my little burg?"

Shel hadn't planned to answer that question any more than she'd planned to answer questions about her past. "Looking for an old friend."

"An old friend."

"She could be in trouble."

Milford looked skeptical. "Trouble?"

"Is there an echo out here?" Shel grew impatient. "Look, run your checks, run your town—do whatever you want, but I'm freelancing, so I'm staying here for a bit. Get over it."

Milford studied her a moment. "Fair enough."

"Anything else?"

"You got a license for your 'freelancing' thing?" Milford hooked air quotes.

"I have a gun permit."

"Any moron can get a gun permit. I'll take that as a no on the license."

"Take it however you want. I'm not looking for trouble here."

"They never are," Milford muttered. She turned to go, but dropped back a second time. "One more time—why were you running around in the middle of the night?"

"I heard a noise across the street, I told you, and I went over to check it out. I thought something might be wrong."

"Fair enough," Milford repeated what seemed to be her favorite phrase. She stared out at the murky pool again. "Don't go wavin' your gun around my burg though, you hear?"

Shel only looked at her. Milford was looking over her shoulder at the pool.

"Get yourself some strong bleach water and scrub that insert and tiles. Let it drop into the bottom, fill it up. You'll shock it and run the pool pump for a few days anyway. That'll clear it."

"Thank you, Officer," Shel said, disgust obvious in her tone.

Milford started toward the side of the house. "And here's your pump over here."

Shel was aggravated that she actually needed to know its location. She begrudgingly followed the cop to the side of the house and together they stared at a contraption that looked like a giant oxygen tank. Shel wondered suddenly if she was in over her head. She didn't need a pool, or its accompanying hassles.

"Now just unscrew this," Milford narrated, giving the plastic cog a spin. She removed it, handed it to Shel. "Then you pull this top off, and there's your filter."

"Jesus..." Shel gasped.

They both gasped at the overwhelming fetid odor, waved their hands before their noses, eyes watering thanks to the stench.

Milford, appearing to muster her bravery, reached into the contraption and removed the slimy filter. She stretched her shirt collar up to cover her mouth and nose, then proceeded to talk through it, her words muffled. "Looks to be intact and that's good. If it wasn't, it could set you back a hundred bucks or so."

Shel was amazed at the woman's seemingly endless knowledge of strange things. "You a pool cop, too?"

Milford ignored her. "Just spray this thing down until it runs clear, and from the looks of it, that's going to take a while. Replace it and turn it on. That's the key. The pump must be turned *on*."

"I take it that it wasn't," Shel said, scratching her chin.

"Lord, girl. You don't know a thing about swimmin' pools any more than you know how to dress for south Florida." Milford flipped back the lid on the switch box and adjusted a dial inside. She tapped it to get Shel's attention. "Run that pool full of water and then hit this switch, but not till it's full, you hear? Drop in all your goodies and do a pH level in a couple of days."

"Okay."

Milford looked suspicious. "You have no idea what a pH level is, do you?"

Shel looked away. Milford recapped her crazy head of hair and started to leave through the side yard.

She called behind her, "Good luck."

CHAPTER TWELVE

By early evening, the pool was technically clean, but heavily clouded with chlorine. Shel padded out into the backyard to check the water level, clean bare feet stepping carefully across the uneven patio to avoid stubbing her toes. When she was satisfied that it was filling properly, she sat down on the back step and took a swig of cold beer.

The sun was setting, thoroughly pinking the sky in its wake. Shel figured since she would soon be gone, it wouldn't hurt to see the sunset a time or two from the beach. This sneak peek of day's end promised a spectacular show given the mere slice of sky above the tree line. The night was navy blue and the moon looked fuzzy. She got a strong whiff of chlorine and blinked, realizing it wasn't the moon at all, but vapors rising off the pool. She took a final swig and went inside.

The house across the street had been quiet all day long. As per usual, Kathleen had arrived home shortly after five with Fortier's daughter, and had once again disappeared inside. Shel sauntered over to the countertop, set the bottle in the sink and gazed over paperwork she had spread all over the place.

While the pool was filling, she'd gone to the library where the Internet was free. She'd intended to Google the location of City Hall with the intention of paying the records office a visit to find out who owned the yellow house across the street. When she'd found a Collier County city property directory online, she felt like she'd struck pay dirt. She loved the idea of avoiding a trip to such a public office. With the lingering presence of Officer Milford, she was already closer to one civil servant more than what made her comfortable. Within fifteen minutes she had the name of a listed owner, SLW, LLC, a business with no website and no listed address, only a telephone number. She could also see that SLW, LLC owned sixteen other properties, all seemingly similar modest cottages in the same type of beach neighborhoods. She printed out mini profiles on each property.

She stared at the screen a bit before punching the number into her new phone, courtesy of Richard Fortier. It didn't bother her that it was after nine o'clock, in fact, she preferred the late hour. A business would have a recorded message or voice mail, and either one would give her a bit of information about what kind of company was behind the cryptic acronym. To her surprise, a real, live voice interrupted her internal prattle.

"Hello? Can I help you?"

Shel froze, in part from the fact that she'd actually reached a human at this hour, but also because it was a familiar voice. She couldn't believe it was possible.

"Hello? Anyone there?"

"Hello," Shel half-whispered in the event the woman on the line was as good at identifying voices as Shel was. "I'm sorry it's late."

"We're always here to help." Yes, she definitely recognized the well-spoken, polite-sounding woman. "Who referred you, please?"

Referred her? For what?

"Mmm…" Shel covered the phone as she quickly exited the kitchen, sidestepped the cat, and within seconds was in the bedroom. She snatched her jacket off the bedpost and violently shook the garment. Her pen and leather bound notebook went flying from the pockets and two bucks feathered onto the bedspread. Shel barreled into the closet and snatched the plastic hotel laundry bag and hurriedly dumped it on the bedspread. "I can't say…"

"Can you tell me your name?"

"I was, uh, given this number by a friend." Shel wanted not only to keep the woman talking, but hopefully to say something—anything—that would indicate the nature of her employment. She shook dirty laundry all over the bed and quickly sorted through the heap.

"Are you still there?"

"I am. I'd rather not say who gave me your number." Shel drew the conversation out as much as possible. She hurriedly plucked and discarded each item from the pile, littering the floor with the castoffs. "He's a confidential person."

"He?" It had to be her. Smooth-sounding, deliberate, intelligent, hint of Midwest accent... "I'm happy to assist you, but I will need that name."

Shel panicked, hoped the woman couldn't hear her breathing heavily. She found her jeans stashed at the bottom of the bag, pulled them out, and yanked at the pocket linings until they were inside out. A wrinkled, white business card fell onto the bedspread and she snatched it up. Running her finger over the rubberized gallery embossment, she flipped it over and froze.

"How do you think you can help me?" Shel asked after a lengthy pause.

"I have many contacts," the woman calmly replied. "It's okay. This is a guaranteed safe line."

"I-I'm sorry to have bothered you," Shel whispered. She hurriedly punched the off button on the phone then scrolled through the abbreviated call history. Heart pounding inside her tight chest, she dazedly dropped on top of the bed, amidst the strewn clothing.

Blinking, as if she could somehow sharpen her focus and prove herself wrong, she compared the handwritten telephone number on the card's backside to the digital one on her phone screen. They were the same.

She'd just talked to Silvia Frances.

"Many contacts? She some kind of madam?" Shel muttered. It seemed absurd, but possible. But the woman assured her the line was safe. "They sell drugs...?"

Was Silvia Frances the owner of SLW, LLC? Was she an employee? Shel was well out of practice for such problem solving. Realistically, the employee guess was probably correct; perhaps Silvia Frances was a realtor or a secretary or personal assistant for the individual behind SLW, LCC. Perhaps *she* was SLW. Maybe Silvia and Kathleen were in cahoots on a scam—the possibilities seemed endless...

Her fugue state was interrupted by a low buzzing sound coming from the front of the house. Dropping the card onto the bedspread, Shel rose up and snatched her gun off the nightstand. She quietly followed the dull hum that sounded like a dying neon sign and grew louder with each cautious step she made to the foyer. The sound of her nervous breathing filled the otherwise quiet room. She nudged aside the thin blind on the front door and peeked out. Her shoulders fell and she dismissed a great sigh that was one part annoyance, one part relief.

"What now?" She secured the safety on her gun and tucked it in the back of her jeans waistband then smoothed the hem of her shirt to conceal it. She opened the door. "Officer Milford, what a pleasant surprise."

"Your doorbell is broke," the woman calmly announced. She wore green shorts and a matching striped top, but even in her civvies she looked regimented. She pressed the illuminated button a half a dozen more times, causing it to emit the same low, annoying and highly ineffective buzz. "Hear that? Somebody disconnected the speaker. Better fix that."

Shel watched her, willed her pounding heart to calm down. She hoped she looked status quo and not a nervous wreck. "Pool cop... doorbell cop..."

"Har-har." She walked past Shel and entered the living room.

"Come in," Shel said, after the fact.

"I might, thank you." She turned to face her reluctant host and waved a small box. "I brought you something."

Shel bypassed the living room and instead went into the adjoining galley kitchen. There, she ditched her gun on the countertop and went to the refrigerator. She opened the door and leaned in, relishing the icy blast that swept over her until every bead of perspiration was thoroughly chilled. When she felt better and her breathing was back to normal, she called out to the cop, "You want a beer?"

"It ain't a cheap one, is it?"

"The very cheapest." Shel swiped two off the top shelf and popped the caps before returning to the living room. She presented one to Milford, who was still standing in the middle of the room. Given the woman's bold entrance, it seemed funny she hadn't already sat down and made herself comfortable. She motioned toward the sparse furniture. "Care to sit on the dusty couch?"

"Don't mind if I do." Milford plopped down, creating enough of a cloud to thoroughly powder the place. When it cleared, Newton had appeared on the coffee table before her, like a magic trick, waiting to investigate their first guest. He leapt onto the couch next to her and purred loudly. "Well, hello kitty. What's your name?"

"That's Newton. He's an idiot."

Milford scrubbed the cat's neck with her fingertips. "Hello there, Newton."

Shel scooted the cat off the couch before she sat down in a chair across from the cop. "Scram, cat." She glanced at her guest. "I'm at the end of my allergy meds with that one."

"Either him or this decrepit furniture." Milford chuckled, nodded toward the coffee table where she'd tossed the little box. "Gotcha some pH strips for the pool."

"Okay…" Shel warily eyed her, picked up the test kit and set it down again.

"You're welcome," Milford emphasized.

"Thanks," Shel said, unsure of what was happening.

They drank their beers for a few seconds before the cop looked at her and smiled big. "So, tell me again why you're in Naples."

Shel rolled her eyes, also set her beer on the table. "Is this official cop business?"

"No, ma'am," she answered, shaking her head. Her interest remained unapologetically strong. "Whose dime you on?"

"It's really none of your business, no offense." Shel took another long swig and allowed her gaze to float past the woman's shoulder, out the window to Kathleen's house. She took another swig, made her best effort at appearing indifferent.

"None taken," Milford calmly answered. "I'm trying to decide if you're walking on the right side of the law. That's all."

Shel borrowed Milford's favorite line. "Fair enough."

"You said you were looking for a friend, or was that also a lie?"

"I'm sure she's a friend to someone."

"Now we're getting somewhere." Milford looked pleased with herself. She set her beer on the table between them, leaned forward, eyes sparkling. "What's the case?"

"That's confidential information." Shel rose from her place and went back to the refrigerator. Though their beers weren't close to empty, she grabbed two more just to put some distance between them, again letting the refrigerator cool her. Everything about the night thus far had her feeling anxious. Perhaps another beer might soften Officer Milford, make her ease off whatever harebrained questions she intended to ply her with. Shel was tired of her polite interrogations. As there were only two more beers in the refrigerator, she doubted she'd get far on the idea, but at least it might keep things hospitable.

She grabbed the bottles, popped the tops a second time, and headed back to the couch where Milford was seated looking patient, but expectant. Shel set the fresh beers on the table, then again took a seat on the opposite couch. She took a long pull off her old bottle, quickly draining it, but Milford's eyes remained intently focused on her. Shel knew she should say something. She set the empty bottle aside and settled back against the couch. The silence had her making an unnecessary explanation.

"Look, I don't want you to get involved because then you'll go all cop on me, and quite possibly screw up a delicate situation."

Milford's eyebrow arched. "Such an abundance of confidence you have in folks."

"Well, that's generally the way things work for me when *folks* get involved." She hooked air quotes.

"Somehow I doubt you ever let anyone else get involved."

Shel pretended to think it over then shot her a smile. "Nope."

"You've made what we call a presumption about all people in general, which speaks to trust issues over actual experiences." Intrigued, Milford settled back on the couch, touched her chin, looking every bit the part of a cop-shrink Shel had once been ordered to see. "Being that you think you know so much about people, what is it you think you know about me? Go on, knock me out with your insight, hotshot."

Shel hesitated only a second. "I see a middle-aged woman working in a small town with very few friends."

As Milford didn't appear affronted, Shel pushed the envelope. "I'd say once upon a time you had a better job than this gig, also in Louisiana—I recognize the twang—then you got injured. You've got a slight limp," Shel motioned toward her guest's leg. "Probably wounded in the line of duty. So you searched until you found this one-horse town. Not much action, but hey, it beats a desk job."

Milford studied her host without reaction.

"You've likely been here a dozen years too long, treated like an outsider, a less-than public worker serving a greater-than crowd. And long about now, the boredom of it all is about to kill you. At night, you probably drive to the outskirts of town, back to a trailer park that is full of retirees and too many plastic flamingos."

A long silence hung between them. Shel felt smug about her assessment.

"Motel." It was Milford's first contribution to the narrative. Shel arched an eyebrow which prompted the cop to clarify. "The Gondolier. Ten-room motel about a mile from here. I hate a trailer park."

"How long have you been there?"

"Ten years or so."

Shel raised her beer in cheers, openly lauding herself for the close reading.

Milford's look was one of genuine amusement. "You think I'm bored?"

"Desperately bored. Then along comes me—also an outsider, also a cop, also injured—and you want in."

"Former cop. There's a big difference." Milford's tone made that point very clear.

"I'll give you that."

"I'm from Baton Rouge," the cop supplied. Shel grinned, again lifted her bottle in a self-congratulating way. Milford ignored the move, continued, "Speaking of twangs, where's yours, Ms. Shreveport?"

The mention of her accent—or lack thereof—had her thinking about Kathleen's odd and purposeful dialect and Silvia's perfect Midwestern accent. She realized she'd let too much time pass before answering, as the cop was now staring at her expectantly. "It's in Michigan, where I left it twenty years ago."

"At Kalamazoo where you started or Kirtland after you flunked out of Kalzoo?" Milford shot her a wink. "You're not the only one who minds the details."

"So we both fancy ourselves master detectives." She pointed her beer in the cop's direction. "Kalamazoo was one big party for a kid raised in a group home, but you probably knew that, too."

If Milford had known that fact about her, she didn't let on. "So, what are you working on?"

Shel rolled her eyes. "Jesus, Milford—you're relentless, bordering uptight. I'll bet you haven't been laid in a dozen years."

"Which just proves you don't know everything." Across the street, Shel noticed the living room light turned off and a bedroom light turned on. Her gaze flicked back to the smiling cop. Apparently, Milford didn't miss a trick. "So, what's her name?"

Hopelessly defensive of her case as well as her own privacy, Shel stiffened. Grimly, she studied Milford, whose smile was only broadening by the moment.

"Look, hon, I'm not as old as I look. Not as dumb, neither." Milford tipped her bottle, drained it. She set it on the table between them. "If she wasn't something special, you'd have checked yourself into a hotel for your little stakeout. Instead, you set yourself up here." She lifted her indelicate frame off the couch, and continued to talk as she slowly headed for the door. "If she wasn't something special, you'd have hauled her ass back to Louisiana a long time ago. I mean, that's what you do, right? You're sort of a glorified bounty hunter."

"Only without much glory." Shel also rose and followed her, coolly working up an impromptu bluff. "Besides, you've got it all wrong."

She opened the door for the cop, grateful for the impending reprieve.

"Well, maybe she's not special. Maybe she's just...intriguing."

"Hmm." Shel tapped her chin thoughtfully, mimicking Milford's earlier gesture. "I believe you said it best—that's what we call a presumption."

"You call it whatever you want, I call it instinct."

Shel watched as Milford stepped across the threshold, but the woman didn't depart just yet. Instead, she stared in the direction of Kathleen Fortier's house, wearing a knowing grin. "I might be old and nosy, but I know what I know. Someone has to be plenty intriguing for me to have that level of interest."

"You're right. You are nosy." Shel tried not to look rattled at the cop's confidence or the fact that she appeared to be zeroing in on Shel's mark. She hoped Milford was utilizing guesswork over actual intuition. She didn't like the idea of anyone thinking she was getting soft on someone, particularly not the potential payoff of a lifetime. Renting the place was good business, plain and simple, nothing more. Shel swung a drastic subject change with hopes of throwing her off. "So Milford, what's your excuse?"

The cop stopped at the door, shot her a bemused look. Shel slid in front of her, blocking her exit. She lowered her gaze and boyishly batted her long lashes at a cop even more tomboyish than she. Employing a poor version of sexy, she asked, "Why are you hanging around me? Do I intrigue you?"

Milford threw her head back and laughed hard. "I stopped letting feisty little things like you intrigue me years ago. Requires too much energy."

"Yeah?"

"Yeah." Unaffected to an insulting degree, Milford stepped around her. "I'm just curious, that's all."

For a split second, Shel envisioned a younger, sleeker, gun-toting Milford in her prime, chasing women. It caused her as much laughter as she'd caused the cop when she'd made the absurd suggestion about her level of intrigue.

She recovered and followed the cop outdoors to her ride, which turned out to be a Harley. The woman hefted a short leg over the machine, struggling despite the fact that it was as low and wide as she. Shel made an apprising half-circle around the bike then nodded.

"Nice wheels, Milford."

"All part of my charm," the cop answered. She shoved in the key and with a few twists of the throttle, the bike declared its throaty roar across an otherwise peaceful night. Milford flicked her wrist several more times for drama, an action that quickly went from being impressive to just plain too loud. Shel cupped her ears and wondered if she was getting old.

"Show-off!" she called over the racket. The cop laughed and gently peeled out of the driveway, just enough to shower her host with tiny bits of gravel. When the noise had faded into the distance, Shel blinked and batted away the last remnants of Milford's dusty departure. When she could see clearly, Shel gasped. Front and center in her line of sight was Kathleen Fortier. Dressed in a bathrobe, she stood in her own yard, glaring at Shel.

"Goddammit," Shel whispered. She gasped, helpless to prevent her startled reaction. She quickly composed herself and set forth to make inquiry or apology—whatever was required—but stopped short when moonlight glinted off something at Kathleen's side. Even from her place she could tell it was about a twelve-inch butcher knife.

Shel took a hesitant backward step, despite the fact there was a road and full yard between them. She steadily moved toward the house, still locked in Kathleen's dull gaze.

"Fuck, me," Shel muttered to herself. She cast several glances Kathleen's direction as she quickly went back to the house. By the time she gave a last look, the woman was gone.

Shel closed then locked the door. Breathing heavily, she leaned against the doorframe wondering if she'd just got her first look at the real Kathleen Fortier. If so, it was scary. She hurried around the house, checking the back door, even the windows. The house was quiet and clear. She brought a kitchen chair back with her to the foyer and wedged it under the doorknob of the front door.

Rationale would say that at barely over five feet tall, Kathleen Fortier lacked mass or muscle to do too much damage, but the image of the petite woman clutching a butcher knife was rapidly defeating every argument Shel could conjure up about the woman, tiny or helpless appearing or not. After ten more minutes of checking windows and doors, Shel reluctantly went to her bedroom.

Laundry remained scattered across the bed and she swept it off into a heap in one stroke. She started to shimmy out of her jeans, but thought better of it, instead choosing to lie atop the bedspread fully clothed. Her gun was already on her nightstand, at the ready, safety disengaged. She reached behind her and turned out the lamp just as Newton leapt onto the bed. The cat proceeded to make a nest of the bedspread and then settled in for the night.

Shel didn't succumb to sleep quite as easily. Not only was her deranged neighbor on her mind, but so was Officer Milford. Judging by the cop's Q and A session, Shel figured Milford wasn't looking to make a bust; probably she was just as bored as Shel had accused her of being. Oddly, the silly cop was starting to grow on her, annoying habits and all, but now even that didn't matter. Prior to the last half hour, her largest concern was Milford's curiosity and how it could screw up her investigation. And possibly a child's safety was in question. Now, everything had changed. She wondered if she should worry for her own safety…

One look at her knife-toting neighbor's bat-shit crazy behavior, Shel was finished. Fortier could have his kid and Kathleen could get what she had coming her way in whatever lockdown psych ward her husband had selected for her. Shel would have her money and never give the woman, the kid, or the whole damned place another look.

CHAPTER THIRTEEN

Shel didn't even bother with the bike or following her mark; however, she did spend a few moments thinking about Mrs. Fortier's bottom, delicately swaying with each pump of the pedal for as long as she could keep up. The woman had the ass of a fifteen-year-old girl, a thought that often crossed her mind simultaneously with the knowledge that it was inappropriate as hell. Especially now, given the latest occurrence.

Instead, Shel left home before her neighbor could even think to push her bike down her driveway. In her car, she drove eleven blocks until she could see soaring white bell towers over the lush palms that lined Ninth Street. Guided by the landmark, she turned into an alley and idled into the parking lot of the Unified Church. She selected a space behind the long line of shrubbery, parked and waited.

A few minutes before eight, Kathleen Fortier pedaled into the parking lot just as Shel predicted she would. She ducked slightly behind the wheel, thankful for the buffering row of low hedges. From her vantage point, she watched Kathleen unfasten the child from the seat and remove her tot-sized helmet before carrying her into the church. The kid clung to her mother's neck, and even from across the parking lot Shel could see her eyes, typically wide with mistrust.

Shel hadn't slept, having spent her night wide awake, creeping around the house at the hint of the smallest noise. Kathleen's latest stunt had thoroughly freaked her out. Shel chastised herself for not having acted sooner. The child always wore an uneasy expression that was surely born from some trauma. Prior to now, Shel figured either Fortier or his wife could be responsible for the child's wary look. Now she was firmly on the side of dear old dad and in a quick hurry to get the child's location to him, as well as collect her money.

Shel thought about her unintentional telephone conversation with Silvia Frances and wondered what trouble she and Kathleen could be creating in Naples, Florida. All of it had Shel again wondering why she'd not turned it all over to Fortier much sooner. She'd have put it behind her now and have a nice bounty lining her pocket for having done so.

She thought about this as she snapped half a dozen pictures of Kathleen and Harper on Fortier's cell phone. He'd want proof his daughter was okay.

Helpless to her own appreciation for pretty women—no matter how crazy they may be—Shel snapped a few extra pictures of Kathleen getting on her bike and pedaling away again, nicely employing that tight backside of hers with every move. Shel didn't have time to follow her just for the view today; there was business at hand. She already knew Kathleen's next stop would be the art gallery where she'd remain until Silvia Frances dropped the child off at five, sharp. Oh, the danger of patterns.

Shel quickly reviewed the pictures before erasing the ass shot. When she was satisfied the ones of the child were clear, she started her car and backed out of the parking space. As she coasted toward the exit, Shel braked hard enough to lurch forward. Frozen, she stared at the subject of her intense interest. There, next to a sign marked Faculty Parking was a silver Volvo wagon. Shel pulled her notebook out of her pocket and compared the license plate number to the one she'd recorded days ago in front of the gallery. Indeed the car belonged to Silvia Frances. Could SLW, LLC be the church? The preschool…?

Shel stared at the wagon a bit longer, wondering who was proving to be the bigger mystery—Kathleen Fortier a.k.a. Addison James, or Silvia Frances. Shel blinked her eyes tightly shut, as if she could physically rid her mind of the nonstop what-ifs. None of it mattered anymore; today was the start of her new life, and it was a change being directly sponsored by Richard Fortier.

As if she were afraid she'd change her mind, Shel grabbed the phone and pressed call on the single pre-programmed number. Struck with a sudden bout of old paranoia she hung up before it could ring even once. She was again focused on her credit card activity and the notion that Fortier could already be ahead of her in the game, possibly screwing her out of her take. Stronger than her desire to get right with the world was her resolve that she would not be left high and dry. Before making her golden find formally known, she wanted collateral.

Back on Third Avenue, she lingered in front of her own rental house, staring at the now empty yellow cottage across the street. She recalled Bartender Rob telling her it was a tourist town for winter people, and it was summer. There wasn't a soul in sight. She counted five minutes and still not a single car had passed, not even a random dog walker.

She jogged across the street and around to the side of Kathleen's house. She unlatched the flimsy wooden gate and let herself into the backyard.

She watched her footing as she followed the flagstone path bordered by uncontrolled purple bougainvillea. Other sweet-smelling vines sprawled the grounds and crept up rickety, nearly-rotting trellises propped against the house and fence. It successfully transformed the backyard into a nice, woodsy fortress. In the middle of it all was an old, uneven bricked patio. Above it, an umbrella of blooms dripped down from a splintery arbor. Two metal lanterns with burned-down candles dangled from the center only a few feet above a child's picnic table. In all, the landscaping was lush, unkempt, and nothing short of charming.

Shel desperately attempted to not picture Kathleen in one of her carefree skirts, standing in the midst of the equally bohemian backyard. She instead focused on the back entrance. The house had been built at a time when security wasn't even thought of. Only a single power line was attached to the house, which gave her reassurance that nothing else had been added after the fact. There probably wasn't even a telephone line.

The glitch in her planned intrusion wasn't a technical one, which Shel probably could have managed, but rather a manmade security "system." Each window and the sliding patio door were lined with a row of blue marbles, evenly spaced, glistening in the sunshine. A narrow door off to one side seemed like her best point of entry, but it would require removing the screen or breaking the doorknob, and Kathleen would know someone had been there. It was likely she would take the kid and split and then bye-bye payoff. It was that concern, coupled with the notion that Fortier might try to stiff her, that had her doing a B&E at the small house.

Shel chose the sliding door and easily picked the simple lock and jiggled the door open, sending blue marbles rolling every direction. Shel crawled around the floor collecting and replacing them, just as she'd found them. She definitely wouldn't be exiting the same way, but she'd worry about that later. By her count, she had a good part of the day to ransack the place, if she so chose.

She stood in the kitchen that, small as the house was, afforded her a decent view of the entire place, sans the hallway and any subsequent attached rooms. The place was clean but rather boring in décor, and again Shel couldn't help notice it looked thrift store furnished, which had her momentarily feeling guilt for having broken in on this particular mission. Almost as quickly, a vision of Kathleen with her empty stare and gleaming knife blade came to mind. It haunted her now just as it had the entire night before, robbing her of a decent sleep. A familiar coldness crept over her, resuscitating feelings of vengeance and a mistrust she'd previously vowed to put behind her. People could not be trusted.

Kathleen's expression had grown steadily more deranged with each flashback, the knife even longer, her stance more menacing. Add to that the potential of Fortier's betrayal and Shel was fortified for her mission, determined not to be left without her bounty, even if it meant taking it herself. A woman of Kathleen's means would not be without a stash of money or jewels. Even middle-of-the-road jewelry would fetch some value in a pawn shop.

A preliminary search of the kitchen yielded a few orchard green plastic plates and a handful of mismatched glasses, reinforcing the thrift store notion. She rummaged through the pantry, going so far as to shake boxes of macaroni and even a coffee can. No hidden money there. She poked into the refrigerator, but there discovered only juice and a carton of milk. She closed the door and turned around, her eyes landing on a childproof lock looped over the only low cabinet she hadn't checked. She went to work on the contraption, finding it ironic that although she could successfully pick the door lock, she was having difficulty disarming a piece of looped serrated plastic. At last it gave and she yanked the cupboard open. A single jug of wine sat on the only shelf. Puzzled, she waved her arm around the deep recesses of the cabinet but found only dust.

"That is what you're protecting…?" Shel angrily replaced the lock and stood, making a final glance around the kitchen. "For all your money, Mrs. Fortier, your food selection is repulsive and your wine is cheap."

Shel marched across the living room, pausing to check a tiny flowered wood box on the shabby coffee table. She flicked back the lid to reveal childish trinkets—plastic rings, fake baubles, and a myriad of paper hearts with "mom" scrawled on each in a childish hand. Shel slammed the flimsy lid shut as if touching the box might threaten her resolve. She set it back in its place and continued on her mission.

A narrow hallway just beyond that led to two small bedrooms. The smaller contained a full-size bed with a drab coverlet, a nightstand, and simple chest of drawers. The furnishings were spare, a half step up from prison issue.

"Sixth grade camp was swankier than this," she muttered. In the corner, a sweater was draped over the mirror attached to the chest. Shel ran her hands through the soft fabric of the pockets. Nothing. She opened the closet door and examined the few items dangling from hangers. The clothing was airy, plain and very simple, the exact opposite of what she'd seen in the woman's New Orleans closet. No tightly wedged wardrobe here. No suitcases or trunks, only a single pair of canvas, no label tennis shoes that may well have come from Walmart. Shel stared at everything which was…nothing.

She closed the door and went to the chest, opening each of four drawers, but finding only a few pairs of shorts and T-shirts. The topmost drawer contained cotton panties. Shel stared at them for a bit before reluctantly scooting them aside. She tried not to notice the soft fabric or imagine what they looked like when they were not laying in the drawer…

She swallowed hard and slammed the drawer shut. She checked beneath the bed. In all she found nothing.

"Where do you keep your precious jewelry, Mrs. Fortier? Family heirlooms—anything." Shel was simultaneously growing more curious and angry. "Where are you hiding the good stuff?"

She yanked open the nightstand drawer and found a box of store brand tissues. Everything about the room said she was as transient as Shel, and again she wondered if the woman was only on a stopover for a job.

Shel stormed out of the room and directly into the child's room, which was larger and significantly brighter than the other. In fact, it was the only room in the house painted a color other than institutional white. The walls were sunny yellow, adorned with several paintings that froze her in her tracks. Although she needed no additional confirmation that she'd found the missing mother-daughter duo, several original Kathleen Fortier paintings of those funny New Orleans houses hung on the walls, complete with the infamous curling K signature.

Shel set about snapping camera photos of the paintings. Some of the houses had stars sparkling in the windows while others had hearts and rockets bursting from their chimneys. Each bore the trademark yellow sliver of a moon. Shel shook her head at her good luck. She'd give Fortier all the evidence he needed that she'd located his child.

A thick pile rug in the center of the room had a few dolls scattered across it. The toddler bed was a huge downgrade compared to the swank one in the child's former nursery, yet captivating as it had been hand-painted with whimsical yellow moons, stars and smiling flowers. Shel spun a slow circle in the center of the room, taking silent inventory. It appeared the paintings were the only jackpot to be discovered and they were, in fact, worth far more than the grand total of the house's entire contents. Taking them would be pointless. Art was tricky; if additional paintings surfaced on the market, Shel would look like the obvious thief. Should anything happen to Kathleen and her daughter, Shel would also be subject to that scrutiny.

She noted that the kid had nicer clothes than her mother. A row of tiny shoes and sandals lined part of one wall and the only closet was nearly filled with simple sundresses. It looked like the child was clearly priority in the house, which didn't support Kathleen's odd behavior or her husband's nasty description of her.

Shel glanced at another row of blue marbles lining the high windowsills.

"Why so paranoid, momma? Someone after you?" With some humor, she quietly added, "Besides me?"

The thing about paranoid people was that they usually hid their valuables. It angered Shel that she'd been unable to strike pay dirt. She checked under the toddler bed then the mattress before returning to Kathleen's room. She drew back the sheets and swept her hand under and between the mattresses. Replacing the covers, she felt a hellish level of frustration.

She made another pass through the living room and the kitchen table with two mismatched chairs. She felt under the table to see if anything had been taped there and again she came up empty. Basic furnishings, minimal clothing, no personal effects to speak of—it was hardly a suitable setup for a millionaire's wife. Even the silverware was metal with plastic handles, the kind one would use for a picnic. Shel double-checked everything to make sure she hadn't missed a trick. There was still one more room. She headed for the small bathroom.

It was in this room she discovered her exit strategy. The only window in the entire place that wasn't lined with blue marbles was also five feet off the ground, over the bathtub, and certainly no easy way to leave the premises.

"Jesus," Shel muttered to no one. She proceeded to check the cabinets, empty a travel bag, even checked the tank on the toilet. "This is…unbelievable."

There was nothing to do but leave. She stepped up, placing one foot on each side until she was straddling the bathtub. She unlatched the window, but it didn't budge. She dug her fingernail into the line of caulking and began peeling it back, littering the porcelain below with white, rubbery slivers. She pounded the heel of her hand against the window until it opened a few inches. Working the stiff rusty bend, she was almost breathless by the time it was fully open. Shel dropped down into the tub and gathered all the discarded bits of caulk and shoved them into her jeans pocket. She looked back at the high window and groaned. "This should be fun."

She again straddled the tub and pushed off with her toes, slowly, but effectively lifting herself in a chin-up. Shel swung her leg high and boosted herself the rest of the way, hunching low to get through the long, skinny window. She shimmied across the threshold then fell to the ground outside, knocking the wind clean out of her lungs.

She caught her breath and stood, hobbling first, then made the reach on tiptoes to push the window shut. It made a whoosh-thunk sound, probably showering the tub with caulking particles all over again, but now she was too angry to care. She limped back around the house, to her own place across the street.

Shel didn't go inside for fear that she'd lay down and never get up again. Instead she got into her rental car and headed toward the beach. She parked outside Naples Seaside Resort and within seconds she was standing in front of the concierge's desk.

"Welcome back, madam. How can I assist you today?"

That he said welcome back and didn't call security said that her ludicrous charges from her previous stay went through the powers that be at American Express Black. She withdrew the card and her driver's license and handed both to the man.

"What's the max I can draw off this thing?" Shel asked him. Then, if only to add an ounce of intended credibility, she added, "I want to restock my wine cellar back home."

He looked thoughtful as he examined the card. In a quiet voice he told her, "This is the highest order card one can receive, as you know. I'm sure the benefits are substantial. Would you like me to find out for you, madam?"

"Yeah, I would," she said, already feeling relieved. "Will that take long?"

"Not too long," he politely replied. "Would you care to wait in the lobby or the bar?"

A flurry of workers was wrestling around a project in the main lobby, and Shel nearly told the concierge she'd be in the bar. But then she saw her. Kathleen Fortier was in a small huddle of uniformed hotel workers, framed art all around them.

"What's going on in there?" Shel didn't attempt to mask the surprise in her voice.

"The hotel features art from a variety of local artists. They're making the monthly switch at this time." He pointed toward the bar. "If it's too noisy for you, feel free to have a complimentary drink in the bar. I'll come find you there when I have your information."

"No, it's okay," she said, still staring at the workers and their appointed artistic ringleader. She was already walking toward them as she said, "I'll make my way back around to you."

Shel slipped through the lobby and settled into a corner library-style nook seat with high leather backs, designed to provide its occupants utmost privacy. She had a limited view of Kathleen and watched her from a safe distance. The woman appeared to be laying out directives, pointing at the walls, and showing her new minions something on a clipboard. Shel couldn't believe the coincidence. She recalled her conversation with the local art gallery owner and his nice little speech about respecting people who wished to remain in the background. At the memory, Shel smirked. Kathleen Fortier was hardly in the background now. In fact, this particular hotel was heavily concentrated with wealth and society. Thinking about Fortier's warnings about his wife, Shel wondered if Kathleen was presently on the hunt for another sucker to scam. If so, it would go far to prove Fortier was telling the truth about other things concerning his wife and Shel could catapult past her infatuation with the woman, turn over her location without a guilty feeling in the world.

She stared at the beauty with the clipboard and sighed. If only Shel had help—someone who could pose as a mark to see if Kathleen would take the bait.

The soaring ceilings and marble floors created an echo that made it impossible to hear what was being said no matter how hard she strained; however, she overhead a closer conversation and instantly recognized the voice. She made the decision to capitalize on a previously played bluff.

Shel quietly milled through the rows of ultra-private booths until she found Bartender Rob. Dressed in a French terry shirt and white tweed shorts, he was deep into whatever role he was playing for the older woman sitting across from him. His smiling, beautiful face practically melted to tears when he saw her, causing Shel to wonder what he was up to. The place seemed to be ripe with scammers. He quickly excused himself and approached her.

"What's up?" he asked her in an impatient whisper. "Did I do something? Why are you back?"

"Did you do something?" she asked, putting his fear to good use. Paranoia seemed to be the soup du jour. After a second she patted his shoulder. "Relax, Rob. I'm only admiring your work. You really know how to get the ladies, don't you?"

Clearly frustrated, he said, "If that's all you wanted you could have admired my work from across the room."

"Not really. Would you get a load of the size of these things?" She pointed at the towering units with hand-carved shells all around them. She leaned to one side and gave a little wave to his friend still seated in the cozy booth. "Cute," she said, her voice ripe with sarcasm. "So, what kind of money you expect to make off her?"

"What can I do for you?" he more begged than asked.

"And what's with this getup?" Shel said, ignoring his inquiry. She pinched his expensive sleeve. "Mr. Peterson would be plenty interested to know you're a kept man many times over, all courtesy of his hotel. If I'm not mistaken, that makes him like…your pimp or something. Big trouble there…"

The mention of his boss's name seemed to visibly shake Rob. In truth she'd never laid eyes on the man except for the labeled picture in her welcome brochure.

"I'm cooperating."

"Who's the dame?"

"A friend."

"A friend." She sounded like Officer Milford, but didn't pay it notice. She was preoccupied with a move she was formulating on the spot. "I need a little favor. Now."

He looked put out. "Seriously? I'm in the middle of something here."

"Yes, and I'm sure it pays well," she said, giving him a look. "You got more of this kind of thing here? These snazzy rich-guy duds? Something that doesn't look like you just rolled off the tennis court?"

Looking aghast, he looked behind him at his awaiting date, giving her the one-minute sign. He faced Shel again, his friendly demeanor gone, but his exasperation intact. He admitted, "I might be able to get my hands on something."

"Make it fancy. And expensive," she added. "Let's go."

"I'm going to need a minute," he whispered. "I can't just leave her."

"Tell her you'll meet her in an hour."

"But she's my…" He shrugged, nodded, and made several foolish looking gestures to indicate money.

"Oh, she's going to hook you up with the duds?" Shel pretended to be impressed. She winked. "Smooth. Gotcha."

He made his reluctant proposal. "Meet me outside the gift shop in fifteen minutes."

"Don't be late." As he started to go, she whispered loudly, "Shake your moneymaker."

Fifteen minutes later, he emerged from the boutique that was hardly a modest gift shop. Wearing a pair of white, freshly minted slacks and an upscale polo shirt, he looked every bit the part of one of the patrons rather than a tiki bartender. She made a low whistle. "Bling?"

"Pardon?"

"Fancy watch? Like a Rolex? You need to look very legit for this assignment."

They walked down the marble hallway until he broke off and ducked into a smaller, private hall. There he exchanged a few words with security, an older woman—his specialty—and within moments she'd buzzed him through another door.

He returned shortly and caught up with Shel. Unable to hide his pride at what he'd accomplished, he proudly displayed his arm for her to see.

She squinted at the watch, sounded disappointed when she asked, "What is that?"

"It's Harry Winston," he told her. "On loan from the main safe, so I have to hurry or it's my ass."

"They didn't have a Rolex?"

His eyebrows practically hit his hairline. "It's *Harry Winston*," he repeated, as if she'd possibly misheard him.

"I'll take that as a no." Quickly getting over it, she laid out her warning. "Now, this woman knows her rich shit, so don't try to have a conversation about anything unless you truly know what the fuck you're talking about."

"Okay," he nervously agreed.

"Do you know anything about art?" He shook his head. Shel went on. "That's okay. You're the lonely, sexy, wealthy guy who wants to learn everything there is to know about it and you want to learn it from her. Don't come on strong like you normally do. This requires subtlety. She's an operator, much like yourself, so don't get too familiar or she may call your bluff."

They rounded another corner. An older woman had linked arms with her husband, but when they passed, she shot Rob a flirtatious glance. He waved at her.

"You're despicable, you know that?" Shel said before quickly shifting back to his mission and its accompanying directives. "That baller stuff may work with the older dames, but not this one. For this one, you're a sensitive loner with all this damned money. Make yourself appear downright vulnerable—I need to catch her trying to scam you, you understand me? Do not screw this up."

"If you don't have faith in me, why did you come find me?" He stopped walking, forcing her to do the same. His impatience was showing. "Maybe you want to stick your hand up my ass and make me your puppet."

"I don't relish the thought, but it would be easier," she admitted.

He rolled his eyes. She walked on and he reluctantly followed her to the main lobby. They stopped near the back, watching workers unwrap art and situate displays.

"The funny little guest house and alleys paintings are hers. Don't compliment anything on that wall unless it's hers, you understand me? You'd love it on every wall of your pretend big-ass house."

He nodded.

"And do not talk about money, you hear me? Do not—"

"Baby, the only people who talk about money don't have enough of it." He was suddenly at ease, owning the role. Shel breathed a soft sigh of relief.

"Good luck. She's over there." She pointed out Kathleen Fortier. He seemed to look right past her.

"Where?"

"The beautiful one, genius," she mockingly told him. "With the blond pixie."

Shel studied the woman wearing gauzy white pants and a simple yellow T-shirt. Her bleached hair was stylishly mussed and wrapped in a matching sheer scarf that fell to the backs of her knees. How could he not know which one?

Kathleen made a slow turn, obviously demonstrating to her helpers what frames were to be placed where. Shel took a backward step, shielding her identity behind a potted tropical tree. Through the palms she could see Kathleen's lovely face, which didn't look nearly as crazy in daylight. Rob saw her at the same time. His eyes sparkled winningly when he touched Shel's arm and said, "I've got this."

His approach was spot-on, pretending to be engrossed in the art, standing perilously close to where she stood, bright eyes aimed at one of her paintings. It was the perfect setup for her to brush against him, which she did, and for him to turn shy and apologetic, which he did, and very convincingly.

From her safe vantage point, Shel quietly monitored a conversation she could not hear over the noise, supplying her own script for her amusement.

"I am deeply drawn to this shit. Whoever could have created such masterpieces?"

Across the room, Kathleen shyly smiled.

"Why, it was me, silly." Shel again inserted her own words when the woman's lips moved.

Though it seemed a bit soon, Rob was obviously making his move, an action that caused Kathleen's kindhearted expression to change to a worried one. She motioned toward her workers.

Shel continued to supply their words. "Go with you? Why, I couldn't possibly leave my minions."

Rob motioned toward the patio doors.

"Oh please. Run away with me, my beloved."

"I could never—" But Shel dropped her silly imitation when Kathleen followed him right out the glass patio doors. In her usual voice, she uttered, "Holy shit, she bought that act..?"

Shel noticed a woman standing near her, curious eyes beneath a furrowed brow. She felt her own cheeks warm. She cleared her throat and touched her ear, hoping to give the woman the impression she was speaking into a Bluetooth rather than talking to herself.

Rob's plan was definitely working, but Shel was in disbelief that Kathleen had so easily taken the bait. She watched the pair leave across the patio and out of her line of sight. After all, it was the desired outcome, wasn't it? The woman was as big a fraud as her husband claimed. Shel could turn over the location and collect her money without any attached guilt.

Feeling oddly melancholy, Shel retreated to the same high booth where she'd earlier spied on Kathleen conferring with workers. A bartender trolling the area caught her eye and she waved him over.

"Vodka tonic." Her voice sounded monotone.

She stared numbly at the glass doors for several minutes before making herself look away. With unexpected disappointment she realized Rob was experiencing great success doing exactly what Shel had asked of him.

On the good side, Shel now had options if Richard Fortier didn't pay up. As she wasn't one to get her hands dirty kidnapping for ransom, she was perfectly able to hold out on providing him Kathleen's exact location. Originally, that had been her only plan. Well, that and maybe some insurance money or jewels from Kathleen's house, a plan that hadn't panned out at all. Now, with the help of Rob, she was coming to believe there was a shadier side to Kathleen. She could threaten Kathleen about disclosing her location to the unhappy hubby. Kathleen could then either pony up whatever money she'd hidden, and there was surely some somewhere, or if that failed, there was always a third option.

Option three involved widening her net; she'd go after Silvia Frances. She'd throw out a few decent bluffs—an expert tool of Shel's—and get to the bottom of the women's connection. If Silvia were a partner in crime, how bad it would look for her, working in the community church with children? Silvia's wardrobe wasn't cheap either, so she either had a place in society or she was running her own scam, assuring there would be value in Shel's threat.

If all else failed, there was always the list of victims that Richard Fortier had provided her. Certainly no highfalutin fellow would want to risk reexposure to scandal and embarrassment. Yes, by all outward signs things were looking up. So why then did Shel feel so awful?

She stared at her watch, not bothering to acknowledge the server when he set a drink on the table before her. Half the liquid was gone in one swig. She closed her eyes and let the booze warm her system. In moments she felt looser. She downed the balance of the drink and shoved the glass aside.

Feeling slightly off kilter, she clenched her eyes shut. She felt alone and empty, not exactly the good feeling fresh start she'd envisioned. Perhaps she'd been foolish to dream about such. Still, she would make damned sure she got her money, with or without a side of redemption.

She opened her eyes and motioned to the floating waiter, and within moments he'd brought her a fresh drink. She chucked her hand in her pocket for cash.

"Should I start a tab for you?" he asked.

Shel started to put her money away then thought better of it. It was still early and nothing good could come from being a sloppy drunk. She commended herself for having not lost all perspective. She counted out a few bills. "That'll be all. Thanks."

More than an hour later, she was still waiting. Her head ached, made worse by the noise the lunch crowd brought. They were a hoity-toity set of people if ever she saw them, probably women's leaguers or Rotarians. She felt a flash of guilt for her cynical thinking. In truth, nobody in Naples had been even slightly rude to her. Well, nobody except for the nosy cop.

Only when she rose out of her seat did she remember her earlier death-defying jump from a too high bathroom window. Slightly wincing, she did a gentle stretch before heading toward the concierge's desk.

The same gentleman beamed his pleased smile her way. "As you can see, the Lady is in quite good standing."

She glanced at her approved cash advance line, hoping her eyes wouldn't physically bulge from their sockets. She swallowed, licked her lips, and put on her best casual attitude when she said, "Thank you."

Her hand trembled as she filled out the dollar amount. She studied it and briefly considered tacking an extra zero on the end. In the end, she figured it might make her look desperate and possibly sound unnecessary alarms with the hotel staff or worse, the credit card company. Fortier would get word in no time. She slid the request for ten grand back to the gentleman, who nodded and carried it off to the office. Twenty minutes later she left the desk with cash in her pocket. It wasn't a hundred grand, but it helped alleviate the sting of finding absolutely nothing of value in Kathleen's tiny house. Besides, if she followed her newly formed plan, she'd get what she had coming to her, perhaps more.

She paused in the hallway in front of a chalkboard sign posted outside a restaurant that was casual compared to the other swank eateries. The host seated her in a corner booth and soon she was dining on a heaping roast beef on rye with a side of "hand crafted" chips, reminding her that Naples was nothing if not artsy with its food.

In the middle of a particularly large mouthful, Rob slid into the seat across from her.

CHAPTER FOURTEEN

"She is one tough nut to crack, I'll tell you that much." He grinned and made a low whistle.

"But you did? Crack her, I mean?" Shel said after swallowing her too-big bite. It felt stuck in her throat. Still surprised to see him, she'd expected she'd seen the last of him. For a while, she wasn't even sure why she'd bothered hanging around. The thoughts spun through her head as she sipped her water then pressed forward. "Did she pursue you? Were you able to—"

"Give me a chance, would you?" He playfully wagged his index finger at her, like a parent admonishing a naughty child. "First, let me commend you for being a clever little wench. That's some shtick—find a sucker with a record and hold it over his head until he dances like a monkey? I gotta hand it to you, I didn't see that coming."

Her expression was deadly serious. "What are you talking about?"

"It's cool. You've got a little larceny operating in you. Don't we all?" He paused dramatically as he leaned back against the booth. His Cheshire grin didn't show signs of fading. "Of course, I was insulted at first; you did use me after all. If you needed a wingman, you could have just asked."

His nonsensical accusations were causing Shel to quickly lose her patience. She narrowed her gaze. "I'm forming my own notions, but let's find out how large an idiot you really are, Rob. Did you follow our plan at all? Did you even attempt to scam the scammer, *at all*?"

"Yes and yes. Girl's got no game and she's got no cabbage."

Shel shook her head. "What?"

"No dough." He rubbed his fingertips together. "No bread, no moolah—zip. My guess is she's a starving artist. Not well traveled, no jewelry, and her clothes are three seasons old, if you know what I mean."

Shel didn't. "Cite your supporting evidence."

"She's classy, but not sophisticated. Think about all the things you'd do if you were an artist with means." He nodded, obviously pleased with himself. "You'd go see the great works in sweet places—Musee D'Orsay, Bushwick Galleries—I dropped it all. She has a working laymen's knowledge, probably from books."

"How do you know about it?"

"Books. It's always easy for me to spot a faker, though I can't say she was trying to fake me out." He appeared momentarily puzzled. "Girl acts like Florida is the first sun she's ever had on her face. Had she not been so well spoken, which speaks to decent education, I'd have pegged her for being fresh off the farm. Oh, and she was very wary of me."

Shel tensed. "She made you, you moron."

"No." He shrugged. "I mean she could have, but I doubt it. Her reactions were too spontaneous, too legit. Seemed more like the brand of wariness you have when small-town folk have warned you about city-slickers."

"So you're a profiler now?" Shel rolled her eyes and quickly got down to business. "I thought you were a pro at this pick-up biz. If she were so fresh off the farm, you'd have her by your side by now. You failed."

"Oh, I did not fail. Picking up is my business—it's what I *do*." He seemed very serious about that point, and leaned forward to make it. He continued in a quiet, firm voice. "I gave her my best low-key moves, employed some smooth don't-know-much-about-art-shit moves, and even offered to buy her dinner. No traction. But that's still good news for you, right?"

"How could there possibly be good news for me?"

"She's an obvious lesbian. There you go." He again sat back, proudly crossing his arms across his chest. "My work here is done."

When every last piece of his odd summary had clicked into place, Shel felt her cheeks burn. "You're an enormous idiot, you know that? You think that's what I'm after here? A piece of tail?"

"No shame in bringing on a professional consultant." He glanced toward the ceiling, as if he were considering it all. "I admit, even an unwilling wingman is better than none at all. I applaud you. Nice work."

"She told you she is gay?" In her wildest imaginings she couldn't hear those words come from the feminine woman's sweet lips.

"Not with words, but why else would she turn me down flat?" He chuckled, his healthy ego on full display for Shel. "Please—get real. Never happens."

"Let me see if I comprehend." Shel continued glaring at him. "Despite my clear directives, you thought the mission was to find out whether or not she was straight."

"This is odd advice coming from me, but I'd go for it even without the money. She is pretty damned amazing to look at." He swiped her water glass and started to take a sip, but Shel reached a hand out and stopped him. The water sloshed over the rim and onto the table between them.

"God only knows where those lips have been." She set it back down and sighed with disgust. "Thanks for nothing."

Instead of being put off, he appeared to sympathize. "Look, it's clear that cops make no money..." He paused and gave her outfit and hair an exaggerated gander to make his point. "You look like you're used to it by now. True this dame hasn't got a pot to piss in, but she's swell. Go after it."

Disbelieving her ears, Shel repeated, "You have seriously fucked this up."

Appearing immune to her insults, he continued. "I'll warn you that she's got kid-baggage, surprise-surprise." He shivered. "Only good thing about kids is visiting the place where they started."

She tossed the crude words around her brain and shook her head until it hurt all over again. "You're really a pig."

"You sent me on a job for your personal benefit, and I'm a pig?" He appeared to easily shrug off her opinion of him, whispered, "That's the pot calling the kettle black isn't it, Officer-Detective?"

"You utterly failed the job I gave you."

"And you're happy I did," he cockily declared. He started to lean onto the tabletop, but looked as though he thought better of it. Dusting pretend lint off his sleeves, he grinned. "Almost forgot, they said I could return these for cash."

He slid his sleeve back enough for her to see that indeed, the tag with all its zeroes was still intact. Rob beamed with pride at his alleged brilliance then glanced at his borrowed watch. "Gotta run, but thanks for cutting me in. It was fun."

"Fun?" She felt like she was in the *Twilight Zone*.

"Yeah—we could be a real team, you and me. I could be, like, your gaydar." He slid out of the booth and stood. "Feel free to bounce all your potential hot-ass dates off me. There's bound to be a flunky in there somewhere. With chicks like that, money or not, I live for the day."

Long after he was gone, Shel still stared at the doorway. While it was true that Kathleen Fortier was at least two decades younger than his youngest sugar mama, she'd felt too stunned to even properly insult him with that fact before his departure.

Her initial disappointment had taken a brief foray into excitement to which she was neither entitled nor would she ever benefit from. Rob had been right about one thing: women as educated and gorgeous as Kathleen wouldn't give her a second look. The reality was that for her, snagging a woman like Kathleen would require more than a wingman—possibly it would take an entire flight crew.

On the heels of that bunch of ridiculous notions, she came full circle to Rob's certainty that Kathleen was a basic pauper. In her earlier search of the woman's house, Shel hadn't recovered a dime let alone diamond. His mention of her not being well traveled didn't much concern her; there could be a million reasons why someone would choose not to travel. He'd mentioned the possibilities of what would an artist do if she had money, and although Shel could hardly believe she was following the lead of a professional scam artist bartender, she was compelled to work along that same vein.

What would a creative person hope to provide for their child?

Inevitably her thoughts went to the young mother delivering drugs all those years ago.

"Mothers always hope their child will do better," she'd said, *tired eyes shining. In a whisper she added, "Anyhow, it's surely what I hope."*

Shel clenched her eyes tightly shut as if she could physically purge the memory. It still pained her after all these years.

Kathleen, if she were a decent mother, would also want better for her child. The woman herself could create beautiful things; she'd want to give her daughter an artistic environment in which to thrive. Yet the yellow cottage lacked art, even books. There were no paints, not even a radio for music or television on which to watch a movie. Given monetary limitations, was it possible Kathleen attempted to "do better" by her child, if only by way of nursery décor? She thought about its brightly painted walls, simple, yet stimulating toys, and the fact that the walls were adorned with the only pictures in the house. If Shel ignored the warnings of Richard Fortier and went strictly with gut instinct, the answer seemed clear: Kathleen was giving her daughter everything she could. It so happened to be that her everything just wasn't much.

Then again, maybe she simply provided the kid just enough stuff to get her to shut up. Like that, Richard Fortier's claims were infiltrating her already shaky objectivity.

Why wasn't Kathleen asking for that ransom? What was she waiting for, and why?

Being held for ransom isn't supposed to be a cultural experience, her inner con artist butted in next. Turning the whole damned nutty bunch over to the authorities is what's best for the kid—or so urged the last dregs of the old cop inside her.

Her eyebrow arched as she considered what it would be like to nail Mrs. Fortier should Rob's suspicion turn out to be an accurate one…

"You fucking nutty bitch," she quietly, firmly said aloud, emerging from her internal rambling. She was staring at her now cold sandwich and she wasn't alone. The waitress stood over her wearing a confused look. Shel scrubbed her hands through her hair and quickly apologized. "Sorry—I was…talking to myself."

The young waitress looked uncertain and her voice wavered when she asked, "Is there something wrong with the sandwich?"

"No, no." Shel fished her wallet out of her pocket and found a few bills. "Could I get this wrapped?"

CHAPTER FIFTEEN

By the time she stumbled through the door of the Third Avenue house, streaks of pain were shooting up her leg, into her lower back. If history had its way, she'd be stiff as a board within a few hours. The way it already felt, she worried that this round might really be a doozy. Shel toed her shoes off, and with the agility of an aging arthritic, slowly changed into sweatpants and T-shirt. Two Tylenol later it was time to lie down.

She considered the bed then the couch, but both would be too soft. Should she lie down, she might never get back up again. She eyed the wide, flat coffee table only a moment before gingerly lowering herself onto its top. Holding her breath, she willed it not to collapse under her. Within seconds, she'd deemed it relatively solid. Legs dangling over the edge, she took short, shallow breaths and stared at the whirling ceiling fan. Her eyelids grew heavy.

She woke to a dull buzz coming from the front of the house. It was now dark and she blinked to adjust her vision. One upward move reminded her why she was there in the first place. The buzzer came in long spurts and was quickly growing annoying. It could be only one person.

"Come on in," she called in a scratchy voice. In seconds she was staring at Officer Milford standing over her, a six-pack of beer wedged in the crook of her arm. Shel sighed. "Well, Officer Milford…surprise, surprise."

"I could have been a serial killer."

"Too bad you weren't," Shel muttered. She clenched her eyes tightly shut. "I might have been put out of my misery."

Milford tsked. "You down in the back, hotshot?"

"What makes you say that?" Shel cynically asked, wincing as she again tried to sit upright. She gave up and pointed toward the kitchen. "Could you get those tablets on the counter left of the stove? And bring me one of your beers, would you?"

Milford looked at her with unease before disappearing into the kitchen. She returned seconds later with a glass and the requested pills and stood by as Shel tossed them down with what turned out to be water. In the near darkness she'd been tricked. "That…is not a beer."

"You had me worried."

"Shouldn't have been," Shel said. She swiped her hand across her lips. "I drink beer all the time."

"You know what I mean." She referred to the requested tablets, which turned out to be imprinted with the word *Tylenol*.

"Jesus, nobody trusts anybody anymore." Shel handed the glass back. "Could I get that beer now, please?"

"How'd you hurt your back?"

"Breaking and entering," she truthfully answered.

"Very funny," Milford said, her rusty voice rising up a notch. The cop fished two beers out of the cardboard carrier and popped the lids. She handed one to Shel, who was now sitting on the couch, but massively pained at her effort to do so. She took a long pull off the beer. Milford, who'd been standing by, seated herself on the facing couch.

As they drank their beers in silence, Shel mentally reviewed her unusual day and wondered how much of her back pain was physical and how much was stress. Fortier had yet to return her call and his estranged wife was proving to be the mystery of the century. Judging by the pain in her back, she wasn't going to be able to do much about any of it soon.

She broke their silence, her tone bordering disgusted. "You want in or what?"

"I'm in," Milford coolly said. "I'm in sitting on the couch, about to drink a second one of these beers. You want another?"

Shel nodded and Milford collected bottles then delivered a fresh round.

"How long you been in Naples?"

"Long." Milford stared at her. "This illegal work?"

"No, but it's tricky."

Milford narrowed her eyes. "Define tricky."

"You ever heard of SLW, LLC?"

Milford wanted more information up front. "First, what's your case?"

They stared at each other in the growing darkness for several seconds before Shel muttered every curse word known to mankind. After a follow-up of exaggerated eye rolls, she said, "Christ, Milford—where's your sense of adventure?"

"On hold." Milford stared her down. "Continue."

Shel wondered how telling could hurt anything. After a brief hesitation, she quietly began. "A prominent art gallery owner in New Orleans hired me to find his runaway wife."

"Why'd she run?"

"Not my concern." Almost immediately, Shel amended her statement. "Doesn't matter, anyway. She took his daughter, a four-year-old. He says the mom is deranged, a real danger to the kid."

"And you took him at his word." It wasn't a question. Milford looked very reluctant. "I hesitate to ask, but you're not planning to kidnap—"

"No," Shel cut her off. The cop let out the breath she'd been holding, motioned for Shel to continue. "My job is only to find her and report to him her location."

Milford seemed to be thinking it over. She stood up, sauntered toward the window and gazed outside at the dark street. She tapped her beer bottle lightly against the front window indicating the house across the street. "I take it you already know their whereabouts."

Shel nodded, an unnecessary move in the darkness. "I've got copies of all the legal paperwork and there's committal papers waiting for the wife when he finds them." She paused a second. "There's good money on the line."

"So what's your holdup, hotshot?" The cop's tone said she was testing Shel's sense of integrity. She came back around and sat down across from the troubled woman.

"Something seems…off."

Milford cut right to it. "Is this a case of conscience or puppy love?"

She blinked a few times. "A person should know what they're really looking at before they take a woman's kid away from her." And when the cop seemed ready to test her selection of terms, she impatiently revised it. "*Alert* the father who will then take the woman's kid—c'mon, Milford, don't be so technical."

Milford sounded deadly serious. "It is technical. You need to mean what you say and say only what you mean, particularly in cases like this one."

That she went silent said the cop was at least mulling it over. Shel prompted her along. "I will give you the details of this case, but I swear to God if you screw me over or let the cat out of the bag, I'll kill you. And yes, I meant what I said."

"I'm not going to break the law." Milford was firm on that point.

"I'm not asking you to do that."

"Exactly what are you asking me to do, pray tell?"

In a matter of minutes, Shel had briefly filled the woman in on the case details, including the events of the day with Rob the shady bartender.

"You believe him? This guy fancy himself a cop or something?"

"No." Shel chuckled. "He's just an observant friend."

"Be careful who you confide in."

"Including you?" Shel coyly asked.

"Especially me." Milford was again quiet. Finally, she said, "I've never heard of this SLW, LLC, but I can do some checking."

"And what do you think about Silvia Frances?"

"Where's your computer?"

"There's no Internet."

Milford held up her telephone and gave it a midair jiggle. "I bring my own Internet."

Shel started to stand, but the pain stopped her. Instead, she motioned toward the bedroom. Milford left and came back with it in seconds. She fired up the personal hotspot and clacked around a bit. The light from the screen illuminated her expression of disappointment.

"Looking at the preschool website and she's on the board. I guess she skipped picture day." Milford spun the computer around for Shel to see. "Surprise, surprise."

Sure enough, in a row of professionally photographed pictures, Silvia Frances was represented by an ambiguous blue outline and the caption *N/A*. The women were quiet each caught up in their own thoughts.

"I'll see if she has a record, voting card, residence, that sort of thing."

Shel didn't look terribly hopeful about their prospects. She rubbed the small of her back, whispered, "Probably not her real name. Seems to be a trend around these parts, just ask Addison James."

"You've got yourself quite a case here, my friend."

"I know." Shel looked at her in the darkness. "So, are you going to help me or what?"

"What's in it for me?"

"Escape? Adventure…?" And when that didn't seem to do it, Shel rolled her eyes again. "What's your price?"

Milford stared at her for a while before finally softening a bit. "You stick with my code of ethics, which means no law breaking, you hear? And I'll do it for the pure delight of it." Her sarcastic tone and perturbed expression said she was wondering what she'd gotten herself into. She shut down the computer and punched a button on her phone before she stood and headed for the door. "Maybe an occasional beer or two."

"Thanks, Milford." Shel meant it. It was an odd feeling having someone else on board with her. She got the feeling Milford worked alone, too. She wasn't sure how well they'd get along. The thought of it made her ask, "What made you say yes?"

"The Tylenol." She opened the door, but didn't go, only stared across the street.

"I'd at least like to know what's going on with those ladies—Ms. James and Ms. Frances. From your story alone, I'm guessing theft or trafficking or something else that requires a bogus corporate name. I don't like the idea of it happening here, right here in my little highfalutin backyard."

Shel motioned toward the yellow house. "Well, if she's hiding anything, it's only secrets. Her place is clean."

"I did not hear that." Milford leaned back inside and pointed a finger at Shel, her voice suddenly stern. "And that kind of thing won't happen again if you hope to get any help out of me. You need to know that."

Shel nodded and watched Milford leave. She peeked out the window, watching as the cop lumbered down the sidewalk and into the driveway and hitched up the waistband of her jeans. Milford swung one short leg over a motorcycle and straddled the seat of her Hog and started it up. Shel let the curtain fall back and listened as the cop rode off into the night, only a fading deep *put-put-put* echo in her wake.

She knew Milford was right. Old Naples was exclusive— too much so that a starving artist could move in, secondhand furnishings or not. That meant there was money somewhere or at least the prospect of it. Add in the false names and air of secrecy and something was off. It felt like more than a child custody war or even blackmail.

More and more, Shel's thoughts were centered on what they might discover about her baffling neighbor. A genuine sense of foreboding hung over Kathleen like a dark cloud. Shel's objectivity felt shakier than ever thanks to absurd, lustful thoughts she was having about her employer's wife—God help her—making it difficult to tell if her own instincts were trying to tell her something. It felt that way.

The cases she'd taken over the last few years had primarily involved outwitting dimwits. There wasn't much need for employing morals, values, or even emotions for that matter. By now, given the surplus of stupidity she'd witnessed, her gut instincts were so firmly insulated by cynicism she wasn't sure she'd recognize them if they slapped her in the face.

That's why she needed Milford. While the cop's pared down lifestyle had her at risk for being terminally boring, her simplified view had given her an uncanny knack for easily distinguishing right from wrong. Shel could tell. She found herself admiring Milford's low maintenance, peaceful existence. Boring or not, she'd bet the woman slept well at night, which was more than she could say for herself.

She rubbed her eyes and glanced at her watch. It was after ten o'clock and the house across the street was dark, right on schedule with a town that rolled up its sidewalks at dusk. The night air was considerably less stifling than when she'd lain down in the first place. It wafted through the screened windows bringing with it the sounds of crickets and an occasional frog croak, setting the tone for restful slumber. But Shel knew better.

CHAPTER SIXTEEN

Though she hadn't been in a pool for years, Shel sat at the edge of the backyard pool wearing the closest thing she had to swimwear: sweat shorts and a T-shirt. She gently lowered herself into the shallow end and slowly began to move about. Low-impact exercises, Milford had instructed her after summoning her from sleep with the faulty doorbell. It was the second such time in less than twenty-four hours. As she'd watched the bedside clock until nearly four a.m., Shel was angry about the disruption at first. She quickly forgave the visit when she realized it was already early afternoon.

Milford had stopped over during her lunch break with no real update on the SLW, LLC mystery. In truth, Shel knew the cop was checking on her sordid state of mind and rotten back. She promised Milford both were improving.

Moving around the sun-warmed pool felt like trying to walk off rigor mortis. She waded slowly through the shallower end and discovered that after several minutes, she was feeling slightly better. She continued gentle movement, hoping for continual improvement, but recovery was only marginal. She gave up and free floated with her face to the sunny sky.

It was funny, relaxing in the pool she'd cleaned and filled, out back of the home she'd rented in a real neighborhood, and it all felt terribly domestic. Never before had she the slightest desire to be stuck in one place or have a home. She was used to hustling just enough jobs to pay rent on maybe four hundred squares in the city. Compared to that, life in the slow lane in Naples didn't seem too bad. She considered she could get used to it, while alternately wondering if Naples' brand of small-town quiet could eventually cause her to go stir crazy. Perhaps she'd become like Milford. It changed the feeling of her momentary lapse to domestic fantasy and she grimaced.

She knew better than to get used to feeling even remotely settled, particularly here. She wasn't the type. Anyway, she'd be done with the seaside town soon, only the leftover white sand in her shoes to show she'd been here at all. Possibly there was money ahead. Definitely there was freedom.

Shel stayed in the pool until her skin was sufficiently pruned and pinking. She gently hoisted herself onto the aluminum ladder and slowly climbed up and out then leaned against the porch railing to let the sun dry her.

At a child's shrieking scream she forgot about her back. With a strength and speed she didn't even know she was capable of, Shel ran around the side of the house toward the street. Another shrill scream had her running full force across the street. In seconds she was hammering her fist against the front door. If harm came to the child living there, Shel would be to blame. Her stomach was in knots. She wished she hadn't seen enough in her career to know how vulnerable kids truly are.

She pressed her face against the front window, but saw no movement. She abandoned the front porch and ran along the fence to the gate. When the latch stuck, she impatiently rammed the flimsy wooden door with her hip until it burst open. It loudly slammed against the fence, splintering around the rusted latch and in three long strides she was standing in the backyard.

The child's tiny hands were wrapped around a garden hose, the stream of water aimed directly at her mother. Mother and daughter were obviously startled by Shel's sudden appearance, her intense expression, the sound of the gate—all of it. The child lowered the hose and stared at the intruder, gaping.

"Off," Kathleen commanded the child in an unexpectedly chilly voice. The stream of water died. Kathleen's hands went to her hips and she took a bold step toward her neighbor, implying that she was prepared to defend herself and her child. Given her petite size it seemed absurd. Still, she had a right to be angry.

Shel stood breathless, staring at the soaking wet woman. Uneven blond strands were damp and sticking to Kathleen's cheeks and lips creating a funny frame for the otherwise perfect face. Helpless to her wandering eyes, Shel's gaze moved lower, falling over the damp T-shirt that hardly disguised perfect, erect nipples. Trying desperately to look away, she lowered her eyes further, only to land on the gauzy skirt now almost transparent as it clung to the woman's petite curves. Kathleen's icy demeanor remained intact, as conveyed through her stance and the hard look in her aqua eyes.

"Can I help you?"

After hesitating longer than she would have liked, Shel muttered, "I heard a commotion."

Her skin prickled in a light breeze and for a moment, Shel thought Kathleen's chilly demeanor was contagious. Only then did she realize she was still in wet clothes. In fact, Shel's attire was only a partial improvement over what she'd worn the first time she'd barged into their lives.

Kathleen's arms crossed in front of her damp T-shirt, effectively reducing the wonderful view. "Are you always on high alert?"

Feeling foolish, Shel looked away. Her face felt warm either at her embarrassment or her adolescent musings concerning Kathleen's wet shirt. She slowly nodded. "Maybe."

"Are you a cop or something?"

The question caught Shel slightly off guard, but no more than anything else that had transpired in the last two minutes. She looked at the child, still standing there with the hose nozzle clutched in her hand, staring at the women. Shel wondered what the kid was used to seeing and couldn't stomach the thought of adding more insanity to it. Her tone indicated surrender when she said, "Just a nosy neighbor."

Kathleen turned toward the child. "Harper, go inside. Now."

The child promptly dropped the hose and without question, did exactly as she was told.

"Harper…" Shel hadn't meant for the word to make its way out of her mouth. It was the final piece of what was truly unnecessary confirmation that all the players were accounted for. Kathleen remained staring at her and Shel raised her hands in faux surrender. "I'm going."

She took a few steps toward the gate, but thanks to her grand entrance complete with splintering the wood, it had shut too hard and now wouldn't budge. Desperate to avoid making an exit as brazen as her entrance, Shel quietly struggled with the latch. Every ache and pain trickled back into full strength until even jiggling the gate was intolerable.

Kathleen was suddenly at her side, working at the dilapidated latch. Her arm brushed against Shel and she flinched, as if Kathleen's very touch caused her even more pain than her back ever could.

Kathleen didn't seem to notice the impact she had on her unwelcome visitor. She continued to struggle with the latch, her damp skirt swaying with her movement, revealing the barest hint of lovely midriff when she finally bumped the gate with her slim hip. It slowly swung open.

Shel felt a dangerous kind of warmth building inside her. The woman was having an extraordinary physiological impact on her, yet Kathleen didn't even seem to notice.

She turned to face Shel, and they stood there enveloped in an awkward cloud of silence. "Thank you," Kathleen finally said.

Confused, Shel shook her head. "I'm sorry?"

"I was rude—I've been rude since the first…" Her voice trailed off as she obviously collected her thoughts. "Look, I can see you were just looking out for us. I guess I'm not used to neighbors."

"Me neither," Shel quietly confessed. "And you weren't rude. Not much."

Damp strands of dyed blond hair clung to Kathleen's cheekbones and tickled swollen pink lips. She seemed to thoroughly analyze each word before she spoke it. It was with tremendous trepidation that she finally extended her hand to Shel, but there was no warmth in her eyes. "I'm Addison."

Shel's own hesitation was also caused by apprehension, but for different reasons. Kathleen had called herself Addison. Shel wasn't sure she'd ever seen such beautiful lips lie so openly to her face. Shel took the delicate hand in her own, almost melting at the woman's soft warmth.

"Nice to meet you, Addison." Though she'd already introduced herself nights earlier, she did it again. "I'm Shel, your…neighbor."

"Nice to meet you."

The look on Kathleen's face said she still wasn't fully invested in that statement, but rather politely reciprocating. Still, it was better than nothing. Shel realized she was still holding her hand and quickly let go. She started to take a backward step, but shooting back pain caused her to limp. She grabbed her side and issued her "new" acquaintance a compulsory tight-lipped smile.

Kathleen's brow furrowed in concern and she took a halfstep toward her uninvited guest. "Are you okay?"

It was a loaded question. In fact, she felt she was very much not okay. Shel stared at her neighbor a moment longer, then hurriedly left without explanation or goodbye. Clutching the small of her back, she limped across the front lawn, across the street and back to the green house—anything to get herself as far away from Kathleen—*Addison*—as possible.

She occupied her thoughts with anything she could to resist thinking about the woman's warm, soft touch, wispy hair or see-through skirt. Why had Kathleen chosen to change her own name and not her child's? *Because children don't lie well*, Shel answered her own interrogation—*it's not in their nature*. Shel had all her proof; she'd found them both. Technically, the only thing left to do now was to turn them over to Richard Fortier.

Shel pushed through the front door of the little house. She needed a cold shower and hoped it would be enough to douse the inexplicable fire that Kathleen seemed to have ignited deep within her.

On her hurried route to the bathroom, a vibrating sound caught her attention. She scanned the room and saw Fortier's cell phone buzzing across the top of the nightstand, hazardously nearing the edge. She snatched it before it could rattle to the floor and squinted unnecessarily at the tiny screen. Of course it would be Richard Fortier.

She wondered if he had telepathy. Frozen by her paranoid thoughts, she held the phone until it went silent. As she'd neglected to set up her voice mail account, he wouldn't be leaving her a message. She was about to set it down when it vibrated in her hand once again. Wincing, she licked her dry lips and pressed the button.

"Mr. Fortier," she said.

"Have you found my little girl?" he eagerly asked. "Did you find them?"

Her heart hammered against her ribs and her throat grew tight. She'd found her all right—she'd just eyeballed his wife's breasts in a tight, damp T-shirt after spending days studying the woman's fine ass on a bicycle—*sure*, she'd found them. Shel first wondered why the delay for his call, then, given the suspect timing, wondered if he had a better tracker on that phone than she'd credited him for.

"I'm working on it." She whispered the lie, scrubbed her hand through damp hair, and continued to listen to his shallow breathing down the line. Still limping, she slowly paced the room, her voice low. "I am making some solid headway. I promise you that much."

"I know I said I wouldn't call, but I'd hoped you'd call with an update."

She clenched her eyes shut, utterly unprepared to answer his questions. "I was going to check in with you tonight. There's still no news."

"Harper needs to be home with her daddy. Her birthday's next month." His voice was slightly slurred, his southern accent more deeply pronounced. "I need her here."

"Mr. Fortier, are you drinking?"

"I'm not sleeping well," he said, disregarding her question. She listened as he prattled down the line, his heartache evident. Shel rubbed her temples and nodded, as if he could see her. He wrapped up his call with a plea. "Please. I'll double the money—whatever it takes to get my Harper home."

Double the money? Would he remember that promise once he sobered up? Would she try to collect it once she snapped out of her lustful haze…? Shel's nerves caused her to pace more quickly. "I will make every effort to do right by your daughter."

And that was true.

"Please, that's all I'm asking of you."

She ended the call, clutched the phone, staring at it. She finally powered it off and replaced it on the nightstand.

* * *

In New Orleans, Richard Fortier pressed the off button before handing the phone to his attorney.

"How'd she sound?" Dubois eagerly asked. "Any progress?"

Fortier appeared melancholy. "She was vague."

Dubois seemed concerned. "I know you have a great deal of confidence in this woman, but perhaps we should send in someone else."

"Let's give her time." Fortier sipped his drink, eased back in his chair. He looked like he was questioning his own words. "What's it to you? You still get paid."

"I'm just one for making things happen, not sitting around feeling helpless. We've put all our eggs in one basket. Should we send in someone else? Perhaps a man this time? I can get some names—"

"That's the problem with you," Fortier sputtered. "You can't send a man to do what is most definitely a woman's job."

A small smile flexed on Dubois's lips. "Are you sure you're not over-crediting maternal instincts?"

Fortier studied his associate for a long time. As he tended to whenever subject to scrutiny, Dubois felt nervous.

"There are female instincts other than maternal," Fortier curtly informed him. He tapped his glass for a refill and Dubois obliged like a well-trained dog. Fortier took another sip, looked lost to his thoughts as he added, "I assure you they are just as powerful."

* * *

Shel's second attempt to get to the shower was thwarted by the doorbell she was beginning to detest. Aggravated, Shel moved slowly toward the annoying buzzing door and swung it open to find Officer Milford leaning against her doorframe. "Doorbell's broke," she reminded her host.

"Stop pushing the fucking thing." Shel waved her inside. With sarcasm, she said, "You're becoming quite the frequent flyer, Milford. Why not check out of the motel and just take the second bedroom."

"You got a second bedroom in this dump?" Milford abandoned the doorway, shuffled down the hall a bit, pretending to check it out. "Nah, I don't do well with roomies. I bet you're a terrible one anyhow."

The tired-looking cop wore plain clothes, this time matching yellow stripes and solids, causing her to resemble a short circus tent. She carried with her an environmentally friendly canvas grocery bag that she set on the coffee table. She wrinkled her nose as she noticed Shel's still wet clothes for the first time. "What the heck's got into you?"

Shel ignored her question. "I just got off the phone with Fortier. He's impatient."

"What's that got to do with your wet clothes?" The cop plopped down on the couch. "And what'd he want?"

"He wants his kid back. He was a drunken, sad mess." Shel perched herself on the edge of the opposite couch, cupped her hands over her mouth and sighed. "Surreal. One minute I'm standing in the woman's backyard, watching her and the kid have a water fight like they're normal people, and the next I'm listening to her husband bawl down the phone line about his miserable, child-stealing ex. You're right—something's off."

"You were in their backyard?" She reappraised Shel's thoroughly soaked condition, added, "Kid's got one heck of an aim on her for a four-year-old."

"She didn't do this," Shel impatiently told her. She got back to the issue. "Look, I'm just saying it doesn't seem to me that the little woman is holding out on him, using the kid for some kind of money grab. She's no peach, but she doesn't strike me as being a kidnapper and she doesn't seem nuts. A little paranoid maybe, but not to a clinical degree." Her thoughts went to the incident in the front yard and the gleaming knife. She addressed it absently, almost helplessly. "That knife could have been for protection. She's scared."

"Knife? What knife?" Milford lowered her gaze. "Crazy people never think they're crazy, and they're very good at convincing others of it, too. You know that by now."

"I do know that, but the point of bringing you in on this is not only for help, but some objectivity." Frustration was building within Shel. "Otherwise, I could already have the kid back to Fortier by now with a wad of cash in my pocket and you and I wouldn't be having these late night talks."

"You sure the point of these late night talks of ours isn't to punch holes in the notion that Mrs. Fortier isn't wacky up to the eyebrows so you feel a little better about wanting to get her in the sack?"

Shel glared at her. "Are you delusional?"

"Are you?" They stared at each other for a long time. Milford finally spoke. "I'm just saying if the point is to be objective, then let's be objective. Maybe Mrs. Fortier is a lunatic. Maybe Mr. Fortier is…" Her voice trailed off and she shook her head. "What do we think he is, anyway?"

"Don't know yet." Shel rubbed her eyes with the heels of her hands until everything sparkled. She was exhausted. "I honestly can't answer that, but I can tell you I didn't much like the guy when I met him. Arrogant…odd."

"Then why'd you take the job?" Milford quickly answered her own question. "Oh yes, the money."

Shel attempted to relax her defensive stance, but flinched at a pain in her lower back. The cop noticed.

"That reminds me." Milford leaned up and dug around the inside of the grocery bag. She tossed a box on the table in front of Shel. "Somebody recommended this. Tea made especially for bad backs."

Shel picked it up, stared at the box in the dim light. "Milford, this is green tea drops to make massage oil."

They both cringed at the notion, a much-needed tension breaker. Finally the cop chuckled. "You can forget about that, hotshot. I know less about a back massage than I know about buying tea." From the same bag she produced a six-pack of beer. She twisted the lid off one and handed it to Shel. "I didn't have you much pegged for a tea drinker, anyhow."

Shel accepted the beer and took a long, icy swig.

"I'm only buying this beer because you're down in the back. You owe me big-time." Milford helped herself to a beer. "So tell me why you were across the street."

"There was more commotion over there." Shel settled back, cautiously guarding her sore back. "Turns out they were having a water fight, but I had to check it out. That's just me, utilizing that objectivity you think I've pitched overboard in the name of lust."

"Fair enough, you're objective." Milford raised her beer high in salute then took a sip. "So, let's talk about the jam I nearly got myself into today looking for the goods on Silvia Frances."

"What kind of jam?" Suddenly their evening meeting had purpose. Shel set her beer aside and gave Milford her full attention.

"The kind you get when you start poking around for information on a person who's in the Witness Protection Program." The cop shot her a nasty look. "That kind of jam."

"Really. What's her story?"

"Dunno. That's why it's called a protection program." She let out a long sigh. "Apparently I did enough snooping around under Silvia's new name that I got noticed. Somebody calls up my lieutenant inquiring about my sudden interest, and I get my ass chewed up and spit out along with a little vocabulary review. Words like administrative leave, and so on."

"Tell me they did not suspend you." Such an action would dramatically change the landscape of her case. If Milford couldn't get to that precious privileged information, bringing her in was for nothing. "Without access—"

"Thanks for your concern for my great big, important career." Milford made a little humph noise. "Don't worry anyhow. He's a tough guy who just likes to hear himself yell."

"So that's the end of the line with Silvia Frances," Shel said, summing up the glum situation.

"It is without raising more official eyebrows." Milford leaned forward, rested her forearms on her knees and lowered her tone. "However, that is not the case with SLW, LLC. Steven Winston is behind that one, but I can't figure the tie-in with the Frances woman."

"Good job. It's a start." Shel thought quickly. "Silvia Frances drives a car—a silver Volvo wagon, older model. You want the plates?"

"I do not want the plates," Milford firmly warned her. "I think I just mentioned I don't need another red flag."

"Then I could follow her home."

"Yeah, then she can call me herself and I can arrest you. Good way for all of us to get nice and acquainted." She drained her beer, replaced the empty bottle in the carton. "I don't know what they call it in Louisiana, genius, but here in Florida we call it stalking."

"I'm just saying whether she owns or rents, she's got something in her name—a place to live at very least. Let's find out what and where."

"Computer?" Milford had already started for the bedroom when Shel nodded. The cop returned with the computer in tow. She set it down on the table and fired up her phone's hotspot. With the laptop perched on her lap, she Googled Steven Winston of Naples, Florida. "Let's see what we've got here."

The search yielded only three hits, which puzzled Shel; all were images of Mr. Winston cutting ribbon in front of a park-like setting with no real story attached excepting the text identifying that it was him standing next to the town's mayor. She got the clear impression that he had money which wasn't big news. Most everyone in Naples did. There was no information about the man owning properties or his own residence.

Shel scratched her head. "I could Google myself and come up with more information than this guy." Shel tapped the magnify button for a closer look at the inscription on the plaque. *Miranda Winston Memorial Park*. "Who is that? Wife? Child…?"

"I don't know about you, but I'm wiped for this night." Milford rose up off the couch. She picked up her phone and Shel nodded that she was finished. "Let's reconvene tomorrow when we've both had sleep."

Shel stopped her. "Give me one more sec with this Internet signal. Maybe I'll find some nice bedtime reading."

She plugged the name Miranda Winston into a search engine and within seconds had saved several screen shots for later reading. At last she nodded. "I'm good."

Milford pocketed her phone. "As for this Frances woman, let's not forget that she might be nothing more than a friend—a dead-end. Let's focus on the kid and your crush across the street."

Shel shot her a look of warning, but asked, "What's your plan?"

"I'm going to do some light checking on Mrs. Fortier tomorrow—had no time today. I'd gotten myself into enough trouble and I do have a job, remember?" She headed for the front door. "I'll keep an eye out, but not so much I end up unemployed and sleeping in your spare room."

"Sounds good." Shel painfully rose up off the couch and followed her to the hallway. She let her friend out and locked the door behind her. In seconds, she heard the Harley fire up and zoom off into the night.

She limped through a shower before slipping into a T-shirt. She crawled into bed with her computer that now contained a saved collection of relatively large documents pertaining to Miranda Winston. It looked like tedious reading and Shel was tired. She hoped it wasn't a meaningless tracing of ancestral roots or other insignificant material.

The first bit of information was merely vital statistics, enough to tell Shel that the woman had died forty years ago at the age of thirty-four.

"Hmm," she murmured. "An aunt, perhaps?"

She opened another screen shot, this one a newspaper article providing slightly more information than the first. The content included news of a murder and a trial, in no real detail. Still it was something and suddenly Shel felt slightly more awake.

The next file was an obituary for Miranda K. Winston Clark, about two inches square and very blurry in quality. The presence of rough edges of the surrounding articles indicated that it was also an original newspaper section that had been scanned into the computer. It gave minimal survived-by details that included the mention of a young son and her husband, Donald Clark of the famous Clark Paper family.

"Jesus, could Steven Winston be that kid...?"

Shel quickly reread the tiny article; it seemed peculiar that the son's name had been omitted, but Shel was surer by the moment it was Steven. It seemed very odd that it was such a modest death announcement given the couple's obvious wealth. She closed the article and selected another.

The stories got progressively more interesting and this one was a five-year anniversary report of a murder including details of the original investigation. Shel scrolled down line by line, reading carefully. Twenty minutes later she was left shaking her head, mesmerized by a brutal crime that had taken place in Naples years ago, when it was an even smaller, quieter seaside town. It smacked of cover-up and scandal and included domestic abuse allegations directed at Donald Clark. He was heartily defended by his family, of course, and the issue of the woman's death never went to trial. Townspeople and retired cops commented on the horrific, bloody event, and interviews with Clark family members were predictable. Five long years later, they still bad-mouthed the dead woman as if she'd asked to be killed.

Over and again the townspeople expressed their shock at how quickly the case had been dismissed as an accidental death. Brief public outcry bashed local officials for having given Donald Clark special treatment on the basis of his family's wealth. The police force responded only with no comment. With Miranda K. Winston Clark safely in the ground, her voice forever silenced, Donald Clark and the rest of his pretentious family had taken their vast wealth and swiftly left town.

Shel found it unusual that there wasn't even a passing mention of Miranda's son. She wondered what became of the boy.

"What a sham job," she quietly said. Newton leapt onto the bed next to her, pawed and clawed a circle in the blankets in front of the laptop. She addressed the cat as if he cared. "That's the power of old money right there."

There was only one saved screenshot remaining, and after a few seconds of reading, it was clear to Shel that she'd inadvertently saved the best for last. This one concerned a civil court case a few years later. At the outcome of this trial, Donald Clark did finally pay for the crime, though not with time in jail, but with real cash money. Possibly to protect the balance of the family assets, the Clark family had legally distanced and disinherited Donald Clark. The once flamboyant heir had plenty of money hiding around the globe and it appeared that the prosecution had found it all. The plaintiff was listed under a corporate name, SLW, LLC. Shel's eyes nearly dropped out of her head. There was no word about who was behind the corporation, only that much later, Donald Clark died alone and penniless.

She closed the laptop and set it aside then scooted the cat to the end of the bed to make room for herself. Easing back against the pillows, she lay there attempting to sort through her jumbled thoughts.

She considered all the players. There was Steven Winston— probably the SW of the SLW acronym. Then there was Silvia Frances, the camera shy preschool administrator. Maybe she worked for him; maybe he didn't even know her. Considering the fortune Shel suspected Winston had legally extracted from Donald Clark, it was easy to see how the man could keep sixteen properties scattered about town. Of course, if he had that kind of dough, he'd also have a league of people and investors—so why the tiny cracker box-sized houses in a single seaside town? Why not spread out, or invent things, or invest in technology, or any number of potentially lucrative investments? And where did Kathleen play into this mystery?

Her mind churned through the endless possible scenarios until, exhausted, Shel nodded off to sleep.

CHAPTER SEVENTEEN

Restless sleep dragged Shel from one dream to another, each starring her neighbor in various states of dress, wet transparent skirt, wet T-shirt, no T-shirt…

More than once Shel had awakened in a pool of her own sweat, panting hard, clutching her chest, wondering if having the woman so close in proximity might cause her a heart attack, or at very least, a panic attack. By six a.m., she was literally hosing off in the shower.

As she slowly stripped the bed and tossed damp sheets into the wash, she seemed to move better. Using her newly acquired knowledge about Steven Winston, she formulated the day ahead. She needed to learn something about Silvia Frances to connect the dots. While she drank her morning coffee, she factored a trip to the library into her day. A visit to the Collier County Clerk of Court was in order. Not only might she discover something more about the properties owned by Winston, but Silvia had a car, and behind every license plate there was a registered owner. She wasn't worried the search would leave a virtual bread crumb trail leading right back to her. Unlike Milford, Shel was a civilian, and there was no law against being nosy.

After she was certain Kathleen was well into her daily routine, Shel toted the Addison James painting outside and secured it in the hatchback of her car. She then drove to the hospital with every intention of making the donation to their children's wing. It was important that if Silvia checked out her story, the painting was where she promised her it would be. If need be she'd contact Silvia under the pretense that she needed more art. Of course this call, if necessary, would be placed from a pay phone as she'd already blown her cell number on the late night hang-up. Details.

Her first stop was the clerk's office where she requested information on one of the other properties on the extensive list of those owned by SLW, LLC. Shel was trying to get an idea about the type of people who lived in these modest little homes. Perhaps they all had something in common. An elderly woman with blue-tinted hair and bifocals gave her attitude and information she already had.

"SLW, LLC is a corporate name. I'm trying to find out who actually lives at that property address," Shel politely explained.

"We only have record of property owners." She started away without as much as a thank you or goodbye. In conducting her grand experiment Shel had unwittingly selected a bad participant.

"Ma'am? Just another second of your time, please?" She refused to be rude to an old person no matter her curt behavior. Shel forced a smile and started over again after the woman reluctantly shuffled back to the counter. "You're sure there's no listing for a tenant at this address? If the property owner has tenants, aren't they registered anywhere? Perhaps a tax collection document or something?"

"That's between the landlord and the IRS." She put one weathered hand on her bulky hip. "And, if they're family friends or someone not paying rent, you've hit a dead end. Contact the owner."

"SLW, LLC…" Shel murmured. She then impulsively asked her, "Ever heard of it?"

"Contact the owner," she repeated, and when Shel started to speak again, the woman raised her voice and abruptly finished their conversation. "Good day." The woman spun on the thick heels of her orthopedic shoes and marched away, leaving Shel alone at the front counter.

"Thank you for your help," Shel said to no one. She walked away muttering things not normally muttered about old ladies with blue hair. There was no asking her about the car plates. It was a wasted trip.

At the hospital she encountered another of many obstacles the day seemed to be throwing in her path. The office that handled donations was being manned by a temp, as the administrative staff was locked up for the day in meetings. Shel's attempt to leave the painting was met with the woman's cool insistence that proper protocol must be followed, including tax forms and multiple signatures and witnesses on a variety of releases. It seemed ironic to her that her donation would be entirely on the record while a house tenant would not. Frustrated, Shel took the painting and left, two fails under her belt thus far.

Her next stop was the Naples Seaside Resort. She parked, grabbed her canvas satchel and headed straight through the sand to the tiki bar. Rob did a double take when he saw her approach and was holding his hands up in a stop sign before she could even have a seat.

"No can do. I'm on the boss's clock right now." He pantomimed punching a time clock and grinned. "I can't possibly be your rent-a-stud for another three hours."

"That's an interesting greeting." Shel squinted in the sunshine and proceeded to take a seat at the mostly empty bar. She looked around. "Can I make this my temporary office?"

He shrugged as he pulled a bar towel off a rack and dried some newly washed glasses. "What a hose-job. One day I'm a priceless help and the next day, garbage."

"Nonsense, I need you." Shel didn't look up at him.

"Cool." He stopped what he was doing and came to stand before her. "What's the job? A flunky this time, I hope?"

Shel's fingers clacked away at the keyboard, but she could feel him staring. "I need your wifi password anyway."

Obviously disappointed, his shoulders fell. "Seaside-dot-naples, all lowercase."

"Thank you." Shel made the entry and waited.

"So, how's things with the poser?" He grabbed a towel and went back to drying glasses, shooting her an occasional look. "You make any headway?"

"Not much," she lied. The computer came to life with full Internet access. Shel dumped the contents of her satchel on the stool next to her and rifled through the papers until she found a particular stapled set. It was the "hit list" that Fortier had given her on her last night in New Orleans—the names and contact information of all the alleged victims of Kathleen Fortier's scams. Presumably, they'd been plied with large amounts of hush money.

"Whatcha working on there?" Rob pestered.

"Not much," she only repeated. The first name on the list was Ford Franklin and she hurriedly entered it into a general search engine along with his city name. Nothing. She added the physical address listed on the page. Soon bits and pieces of parts of his name populated the search, but no solid hit. Unusual, given the amount of identifying information she had on the fellow. She flipped the top sheet back and started on the second male listed. She was vaguely aware of Rob moving to the other side of the bar, working his angle on a woman of about seventy. For his momentary distraction, Shel was secretly relieved.

Four hard copy pages later, she'd yet to discover a single firm lead on any of the men in her packet. Some names matched the names of individuals, but in other parts of the country or world, and didn't have positions or the type of wealth that would make them good candidates. Phillip Rogers II, for one, was a retired, ninety-year-old grocery clerk residing in Queens.

Time and again, Shel cross-referenced the names with New Orleans, Louisiana, art, society, philanthropist, news, and donor. The donor did get a hit on Reginald LePlatt, but only because he received a multiple pints button for donating blood at a center outside Seattle.

"Ridiculous," Shel muttered.

Rob was buzzing around the bar. His elderly customer was long gone and he now tended to a few afternoon ramblers happening by. As these were guys close to his own age and not a member of the wealthy geriatric set, Rob refrained from putting on his usual ridiculous show. Shel almost hated to interrupt, but waved him over nonetheless. He gave her the one-minute sign. Sighing, she grabbed her phone and punched in the number listed as belonging to Ford Franklin. It went straight to an automated message stating she'd misdialed. She hurriedly did the same with a few more and got the same thing. Caller number six picked up.

"Can I speak with Reginald LePlatt, please."

"I'm afraid you've got the wrong number," the voice on the line informed her.

"Wait—sir?" Shel feathered the papers out before her. "Can you tell me if I've reached Ford Franklin?"

"I'm sorry."

"How about—"

"I'll save you the trouble," the man on the line said with a gentle chuckle. "I'm Mario Jimenez."

"Mr. Jimenez," she said, doing a quick shuffle. It didn't match any of the names. She sighed. "Thanks for your patience, sir. Have a good night."

She set her mobile phone on the bar top and stared at it, running her hands through her hair. She wondered if it had gotten late before realizing that dark clouds had rolled in, casting a sepia tone across the place. During her phone frenzy, Rob's friends had left. In the midst of packing up the bar against the storm, he noticed Shel's vacant expression.

"Relax. We're just revving up for an afternoon shower. Damned hurricane season." He glanced toward the gloomy sky. "Looks like this storm could be a doozy."

"Oh yeah?" Her papers started to flutter in the breeze which was rapidly picking up. Rob came to the rescue, promptly providing shot glasses for paperweights. "Thanks."

"So? You gonna tell me why you've made my bar your office all afternoon long?"

"Following up on leads that turned out to be…bogus."

"Anything to do with your lady who likes ladies?"

"She's not my lady, she's my case. I told you." She shot him a look then sighed. "I just wasted the afternoon calling all these numbers."

Thankfully, he listened to her brief rant without specific questions. "No go, huh?"

She shook her head. "All shit. Lies."

"I believe you've been duped on this case, my friend. I hope you collected your money up front." The wind picked up again, and Rob pressed his forearms on top of her paperwork. He glanced over his shoulder at the quickly moving clouds, but remained patient. "Was it going to be a good haul?"

Shel thought about Fortier's tearful call, a child's pink bedroom in New Orleans, the slime-ball attorney dressed in fine threads, and how bad it all felt for reasons she could not explain. Just as easily she recalled Kathleen's cold behavior, the possible kidnapping, a kitchen knife gleaming in the moonlight, her soaking shirt and pert nipples…

She shook her head, more to rid her brain of the nonsensical thoughts that swirled there. "Liars. I just haven't figured out the lie."

They were quiet for a bit. He seemed bothered by her trouble. In a surprisingly charitable move, Rob asked, "Can I help?"

"You got truth serum?" The words were barely out of her mouth when a big wind blasted through the tiki hut, strong enough to rattle the makeshift paperweights. Rob collected her flying paperwork and Shel grabbed her computer. He quickly dropped and latched four large wooden shutters. Sand had begun to whip around them in funnels, like mini tornadoes, and he squinted and pointed toward the hotel lobby. Dodging large, cold raindrops, they made a mad dash to the main building.

Safely inside, he handed her papers back to her. In his rush, he pressed something else into the palm of her hand. She studied it in the dim, elegant lights of the lobby.

"Truth serum," he supplied before she could ask. He grinned, proudly. "Well, almost."

Shel immediately recognized the chalky pink oval housed inside its tiny bag. She raised her eyes to his. "What the hell…?"

"Call it your little helper." He folded her hand over the pill and patted her knuckles, grinning. "On the house. No worries."

"What I mean is what the hell are you doing giving a cop a controlled substance? Are you crazy?"

"We're friends by now." His smile faded somewhat as if he suddenly wasn't altogether sure of that notion. He recovered, his enthusiasm for his project renewed. "Look, get in good with her, slip her the Perc, loosen her up and let her ramble."

She stared at the Oxy in her hand and swallowed hard. Her thinking was a world apart from the scenario he was suggesting. With her aching back, battered confidence in her detective work, and screwed-up emotions concerning the case of her insanely sexy neighbor, the allure of the drug was tremendous.

"Keep it off display, would you?" He again folded her hand to cover. "We don't want to piss off my source."

"You get drugs for your clientele?" she half whispered.

"I get them whatever they need. We live in the prescription capital of Florida." His blue eyes glimmered in the low light, and he spoke in a surprisingly bold manner. "I'm doing you a solid here. Are you going to be an asshole about it?"

He didn't blink. After a second she shoved the tiny bag in her jeans pocket and looked around to see if anyone had witnessed their "transaction." Rob's wide grin returned. "Maybe you'll get some of your answers. I hope it goes in your favor."

He patted her shoulder and walked off, carrying his cash box toward the employee's hallway.

Shel hoisted her satchel onto her shoulder and once again darted outside into the elements. She was thoroughly soaked by the time she reached her car and wondered about the condition of her computer housed inside the flimsy canvas bag. She carelessly tossed it into the backseat and sat behind the wheel, watching the rain pulverize the windshield for several minutes. The noisy sheets made her feel sheltered and anonymous. With more excitement than she was proud of, Shel pulled the pill out of her pocket and felt a measure of revolting relief that it was thoroughly dry in its plastic house. She hungrily rubbed it between her fingertips, feeling its outline like a depraved blind person reading a lifesaving message in Braille.

"Years I spent getting you off my mind, and now look."

Her whispered words weren't hostile, but rather waxing poetic. She stared at the Percocet until her eyes watered, then pushed it back into her jeans pocket, her heart pounding almost as loud as the rain.

Starting the car, she slowly backed out of the flooded parking lot. Once on Gulfshore Boulevard, she cranked up the music to drown out her bad thoughts. Above her, a crack of lightning split the black sky. Naples was embroiled in a torrential downpour.

The wipers on the car could hardly keep up. Despite the compact rental being a newer year and model, its tires were sub-par and drifty. It seemed at any moment the car might possibly float right off the road and into the ditch which was filling up with flash floodwaters. She drove slowly, carefully, concentrating on the yellow center line barely visible in the rain.

As most of the smaller roads had quickly flooded, she kept the car on the main streets, unable to find another clear pass until Central Avenue. She made the turn and followed it up almost to the library and prepared to take a left. At the stop sign she used her shirt sleeve to wipe a big circle in the window fog. She started away from the stop sign, but slammed on her brakes, the entire car lurching with a dreadful squeal.

Kathleen Fortier was in the crosswalk in front of her. She was soaking wet and pushing her bike, Harper still strapped in back. There wasn't a thing to protect the toddler from the elements beyond the standard safety helmet.

Shel threw the car in park, hit the hazards and tapped the horn. She jumped out of the car and ran toward them.

CHAPTER EIGHTEEN

"Get in!" Shel called over the steadily pouring rain. It was difficult to see Kathleen's expression in the whiteout, but she sensed her hesitation. It really wasn't the time or place for gentle coaxing. Shel charged toward her neighbor and clutched the handlebars of her bike. She called to her over the storm, "Get her! I'll get this!"

Kathleen unfastened the child from the seat and with some difficulty, lugged her to the car. Shel pushed the bike toward the hatchback, but immediately realized her Addison James painting was there, faceup for the world to see. She hurriedly unlatched the floor cover and was grateful to discover the spare tire was missing. Utilizing the extra space, she hastily crammed the painting beneath the floorboard, covered it and gently placed the bike on top of it all. She jogged to the driver's side and got in.

She brushed the rainwater and bangs out of her eyes and killed the hazards. She took the car out of park and slowly started for home. After a few blocks, she broke the silence. "You bike everywhere?"

"I don't drive." Kathleen's answer could barely be heard over the sound of the wipers.

"How come?"

She shrugged, said, "I don't have a car."

Of course she did not. Cars meant registration which meant information and insurance, both requiring ID and background and credit checks, none of which the woman would have living under an assumed name. Shel nodded. She turned the corner onto their street and pulled into Kathleen's driveway. Without a word, Kathleen jumped out of the car and rushed the child inside.

"You're welcome," Shel said to the empty car. She opened the door and stepped back into the pouring rain to retrieve the bike from her hatchback. Blinking against the rain, she rolled it onto the woman's front porch and turned to go when she heard the door open behind her.

"Here," Kathleen said, handing her a towel. Soaked as she was, it was a pointless, but kind gesture. Shel stood staring at her a moment before accepting the towel. She blotted her face and neck, handed it back. Kathleen raised her voice to be heard. "I appreciate the ride."

"Sorry I didn't get to you sooner."

Kathleen seemed fixated more on the weather than Shel's words. Though quiet, her haunted tone sliced right through the sound of the rain when she said, "I don't like storms."

That would make sense if Kathleen's parents truly died during the ultimate storm. Shel felt herself inevitably softening toward her, while at the same time remembering that the Hurricane Katrina story could also be a lie.

"This is normal. Not much to worry about." Shel's answer was interrupted by thunder that started with a low rumble, then escalated. She looked through the curtain of rain over her house that was turning gray with nightfall. She had to yell over the steady cadence of rain pounding against the tin roof. "I'm sure this old neighborhood has seen a lot of these storms. We probably won't even lose power."

As if on cue, lightning branched across the dark sky followed immediately by a thunderous crash. Every streetlight, as well as the lights in Kathleen's house, went black. Shel was zero for two.

"Then again…" Shel muttered practically to herself. She heard Harper's worried cry from inside the house.

"It's okay, I promise. I'll be right there." Kathleen tossed the wavering comment over her shoulder and looked more than nervous herself when she again turned to Shel. "Looks like it's going to be a long night. Well, thank you again."

"Wait." Shel put a hand out, stopped her from closing the door, much as she had the first night they'd met. "Do you girls have candles, flashlights—anything?"

Kathleen hesitated a moment before shaking her head. Shel did an about-face and ducked back into the awful weather. Minutes later, she returned with her haul and was ushered in by a surprised-looking Kathleen. Sopping wet as she was, Shel didn't budge off the inside front doormat. She handed over a dripping brown paper sack and again turned to go.

"What's in here?" Kathleen asked, surprised at the weight. She began to poke through it guided only by the dim light coming in from the windows.

"Emergency flashlight and candles from a kit the owner of my rental house left behind in a closet. The batteries look okay. I hope the matches are the camping kind because they're wet by now." She wiped the beads of water off her forehead. "Also, there's some cheese and crackers—the kid's got to eat and there's no power."

"What will you use for light?"

"I don't mind the dark. I'm comfortable there."

"I wish I could say the same thing." Kathleen's eyes flitted about. "I just think it's silly to give us all your candles and stuff, especially when you've just moved in."

She presumed the statement masked a truer one, which was that Kathleen hated to be alone in a storm. She looked down at her own rain-soaked clothes once again and then back to Harper who was teetering on a stool, flashlight already in hand, aiming the beam of light into the soggy paper sack. The heaviness of the metal casing made for awkward handling for such a small girl, but the child was persistent, and she wore a curious expression as she removed a particular item and held it up for her audience. In the tiniest possible voice, she asked, "What is this?"

Intrigued by the first words she'd heard out of the child's mouth, Shel gently answered her. "That's, uh, basically it's spray cheese, the best, purest form of junk food on the planet." Shel's lips tipped up into a half smile at the child's inquisitiveness. She then glanced at Kathleen and attempted to defend her junk food in advance. "Probably not the building blocks of nutrition, but the kid will dig it. Maybe it'll be a nice diversion." She glanced at the window, indicating the storm.

"Spray cheese?" The child was suddenly extremely interested in the concept. Her normally dull eyes seemed alive as she considered the possibilities. Diversion accomplished.

"You spray it on a *cracker*," her mother told her, eclipsing any childish ideas she may be conjuring about covering walls—or even people—with cheese.

"Or…your fingers," Shel put in. She gave half a shrug, quietly admitted, "I mean, a cracker is just the middle man, right?"

And though she probably had no idea what that meant, Harper eagerly nodded.

Kathleen swung the tot off the stool and safely delivered her to the floor. She handed her the flashlight. "First, why don't you go dry off and put on some pajamas."

The child tugged her mother's sleeve until she bent to allow Harper to whisper something in her ear. In return, Kathleen shook her head, told her. "No honey, no bath tonight. We've already had a shower."

The child seemed more than pleased at this news.

"Go get dressed, then you can have the…the spray cheese," Kathleen gently assured her. She held out the flashlight for her. "Take this with you so you can see."

The child accepted the flashlight, struggling to hold it in front of her as she hurried toward the hallway.

The gray sky provided minimal light as Kathleen walked around to the other side of the counter and began rummaging through drawers. She nervously addressed her company as she did so.

"I might have dry matches." She glanced at Shel still standing in front of the door in dripping clothes. "Oh—you could hang your shirt on that kitchen chair and have a seat, if you want."

Kathleen was solidifying her previous unspoken request that Shel stay. Her guest slowly removed the flannel shirt she'd worn as a jacket, appropriate for the southern Florida climate. Still she didn't budge from the mat, fearing she'd leave a trail of water. She feared many things.

Kathleen noticed her standing like a statue and gave her a quizzical look. Shel explained, "I don't want to get your stuff wet."

Kathleen suddenly looked foolish at the realization that she was asking the woman to make herself comfortable in a most uncomfortable state of dress. Matches in hand, she lit one candle and pulled a jelly jar out of the cabinet and put together a makeshift candleholder. She lit a second candle off the first. Then, shielding the flickering flame with her hand, she gracefully moved toward the hallway. "Just a second."

She returned in seconds minus the candle, carrying a bathrobe that she handed to Shel. It was the same one Kathleen had worn the first night they'd met. Shel nervously accepted the robe, squeezing the soft material between her fingers. Her hesitation was obviously making her hostess uncomfortable.

"Will this do? The bathroom is down the hall. You can't miss it in this small house."

Shel was unsure what to make of the sudden bout of hospitality her neighbor was displaying, if only prompted by the storm. Helpless to her own curiosity, Shel slipped out of her drenched canvas tennis shoes. "I'm afraid even my socks will leave prints."

"It's okay. We all are."

Shel took wide, careful steps in the direction Kathleen had indicated, feigning naiveté about the layout of the house. Once there, she saw that Kathleen had wedged the candle in the wall-mounted toothbrush holder. Its flicker softly illuminated the tiny room. Shel quietly closed the door and looked around. She couldn't resist nudging the shower curtain back to get another look at the height of the window through which she'd made her stunt-move escape.

"Whew," she whispered, letting the curtain go again. She took off her jeans, T-shirt and socks. She stared at her reflection in the mirror at her soaking underwear.

"No," she softly said. It was a compromise she refused to make, no matter how uncomfortable they were. She pulled the robe over her shoulders, enjoying the soft sensation of its fabric against her skin. It smelled fresh, like clean sheets or baby powder. She wondered if it was fresh out of the laundry or if Kathleen had recently worn it. The latter thought ignited a quiver in her stomach. She tightened the sash, ran her hands through wet hair until it looked reasonable. She stared at her near-gaunt form and haunted expression in the mirror.

Gathering her clothes and the candle, she quietly headed back into the front room. Kathleen had changed into some kind of casual sundress—the woman seemed born to be clothed in airy dresses—

and she was patiently waiting next to her tot who was seated at the counter. The can of spray cheese was squarely in front of them, and Harper wore a serious expression that Shel thought seemed uncharacteristic of a child her age.

Shel laid her wet clothes on the doormat and somewhat embarrassedly glanced down at the robe. She pulled the pink lapels closer together and crossed her arms in front of her.

"We figured maybe you'd want to do the honors." Kathleen motioned for her to join them in the tiny galley kitchen.

Shel's hesitation had little to do with her standing in a robe in her mark's house, but spoke more to her social awkwardness acquired after so many years of working and being alone. She moved toward mother and daughter, feeling the weight of their very different gazes, one reflecting a mixture of concern and apprehension, the other, diminishing leeriness coupled with new curiosity.

Shel picked up the can, flicked the cap off and tore off the safety ring. Shooting little sideways glances at the toddler, she internally marveled at the kid's intensity. It was a familiar brand of distrust on the child's face. The last time she'd seen it was on a same-aged child, those years ago, right before…

"Are you okay?" Kathleen quietly asked her.

Shel realized she'd clenched her eyes shut in an effort to block out the awful memory. She felt her cheeks warm and nodded.

"I sometimes get headaches during a storm. I'm fine." It was a lie, but she hoped she'd managed to shift the attention off her. Still, the dreadfully serious mood remained in the house. She attempted to work on that next. She gave the kid her best smile and ceremoniously raised the can. "You ready for this?"

"I am," Harper whispered.

"Hold out your pointer finger. Keep it steady."

With some hesitation, the little girl did as she was told. Careful not to actually make physical contact with the child, Shel pressed the tab and ran it above the little finger, forming a fat, squiggly worm of bright yellow processed cheese. By the time she finished, Harper was wiggling around on her stool with the closest thing to delight she'd seen out of the tot.

"That's all there is to it," Shel told her. "Now you can eat it."

Harper promptly stuck the pudgy, cheesy finger into her mouth and her eyes went wide. When she'd finished licking every last drop, her mouth was outlined in yellow and she was wagging her finger for more. Her antics caused both women to chuckle.

"Sure," Shel easily caved, painted another cheese line on Harper's finger.

"Well, congratulations," Kathleen quietly said. "You've successfully introduced her to the wonderful world of preservatives."

"Awesome, right?" Shel glanced her way, whispered, "It's like crack for kids."

"You eat this stuff? I mean you bought it, right?" Kathleen took the can from her, studied it in the candlelight a moment before spraying a bit on her own finger and licking it off. It was an innocent, yet erotic move. She nodded approvingly. "I can see the attraction."

Shel took the can back and sprayed another orange line on Harper's finger. She held it out to Kathleen. "Another hit?"

"I'm good, thanks." Kathleen bit her lip, and licked little bits of remaining cheesy residue off her fingertip.

Shel forced herself to look away. Whether she was licking her lips, fingertips, batting her too long eyelashes—even the smallest things Kathleen did were sexy. Particularly given the candlelight, the clingy dress, the raging storm…

They avoided exchanging looks for a few more minutes until Kathleen at last proclaimed snack time to be over. Only when her smile disappeared did the women truly realize how much the kid had been enjoying the simple fun. Shel quickly capped the cheese can and handed it off to her mother.

"So, that cheese is yours and you can finish it tomorrow or something. What do you say?"

The child appeared to consider this and was seemingly satisfied with that idea. Kathleen helped her down from the stool and steered the sleepy—and sticky—child toward the hallway. "I'm going to wash her up for bed."

The rain was creating a surprisingly refreshing draft that was pushing right through the screen of the window Kathleen had opened. It easily cooled the tiny house. Still, the nasty weather was noisier than any kind of air-conditioning. She tossed a look toward the front door, then down at her unusual attire, feeling antsy all over again. "I should probably get going anyway."

"Hold on a minute," Kathleen called to her. Shel heard her laying out directives to Harper about washing her hands and face.

Then Kathleen popped back into the kitchen and wiped her hands on a towel. Clearly stalling, she said, "You don't have to rush off. I mean, you can stay, if you'd like."

Though it would be a splendid opportunity for Shel to get to know the woman better, she was nearly naked, wearing a highly fragrant bathrobe, standing in the house belonging to her sexy, and quite possibly nutty, neighbor. She prepared to make her excuses rather than continue to tinker with already flimsy boundaries that divided her personal and professional objectives.

Her moment of indecision must have made Kathleen uncomfortable. "I've got drinks that aren't juice boxes." As if to prove it, Kathleen walked into the kitchen and unfastened the childproof lock with far more ease than Shel previously had the day before. Kathleen lugged an oversize jug of wine out of the low cabinet and Shel pretended to be surprised. Kathleen set it on the countertop and brushed her thumb across the lightly dusted handwritten label, squinting to read it in the darkness. "I've never opened it. A customer brought it to me at work. He makes it himself."

"Really? A barter system?"

"Sort of, yeah." Kathleen raised the bottle and held it against the dim candlelight, swirling it for inspection. "It could have floaters."

Against her better judgment, a decision was made. Shel nodded. "I'm good with adventurous cocktails. You get her ready for bed and I'll find some glasses."

Kathleen looked somewhat embarrassed. "They aren't so much glasses as they are, uh, little jelly jars."

Shel also knew that, said, "I'm on it."

Kathleen started out, but stopped quickly. "You mind if I let her take that flashlight to bed?" She pointed toward the hallway, looking concerned. "She won't sleep without a nightlight and I can't leave her a candle. She's just had her first experience with spray cheese— she might think she's invincible."

Shel cracked a genuine grin. "Good idea."

"I just have to read her a little story."

"Go. Do what you have to do." Shel turned toward the cabinets and opened a few doors until she found the "wineglasses."

She glanced behind her, but Kathleen had already gone to attend to her daughter. Scrunching her nose a bit, she raised one of the glasses to the candlelight to examine the curious design.

"Tweety Bird," she mumbled. The other was Sylvester. She arched an eyebrow, continued talking to herself. "Of course."

Shel pried the lid off the wine and poured even amounts into the tiny glasses. She gave hers a whiff, swirled it, cautiously sipped it and deemed it somewhat tolerable despite evident floaters. She dipped her finger into the purplish mix and fished out one of the questionable particles, and upon closer examination concluded that it was just grape skins that had escaped the sieve. She downed the rest of the short glass and set it aside, shivered as the sour flavor caught up to her. She poured another glassful, leaned against the countertop and looked around.

Kathleen Fortier didn't appear to be a millionaire any more than she appeared to be a monster. She was a bit standoffish, but there was no law against that. The child appeared to be well cared for and well dressed. Her seemingly timid behavior hinted that she may have been traumatized, but the way she'd clung to her mother that morning at the preschool spoke to separation anxiety from the woman. She'd seen it before in classic cases of kids who'd been victimized. But who'd made her a victim? She recognized Harper's behavior from somewhere else, too. The overly-cautious demeanor and those haunted, distant eyes also belonged to Kathleen.

Shel glanced around the kitchen at the plastic childproof locks on the bottom row of cupboards. Hell, even the outlets had plastic safety covers. Perhaps Kathleen Fortier had had a lobotomy; perhaps she had amnesia. Either way, she was nothing like the person her husband had described. He was probably the liar—but why all the lies? What did Kathleen have that he so badly wanted? Why did she want away from him? Shel was desperate for the truth.

She found herself staring at her pile of wet clothes heaped on the doormat. A bad, slow-growing idea was gaining momentum as she crossed the floor and retrieved her jeans from the heap. She unrolled them and plunged her hand into one pocket, withdrawing the tiny bag. She peeled apart the zipper opening and shook it into her hand and caught herself staring at it for too long. It was easy to remember the warm, cozy feeling they used to give her—a nice, fuzzy, floaty relaxation.

During her days as an undercover, she'd witness fellow punks administering various drugs to one another because it made them "chill." She didn't fully understand this until after she'd been shot.

How nicely Percocet had come to her rescue, settling in, cozying up, lessening the pain—physical and emotional—and indeed she *chilled*. It was with drug-enabled courage that she'd told her boss where to shove the job without giving it a second thought. Percs made her loose, careless...

She set the pill on the counter and chucked the empty plastic bag into her wet jeans pocket, then reballed and dropped her clothes back onto the mat, just as they were. Operating in stealth mode, she padded back to the counter and began to move around the kitchen, hunting through the drawers for a spoon. She located one and used it to crush the pill into tiny granules, careful not to send any particles flying. She brushed them into a neat pile then dumped about half, then on second thought, a little more into Kathleen's glass.

She mentally reviewed Percocet, or Oxy, as they'd called at the clinic where she'd detoxed. Aside from its sedation and pain management, the drug created a dangerously low dip in brain function. Lying was a very high-level functioning activity. She figured for the average, nonaddicted person of small stature, Percocet would serve as a low-level truth serum. It was just as Rob had intended it to be. At very least it would dramatically lower her host's inhibitions.

Shel disposed of the residue in the sink drain and ran water to wash it down, then scrubbed the countertop clean with a paper towel. She twirled the spoon in the glass, careful to avoid clinking against the sides. She ran the spoon under hot water, dried it, and replaced it in the silverware drawer. Shel raised the glass, examined it against the light. Were it store-bought wine sans the floaters, the operation would have been a total fail.

"That for me, I hope?" Kathleen's voice caused her to lurch, even slosh the wine a little. Shel quickly recovered and handed the little glass to her smiling hostess. They raised and clinked glasses and Kathleen took a sip. She grimaced then weakly smiled. "It's not the best wine I've ever had. In fact, it's rather bad."

"It'll do," Shel said. She held her own glass to the candlelight, gave it a good look. "You said you got this at work?"

"Yeah. Maybe I should have left it there." Her eyes flitted to the front window and the storm raging outside.

Shel moved to intervene before the woman again became lost to her concern over the weather. She motioned toward the couch. "You want to sit down?"

"Sure. Yes."

Kathleen transported their meager light source, followed by Shel who was toting the jug of wine. They arranged the glasses and oversized rustic decanter on the table in front of the couch. Like clockwork they sat down, each carefully minding her personal space, though likely for different reasons. Shel cautiously sipped her wine, which wasn't good, but surely better than Kathleen's. The crushed half-pill would have hers tasting very bitter. Shel kept her voice low as to not disturb the child in the next room. "So where do you work that they pay you in wine?"

Kathleen chuckled unexpectedly then smiled. "The art gallery near the city dock. They generally don't pay me in liquid, thank God, or else I would be insulted by this particular…" Her voice faded and she held her tiny glass up to the candlelight, swirled it, floaters and all. "What do you suppose this is, anyway?"

"Something comparable to bathtub gin." Shel gave an innocent shrug after winning yet another sweet laugh from her hostess. Encouraged that the woman was feeling more comfortable despite the storm, she added, "Great glasses, by the way."

"Here's to Goodwill, right?"

Shel wondered if the medicine was already at work. She raised her glass and tipped back another sour sip, all the while wondering why a millionaire's wife would be buying jelly jars from Goodwill and sipping bad, homemade wine. Kathleen eyed the drink with suspicion, causing Shel's heart to beat a bit faster. Kathleen's floaters were obviously white, and Shel wondered if she'd noticed the difference in this poor light. Shel lifted the jug and quickly poured another inch into both glasses with hopes of further diluting the white specks. Kathleen arched an eyebrow.

"I see you're a woman who likes to live on the edge, floaters and all. How brave of you."

"Indeed," Shel said, lifting her own glass again. "Cheers."

Another sip, another round of shudders.

"So, what do you do at the art place?" Shel asked upon her recovery.

"At the art gallery," Kathleen politely emphasized the correction. She smiled. "I paint."

"You're an artist?" Shel faked a reasonable level of surprise at the news. "Impressive. Are you good?"

Kathleen shrugged. "I hope so. It'd be nice if Addison James could sell enough work to keep the kid in juice boxes."

It was an odd third-person remark that sounded more like a wish than an actual statement. Shel mentally filed it away and moved ahead. "How long have you been in Naples?"

"Not long."

"Where are you from originally?" Shel tested the strength of the drug and the level of Kathleen's resistance to it.

"Florida," Kathleen answered after a few seconds. Shel tried to avoid looking outwardly disappointed. She questioned the strength of the pill and then considered that Kathleen might be such a seasoned liar, she believed her own lies. Not even real truth serum could bust through a deluded frame of mind. The quickness of her reply had Shel again leaning toward Richard Fortier's side of the story once again. It was tough to keep score. Just as she was wishing she'd had two pills instead of one, Kathleen spoke up. "So I was glad to come back."

"Oh?" Slow growing hope was building within Shel. "Where else have you lived?"

Kathleen frowned, and after some hesitation answered, "Louisiana."

"Good." Shel's strange reply was issued in a low, comforting tone. She subtly encouraged her conversation. "Let me guess— you were one of those girls who got hitched and forever left your hometown behind?" When Kathleen gave her a funny look, Shel explained, "That's the way it usually goes, right?"

"I never wanted to leave Florida," Kathleen firmly answered. She looked Shel straight in the eyes, said, "And I've never been married."

CHAPTER NINETEEN

Shel stared at Kathleen, trying to comprehend the lie that had just tumbled from such perfect, lush lips. She shook her head.

"But you have a child."

Kathleen bit her lower lip and demurely smiled. "Well, anyone can have a child."

"I s-suppose," Shel stammered, making quick physical assessment of the woman sitting beside her. Kathleen's pupils were dilated, her posture was notably more relaxed—it *appeared* the drug had taken effect. It wasn't a perfect system. Shel didn't care that her next question was a bold one. "Then how did you…?"

"How are those things normally done?" She was again being coy, but Shel was quickly tiring of her flirtatious game. The game part of it annoyed her; the flirtatious part turned her on. Both reactions were making her angry at the moment. Perhaps Kathleen could tell. She ceased the batting eyelashes and coy behavior, softly admitting, "I was in a relationship, but it went bad."

"How so?"

Kathleen looked away, reached for her pseudo wineglass and took the last sip. "It just did."

Shel pressed on. "So the father has visitation rights, I take it?"

"The biological father has no right," Kathleen suddenly snapped. Her stance and expression were defensive, yet different from what Shel had witnessed when they first met that strange, late night. This was a combination of hurt, fear, perhaps a hint of righteousness, and those aqua eyes contained nothing short of plain hatred for the man about whom she spoke. Shel held her cold gaze unflinchingly until at last Kathleen said, "He takes anything he wants and he always wins, but not this time."

"This time?" Shel's breath caught in her throat. She carefully pursued the odd comment. "Tell me about the other times."

Kathleen looked away, recouping her composure, her eyes quickly softening nearly to tears. Now it was her turn to blink and stammer. She appeared to be attempting to collect her thoughts and habitually ran her fingertips along the plunging dress collar. In the dim candlelight Shel discovered a very useful tool: Kathleen Fortier got blotchy when she was nervous. Hives.

Shel pushed ahead, leading with a promise that was a bold-faced lie. "I'm not going to judge you. You can tell me."

Kathleen abruptly yawned and slowly blinked, and Shel realized that it was likely she'd unnecessarily drugged a woman who was already too easy to read. She set about doing damage control, gathering their glasses and taking them to the kitchen sink. There she rinsed them thoroughly, scrubbing her finger along Kathleen's jelly jar glass, eliminating the last of the pill residue. She rinsed it several times before filling it with water. She quickly crossed the small room and handed it to Kathleen, calculating only a small window of time before the woman nodded off. Shel forged ahead.

"Start by telling me why you left Florida in the first place."

"I was very young." Kathleen said after several welcome gulps of water. A melancholy expression came over her as she launched into her quiet narrative. "My parents were killed in an accident and I went to live with an aunt and uncle in Louisiana. I'd never met them before landing on their doorstep."

Shel noticed Kathleen didn't again touch her neck, but it remained blotchy making it difficult to know if it was the lies, the wine or the South Florida heat without the benefit of electric air.

"How old were you?" Shel encouraged the conversation.

"Twelve," Kathleen sleepily answered.

"Were they good to you?"

"They were okay. They just didn't really know what to do with a kid." She looked away, her eyes telling of great pain. "They weren't very good comfort to me after my parents died, but they were there, and that counts for something."

"That must have been a sad time for you." Shel wanted to keep her talking. "What did you do?"

"I painted. I wanted to be an artist like my mother. I eventually got an art scholarship and I enrolled in college."

"Your mother was an artist. I like that," Shel said with genuine admiration. "And your Louisiana family, do you see them now?"

She shook her head. "They died in Hurricane Katrina."

Her story lent validity to Fortier's tale and certainly gave him points. It was tough to believe that a madwoman could possibly be wrapped in this beautiful package, sitting next to her on a couch in Naples. Still, Shel would be foolish to discount the notion. She spoke up, offering her condolences. "I'm sorry."

"That was long ago." Kathleen appeared distant. "Do you believe everyone gets what they deserve?"

"I'm sorry? Explain that one to me." Shel leaned slightly forward, but failed to capture Kathleen's gaze. "Do you mean your relatives deserved to die?"

"No, oh no..." She was barely making sense. "Do you believe in karma?"

Helpless to her own honest reaction, Shel answered, "To some degree I feel I've lived karma."

"I hope I haven't. I'd wonder what I'd done to deserve..." Kathleen's voice drifted off reflecting an apparent change of heart concerning what she was about to say. Her eyes flicked back to Shel. "Never mind. It's really nothing."

Kathleen's speech had become slightly slurred, which made Shel nervous. There was more information to be harvested and this was her best—possibly only—chance. Again she grabbed the glass and refilled it in the kitchen sink. She returned and handed it to her hostess, who drank the water like she'd just come off the Sahara.

"More?" Shel asked her.

Kathleen shook her head and Shel sat down next to her. She noticed the woman had scooted somewhat closer to her, which also had her nervous, but Shel pressed ahead with her mission. "I have a question for you."

In such close physical proximity, there was no room for lies. Shel alternately monitored Kathleen's expression and her hive-prone skin in the candlelight. She lunged ahead. "The night I came over here—after the scream, what had happened? Tell me the truth."

Kathleen's lips moved, but no words came. Finally, she whispered, "Harper."

"What's wrong with Harper?"

Kathleen grew tearful, whispered, "She has nightmares."

Shel knew the feeling all too well, but wondered what the child could have seen in her young life to inspire such trauma. "What kinds of nightmares."

"About…someone breaking into the house. Then he tries to hurt us."

"Why?" Shel scooted slightly closer, kept eye contact. "Why is she afraid?"

"For the same reason I am." Kathleen's voice broke.

Shel refused to dismiss her gaze. "Who scares you so much?"

Her own eyes locked on Kathleen's, but Shel was continually sidetracked by beautiful lips that were flushed and swollen from bad wine. She found her gaze drifting lower as she imagined what soft curves existed beneath the thin, shapeless dress. She tried to put it out of her mind given the importance of her task.

"I can't talk about it." Kathleen's low, disturbed voice indicated she'd probably only meant to think, not verbalize the statement.

"Please, trust me." It was an absurd statement coming from Shel, who'd neither trusted, nor received real trust in her life. Her sudden unexplainable shift of instincts occurred in congruence with her rapidly realigning allegiance. It terrified her. Her stomach fluttered at the sound of her own raspy words. "I'd like to help you."

"I know you mean well," Kathleen said, never removing her stare from Shel. "But I'm afraid nobody can help us."

Shel's eyes felt dry and her mouth twitched. Her body felt tingly in an unfamiliar physical response to an urge so strong, it was downright painful.

The underlying insecurity in Kathleen's eyes was steadily devoured by her apparent desire to share her secret. At last she said, "Someone was quite awful to us."

Shel reached her hand across the couch and covered Kathleen's. It was obvious that drugged, Kathleen's restraint was perilously out of check. She craved comfort and Shel craved nothing more than to provide it. She willed herself to put the notion aside for the sake of the case, but found herself speaking out of turn.

"Come here," she whispered. She swallowed hard, awkwardly slipped an arm around Kathleen. Her next words were undoubtedly the most foreign to tumble from Shel's lips. "It's okay."

Kathleen's eyes never left Shel's. Whatever internal war waging within her at last reached its conclusion and her shoulders caved slightly forward. Shel gently nudged her closer still until the woman's rigid body was against hers.

"Breathe," Shel whispered.

Within moments, she felt Kathleen relax somewhat. Kathleen raised soft eyes to Shel and at once the space between them vanished along with every last drop of self-possession. Warm lips collided, sending tongues exploring, first tentatively, then hungrily. Shel weaved fingertips through Kathleen's still damp hair, encouraging and deepening their connection until their lips parted and they gasped for breath. Eyes searched each other, channeling and receiving unspoken permission to advance their passion. They kissed again.

The warmth felt beneath Shel's robe resonated throughout her entire body, causing harried, awkward movement on her part. She moved her arm behind Kathleen and easily scooped the woman onto her lap. With small encouragement, Kathleen gracefully straddled Shel, hiking the hem of her sundress up enough to lean into her. Shel untied the robe sash and parted the opening, allowing Kathleen to writhe against underwear that was damp from both the rain and their escalating passion, making her wish she'd removed them after all.

Kathleen emitted a needy moan and Shel shifted her leg slightly to allow her to press even closer. She ran a hand along the springy elastic top of the Kathleen's sundress then pulled it down to reveal her soft flesh. The candlelight created a glowing outline of Kathleen's thin form and softly illuminated perfect breasts. Shel cupped one then dipped her head enough to capture the hard nipple in her mouth. She suckled her, cupping a hand beneath Kathleen's bottom, assisting her rhythmic movement. Shel felt an explosion rising within as Kathleen groaned.

A sharp scream disrupted their frenzy. Their bodies tensed and ceased all movement. Kathleen quickly pulled back and nearly toppled off Shel's lap. Her eyes were wide with horror as the sum total of their frenetic actions seemed to hit her. With muttered apology and obvious embarrassment, she covered her front, pulling up the top of her dress as she stumbled and recovered and then hurried off in the direction of the child's bedroom.

Left alone, Shel gazed down at her own disheveled state. The robe hung open revealing her long, pale body, and plain, standard-issue white underwear. Her head dropped against the back of the couch timed to her remorseful sigh. She'd been abruptly expelled from a passion best never engaged in the first place. Slowly, she stood and straightened and retied the robe sash, mentally consoling her sex-starved body. No matter her painful discomfort, Shel could see past the physical urge enough to realize it felt different. It wasn't about sex. It was something more.

She ran her hands through damp hair, rose up and padded down the hallway and stopped in the doorway of the child's bedroom. She was prepared to make an apology and bid them goodbye, probably never to see either of them again. In the darkness, she saw mother cradling her child, speaking soothing words against the sounds of the softening storm. Between pressing kisses on her daughter's forehead, Kathleen's eyes momentarily flicked to Shel. She didn't address her, only continued comforting the child from her apparent nightmare. Shel lingered a moment before returning to the living room.

Still trembling from the disruptive screech as well as the almost-sex, she sank onto the couch covered her eyes with one arm. She wondered what had gotten into her. Fortier was her client; Kathleen was his wife. Or not. Jesus, the lies…

The sound of soft footsteps drew her out of her confusion and she felt the weight of Kathleen's body as she sank onto the couch next to her. Without moving, Shel said, "Tell me what's going on with you and the kid."

After a brief silence, Shel took her arm away and turned to face a drowsy, tearful Kathleen.

"Maybe you should go," she softly suggested.

"You don't want that."

"I do. I think you should go." But Kathleen's voice lacked even a hint of conviction.

"Your ex is after you." It was the prelude to an all-out confession Shel was prepared to make on the spot. She'd tell Kathleen why she was really there; warn her there was trouble. She'd do the woman a favor, then cut and run.

To her surprise, Kathleen cut her short with her own admission.

"He is after us. We're in a protection group, but I know it's only a matter of time before he finds us."

Shel sat up, suddenly alert. "A group?"

"An underground railroad of sorts for battered women." Kathleen said the words with difficulty. "They brought me here and gave me a chance to start over. I'm not to speak of it. It's the only condition of their help."

Shel blinked and started to speak several times, but lacked the proper words. Her eyes invariably went to Kathleen's neck so she could gauge her perceived truthfulness. It was blotch-free, peachy, beautiful…

Shel went after it, encouraging the confession. "Who the hell is your ex that you'd have to run away?"

"A bad man," Kathleen said, wringing her hands. Her voice was monotone. "It's best you not know…"

"Wait—stop." Shel was confused. "How can I be incriminated for trying to protect you from your controlling abuser?"

"You don't understand—it's not me he wants."

"It's your daughter, right?" At the risk of scaring Kathleen off, Shel attempted to remain vague now that her own confession was off the table. She felt relief at the strong possibility that Richard Fortier's tales about his wife were wrong. *She wasn't even his wife.* Hatred for the man flared within Shel. And to think she'd been prepared to help him in his abusive plot. "It's a power play. The son of a bitch wants Harper to get to you."

"He's even worse than that. He wants Harper to get at his money," Kathleen said.

Shel looked puzzled. The storm had calmed and now only leftover intermittent flashes of light lit the room, giving her infrequent glances of Kathleen's terrified expression. In a whisper light voice, Kathleen said, "He wants his ten million dollars back."

CHAPTER TWENTY

Shel sat, mouth gaping.

"You have ten million dollars?" she asked when she finally could.

"No."

Shel felt a headache creeping up on her for reasons that had nothing to do with bad wine. With some impatience she said, "These cryptic answers are making me crazy. Can we talk here, please?"

"My ex—"

"Name," Shel firmly requested.

Kathleen looked conflicted. "Richard."

Shel was overwhelmingly satisfied to know that without a doubt, Kathleen had told her the truth, if only in the way of a first name. She nodded, prompting her to continue.

"He carries himself off as an art connoisseur, but he's nothing more than a con and a thief."

"Explain that."

Kathleen plainly stated, "He sells fake art."

She hesitated. "You mean to tell me people don't know any better?"

Kathleen shook her head. "He's fooled people and companies…"

"Must be damned good fakes."

"It's hard to detect a good fake without X-ray and carbon dating. Particularly lesser known works." Her slurry words and dazed look had her appearing downright woozy. "It's a hit-and-run operation fronted by a longtime gallery with a nice little reputation."

Shel knew exactly which gallery. She studied the woman sitting beside her and tried not to let her soft skin, the faraway look in her eyes, or the fact that she'd nearly been inside her only minutes earlier, ruin her objectivity. It was…hard.

"You're telling me your guy is good enough to create art and pass it off as being something by one of the greats?"

"No. He only handles the business end." In a near monotone, she quickly added, "And please don't call him *my* anything."

On that point, Kathleen was firm.

"Where does he get passable phonies like that?"

Kathleen hesitated and when she answered, her voice was a mere squeak. "Me."

Shel blinked several times, trying to decide if she'd heard correctly. "You create fake masterpieces?"

"Some." Kathleen's eyes flitted upward momentarily. Her eyes flicked toward the ceiling as she proceeded with her recitation, as if by rote. "Nothing too obvious; nothing too obscure. Stick to household names—Monet, Chagall, Renoir—the market is flooded with fakes. Good accompanying documentation is everything."

Shel stared at her in disbelief, whispered, "How do you do it?"

"Re-creating the artist's signature style or brush strokes." She made a pantomime of a sweeping paintbrush. "A little light treatment process for aging and it's hard to tell the difference. Deals brokered under the table, referred to an expert—"

Shel was quickly coming up to speed on the process. "And the expert is an associate of yours."

She nodded, obviously feeling the full weight of her shame. At that moment, every welled-up emotion appeared to surface and Kathleen sobbed, looking as though she could easily fall apart right then and there.

"Okay, hold up," Shel said, unnerved by the sobbing woman. She started to move toward her, but abruptly stopped. Sex she could do; physical comfort was not her strong suit. Not by a long shot. "Stop, already. This isn't helping anything, honest to God."

"He will find us, he's done it before. I was stupid to think we'd be safe…"

"Stop it," Shel told her, softly at first. When the woman showed every sign of falling into full-fledged hysterics, she captured Kathleen's face between her hands and forced her to look into her eyes. Utilizing a far more forceful tone, she repeated herself, "Get a grip *now*."

A few sobs escaped, but she had Kathleen's otherwise undivided attention.

"Tell me, is Addison really your name?" Shel asked her, almost hopeful that she would receive a lie for her answer.

"No," she whispered. "It's Kathleen."

"You're telling me the truth."

"Yes."

"It wasn't a question," Shel muttered. She released her hold, but remained staring at her. "When you say he's found you before, what do you mean?"

"I ran before, when it was only me, years before the baby." She snuggled bare feet beneath her, appearing suddenly chilled as she repeatedly ran hands along her bare arms. "Right before the big hurricane he was arrested on fraud charges. As soon as he was gone, I ran. But he came back."

"He got out?" Shel was missing something. "He escaped? What are you saying?"

"Hurricane Katrina was such a confusing time." She shrugged and swiped at her tears with the back of her hand. "I never asked. I didn't want to know too much."

"You said you ran. How did he find you?"

"He's very good." She stared at Shel a moment, as if deciding how much information to entrust to her. She quietly said, "He paid a visit to my relatives—the ones who took me in as a child."

"Oh no," Shel said, grimacing, hardly wanting to hear the outcome of the tale. It was hard to imagine what he'd done to convince them. "Did he threaten them?"

"I truly believe he killed them."

It was a sobering accusation. Shel was taken aback. "That is a very strong allegation, my friend."

A hard look of mistrust came to Kathleen's eyes, but almost immediately her shoulders sank and she shook her head, a look of utter hopelessness coming over her. "And I don't have any proof.

After Katrina, my relatives were the only ones in their neighborhood unaccounted for. Their bodies were discovered across town, which also made no sense. Blunt force trauma was listed as cause of death. Their bodies were…" She shuddered, quieted even more. "It was hard to tell. The authorities contacted me and I went back to bury them."

Shel supplied the inevitable finish. "He was waiting for you." Kathleen nodded. "Did you contact anyone about this? The police?"

"It would have come down to my word against his. Many records were destroyed in the storm. Even digital became a hacker's paradise. Add that to the special relationship Richard had with the local cops."

Shel fished for confirmation. "Payoffs?"

"Many were on his payroll." Kathleen looked haunted. "To this day, Richard continues to boldly live where he always has, right in the Quarter."

The rain had completely stopped and the room was quiet.

"No wonder you think no one can help you."

"No one can." Kathleen wore a dazed look, her voice slightly cracking when she said, "It's just a matter of time. I'm afraid I'll never be free of him…"

Her desperation felt contagious. Shel wanted to talk about the stolen money and the extent of Kathleen's involvement, but her need to calm and comfort was overpowering.

"It'll be okay," she softly told her.

"Harper has seen so much. She has nightmares about him—I don't know how much more we can take…" Addison buried her face in her hands.

"It's okay." Shel hesitated only a second before again slipping an arm around her. She scooted her close, tightly encircling Kathleen's body. She wondered if she could physically keep the woman's world from falling apart all around her.

Shel ignored visions of Fortier dollar signs sprouting wings and flying away. She held Kathleen close, stroking her back. The comfort that she'd initially only mandatorily provided had changed, softened, and segued into something that felt inexplicably natural. She felt like she could hold Kathleen forever.

"It won't happen again, Addison," she whispered. "I promise you he won't get you."

CHAPTER TWENTY-ONE

Shel awoke with wisps of a pixie haircut tickling her nose and slowly came around to her surroundings. She was still on the couch in the living room of the yellow cottage, a bit of sunlight pushing through the shutters. Shel studied Addison's beautiful form for a while before kissing her awake.

"Addison," she whispered, softly at first. She repeated the name several times to get used to the sound of it and decided it was a better fit than her old name anyway. As far as she was concerned, Kathleen Fortier was forever gone. The woman tensed in her arms, as if the memory of the night and all its meaning were catching up to her. Shel held her firmly, but gently. She stroked her back, spoke reassuringly. "Hey, how are you this morning?"

Addison squinted against the daylight, rubbed her temples. "I feel…funny."

Shel knew it was the medication, and blew past it. "You had a rough night."

"I had some bad dreams," she admitted without looking at her.

"A few." Shel thought it was the understatement of the century. All night long Addison had tossed and mumbled. In light of all she'd learned, Shel felt more than a little guilty about having unnecessarily drugged her drink. She vowed never to pull such a ridiculous stunt again. She checked the woman's eyes this morning and felt assured that they were good and clear. Still, Addison was edgy. Shel reached over and brushed hair from the woman's eyes. "I want to make sure you're okay about everything we talked about last night. It's safe with me."

"I don't remember much, to be honest. I'm not much of a drinker." She bit her lip. "I told you everything, didn't I?"

"You told me a bit. I'm sure there's more." Shel pressed a kiss on her forehead, gave her a squeeze. She glanced at her watch. "What time do you have to be to work?"

Addison turned Shel's wristwatch so she could see it. She gasped, suddenly moving quickly. "Harper has to be at preschool in fifteen minutes!"

"It's okay." Shel was about to offer her car but quickly remembered that it was a rental on Fortier's card and likely easily traceable. No reason to boldly park it in front of the art gallery. Plus, there was still an Addison James painting hidden in its hatchback. She decided she'd properly ditch the painting and turn the rental car in today. Maybe she'd go so far as to book a bogus flight out west. Anything to temporarily throw him off their trail… She reined in her thoughts, said, "I'll drop you girls where you need to be today."

"But we won't—"

"And then I'll pick you up when your day is done," Shel said, cutting short any protest. She smiled at her. "I'm persistent. You might as well say yes."

"That's a lot of running around for you." That Addison's stance had notably softened told Shel that she liked the plan. A puzzled expression came to her face. "What do you do for work that you have so much time on your hands?"

The question would have arisen sooner or later. Addison had come clean; it was now her turn. "I'll tell you about it tonight, how's that?"

"But your job is nothing illegal, right?"

She thought about her shady undercover operations, the fact that she'd drugged the woman standing before her, the same woman whose ex's money was supporting her present lifestyle. In spite of it all, she shook her head. "No."

It was a backward step in her new life, but a necessary one, she felt. She didn't want to risk the trust that had been extended to her thus far. *Lying to protect trust.* She internally cringed at the horrible concept.

"I'm sorry. That was a dumb question," Addison said with apology, further adding to the guilt that Shel was already feeling. "If you seriously don't mind taking us, you'd save the day."

"I insist." She released Addison so that she could get ready. Addison rose from the couch and started away, but quickly doubled back and kissed Shel. When lips parted and eyes opened, Shel was left smiling, and muttered, "Good morning."

Shel stood and stretched, happy that her back wasn't protesting her every move this morning despite sleeping upright on the couch. She looked down at her attire—or lack thereof—and took a step toward the hallway.

"Uh, I'm going to run across the street real fast, get dressed and meet you back here in five." In the daylight she took a second look at the thin robe and again noted its pink shawl collar. She pulled it together as close as possible, mumbled, "Really, really fast."

She scooped her still-damp wad of clothes off the mat, unlocked the door and bolted across the street to the safety of her own house. Inside, she pitched the clothes onto the floor, then unfastened the sash and prepared to wriggle out of the robe.

"Well, look what the cat dragged in." The voice jarred her, and despite its familiarity, Shel loudly cursed. Clutching the collar of the pink robe she'd nearly slipped off, she spun around to see Naples's favorite cop. "You left your door unlocked."

Milford was seated casually on the couch dressed in her full uniform. She blotted a dot of jelly from her lips with a paper napkin and brushed a few crumbs off her lap leftover from a pastry she'd been eating.

Breathing hard, Shel clutched the robe lapels together.

"Jesus Christ, Milford—you trying to give me a heart attack or something?"

"That'd be bad considering you've apparently already suffered some kind of brain damage. Anyway something's gone wrong up there." Milford thumped her index finger against her own temple to demonstrate. She gave Shel three long head-to-toe looks, smirked. "Nice threads, hotshot. You mind telling me what the hell you're doing?"

"What are you doing inside my house?"

"I fed your cat." She stood and brushed the last of the crumbs off her hands, then rolled down the top of a paper bag she'd brought with her. "I brought you breakfast, but it looks like you already ate out."

"That's rude. Very rude." Shel wagged a finger at her regarding her wrong assumption.

"Anyway," Milford shot her an extremely annoyed look, but got on to matters of business, "I came bearing news about that Winston guy, the property owner, but you were out gallivanting around with the pretty neighbor."

Shel ignored the remark, nodded. "I've got some information, too."

"I'll go first. Winston's got a bunch of money thanks to a lawsuit about thirty-some-odd years ago."

"Over his mother's death," Shel supplied, hurrying things along.

The cop looked taken aback. "Ms. Hot-to-Trot tell you that?"

"No. Google search." Shel again ignored her commentary.

"Clark Paper heir, as you know by now. Old Man Clark killed his wife right in front of his young stepson."

That part had been conveniently left out of the newspaper. Shel arched an eyebrow.

"Years later, the kid got his own attorney and took him to the cleaners. Won all his money in a civil suit." Milford paused for a sip from her steaming Styrofoam cup. Shel squeezed her eyes tightly shut. "I'm trying to do that math on the statute of limitations."

"And how does one make money off nonpaying tenants?"

"One doesn't. Winston's nonpaying tenants are a mysterious lot. Nobody's on the radar. Even the utilities are in Winston's name."

"I think I know why." Shel glanced at her watch, knew she had to hurry. Still, she knew Milford would be upset if she missed the chance to give her story a payoff, so she asked, "But what's your theory?"

"Glad you asked." Milford retrieved a folded piece of paper out of her pocket and made a show of unfolding it. Shel was growing more impatient by the second. "So we know all his properties are small two-bedroom homes, nothing fancy, and he makes no money off 'em. All this was learned from sweet talking a woman at the tax office." She raised her eyes to Shel, held the tax printout toward her.

Shel took the slip of paper and squinted to read.

"My first thought was prostitution ring. Maybe a kiddie porn ring or trafficking. Just to be sure, I checked for Harper's name in the missing children's database, no hits, you'll be happy to hear."

"Which says her father isn't looking for her via the usual means, just me." Shel tapped her chin thoughtfully.

"So the bottom line is, Winston helps people fall off the map for some reason or other."

Shel handed back the paperwork. "That works with what Addison told me. She claims to be part of an underground system for battered women. It makes sense."

"*Addison?*" It appeared only one word had permeated Milford's brain. "So, you're on a first-name basis with a girl with an assumed first name. How complicated of you."

She raked fingers through messy hair. "It could be that our mission is changing courses."

"You could have been a little more forthcoming about that underground women information before I spilled my guts. That's uneven, is what it is." Milford was off the couch and waiting by the front door. "And it may be that your mission is changing, but I guarantee mine remains the same. I want to verify the story of Ms. Fancy-Pants across the street. Make sure all these fake names are frauds. Doesn't feel right to those of us not thinking with our nether regions."

"Milford, don't let your boredom get you into trouble."

"Looks like I got the shit end of the stick in this deal. I'm doing all the detecting, and you're getting your jollies. Curious how that works."

"Look—I'm trying to earn her trust."

"That's what they're calling it these days?" Milford hiked both eyebrows. "I'm not yet convinced *you're* okay, let alone her."

"For the record, I'm not doing her," Shel said, shooting her a look of disdain. She glanced at her watch, her tone changing. "However, I am playing taxi for her today, so we'll talk about this later. Go with your gut, Milford. Isn't that what you always say? I'm not fucking you over and you know it."

She started for the door, but quickly stopped, turned around. "Here's a question—what happened to the jail records that were destroyed in Katrina?"

"They were destroyed in Katrina," Milford dryly remarked. "The question answered itself."

Shel ignored her dig. "There's seriously no recourse? Backups…?"

"Probably some lucky fools got a new lease on life when that happened. Looking for his or hers?"

"Why would we look for hers?" Shel wore a disgusted expression. "Don't give me grief about this. Can't you see what I'm trying to do here?"

"Yeah," she said. "Her."

"Oh, okay, Master Detective."

Milford opened the door and stepped onto the front step. "It doesn't take a master detective to figure it out. It takes a complete idiot to *not*."

"We'll talk about this later." Shel shot her a displeased look. A new thought came to mind that trumped her aggravation. "Meanwhile, you want to look into something for me?"

"By all means," Milford said in a tone ripe with sarcasm.

Shel disregarded her sarcasm. "I have a list of men who Richard Fortier claims were screwed over by his wife. I called them all to verify, but the lines were either dead or wrong numbers or what have you."

"You're talking out both sides of your mouth, sister." Milford reluctantly accepted the envelope. "In one breath you're saying Mr. Fortier's got this all wrong, and in the next, you're asking me to double-check his wife's scam victims."

"Nobody knows how screwed up this is more than I do, Milford." Shel hurried back into the bedroom to change clothes. She raised her voice to be heard in the living room. "And by the way, she's not his wife."

"You're kidding me," the cop dryly said, sounding not at all surprised. She rummaged through the stapled sheets of paper and chucked the packet into her jacket. "Bet that helped your conscience."

Shel appeared in the doorway tucking her T-shirt into her jeans. Her feet were bare. "Meet me in half an hour or so?"

"I've got roll call. Remember that pesky little job of mine?"

"I do remember," Shel said, jamming her feet into canvas tennis shoes. Untied, she wore them like scuffs when she hit the top step outside. "You tell me when."

She held the door for her guest then let it slam shut behind her. She followed Milford into the gravel driveway. Across the street,

Addison was coming out of her house with Harper on her hip. Watching them, she slowed noticeably.

Now in an even bigger hurry to get across the street, Shel said, "Please, Milford."

The cop turned toward her wearing a disgusted look. "Coffee Cup, inside the hour."

"See you there." Shel started across the street, her shoes still flapping on her feet. She called over her shoulder. "Thanks."

Behind Shel, the cop revved up her bike and rode off.

"Who was that?" Addison's usual suspicious regard was firmly in place.

"No worries."

"Police make me nervous," she mumbled. "She wasn't asking about me, was she?"

"You're in Naples, not New Orleans." It wasn't even an answer, but it wasn't a lie. Shel offered her hand to Harper. The child stared at her for several seconds before quietly accepting her invitation. Surprised at how good she felt about owning even an iota of the child's hard-earned trust, Shel thoughtfully placed her into the car's backseat, wishing she had a child's seat. When she fumbled with the safety belt, Addison leaned in and quietly took over.

As she watched them, Shel wondered how badly Addison would take the news of her own former employment when she finally broke it to her. Worse, she'd also have to eventually divulge her current employment. She wondered how ugly things might get. After all, the woman had basically stolen the child and moved away from her ex. It was clear she would defend her daughter at any cost. It felt like a mission designed to fail.

Shel slipped behind the wheel, but Addison's concern clouded her. She looked at the unnerved-appearing woman, quickly leaned toward her and planted a kiss on her cheek. "She's a friend of mine. Relax."

Shel asked for directions to the preschool then proceeded to unnecessarily inquire about which door to drop them at once they'd arrived at the church. Meanwhile, she scanned the parking lot, hoping with every fiber in her being that Silvia Frances's car was in its place and that the woman was already inside the building. She caught sight of the silver Volvo wagon, parked and empty. She made a loud sigh of relief that Addison mistook for impatience.

"I'll hurry," she promised, gathering the child's things.

"Take your time." Though she hoped Addison would avoid doing just that. She watched the pair enter the school section of the church, drumming her thumbs in a random pattern against the steering wheel for thirty of the longest seconds on record. She grinned when Addison got back into the car. "All good?"

"Yeah," Addison said after brief hesitation. She smiled at Shel. "It is good. And it feels like it's getting better."

Her choice of words warmed Shel. She smiled, but quickly shifted back into business mode. "Look, I hate to bring this up, but your deal with disliking cops, that's because of the way your ex pulled strings in New Orleans, right?"

"I suppose." She looked thoughtful.

"Anything else I should know?"

"Yes," Addison said after a moment. "I hate guns. I could never again live with a gun in my house. I could never live with someone who owns a gun, *period.*"

Shel veered the car into the side street and drove in the general direction of the dock. She glanced over at her passenger, who seemed to be calming down. "You seem pretty adamant about that."

"I am," Addison confirmed.

"Duly noted." More complications.

They made the rest of the short drive in silence. Shel pulled to a stop before the shop then turned to face Addison. She'd already been concerning herself with how she'd avoid Silvia upon picking them up. "I have a few things to do, so I am going to meet you here at five fifteen, is that too late for you?"

"No. Harper usually gets here about five. We'll hang out and watch the fishermen."

Shel knew her schedule all too well. "Can we talk after that? Over dinner?"

"I don't really want to go out, if you don't mind." Almost shyly, she added, "And I do have my constant companion."

"We'll stay in. My place."

Addison smiled. "I suppose that would be fine."

"Good."

She looked momentarily caught off guard. "Should I…bring anything?"

"I think you mentioned a constant companion."

Addison's grin was huge when she left the car. Shel watched her get safely into the shop before she left. Her smile faded by the time she'd come to the first stop sign.

"She's paranoid and hates cops and guns." Shel assessed the situation aloud. She shrugged. "What could possibly go wrong?"

She hit home to grab something before driving to the coffee shop on Fifth Avenue. Milford had exchanged her bike for a Naples police cruiser, standard-issue that took two full parking spots squarely in front of the coffee shop. Shel pushed through the front door and quickly spotted the cop, already seated with coffee, already giving her dirty looks.

Shel blew past all niceties, said, "I need your opinion."

The cop didn't speak, only made the give-me motion with her hand. Shel handed her the manila envelope she'd brought along and waited several minutes while Milford examined the contents. Only when she reached a set of official looking documents did she raise her eyes to Shel.

"Fortier's committal paperwork." She shrugged, kept her voice low. When Milford stared and blinked at her, Shel elaborated. "I told you Fortier said he was having her committed upon her return."

"I don't believe you did." Eyes back on the paperwork. Milford selected a single page and held it up against the sunlight, squinting at it. "Think I'd have remembered a little detail like that."

Shel reached out in an effort to snatch the page, fearing anyone who passed might read the bold letterhead of the psych facility.

"There's something to be said for keeping a low profile," Shel chastised her.

"Yes, there is," Milford agreed. She set the paper back on the tabletop and slid it over for Shel's examination. "This is a pretty real looking watermark."

Shel blinked, muttered, "So you showed everyone in this café."

"You're smarter than this." It was Milford's turn to admonish. She slapped the paper on the table and shoved it toward her. "Why on earth would a man give you the real deal?"

Shel was quickly coming around. She whisked the paper off the tabletop and also held it to the light. A watermark ran the entire width of the paper. She muttered, "You're saying only a fool would let the originals out of his possession."

"And only a fool would think he had." Milford clicked her tongue, gave her a look. "Did you call the doctor?"

"I just figured with all the confidentiality laws I wouldn't—"

"What I mean, genius, is there even a character by the name of…" Milford squinted at typewritten name below the scribbled one. "…Doctor Harlow Farris?"

Shel scrubbed her hands through her hair as she always did when she was feeling nervous or foolish. This time, the latter was the case. "I don't know," she admitted.

"Mm-hmm." Milford flipped through the documents, selecting a few that she set aside. "You're slipping in your young age."

"Fortier had his lawyer right by his side."

"All the more reason to worry about a lawyer who would allow watermarked docs out of his client's custody. Nobody in his right mind would let that stuff go." Milford took a sip of coffee. "Was he even a lawyer?"

"He *did* come up on a Google search," Shel quickly answered, eager to win back points lost on her earlier major error. "Office just off Magazine Street."

"Picture of the man himself or his *law firm* building?" Milford made finger quotes. When answered only by silence, she rolled her eyes. "That's what I figured. You can't put anything past some types. And those docs look plenty official, but if what you say is true, Richard Fortier specializes in official. Not everyone is dumb enough to fall for it." She took another sip, smirked. "But clearly some do."

"I screwed up," Shel said, willingly receiving the intended jab. She fell silent to the background din of bright greeting voices and clinking spoons against ceramic coffee mugs as she considered the many ways she'd messed up the investigation so far. When her vision refocused, she was gazing at the coffee counter where two attendants were smiling, waving a full pot of coffee. Shel gave them a polite wave and shook her head. They looked mildly disappointed.

Milford noticed their pantomime. "You VIP around here?"

"I tip well."

"Let's not forget the possibility that Miss Hot-Britches could still be the scam artist her ex claims her to be. Maybe they all are. Poor kid stuck in the middle—happens more than you'd like to know."

"I can appreciate your objectivity, but I believe what Addison is telling me. My gut instinct says she's legit."

"And your gut instinct has done so good by you to this point." Milford's sarcasm was present but not biting. Concern seeped through her words when she added, "I know you want to believe in her, but where is the proof that you can?"

"She doesn't know about Fortier hiring me and doesn't know what he's told me. Yet their stories perfectly align. Only the villain is different."

Milford appeared to process this. She leaned forward, guarding their conversation from a new batch of patrons who'd just entered the café. "I'd love to see this all work out for you. What I'm not so interested in is seeing you get yourself killed or thrown in the slammer along the way."

"I share your concern and I appreciate that," Shel answered in an equally quiet voice.

"Bad luck seems to follow Richard Fortier," Milford warned. "His gallery made the news this week. *Times Picayune* reported a robbery there. Clerk got shot."

Shel thought of the stuffy little character who ran the place. She wondered if the robbery fit into their ever-changing puzzle. "What's your theory?"

Milford's meaty shoulders rose and fell. "Maybe Fortier staged it for insurance. If things are as you say they are, he's lost his primary moneymaker."

Shel was reminded of Addison's mention of ten million dollars that Shel had yet to fully understand. If Fortier was suffering a sizable monetary loss, that could also account for a fraudulent insurance claim. She'd get to the bottom of that one, soon.

"Good call on that insurance fraud theory. I met Fortier's shop clerk. I'll reach out to him and take the temperature of that situation."

"If his name was Bernard Smith you'll have to contact him via séance. He's dead."

Shel's smile promptly faded. Milford didn't pay it much attention as she stood.

"Do some deeper diving on that lawyer—we want to see his face. Forged documents, bad art deals—this guy is bold. I wouldn't put it past him to throw a fake lawyer at you."

Shel's voice sounded desperate as she said, "It's starting to feel like Fortier's bigger than the law."

"No, he's not," Milford firmly told her, a deadly serious expression coming to her round face. "It always catches up with 'em. Nobody's bigger than the law."

Shel shook her head, muttered, "Milford, I admire your undying passion for the legal system. Let's hope you're right."

"System may not be perfect, but it's pretty good." Milford rose, but leaned over the table, still speaking quietly. "I'll check out the doctor and Fortier's lawyer."

"Thanks."

Milford started to go, but quickly doubled back. "Now that you've challenged my beloved legal system, you got me thinking. A friend on the Fort Myers PD tells me they've got a facial match system tied to the Feds that identifies criminals. You got a picture of Richard Fortier?"

"No," Shel said, disappointed yet again. "If Addison ever had one to start with, she probably burned it. You'd think he'd have pinged on that system in New Orleans if that was the case."

"If we're talking about a smart guy with cops in his pocket..."

"We're giving this asshole a lot of credit that I hope he doesn't deserve." Shel gathered her keys and the documents. "Keep in touch."

CHAPTER TWENTY-TWO

Shel appraised the preparations. The putrid lime-green cottage was thoroughly cleaned, linens included, even the underlying mildew smell had been effectively masked. The only one unhappy with the lemon scent that now enveloped the place was the cat and that was only because Newton had been forced out of his private quarters when Shel had repossessed the smaller bedroom.

In that room, Shel had drawn the plain covers back and placed a stuffed elephant between the sheets, and posed it to look as though it were sleeping. She'd found a rug that she laundered and placed it on the bedside floor, and had thrown open the curtains to brighten the tiny space. With a tablecloth here and a toss pillow there, the entire house had evolved from dull, perfunctory surroundings into something a bit warmer and more inviting. A mixed flower bouquet was soaking in the sink. She hurriedly rearranged them a few times in a larger pitcher she'd found. As a last touch, she plucked two daisies from the bunch and put them in a little plastic water cup. She carried it into the smaller room and set it on the bedside table.

"Better," she muttered to Newton, who'd followed her on the tour. Though initially angry appearing, the cat now seemed downright surprised at Shel's level of interest in, well, anything at all concerning living quarters. Before hitting the shower, she made a final sweep through the house to straighten cushions on the shabby, but now clean, furniture.

She was refreshed, but only physically. Shel had spent the better part of the day inside her head, planning for the safety of Addison and Harper. Though she had formed some ideas, she first needed to know all the enemies in the game. With Fortier, there could be several. It was already starting to feel impossible.

The casual dinner idea she'd sold to Addison had, in fact, been orchestrated down to the last detail. The necessary conversation would likely take them hours past the child's bedtime. Therefore she'd cleaned the room and bought the toy. For dinner, she'd ordered carryout pasta and a nice salad, both of which she'd scooped out of their cartons and placed in bowls she'd found in the cabinets. Double-checking the back door lock—a pool was on the other side, after all—she lit candles and dimmed lights.

A soft rap on the front door sent an unfamiliar flutter through her stomach. Important things were riding on this night.

Addison already wore a wary look. With Harper on the hip of her black sundress, Addison's eyes flicked to the corners of the room before she even entered. Once out of her arms, the child promptly took off after the cat. Her frenzied action had Newton looking every bit as worried as Addison.

"It's okay," Shel whispered, putting an arm around Addison. She gently nudged her toward the main room, aware of her trembling and very obvious fear. "You look beautiful. I like this dress."

"Thank you," she whispered. Hearing her daughter's voice streaming down the hallway, Addison finally smiled. "She'll drive that cat crazy."

"He's already crazy." Shel again nudged Addison toward the dining room. "I took the liberty of getting us some pasta. I hope that's okay. I'm not a cook, as evidenced by my possession of spray cheese. We could have gone out to dinner, but I thought this was more comfortable."

"I only work and do work-related things. I'm not comfortable in public. Not yet."

"You'll get there." Shel gently squeezed her shoulder. She held her gaze a moment before motioning toward the kitchen counter where two freshly rinsed wineglasses and a bottle of wine were waiting. "I let it breathe, did all the stuff the guy at the store told me to do."

"I don't know. After last night—"

"This is no bathtub wine. It's smooth. I think you'll be surprised." Shel quickly looked away, guilt reemerging about having drugged Addison, only to pass it off as poor quality wine. Shel poured two generous goblets and handed her one. They clicked glasses and sipped. After a tentative sip, Addison's eyebrows raised and she nodded her approval. Relieved, Shel smiled. "Good, right? Let's round up that kid of yours and have dinner, shall we?"

As they started down the hallway, a sound came from the second bedroom that was both foreign and intriguing. Both women fell into a light jog, but when they reached the doorway, Harper was sitting center of the guest bed contentedly playing. The cat, looking less than amused, had a stuffed elephant firmly planted on his back. Disgusted expression aside, Newton didn't seem to mind playing the role of horse.

Shel's attention turned to Addison, who hesitantly approached the child, her expression one of mystery.

"You're laughing," Addison mumbled, a slow-growing smile spreading over her face. She shot an over-the-shoulder glance at Shel and smiled. "She's laughing."

Shel watched her fall onto the bed and scoop Harper into her arms, squeezing her close. Addison also laughed, her eyes brimming with tears. "It's a beautiful sound, Harper. It's just a beautiful sound."

"Cowboy Elephant," she said, becoming momentarily serious once again. When Newton meowed, Harper threw her head back in another fit of laughter. "He loves his horsey."

"Where'd you find this new friend?" Addison asked when she'd finally composed herself and wiped her eyes. She squeezed the soft plush elephant and looked at Shel.

Shel had been quietly watching. Her voice was soft when she said, "He's all yours."

"That is very sweet of you." Addison still smiled, and now her stance said she was at last relaxed. Shel immediately noticed that when not guarded, Addison's accent softly reemerged. It made her heart flutter. She watched as Addison stroked between the cat's ears.

Despite having an elephant on his back, he began to purr. "Does this incredibly patient cat have a name besides horsey?"

"Newton, but you can call him anything you want." Shel took a sip of the wine she'd brought in with her, added, "I know I have a lot of names for him."

"You don't like cats?"

"I never gave it a thought one way or the other until I suddenly had one." She rolled her eyes, less than eager to tell the story of how she came to have a cat. It seemed wildly insignificant these days. "What do you say we ditch the horsey-cat and go eat?"

"Can I bring Ellie?"

It was the most Shel had ever heard the child say. She smiled and nodded.

"And the elephant officially has a name." Addison stood and held her hand out to her daughter. "Bring Ellie to the table."

Instead of accepting the hand being offered to her, Harper hopped off the bed and shot past the women, and down the hallway. Suddenly more confident, tiny bare feet thudded across wooden floors toward the dining room. She set her elephant in the extra chair and with the awkward agility of a four-year-old, climbed onto the seat with an extra cushion that Shel hoped would double as a booster.

"I'm impressed," Addison said, upon noticing the sippy cup at the head of Harper's place setting. "Wow, you're good at this. You've thought of everything."

Shel pulled a chair out for Addison, waited for her to sit, then gently kissed the top of her head, lingering an extra second to inhale the flowery scent of her shampoo. She hurriedly took her seat across from the child, next to Addison.

"Ladies," she said, upon noticing all eyes upon her. With as much dramatic flourish as she could conjure, she aimed her words at the child, "And blue elephants, shall we dine?"

* * *

They didn't have to go far to transfer their child-safe dinner conversation to the couch. Shel excused herself to clear the table and set dishes in the sink. She wiped off countertops, killing time to mentally fortify an information-finding plan that seemed to be losing luster in her mind. She wondered if it were too late for Addison to get away from her ex; perhaps Shel had left too solid a trail right to the woman and her daughter.

Perhaps the best thing to do would be send the mother and daughter to an unknown location. If even Shel didn't know where they were, she'd have no useful information if or when Fortier tracked her down…

Shel violently shook her head, refilled her wineglass and drank it all in one long swig. She swiped a hand across her lips and composed herself then refilled both glasses and went to join her guests.

"Right on schedule," Addison whispered when Shel returned to the living room. The child was stretched out on the couch asleep, her head resting in her mother's lap. Addison stroked her baby-fine locks of hair, smiled. "With a full belly, she loses her spunk at eight on the nose."

"You're kidding me?"

"You could set a watch by her."

Shel set the goblets on the coffee table. "Let me move her into the little room."

Addison looked unsure.

"Unless you don't want me to. It's your call, Addison. I just want you to be comfortable."

"I s-suppose," she slightly stammered.

Shel gently scooped the child into her arms and practically walking on tiptoes, gingerly carried Harper to the guest room. She returned in a few minutes.

"I left the nightstand lamp on and put pillows all around her. It's a tall bed. You think I should put some on the floor, too? I mean, in case she rolls off?"

"No." Addison looked simultaneously amused and impressed. "She's slept in a big girl bed before."

"But it's a new place and all…"

"She'll be fine. You're very kind."

"Well, Newton's in there, too. Cat curled right up beside her."

"Sit down," Addison said, patting the space next to her. Shel joined her, taking a sip of wine. Another quick glance down the hallway and Shel sat down. She picked up her glass and took another sip. Addison smiled, said, "She laughed tonight. It sounded…just wonderful."

Which brought Shel promptly around to the subject at hand. "We have to talk about some of the things you told me last night."

Her look of worry returned. "I've said so much already."

"I understand, but with all due respect you levied some pretty serious accusations."

"I want so badly for the past to stay in the past."

"Unfortunately, we have to take the proper steps for that to happen." Shel held her gaze intently. "Otherwise, it will catch up to you. Believe me, I would know."

With a tone that reminded Shel of her old shrink, Addison quietly said, "Tell me about your past."

"Okay." Shel took another sip of wine, but found it now did little to strengthen her courage. She'd rehearsed the speech over and over again in her head, but at no time felt she could properly sell it. She set the glass down and clasped her hands tightly together. "I know how you feel about cops, but that's what I used to be."

When the words fully permeated, Addison's stance noticeably stiffened. Shel's hand shot out and firmly grasped Addison's wrist to ensure the woman wouldn't go anywhere before she'd heard her out. Shel immediately released her hold.

"I want you to stay, but I can't force you. I'm trying to tell you something about me."

Though Addison's guarded posture didn't alter, Shel took the woman's silence as her cue to continue. It was tricky winning the trust of a woman whose own life had been controlled, every move manipulated, all for the benefit of someone else. Shel spoke plainly, looking straight into Addison's eyes. "In Shreveport, I was a cop in an undercover drug unit. I got shot in the line of duty trying to protect a woman and her child."

"Your lover?"

The softly issued question surprised Shel. "No. I barely knew her."

"Go on," Addison encouraged her.

"After that I had some surgeries. There was a lot of medication at my disposal and I took it all. First it was prescription, and when that ran out, it wasn't. It's not like I didn't know where to get the stuff. Thanks to my job, I had connections all over town." Shel felt short of breath and was grateful that Addison seemed to patiently await the end of the story. "I didn't clean up very willingly and I got fired."

"But then you got clean."

"I did," Shel confessed. "But by then I had no job, no place to live and no girlfriend."

"Is there anything else?"

"You said cops make you nervous. I just want you to know that about me because I want you to trust me."

Addison slowly nodded. With a hint of trepidation in her voice, she asked, "What is it you do now?"

The question echoed in Shel's head. Her response fell from her lips in almost slow motion. "I'm…sort of a private investigator."

"Are you on a job now?"

Shel's heart skipped a beat, perhaps two. "Not anymore."

After a lengthy silence, Addison said, "I'm sorry you got hurt. The woman and her child were very lucky to have you."

A hard look came to Shel's eyes and she whispered, "No, they weren't lucky at all."

With her raw feelings on display, and having sufficiently stifled the conversation, she took a deep breath and forged ahead. "Now that you know about me, I need you to tell me everything. I want to help you and Harper stay safe."

Addison set her goblet on the coffee table. The wine had been long forgotten along with any hope for its medicinal soothing effects given the sobering topics at hand.

"So." There was an airy quality to her tone when Addison asked, "What do you want to know about my situation?"

"Let's start with the big question. Have *you* done anything illegal? Anything at all?"

Addison moved her lips, but no words emerged. Finally, she looked at her lap, softly confessed, "I've done some bad things."

CHAPTER TWENTY-THREE

"Tell me everything," Shel prompted, feeling sick to her stomach. She licked her suddenly dry lips, felt her heart skip a beat at the possibilities. "Just start at the beginning. Last night you told me that your husband brokered fake art."

"He is not my husband."

Shel blinked. "Exactly who is this guy to you and how did you end up with him?"

"H-he was an old friend of my aunt's family." Her eyes nervously flicked as if she were giving away family secrets and rapidly losing her courage to do so. She whispered, "I've never talked about this with anyone."

"You never talked about it because you couldn't." Shel gave her hand a reassuring squeeze. "Now you can."

The last bits of daylight had been engulfed by night, and now flickering candles illuminated their surroundings, much as the night before. Addison wore a sorrowful look in her eyes as she slowly unwound her tale.

"I was fresh from art school and unemployed. He had this brand-new, shiny gallery he was trying to get off the ground. He had the business mind and the charisma; I was all about the art. Between us, I figured the gallery would be a success."

"So, he was your boss?"

"At first, then he became my boyfriend. He offered a certain level of…safety, ironically." Addison nervously toyed with the hem of her sundress, admitted, "I didn't quite know where I fit in this world at the time. I felt…different."

It was a feeling Shel understood all too well. She wanted very much to kiss her, but instead softly prompted her. "Go on."

"I considered that I may have abandonment issues from childhood—I considered anything that would make sense of my lack of real feeling for him. But he was happy so I was content. I was convinced that contentment was better than anything else I'd had to that point." She looked at Shel, quietly inserted, "I'd never felt anything for anyone."

"Then what happened?"

"Things began to change. He started bringing his associates around. There wasn't an ounce of integrity among them. They met several nights a week over cigars and snifters. None of them was worse than Richard, but at least he acted the part of a gentleman. Well, to outsiders."

"But not to you."

"No. The honeymoon phase had long ended." Addison winced, causing Shel to wonder what horrors she may be mentally recalling. "One night Richard asked me to join them and give my opinion about the legitimacy of a few works they'd acquired. I'm pretty good at that kind of thing. One was real, the others were fakes. They laughed with delight and congratulated me. Soon after that, Richard started giving me other things to do."

"Like what?" Shel barely let her take a breath. She certainly wanted to be patient, but the more she knew of Richard Fortier, the more worry she had that he could already be on their trail. "What did he ask you to do?"

"He wanted me to alter a painting he'd bought, make it look like the real deal. Richard said it was a joke he was playing on a friend who fancied himself a real art connoisseur." She seemed to momentarily be waxing poetic. "My work pleased him, which was rare. As he'd become a terrible bully, his happiness was a reprieve for me—a real moment in the sun."

Shel tightly closed her eyes as she resisted inserting her opinion about bullies.

"I continued to change up other works of art. But he got into trouble, a forgery charge for documents, not art, oddly." She had a faraway look in her eye. "He served a bit of time then he was back. After the death of my aunt and uncle, I did whatever he said."

"Did he hit you?"

She was quiet for a while before whispering, "Not where anyone could see."

Shel bit her lip, stifling the livid words that threatened to spill forth.

"Also, there were consequences for not honoring his requests about the art." Addison's eyes locked on Shel's. "He brought home a puppy and Harper was very excited. It was a weary week for me as I had many projects to complete for a particular deadline."

"Projects, meaning art fixes?" Shel attempted clarification. Addison nodded. "Go on."

"He said I was sulking and that it made me distracted." She blinked several times as tears surfaced. She almost choked on the horrible words. "He killed the puppy." She moved her hands to demonstrate, tears freely falling. "Snapped its neck...in front of Harper."

"Jesus Christ," Shel whispered.

Addison swallowed hard, wiped her tears, and appeared to gather courage to finish the story. "His message was clear. He would give us anything we wanted, but he had the power to quickly make it all go away."

"And Harper...?" Shel's stomach felt like it was on a spin cycle just imagining the horror the child must have felt. "How did you handle it?"

"I couldn't handle it. We were isolated. And it...it changed her."

"She's post-traumatic, protecting herself just like you are," Shel quietly said. She clasped Addison's hands between her own. "But she can get better—you saw her tonight."

"I was looking for help." She gazed at the candles that had burnt low. "That's when I found the network."

"I'm surprised they wanted to get involved in a high-profile relationship like yours. That's risky."

"I didn't tell them the illegal parts."

Shel was confused. "That might have helped you get permanent protection against him."

"Or it might have kept them from accepting our case. I was desperate. Believe me—nothing of ours would nicely fit in a textbook category. And Richard always said if he went down, we all would. He said Harper would end up in foster care and it'd be years before I'd see her again if ever." Again her anxiety had peaked. "Do you know how bad that system is?"

Shel slowly nodded, quietly pondering that it still might have been preferable to living with Richard Fortier. Still she admitted, "Yeah, actually I do."

Despite her own present intense state, Addison suddenly seemed to realize Shel had secrets of her own. She softened, wiped her eyes, and leaned forward slightly. "I'm so sorry. How insensitive of me."

"It's okay," Shel assured her. "Is there anything else?"

Addison shook her head. "I feel badly about keeping the truth from the network. They were already doing more than they should have."

"I know I'm asking a lot, but last night when you told me you believe Richard killed your aunt and uncle. How strong is that belief?"

"Strong." She said the word without hesitation. "He was waiting at their house after the funeral. I believe he used them as bait to draw me out."

After all she'd heard that night, it didn't sound improbable. It would be a tough haul getting anyone official to believe the dreadful tale. Shel attempted another angle, fishing for anything helpful from a legal perspective. "When he asked you to alter the paintings, could you have said no?"

Addison shook her head, her eyes wide. "He said we owed a lot of money to people for start-up costs for the gallery and they were not the kind of people you wanted to be indebted to." She wiped her eyes with the back of her hand. "He said they'd kill us all. That's probably true. He said do it for our child."

"Tricky prick, preying on a mother that way." Shel tried to control her anger. "He handled the business, but the business was *you.*"

"At first I figured he was right, that we did need the money to pay off the gallery. But later, he was bringing on more sleazy investors and I knew his reasons had changed. We were no longer living hand to mouth; we were living in mansions, hosting social events. He had no intention of ever getting out of bed with those sleazebags. He had a lifestyle to support.

"Richard continued to invest in my education, making me more valuable to him. I was getting better at it. I'd completely lost my ability to say no." She softly chuckled. "For being such a horrible person, he really believed in my talent more than anyone in the world."

"He banked on it," Shel affirmed. She asked, "And you never married?"

"No. I don't even remember when he started calling me his wife. I'd lost my identity anyway. There was no sense in sullying my parents' name with his bad business."

"Did he want to be married?"

"For all I know, he's forged documents that say we are. Nothing really required my involvement." She chuckled sadly at the ridiculousness of it all. Her momentary smile faded, as did the strength behind her tone. "I'm thankful he didn't insist on it. My parents had such a nice marriage. I couldn't possibly make a mockery of it by truly marrying Richard."

"Yet you have Harper." Shel was not only struggling to establish a timeline, but also curious about the motivation behind having a baby with him.

"Richard gets everything he wants." Addison's rasp sent a chill up her Shel's spine, as did her big finish. "And what he doesn't get, he takes by force."

Shel bowed her head, rubbed her forehead, as she considered the sickening implication. She weakly asked, "Have you tried to get away since the big storm?"

"No." Addison leaned forward, rubbed the back of her neck. "He had a game. He'd partially load one of his guns and hold it here…"

Addison made an L-shape with her hand, and pressed her index finger against Shel's temple. She winced, tightly shutting her eyes as she pulled the imagined trigger, whispering a word that threatened to eternally haunt Shel, "*Click!*"

Shel grabbed Addison's hand and pulled it away, looking at the woman through mortified eyes. She pulled Addison to her, held her close.

"He's a monster," Shel whispered into her hair. "A horrible monster."

Addison's tears flowed freely as she cried muffled sobs against Shel's shoulder. When she could, she said, "I had to use the network. I didn't know how else to get away. I hated deceiving them."

"Don't you see? He is a terrorist. You've deflected his blows for so long. There was no way you could have done that alone."

"I did help him steal."

Shel did the mental math on their odds if they simply went to the police with this wretched story. Perhaps they would stand a chance in court with a decent lawyer who hit hard on the abuse aspect. Where would they find such a person, could they be trusted or would they, too, be reluctant to take on Fortier? What would such a thing cost…? It was getting easier by the moment to see why running felt like Addison's best option.

Shel was forming notions of bringing in the government for the fraud, and the possibility of a Stockholm Syndrome for her defense. If he truly were an escaped felon, it might be easier than she imagined; it might not be impossible.

Shel realized that no matter what defense she mentally put together, she'd play hell getting Addison to turn Fortier over to the authorities, thereby blowing her own cover. Plus, confession or not, testimony or not—Addison could still go to jail. She'd seen worse things happen. Fortier had been right about that issue; even a short jail term would have Harper in foster care. She wondered if Addison would even be emotionally strong enough to put up what would surely be a nasty, lengthy court procedure. She wondered if, having been employed by Fortier herself, she'd be eligible for testimony or if she'd simply get thrown in jail for living for years off the government books. None of them were without fault. It would remain to be seen in court whose faults the government disliked most. She shook her head, as if she could physically shake away the legal voices in her head.

"Did your network get you any kind of counseling?"

"Some," Addison answered. "But again, I'd limited my description. Had I elaborated on our situation they may have wanted to legally pursue things. I didn't want to risk being guilty by association. Again, the foster care." She looked desperate. "Can you possibly see what I'm talking about? It's a vicious circle."

"I do understand." Shel released her hold on the woman to see into her eyes. "Still, you could have benefited from some real therapy.

I think you're carrying too much of the burden of wrongdoing. I worry that it would be difficult for you to convince anyone legal of your innocence when I sense you don't believe it yourself."

"I can't go to court. I couldn't very well tell anyone all I've told you tonight. And I certainly couldn't tell anyone that I took that money."

"That's it." Shel's heart did a flip-flop amid her surprise that she'd nearly forgotten about the money knowing it was a conversation they desperately needed to have. The money could fix everything. "Where is that beautiful money? If we can turn it over to the authorities, it may be our saving grace."

"We can't." Her tone was soft, sad. "I gave it back."

Shel's smile faded and she looked confused. "Gave it back...?"

"I anonymously returned it to the people Richard stole it from in the first place."

"Oh Jesus..." Shel scrubbed her head. "We could really use that money right now. What charity?"

"Tree of Life. They feed and educate homeless children. My mother helped start it up years ago. She created the logo." She airily drew a little design with her index finger and sadly smiled. "Having him steal from them was the lowest blow. He sold them on the idea of an art investment that would pay off over the long run."

"But there must be a record of your donation—anything— *something*."

"No." In the dark she could see Addison again wringing her hands. "I stole the money from Richard's safe, carried it out in a duffel, and arranged to have it dropped at donation boxes at two locations, one in New Orleans and the other in Slidell."

Shel's mouth slightly gaped with her awe. "You plunked ten million dollars into a Tree of Life drop box just like that?"

"Not me personally, but a reliable friend. He did it the night I ran. He didn't ask what the packages contained and I never told him." For the sake of detail, she demonstrated the dimensions with her hands. "Plain, brown-wrapped packages about this big, taped and tied with string."

"Who's your drop guy—he could be our proof."

"Bernard Smith, the same man who introduced me to the network. He actually works at Richard's gallery, but I know he can be trusted. He's really the last person anyone would connect to me."

CHAPTER TWENTY-FOUR

Shel's heart lurched. Hearing the deceased clerk's name from Addison's lips was disheartening as hell. It was clear that Fortier had no intentions of stopping until he'd found his would-be wife. She was foolish to think otherwise just as she was foolish to believe she could stop him. The gallery robbery where Smith was killed had indeed been staged. Shel was nervous about other extreme measures Fortier may have already taken.

Addison's expression turned to one of concern. "You look funny, is something wrong?"

Shel realized she'd stopped talking; quite possibly she'd stopped breathing. How was she to reassure the woman she was safe and would not be found, when in fact, she *had* been found. Shel was dizzy with her own culpability.

"No," Shel lied.

"I'm sorry about the money, but it was the right thing to do. Please don't be angry."

"I'm not." Her tone said Shel was utterly depleted. She had no answers. "I just want you to be safe and feel good."

"Every day I feel a little safer." Addison actually managed a small smile. "I feel stronger. And today Harper laughed."

Shel conjured up what she hoped was a convincing smile. Addison easily curled into her side, continuing her cautious, yet upbeat narrative probably designed to convince herself. "I know things look bad. I know my part in all this. I worry about karma or God or fate, but then I met you, and I wonder if I'm forgiven. Perhaps everything isn't as bad as it seems."

No, Shel thought. It's probably actually worse.

"I'm sure we did meet for a reason," Shel quietly genuinely acknowledged. Her head pounded, her chest felt tight. All thoughts of confession had gone out the door. Addison was calm, if only for the moment. There was no sense ruining her rare peace. Instead, she said, "I'd like to help."

"You've already helped me. You're my first friend here."

Addison's eyes were full of emotion and something Shel didn't quite recognize. It felt like trust; she surely hoped it wasn't admiration. She was dead last on a list of admirable people. She realized Addison was still sweetly rambling.

"I do have one other friend here, but she's more like a mentor. She's part of the network. You're the first person I want to confide in—that I've wanted to…" She blinked damp lashes, her eyes nervously darting away, then back to Shel again. She shyly finished, "kiss."

Part of Shel longed to kiss her slowly, see where it took them. Instead, she drew Addison closer and pressed tiny kisses on her forehead in an almost maternal fashion. "I understand everything you're saying, but we need to take serious consideration about getting this right and on the record. I won't do anything you don't want to do, because I want you to trust me."

"I do trust you." Addison seemed to consider it further. "Perhaps that's foolish of me—after all, I've known you for only a short time. But I feel like I do trust you."

The words pained and strengthened Addison at the same time. She spoke plainly, truthfully. "We need to try to make things right in a legal way for Harper's sake."

Addison was quiet and Shel could only hope she was listening as she continued.

"You're using an assumed name, but that won't allow you to own anything of real value, like a house or car."

As Addison didn't appear shocked, Shel could assume she'd already considered these things, probably much more. Addison shifted slightly, as if her discomfort over the subject at hand was actually having a physical impact as well. "I know this."

More notions were flooding Shel's head. "One day, Harper may do something amazing, but you'll still be in hiding. She surfaces, you surface, too. Harper would never endanger her mother, so already she's limited in life and she's only four."

"I know this," Addison said again, more loudly this time. Her chest rose and fell rapidly and she appeared to be in the preliminary stages of an all-out panic attack. She closed her eyes, seemingly willing herself to calm down. Her voice was quiet when she added, "I've thought of all this—I'm *living* this."

"Right now you're surviving, but soon enough you'll want to thrive." Shel tightened her hold on Addison whose stance had gone rigid as her defense. She stroked her back. "You're an artist; she's a smart kid. You both deserve better than that kind of life."

"Hypothetically speaking, what's your plan?" The question was issued in a tone that said she already knew she wouldn't care for the answer.

"I've seen how these networks work, and I have to say, I've never seen anyone take a child underground." Shel dipped her chin, tried to capture Addison's gaze. "How'd that happen?"

"It's against the rules," she quietly admitted, refusing to grant her a look.

"Did you kidnap Harper?"

"She's my daughter," Addison quickly answered, raising her gaze to reveal her eyes flicking with the fire of a protective mother. "She's mine."

Shel held her gaze. "But understand that from a legal standpoint, she's also his. There is no statute of limitations on parental kidnapping. You'd face jail time even if you were sixty."

Addison didn't blink, hesitate or stutter when she replied, "The only reason I'm here is for Harper. If she's successful and happy and able to stand on her own two feet—I can live with jail."

Shel stammered, "W-what about your life?"

"She *is* my life."

The conviction in her voice sent a chill through Shel. The full weight of everything Addison was up against, as well as her unbending devotion to her daughter, hit Shel front and center. She felt breathless and revived at the same time, her admiration for the woman next to her ever strengthening. "You're...a spunky one."

Addison looked bewildered. "Is that supposed to be funny?"

"No," Shel mumbled, again drawing her close. "It just so happens to be that my interest is seeing both of you safe."

"I don't see how—"

She cut Addison off. "Just trust me, please. There might be a way to tackle this legally, but I promise not to do a thing if you're not one hundred percent onboard."

Shel felt her relax, but her own worry-addled brain wouldn't rest. She watched the flickering candlelight cast slow shadows along the walls until she at last felt Addison's breathing level out. She considered the plethora of issues they would face. It felt utterly impossible.

CHAPTER TWENTY-FIVE

A sound, real or imagined, startled Shel from sleep. She quickly scanned the room, recalling where she was, who she was with, and then thought of the candle which had long ago extinguished in its own waxy pool. Shel gently extricated her arm from behind the woman sleeping against her, rubbing the prickly feeling that needled her from having been still for so long. She stood and quietly collected the glasses before blindly scooting sock feet across old hardwood floors. She quietly deposited the glasses in the kitchen sink and headed down the hallway to check on Harper.

The child slept soundly. Shel crept around checking door locks and peering out windows checking for movement beyond moon shadows. She was still processing the fact that the uppity, standoffish gallery clerk was, in truth, a masterful actor. He was Addison's friend and her link to the underground. He was also dead.

She went into the master bedroom and flicked on the bedside lamp feeling sufficiently paranoid that even the dimmest light might put her movements on display to anyone lurking outside. She opened the drawer and stared down at her gun box.

"What are you doing?" Addison's sleepy voice sounded behind her, startling her. Shel spun around to see her petite form leaning against the doorframe.

"I was…thinking." Shel slowly shut the drawer, but apparently not before Addison could see its contents.

"Can I see it?" Addison's sleepy eyes flitted away, surveying the room, its sparse furniture and barren walls. Her eyes came back around to Shel, still quiet, waiting for clarification. Addison clearly enunciated her succinct words, "Let me see your gun."

Shel's stare lingered on her a minute longer before she again turned toward the nightstand. She slowly opened the drawer, removed the sturdy box and set it on the bed. She swished her hand around the drawer, locating the key. Before shoving it into the lock, she looked at Addison who only nodded. The lock made a low click and she drew the cover back on its hinges. Addison stepped closer to the bed and they stood there, staring at the Glock.

"It looks different than Richard's gun," Addison finally quietly remarked.

Shel figured any gun would look different when you weren't the target. She thought about the collection of weapons on display in Fortier's glorified closet and wondered if he'd employed one of those in his twisted roulette game. Shel picked up the gun and the cartridge, making a show of keeping them separate to allay any fears Addison may have.

"It's not loaded until the magazine is in here." Shel indicated the butt of the Glock, keeping it pointed in the direction of the window regardless of the fact that it wasn't loaded.

Addison hesitantly stepped in closer, held out her hand. "May I?"

With an odd sense of reluctance, Shel handed her the unloaded gun. Addison's palm drooped with the unexpected heft of the weapon and she tightly grasped it, her eyes widening, actually marveling at it in its nonthreatening state.

"It's heavier than I thought it would be." She tapped the trigger with her finger in an experimental move then firmly squeezed it. It clicked twice prompting a small gasp. She did this a few more times as if she were acclimating herself to the sound, also now not a threat. Then she held her hand out for the clip. They remained locked in each other's gaze for several long seconds. At last Shel shook her head.

"You asked me to trust you." Addison dipped her chin demurely, softly asked, "Don't you trust me?"

The question was far more loaded than the gun would ever be. Shel did trust her, but it was new, fragile trust. Giving advances on such credit wasn't in Shel's repertoire. Her common sense chanted these facts in the back of her head by habit, but given her immense attraction to Addison it sounded distant and annoying, like a buzzing gnat.

She found herself stepping close behind Addison, enveloping her outer arms, wrapping a hand over Addison's until together they clutched the gun. Her other hand methodically shoved the magazine into the butt of the gun until it clicked. Resting her chin on Addison's shoulder, she uttered her whispered tutorial.

"Lead with your strongest arm and cup your other hand like this." She made a demonstration, aiming toward the window. "Elbows down, find your target. Pull the slide back then squeeze the trigger."

"Is the safety on?" Addison's studious look was reflected in the bedroom window.

"No." Shel made a low, nervous chuckle. "So don't pull the trigger or you'll take out that window and anything behind that hedge out there."

"That's all there is to it?" she whispered.

"That's all."

With her chest pressed to Addison's back, Shel wondered if she could possibly feel her pounding heart. She felt flushed, in part because of their closeness, in part because Addison still gripped a loaded gun. At once, Addison wriggled her fingers away, leaving Shel holding the gun. She turned around in Shel's arms and buried her face against her chest. Immense relief washed through Shel; had she been the world's best con, the woman could have easily turned the gun around on her.

Shel relaxed her grip, ejected the clip, and reset the safety, letting both pieces fall onto the bed. She folded her arms around Addison. Hot tears dampened the collar of her shirt and then Addison began kissing a path up her neck. She reached Shel's ear, whispered, "I want to make love to you."

Shel's stomach bottomed out at the sweetly uttered words, but her surreal joy was quickly replaced with a practical notion.

Addison had lived years of her life bargaining with her ex for her and Harper's safety. Perhaps she was still doing that out of habit.

Contrary to every desire her body screamed with, she found herself taking a backward step.

"No. You don't have to do that, Addison." She attempted to loosen the woman's desperate embrace, but Addison held tight. "I'm going to help you because someone should. You don't owe me anything."

"Owe you anything?" Addison leaned back slightly, her eyes tearful and earnest. "I'm falling in love with you."

Shel forcibly stepped away from her to take several deep breaths. In a near-panic, she turned a half-circle, rubbed her neck. She damned herself for everything, from being conned into the job in the first place, to her new job as protector. She cursed Fortier and cursed the money she now knew she'd never see. He must have known she'd fall for Addison. It was like sending a wild animal after fresh meat, all the while Fortier standing at the ready with his gilded net. She wondered if there was even a single thing about this case she hadn't gotten wrong—a single way in which she hadn't been taken for a sucker.

Shel took two steps toward the bed and hurriedly collected the gun and clip and put it back in its case. The case went into the drawer. She turned the light off and silently stood in the darkness, facing the bed. A heavy dose of anger and sadness congested her chest, leaving scarce room for the breath that labored to fill her lungs.

"Please." Addison's plea was concurrently desperate and sexy. She took a step closer, and rested a gentle hand on Shel's shoulder. "Please."

Shel whirled around with every intention of rebuffing the woman's touch and ill-timed, indecent proposal. In the dim moonlight she glared at Addison. In a whiplash move, her lips were on Addison's, kissing her deeply. Long-building passion ripped through her with a ferociousness she didn't recognize in herself. Her hands ravished Addison's face, neck, shoulders, and breasts. Shel clumsily clawed at the thin sundress material to access smooth skin. Two swift steps had Addison's backside against the wall. With the new leverage, Shel kissed her again, deeply, roughly.

Clutching Addison's bare thigh, Shel made a low moan as her hand moved upward to discover Addison's simple cotton panties.

After days of voracious mental foreplay, Shel had no prerequisites to offer before shoving her hand past the already damp fabric, proof enough Addison wanted her. Eager fingertips plunged into lovely warmth.

She heard Addison gasp, felt her shudder. It occurred to Shel that she was being too rough, too fast. She selfishly cast gentle patience aside, finding it impossible to believe she could inflict pain anywhere as great as what she, herself, had already experienced. Foreign feelings of love and protection warred with lust and need. She gripped Addison harder, her movement growing more frenetic, plunging herself deeper and faster, over and again.

Lost to the sensation, Addison could barely remain on her feet. Her head lolled back against the wall and she cried out. Her body shuddered and wilted against Shel.

In a whiplash turn of emotions, Shel's harsh edges softened and she held Addison close, kissed her. When their lips parted, she steered Addison toward the bed and their depleted bodies collapsed onto the tops of blankets. Moving gently this time around, Shel tugged Addison's damp dress over her head and tossed it onto the floor. She then proceeded to investigate every curve of her lover's tight body, touching smooth skin, tasting a slow, erotic path across her belly then lower.

The rigid seam of Shel's jeans felt painful against her own heat and want. She hurriedly stood and peeled them off, then did the same with her shirt, flinging the inside-out garment onto the floor next to Addison's dress. Slatted moonlight trickled in through wooden blinds, causing her pause to appreciate Addison's beautiful body. She coaxed Addison to the edge of the bed then knelt before her on the bedside rug. She intended to love her slowly, thoroughly. She parted Addison's legs and ran her hands along smooth inner thighs until Addison whimpered with need.

"I want to be yours," Addison quietly declared. "Say it."

Shel was taken aback by the whispered demand. She didn't believe in it; she didn't agree with it. Nobody owned anybody—not her ex, not her former boss, not Fortier—nobody.

"Say that I'm yours," Addison repeated.

Angry at—or at very least puzzled by—her odd insistence, Shel instead roughly pulled at the wet panties, easily removing them. She took Addison into her mouth, tasting her deeply, drawing back only to teasingly flick her tongue. She felt Addison's muscles tense as

Shel plunged her tongue deeply inside again, scooped firm buttocks toward her in slow, rhythmic waves, finding the spot that triggered the greatest response. Addison cried out for the second time in only minutes. Her lovely body quivered and went slack.

Eager to hold her, Shel rose up and nudged Addison's exhausted body to the bed's center. She straddled Addison's legs and looked down at her beauty. Her own head was full of sounds—their ragged breath, the whir of the ceiling fan, muted outdoor night sounds—and she knew her internal prattling had been defeated for the time being. It was lovely and freeing.

Still hot with need, Shel's eyes gazed down and locked with Addison's gaze. She took her lover's hand to her lips and kissed it.

"You are mine." Shel's delayed agreement emerged with surprising grit in her tone. Empowered by sound, she emphasized it again: "*Mine.*"

She kissed Addison's hand then moved it low, looking for confirmation in her lover's eyes. She pressed the gentle, willing hand between her legs, an innocent action that resembled something almost adolescent that filled her with contrasting feelings of wrong and right.

"Please, yes," Addison whispered.

The electricity of her mere touch caused Shel to writhe against cupped fingertips only moments before exploding. Her eyes clenched shut and her stomach tightened as the sensation rolled over her in waves. She felt need, lust, and love on multiple levels. It was a powerful trifecta.

Catching her breath, she collapsed onto the bed and pulled Addison firmly against her. When the fan had cooled their bodies, and when at last she felt physically able to, Shel reached down for a blanket and drew it over their damp, heaving bodies.

While Addison was falling asleep, Shel slowly retreated back into her uneasy mind where voices were already returning to work. She was strengthened against their powerful doubt, fortified by the woman in her arms and her new role as vigilant protector and lover.

Streaks of night illuminated her lover's thin shoulders as they rose and fell with sound sleep. She was safe, Shel would make sure.

"Mine," she whispered once more, confirming her decision aloud. She drew the blanket more tightly around Addison, turned further into her, held her as though her life depended upon it. Maybe it did.

CHAPTER TWENTY-SIX

A pounding on the front door had Shel up too early. She glanced at the bedside clock and saw that it was nearly seven. Quietly as she could, she slipped out of bed and dressed on her way to the door. Milford was on the front step. Shel unlocked the door.

"What are you doing?" Shel whispered.

"You got company?" Milford looked past Shel's shoulder, noted the still partially set table and candles that had burned out long ago. She rolled her eyes.

"Yeah, I do."

"Swell." Milford again rolled her eyes, motioned for her to come outside. Shel stepped onto the top step, arms still folded in front of her. She could smell sex on herself and wondered if the cop also could. "Harlow Farris, the doctor?"

"What about him?"

"Died during Katrina."

Shel's arms limply dropped to her sides. "You're kidding me."

"I wouldn't do such a thing," Milford said. "He remained in his powerless hospital for days, tending his patients."

"He drowned?"

"Nope. Heart attack—he was an elderly gentleman. And he was a mental health doctor, so Fortier got that part right."

"Still…" Shel searched her head for the possibilities. "Did he have a son by chance? A brother or cousin—anyone else who practices medicine?"

"You think I didn't check for that? I'm telling you the only Harlow Farris in New Orleans is six feet under in Lake Lawn, Metarie."

Shel cringed, afraid to ask, but did anyway. "And the lawyer?"

"His license is on file." Milford pulled a folded paper out of her jacket and flipped it out straight for Shel's review. "This him?"

Shel squinted in the early morning light, took the paper, played trombone with it, trying to get a closer look. She finally shook her head. "I can't tell. It's pixilated."

"Picture's a few years old, so that's not helpful." Milford's voice dropped. "Given the circumstances and that most of what she's told you has panned out, I think we better get a move on some kind of plan."

"What do you recommend?" Shel also spoke quietly, although there wasn't a soul around. "There are some details that I believe you'll agree won't make it an easy case."

"Details like what?" Milford's eyes looked tired. "Good Lord, girl. I can't imagine there's more to this twisted tale."

"I'll tell you about it later, promise." They both went quiet. Shel looked contemplative before asking, "There a gun range around here?"

Milford's chin dipped. She blinked.

"That's what's on your mind at this precise moment?" The cop eyed her suspiciously, already putting together her own clues about Shel's inquiry. "How smart an idea is it to arm a woman who is not altogether mentally stable?"

"Milford—what the fuck?" She sprang to her defense. "You just said yourself that you believe. I thought we'd pretty much established—"

"Calm down, hotshot." Milford looked aggravated. "Just how mentally stable do you think people are who endure those types of abuses, huh? You don't have to go to war to get PTSD. I hear the homegrown brand is some of the worst."

Shel took a breath, nodded.

"Despite your good intentions, how wise do you think it would be to haul her to a public gun range with cameras tucked in every crack and crevice? She even got ID?"

"I was thinking someplace quieter." Shel's brow furrowed. She thought about Fortier's fascination with guns, his collection, and his sick game of Russian Roulette with Addison. Milford was probably right about Addison being post-traumatic. If there was a way to make her less afraid of weapons while at the same time giving her some basic gun safety and knowledge, maybe she could help abolish some of that aftershock. Or maybe she was just trying to justify teaching Addison to use a gun to shoot Fortier's ass if he came around, which he probably would.

Milford sighed. "I'm starting to recognize that look by now. I can almost hear your hamster wheel creaking from here."

"Let's just say it's for the sake of basic gun safety."

"Well, let's hope she doesn't get her targets confused."

"Never mind. I'll handle it myself." Shel's visible frustration faded when she noticed how troubled Milford appeared. "You okay, Milford?"

"I am not sleeping for diddly-squat, not that you care." She started down the front house steps, stopped and turned to face her again. "Also, this nonsense is seriously cutting into my love life. Thank fortune it's not damaging yours any. I can smell you from here."

Shel felt her cheeks warm, but otherwise ignored the very accurate implication. "Can I get a hold of you later?"

Milford waved her off as she turned to go. "I'll come by."

Shel watched her leave before stepping back inside. She followed the noise, and more importantly the smell, into the kitchen. Addison had started a fresh pot of coffee and was quietly putting the previous night's dishes into the old dishwasher. Wearing last night's wrinkled dress, she was caught off guard and smiled shyly when she noticed Shel in the doorway.

"Good morning." Shel walked straight into Addison's arms and stayed there for a while. "I'm sorry I woke you so early."

Addison's ever-present paranoia now seemed to fill the room as strongly as the aroma of the coffee. "Was that your cop friend?"

"Yeah," Shel said, equally troubled, though for very different reasons. "She seems to be as afraid of you as you are her, no offense."

"I'm sure." Addison's mood was obviously rapidly making a turn toward depression. "So, you told her about me?"

"Some, but don't worry." When Addison didn't reply after several seconds, Shel defended her decision to share any information with the cop. "Look—she's a law-abiding woman who has no interest in seeing assholes knock women around, and she's not easily swayed by wealth or power. You have to trust me that she's on our side. She's a friend."

"It seems like she doesn't much care for me."

"It's not that…" Shel's words trailed off. It was obvious that Milford was leery of Addison and there was certainly no reason to lie about that, too. Plus, it was good to allow Addison to trust her instincts, something she likely hadn't done in a long time. "She's incredibly socially awkward, but a good person nonetheless."

"I'm trying to trust you. I really am."

"You should trust me." Shel stepped toward Addison, kissed her, whispered, "I am taking very good care where you and Harper are concerned."

Addison nodded. Shel kissed her again.

Shortly, Addison broke away and poured two steaming cups of coffee. She handed one to Shel.

"Have you a plan for us?" Addison took a sip of coffee, avoiding making direct eye contact when she added, "I've been thinking about what you said about living life on the up and up. If it can be done, I'd like very much for that to happen."

Shel was warmed by her confidence and afraid of it at the same time. She could not fail her. As her mind again began to unwind a chattering list of bad possibilities, Shel absently said, "I mean worst-case scenario, we all end up in jail."

"If you knew Richard, you'd know that is not the worst-case scenario."

The haunted words snapped Shel from her thoughts. Her own tone took a serious turn. "Anyone besides your friend, Bernard, that knew about the underground? I'm checking loose ends and breadcrumbs you may have inadvertently left behind. I don't want your ex to get the jump on us."

It was a trickily worded lie. If anyone had carelessly dropped crumbs, it was herself. She was simply hunting for leads, trying to figure out who else might be out there, watching and waiting.

"Only a friend at Loyola. A coach—he was the only other contact."

Shel didn't need to ask for his name, though she was sure that Addison was providing it while her own head privately threatened to explode. Frank Sawyer, a man she'd practically interrogated before leaving the city—a man she'd initially suspected was guilty of Addison's abduction. Shel nodded on occasion to give the appearance of listening, when in fact she was quietly engaged in an internal meltdown.

Struggling to keep the anxiety from her tone, Shel asked, "Anyone else?"

"No. Well, there's a friend here on this end of the system."

Shel presumed she was referring to Silvia. She set her coffee aside and folded the woman into a close, desperate hug.

"I'm sorry," she whispered into her ear while squeezing her tight. Shel blinked her eyes tightly shut, willing tears to remain at bay. She didn't even remember the last time she'd felt so emotional. If she started crying now, she wondered if she'd ever stop. At once, she'd found the best person in her world and had sold her out. Fortier was after her; it was Shel's fault. She simply repeated, "I'm so, so sorry about this."

Addison hugged her back, gently swaying with her like a mother would her child.

"There was nothing you could do," Addison sweetly whispered. "Besides, it'll all be okay. We'll figure it out. We're a good team."

Shel's eyes were wet. She clenched them tightly shut, gnawing at her lip. She nodded against Addison who only held her more tightly and continued administering soothing words. "It'll all be okay. We'll make it all okay."

* * *

It took two minutes and twenty bucks to extract Rob the bartender's hotel room number from the concierge. The look on the gentleman's face was priceless, which told Shel she wasn't the kind of woman who normally plied the staff with cash for the bartender's room number. She thanked him and headed around the back of the hotel and down quite a distance to an older section. This portion was freshly painted in accordance with the rest of the hotel, but it was clear that the units were considerably smaller, spaced more closely together, and not nearly as swank. Shel quickly surmised it was the original wing, too downscale for guests, but just right for staff living on-site.

She found his room number and hammered on the door. He was at the door almost immediately, breathless and bare chested, a blanket slung like a sarong to shield her from view of his nether regions. His blond hair was rumpled and he blinked against the morning sun.

"What the hell…?"

"Good morning, Robert." Shel grinned and attempted to peek around him. "Who's the flavor of the minute?"

Without taking his eyes off her, he stepped outside and pulled the door shut behind him. "Cut to the chase."

"I will. Any of your highfalutin sugar mamas got a gun range?"

"Yes," he immediately answered, as if he fielded such questions every day.

"Whoa, didn't even need time to think on it."

"I am special friends with a woman whose husband is an officer with the NRA."

"I just want you to repeat that statement a few times in your head." Shel gave him a second, but he seemed no worse for wear. "Beauty, no brains. Look—can you pull some strings and get me in? I don't want to go to a public range."

His eyes flicked left, then back. "Yeah. Just you?"

"Me and a friend. Maybe two."

"Yeah." Again, no hesitation whatsoever. "Today?"

"Preferably." Shel noticed a shadow moving behind the window blinds in his room. "You need to call someone?"

Without taking his eyes off Shel, Rob reached behind him and opened the door a crack. "Babs—can a buddy and I use your range today?"

"What's mine is yours, baby." The purred answer came from inside his room.

Shel gazed curiously at him as he stood wearing his blanket sarong. "Rob, you must have a fucking magic wand under that blanket."

"Let's put it this way," Rob started, the sparkle returning to his eye. He leaned toward her, giving her a whiff of a blend of perspiration and something that smelled like orchids, presumably Babs's perfume. He wriggled his eyebrows, whispered, "It takes this whole blanket to keep my wand concealed."

"Okay, TMI." Shel backed away, more than a little creeped out and slightly concerned that he might get overly excited and drop the wrap, thereby revealing the magic. "Can you give me instructions, who to meet—that sort of thing?"

"Meet me in front of the main lobby, noon."

He stepped inside and slammed the door shut before she could ask questions.

CHAPTER TWENTY-SEVEN

Shel went to the police station and summoned her reluctant partner. Together they went to the art gallery. Shel hurried inside where she was again greeted by the owner, this time as a welcome friend. Given that she was suddenly in the good graces of Thomas Taylor, she kindly asked if Addison might have a few hours off. He seemed pleased that his hermit-like employee had a friend and heartily consented.

Milford, Shel and Addison arrived at the hotel right on schedule and found Rob waiting. Shel had already decided that she'd have to come at least partially clean with Addison once she saw Rob, having already sent the guy on a mission involving the artist. It was her dim hope that Addison would be flattered that she'd gone to such lengths to meet her, which wasn't exactly true, but it was a far more survivable lie than admitting she'd sent Rob on a mission to frame her as a gold digger.

Dressed in a baseball cap, shorts and a T-shirt, Rob presented the most casual, age-appropriate look Shel had seen on him so far. Without so much as an invitation, he opened the back door and got in, casting darting glances around the car to accompany his curt greeting, "Hey."

"That's Milford and this is Addison. Everyone, this is Rob."

Rob nodded and firmly shook each woman's hand without even making familiar eye contact with Addison. She exchanged a polite handshake. Perhaps she was simply preoccupied with Milford's presence, but with Rob in his layman's getup, Addison did not seem to make even the remotest connection to the man who'd admired her artwork in the hotel lobby. Shel breathed deeply. It was no wonder he was good at his scam work. She wondered how long her lucky streak could continue where Addison was concerned. Rob instructed them to drive several miles down Gulfshore Boulevard. The mansions grew progressively larger and more elaborately gated as they drove through the exclusive neighborhood. Even Milford appeared taken aback by the swankiest residences of her own town. Rob waved them over to the last mansion on the stellar boulevard, one that was more like a sprawling compound. With gulf waves surrounding it on three sides, it was like an island on the mainland.

Shel pulled up to the call box and looked over at Rob. "They buzz us in?"

"Nope, pull up." He leaned out the back passenger window and punched a code into the box. A green light began blinking and the gates slid open. "Park behind the stables."

"The stables?" Milford echoed. "Horses and guns. Your girl a fan of the Wild West, Rob?"

He appeared to think it over, then grinned big. "I could do something with that. She loves role-play."

"Okay, Rob." Shel shot him a warning look. She parked her rental car and they got out. "Do we need to check in with someone?"

"It's not a hotel," Rob said, chuckling.

Milford caught sight of a young, shirtless man skimming a net across an infinity pool that appeared to splash into the Gulf of Mexico. Nearby, a woman dressed in full formal maid's attire, despite the intense Florida heat, was hand polishing the brass feet of cabana loungers.

"Could have fooled me," Milford said under her breath.

"Right this way." Rob punched another code into the electronics panel near the back door. "These doors are all automatic. They can detect who lives here and *zing!*—they just open. Unless you're family or a servant—or me, in which case you override the system with a passcode."

He led them inside toward a large cylindrical elevator. "And this thing is powered by vacuum, like the little containers that get sucked upstairs faster than those little tubes at the bank drive-through." He ushered them onto the platform and aimed plain words at a speaker panel, "Close door, floor two."

The doors snapped shut and Shel's stomach fluttered as the elevator seamlessly whisked them to the second floor. The speed had her knees feeling wobbly as they exited and she shot Addison a surprised look that was returned. They continued to follow their guide down a long hallway on the second floor.

"Guy who owns the place is a big tech junkie. Every room automatically senses your body heat and adjusts the temperature accordingly. The family room even switches portraits in its frames depending upon who's in there. If it's him, you've got hunting dogs. If it's her, she's got pictures of the grandkids."

"You fooling around with somebody's grandma?" Milford shot him a look of minor disgust.

Rob easily ignored her. "If it were me, it'd be porn."

"Naturally," Shel said, rolling her eyes. They walked down a seemingly endless corridor of all white marble. "Will we get there any time in the next year, Rob?"

On cue, he stopped abruptly, punched in another code, and a door that had been nearly invisible against the marble opened up. Shel cast a look back down the hallway, wondering how many other doors they'd passed without her noticing. They went inside, the door swishing shut behind them. In front of them was a pristine, modern, ten-lane shooting gallery.

"You must be kidding me," Shel said. She did a slow spin, looking at the high white walls that ran deep, with targets arranged in each lane. A counter in the corner was bursting with an impressive cache of weaponry, tagged and neatly arranged. Her thoughts temporarily went to Fortier's gun collection, framed neatly in expensive, velvet-lined boxes. Clearly, the owner of this particular mansion wanted guns to not only be heard, but seen. She remembered Rob mentioning that he was a big NRA member. Shel made a low whistle. "This guy has…everything."

"Not everything," Rob said, grinning and grabbing his crotch in a vulgar move. He approached the banister that separated the shooters from their audience and selected one of the multiple pairs of headgear laid out there. "And he certainly doesn't have cameras in the bedrooms, thank God."

"Showoff," Milford said, clearly tiring of the boy's incredibly overinflated ego.

Her words were muffled by his headgear so he didn't react to her dig. They watched as he selected a cartoonish multiround gun. Milford smirked and also selected a pair of headgear for future use, as, given the preview of Rob's selection, it promised to be a noisy show.

"There's ammo over there," Rob yelled at them, pointing in the general direction of the counter. As if on cue, and older, gray-haired gentleman emerged from the door behind them smiled and nodded.

"Hello, Mr. Rob and friends," he quietly greeted him. "Let me know if I can assist you."

"Hey, Al," Rob hollered, despite the fact that he was the only one wearing headgear at the moment. He turned toward the women, screamed, "Al can get you set up with ammo. I'm getting started."

"Look at that would you?" Milford seemed disgusted. "Everybody's getting VIP treatment in this town except me—even the local gigolo."

Shel pulled her own gun out of the holster that rode beneath her shirttail and laid it on the banister. She looked into Addison's eyes. "Remember what I showed you last night? Let's go through that again."

She checked the clip then led Addison to the target farthest away from where Rob had begun shooting something that looked like a modern-age tommy gun. Its roar was deafening.

"Overkill," Shel muttered, though nobody could hear. They both slipped on headgear. As she had the night before, she stood behind Addison and positioned the gun. Since there was no point in speaking against a background of bullet noise, Shel pantomimed the sequence of steps. She gave Addison little sideways glances, but saw no fear, only concentration in her eyes. When she felt confident Addison was ready, she raised their collective aim slightly, pointing just below the target's center. Together they squeezed off the first shot. Addison's eyes went wide with surprise at the sensation of the gun's recoil. She turned toward Shel. They both removed their headgear, but the noise was ear-splitting. Shel turned around and made a shrill whistle that stopped all movement—and noise—in the large, echoing room.

"Hey, Rob! Can you keep that shit down for a second? We're doing an instructional here."

Milford, still leaning against the banister, rolled her eyes. "Is that firearm even legal, Rambo?"

Rob stared at her, a clueless look in his eyes, apparently only then realizing he still had on headgear. He pulled them down, letting them fall around his neck. "Come again?"

"Just forget it." Milford approached the gun counter where the gentleman still waited, also now wearing headgear. He smiled affably and removed them to hear her. Milford cast a glance over her shoulder. "Looks more fun than the piece I'm carrying. What else you got back there, Tex?"

Shel shot Rob a look of warning about firing his trumped up weapon for a few minutes. She then turned to Addison for a conference.

"I must have misfired," Addison said. "I didn't hold it tightly enough."

"That was just blowback. You get used to it and make adjustments accordingly." She leaned around Addison and arranged the gun in her hands again. "Hold the grip, remember? Lead with your stronger arm. Cup your other hand around, slide this back…"

They fired again, this time closer to the target. Shel nodded and let go of the Glock. "You try it by yourself now."

Shel walked back to the banister where Milford rejoined her, a long-stock rifle in her grip. She wore safety glasses and held out a pair to Shel, who gave her a polite hand gesture refusal. They watched as Addison carefully went through the steps again, this time solo, and squinted toward her target. She fired a shot that went at least five feet above it. After five more such erratic shots, even Rob had retreated to the banister. By now, they were all in safety glasses. After several minutes, Addison stopped firing and turned toward her audience. She looked frustrated.

"I'm terrible at this," she said. Nobody contested her self-assessment. "Let's face it—that was some bad shooting."

"It's a work in progress," Shel told her.

"The important thing is that you look good while shooting up that crown molding." It was the only compliment Rob had in him. Milford didn't even have that.

With fresh ammunition, Addison returned to her booth and continued to shoot everything but the target. Milford alternated talking to the man at the counter and trying new weapons. Upon their return, the counterman laid them aside for what would surely be meticulous cleaning after they left. Fascinated with yet another machine-type gun, Rob went through countless more rounds, and Shel stood in back, watching it all. In a bit, she was rejoined by Milford, sans headgear.

"Look at us, would you? We're standing back here, basically defenseless, while your alleged psychopath shoots everything but the target." Milford glanced Rob's way, made a funny sound, added, "Make that two psychopaths."

Shel didn't react to her sarcasm, only said, "Do you think she could hit something at close range?"

They watched another bullet twang off something in the distance.

"No," Milford plainly said. "So, you come up with any great plans, genius?"

"No, but you should know the other stuff I've learned, starting with the fact that Addison stole ten million off her ex before she split."

"You're. Fucked." Milford's back came off the banister and her message was direct. Shel could tell she was going into full-on cop mood. "You no longer have my cooperation in this matter. I'm bound by law to—"

"Before you get all crazy-cop on me, it was money that her ex stole from a charity—Tree of Life. Bastard sold them a bunch of bad art in an investment scam," Shel quickly explained. "She stole the proceeds and anonymously donated it back to the charity."

Milford slowly relaxed, unclenching her balled fists. "The only reason I am still standing here is because I read about that donation in *USA Today*. Otherwise, so help me, I'd already be gone."

"Thank you." Shel breathed deep, genuinely thankful she still had an audience. "And there's more."

"I'm sure." Milford's eyes flitted toward the ceiling as if seeking heavenly help, then said, "Go on."

"That dead gallery clerk—he was the guy who got Addison into the underground program."

The cop's eyes quickly returned to Shel, all sarcasm gone. "Not good."

"There's another guy, a coach at Loyola. He was the second stop on this whole system." Shel spoke more quietly despite the fact that Rob was engaged in conversation with the attendant. The only remaining noise was the random twangs created by Addison's misfired shots. Shel continued. "I'm not really in the mood to wait for the coach's body to turn up to confirm that Fortier's getting closer to finding his wife."

"You think he's the type of guy to track her down himself?"

"Seems like he hires his help. He hired me, after all." Shel was thankful Addison still wore her headgear. They watched as Rob strode back to his lane long enough to reel in his bullet-riddled target. "Makes you wonder who else is lurking out there, leaving a trail of bodies in his—or her—wake."

"Hence the reason you're trying to gift her with shooting lessons, which don't appear to have taken hold, by the way."

"I noticed."

"Also, I'd be wary of any other *neighbors* who might suddenly appear in your empty summertime hood." Shel had thought of it enough to suspect everyone, everywhere. Milford continued, "This is quite a job you've undertaken."

"I am thinking of a plan, but it's risky."

"Oh, it's only now risky?" Milford shook her head. "Sister, you're into risk up to your eyeballs. How much riskier could it get?"

"I need Fortier to confess." Shel was too deep in thought to absorb her remark. Rob crossed in front of them, again returning to the counter. In the background he waved bottles of designer water at them. Both shook their heads. Shel continued, "If we can get a solid confession on the record about how he forced her to forge the art, maybe she can get a deal."

"You'd need everything to get her off the hook at this point— I'm talking mentions of people he screwed over—the works."

In minutes Addison had emptied another magazine still without putting a single hole in the clean target that sailed toward her on the line. Shel and Milford exchanged glances. Removing her headgear, Addison came toward them, looking frustrated.

"My arms are tired and my head hurts. I'm awful at this." Addison laid down the gun and headgear. "I don't think I could hit anything if I wanted to."

"The good news is you could probably hit anything you didn't want to." Milford's comment inspired silence and a sarcastic look from Shel. The cop shrugged and headed toward the counter to return her borrowed weapon.

"The good news is that you were on the other side of the gun for a change," Shel quietly told her. While she'd hoped that Addison would be a better shot than she'd proven to be, Shel also hoped the experience would boost her confidence. "A gun doesn't make you powerful. Being able to confront the things that scare you, now that's the stuff that makes you powerful. Small steps, that's what we're doing here."

Rob crossed in front of them, heading toward the door.

"My lady awaits me." He wriggled his eyebrows in the women's direction. "You can find your way out, right?"

"Thanks, Rob," Shel told him. When he was gone, Shel again thanked the attendant before heading for the closed door. Just as she'd heard Rob say, she repeated, "Open."

The door slid open with a quick swish like something on *Star Trek*. The trio proceeded down the seemingly endless marble hallway and Shel verbally commanded the elevator to whisk them to the first floor.

"Shotgun, no pun intended," Milford said when they were outside. She slipped into the front passenger's side. Addison didn't protest the call and simply got into the backseat. They buckled up and headed toward the gate, waiting for it to allow them exit to the main road. She chuckled. "What kind of action you suppose that boy gives these women? You mean to tell me all that money can't buy their husbands Viagra?"

"Oh, I'm sure. But God knows where the husbands are employing their Viagra-super powers. Doubt it's at home."

"Tit for tat." Milford shook her head. "What an arrangement."

They rode in silence. Shel dreaded leaving Addison at the gallery, or anyplace for that matter that she would be open, exposed. She parked a few spots down from the gallery, turned and told Milford, "I'll walk her to the door."

As they walked down the street, Shel could feel Addison's anxiety building as the woman cast glances over her shoulder at the waiting cop.

"She really doesn't like me, does she?" Addison finally asked. The cop had the window down watching them, a neutral expression on her face. Nonetheless, she made a curt wave. Addison looked back at Shel, whispered, "She thinks I'm here to cause problems."

"If she thought that, trust me, she wouldn't have gone with us today." Shel took hold of Addison's hands, looked into her eyes.

"Milford and I are working on a good, solid plan, so I don't want you to worry."

"What kind of plan?"

"We're still working out the details," Shel lied. "At the risk of making you paranoid, I want you to watch your back. We can't be too careful about anyone, just in case."

Addison nodded. Shel smiled and kissed her forehead.

"I'll talk to you about it more after work and we'll go from there."

When she'd gone inside the gallery, Shel motioned to Milford who joined her on the sidewalk. Together they strolled toward the docks and a row of wooden benches running along the water. They selected the one farthest away from anyone and sat.

"So what's your great big plan, hotshot?" Milford arched an eyebrow and moved to preempt what would be an unnecessary question-and-answer session. "I heard you."

"We need a confession out of Fortier, as I said earlier. Something official, on the record."

"Well, that would be ideal." Milford seemed too tired to be sarcastic. They gazed at the boat slips, watching oversized cruisers and sailboats bob to the rhythm of the gentle tide. "It's national—probably international—art fraud. The Feds would want to get involved."

Shel was biting her lip, already thinking along the same lines. "It'd be helpful to know someone in the Bureau. We turn this over without the assistance of someone sympathetic to our cause and all bets are off. Addison would go to jail and Harper in foster care before nightfall."

Milford turned to face her. "But if this woman willingly goes to the Feds, her child in tow, armed with this woeful tale and her evidence, she might stand a good chance."

"What evidence?" Shel cut her off.

"Kathleen Fortier's paintings still exist. That's where you started, remember?" Milford smirked. "People *will* be inclined to believe a woman who goes from making several thousand to a few hundred bucks on her work. It says she's scared and she wants away. She walked away from a mansion, you said. Left everything material behind—this ain't rocket science. Give people some credit."

"That argument will last five minutes in court. If that's all she's got, it's not enough to bank on." Shel stared off, looking intense.

"Then there's a matter of parental kidnapping. And just maybe Fortier will luck into a real, live doctor by the time it all hits the fan. One with legit papers."

"Calm down," Milford firmly told her.

"Add that to an expensive attorney and they'll reduce her integrity to crackpot status. She may go to jail; she may go to some kind of asylum." Shel lowered her gaze, studied her sneakers. "As for the underground, they won't testify for her. It's one of the conditions of their help. It's how they protect the group and the women they help."

"Calm down, I said. They don't wash their hands of 'em if they get subpoenaed." Milford shook her head, looked half-crazed. "It's hard to believe you were ever a cop. Besides, this isn't a normal case. Someone here is helping her transition and they let her in with a kid which isn't normal, as you also pointed out. Not something these groups normally do. Those people believe her and they *will* testify if called."

"I hate losing so much control," Shel whispered. "There's got to be another way."

"I'm all ears if you've got a better plan."

"Back to the idea of a confession," Shel said, leaning back against the bench. Her eyes reflected an inkling of an idea. "What if we send her in wearing a mic, have her throw herself at his feet, say and do anything it takes to get a confession out of him? We have cops standing by."

"That's a tremendous leap of faith for cops to make. Cops that— by the way—may or may not have been bought off by Fortier." Milford punched her first holes in the idea. "Next?"

"We could contact the Feds, but not until a good plan is in place. What if we tell them what's going down with the art scams, but only right before we send her in?" She was slowly coming to life. "Could this work? Who do you know, Milford?"

"Let's take a moment to consider that if Fortier's so smart, he's not going to tell her anything she might record. And why else would she show back up on his doorstep?" Milford squinted at her. "You going to just send her in there—nervous as hell—and expect that he will just spill? He's furious. She stole his money. This isn't going to be a joyous homecoming."

"But if she *really* sells it—"

"And you trust she'll put on that brand of Academy Award-winning performance?" Milford scoffed. "If she'd have kept that money it would have helped her case."

"If she'd have been the type to keep the money, she would have been the kind to stay with him," Shel flatly told her. "You and I would not know each other or be having this conversation."

"Understood. But it's going to be hard to get Fortier to give up any meaningful information without something in exchange." Milford gazed off in the distance. "She needs to take him some kind of show of good faith. Doesn't sound like the prospect of getting his only daughter back is going to do the trick. You need material leverage."

"I know," Shel quietly said. "Too bad she couldn't forge pictures of Benjamin Franklin."

Shel felt less than hopeful about the situation. Addison's state of mind was fragile at best, and her fear of her ex was tremendous. Enter the Feds and Shel gauged their chances at success very low. Her head and chest felt heavy.

"Makes me want to take them and run," Shel quietly said. "If I thought I could get her on a plane without getting snagged by authorities, we'd be gone by morning."

"It wouldn't be right, but I can't say I blame you." Milford rose up and stretched, signifying their meeting was finished.

She started toward the car, Shel slowly following along behind. The drive to the station was made in silence. Milford opened the door to get out, but lingered.

"Whatever your plan, don't let it percolate for too long. I got a sneaking hunch she doesn't have much time." The cop sighed, looked at the station. "We'll put our pointy heads together—figure it out."

Shel nodded without looking at her friend as she exited the car. She dreaded going home to an empty house where she would be forced to be alone with her thoughts. Her head was again getting noisy, her internal voice of reason easily losing to the sound of her own guilt and selfishness; both seemed to bellow nonstop. She rolled down the windows and let the wind hit her face as she drove aimlessly in the car rented with Fortier's credit card. She knew she should have returned it, but then she'd have no car. He probably already knew where they were anyway. Perhaps he was watching her now.

Shel drove around until after five. At that time, she returned to the dock and parked far enough away from the gallery she could safely watch for Silvia Frances to deliver Harper to her mother to protect yet another web of lies she'd spun. She wondered if Addison and her child would be much better off if they stayed put in their anonymous lives and instead Shel left. If she could believe for one minute that Fortier's reign of terror could truly end that easily—that he wouldn't find her in Naples, Florida—she'd put the car in drive until I-75 ran out of road.

When Silvia Frances was out of sight, Shel got out of the car and slowly walked toward the gallery. She took deep breaths hoping the salty air would do something to revitalize her. Instead she felt even wearier, her lungs drowned in humidity by the time she arrived at the front door. She pushed it open, jangling the doorbell, announcing her arrival. Addison looked up and smiled genuinely, welcomingly, giving Shel her first clear breath. She went to Addison and hugged her close as if it had been days, not hours, since they'd last seen each other.

Shel leaned back, toyed with the bleach blond pixie haircut that was starting to show undertones of a true color, beginning with the tiny river of auburn at her part. Shel etched every bit of her beautiful image in her mind for safekeeping.

"What's gotten into you?" Addison smiled impishly and her eyes sparkled, a move that put her shyness and charm on full display. Shel captured her hand midair and kissed it. At last Addison gently wriggled out of her hold, locked the front door before grasping Shel's hand and tugged her into the gallery's back room. She chuckled. "Come on. I just don't want Harper painting anything she shouldn't."

The rustic back room spoke to the true age of the building. Its old exposed beams were partially plastered with old art festival flyers. Paintings that would never make it into the showroom adorned the walls and yards of clothesline dangled above their heads boasting an endless array of watercolors, some obviously belonging to Harper. Shel smiled.

She forced her gaze lower to a paint-spattered picnic table where the toddler sat on her knees, wielding a paintbrush across her intended paper canvas and sometimes the battered tabletop. She watched the child stroke various shades of blue and yellow onto the paper, each time drawing her brush back with dramatic flourish. She would stop every few seconds and seem to analyze her work. The blue colors blended well hinting at some natural talent, but Shel couldn't decipher her subject.

"What are you painting, Harper?" Shel quietly asked.

"Elephant," the child announced, again studying her work. She continued painting childish, dramatic strokes of color. Suddenly, Shel could make out the barest hint of ears and a trunk.

"Harper is an impressionist," Addison explained with a smile. She collected a few books and a sweater and pressed them into her bag. She paused to roll two drawings together before sliding them into a cardboard tube.

Shel moved to stop her from capping the cylinder. "Is that something you did?"

"These? No." Addison dumped the pair of drawings back out of the tube and laid them out on the end of the picnic table. She smoothed her hand over them. "Someone brought these to my boss for an appraisal. The gentleman had purchased them in Paris a few years back believing them to be authentic Salvador Dali."

Shel took a step closer, noted the disjointed figures of animals that seemed to be floating in no sensible order. "I take it they're not?"

"No, but it was a close call on the signature." Addison held it up to the light streaming in the low window panes. "An old rumor says that Dali signed his name on many slips of paper to enable his printing company to add the signature to his prints. The printing company rejects the notion, but who can say?"

Shel's interest was piqued. "Why wouldn't he just sign the actual works?"

"He was often between Paris and New York, so sometimes he wasn't where his drawings were going to press. He thought it would be easier." Addison smoothed her hands over the rough edges. "In later years, the press added a watermark to the paper he used so that no one would be confused. Still, there's a matter of his etchings, again with and without signatures."

"Sounds like this guy enjoyed yanking everybody's chain." Shel chuckled. "What's an etching?"

"Sort of a warm-up shot before he did a serious work. Dali was known to give many of his etchings as tips to the staff at his favorite hotel in Paris. There are actually quite a number of them floating around out there, so it's no wonder that's what our customer thought that's what he had. These are close, so it's reasonable."

"You're good at this art business," Shel said, admiringly.

Addison studied the drawings. "The strokes are too abrupt, for lack of a better way to describe it. Too bad, the guy brought us quite a few of them. He was getting them appraised for his will, but when they proved valueless, he just left them all."

"There are more?"

"Yes, these were just my favorites." Addison tightly rerolled the drawings and slipped them back into the tube before going to a large wooden disposal barrel at the back of the room. She pulled half a dozen more of the same off the top, returned to the table and laid them out flat. They all boasted the same odd subjects, anatomical parts, and floating animals. "They're nice surreal works, but alas, they are not Dali."

The wheels were turning as Shel stood and leaned over the drawings, flipping through the stack. "You ever fixed a Dali?"

Addison looked thoughtful before selecting one work. She clipped it to a nearby easel and studied it for a bit. She finally picked up a charcoal pencil, speaking quietly as she made a few soft lines. "I don't do much drawing, but I studied him quite extensively in school." She stopped mid-story, shot Shel a sly smile. "I've been known to perfect a signature or two if the work is believable." Her smile faded. "That's a bad bragging point."

"No, I get it."

Addison was again looking at the drawings. "This one requires some…work."

After a pause, Addison selected another one of the drawings, crossed the room and clipped it to an easel. She stared at it for a bit. For several minutes the room was quiet, only the sound of a child's swishing paintbrush and the scratch of Addison's pencil. Seated at the picnic table, Shel was enthralled. Had Addison not been at work forging a famous work of art, the balance of the scene would have been quite peaceful. After a bit, Addison turned around and stepped aside.

Shel rose up from the bench and moved toward the drawing, which now had harsher lines in parts, counterbalanced by droopier simple subjects.

"I'm not sure what I'm looking at here," Shel slowly said. "But I like it."

"There's more to be done, but it's the humble beginnings of what could be a fair representation of his work, speaking solely about etchings."

"What would one of these go for?"

"The real deal signed and authenticated would go for anything from a few hundred to a few thousand."

Shel cupped her fingertips around her mouth. "You could bring this to a passable level?"

At that moment the jolly-looking gallery owner appeared in the doorway, sufficiently startling everyone. They seemed to let out a collective breath, causing him to grin and apologize.

"Sorry ladies—left my hat." He walked to the sidewall and looked over a row of three hats hanging on hooks. He selected a straw one and placed it on his head, giving it a pat for good measure. He noticed all eyes on him and gave a small laugh. "Everything okay here?"

"Everything's fine. You just surprised us," Addison hurriedly moved to assure him. "Is it fishing night?"

"It's drinking night," he announced, and then seeing Harper there, he amended his statement. "Root beers are best enjoyed on a fishing boat. I'll let the others fish. If they catch anything decent, I may even let them feed me."

Addison smiled. "Have a good night."

He nodded and walked toward the front of the store, doubling back slightly when he saw her handiwork on the easel display. He stood there for several long seconds. "That looks a hell of a lot like a Dali to me. You know, maybe we should send them to Tampa for examination."

"No, I was playing with it, that's all."

"You did this?" He seemed surprised. Shel's heart skipped a beat as he continued to admire her work. "Good strokes, solid figures, nice space." He removed his eyes from the painting and wagged his pudgy finger in Addison's direction. "You could make great trouble for the art industry, young lady."

"I promise I will not," she said. When he'd gone, she quietly added, "Again."

Shel was practically bursting. "You tell me how well this would work."

"Okay." Addison motioned toward the dimly lit main gallery and two old rattan chairs where she could still keep an eye on Harper. They sat down opposite each other. "What's your idea?"

"Milford and I were talking about it. The best way to get and keep you and Harper safe is to get a confession out of your ex. He's not going to do that for just anyone—"

"But you think he'll do it for me," Addison interrupted. She automatically wrung her hands, touched her neck, all the things she did when she was nervous. Her neck reddening by the second, which didn't do much to strengthen Shel's confidence in a plan she was formulating on the spot.

"Perhaps. If you return to him, throw yourself at his mercy, maybe we could get a full confession out of him, then you'd be off the hook." Shel rolled her hand, an indication that she was shortcutting many important things. "The government has been dealing with art fraud for ages. They'll take the bigger fish over the smaller."

"But I performed the actual forgeries."

"Under duress," Shel reminded her. "You could ask for, and probably get, immunity for cooperation and your testimony."

Though she didn't look at all certain of what was being explained, Addison quietly said, "He doesn't want me back, he wants me dead."

Shel tried not to let the words rattle her, for there was much explaining to do, tremendous work ahead of them. "He would listen to you if you had the money or other leverage that was of value to him."

"I don't have the money, I told you, and there are not enough fake Dali drawings to come close to making up for that. Then there's a matter of finding a very sketchy auction house to fence the art even with decent fake documents, and he knows that. The return is small and it's risky."

"Everything about this is risky," Shel said, silencing her. She thought about the multiple drawings that were ready for discard. "Could you do the same thing for a few of those, just enough to show him you'd still do that? I'll worry about how to fake the money. Maybe together it'll make a nice package he can't say no to. Can you try it?"

Shel sympathized with her, knowing how hard it was to go back once you had your heart set on living a life with some integrity. She hated like anything asking her to forge one more piece of art. At last Addison quietly said, "I can do it."

"Good." Shel leaned toward her, planted a kiss on her forehead. "I need you to trust me on this, okay sweetheart? We're going all in. Now, let's get that stuff in the car."

"The drawings?"

"And the pencils and the easel—all of it." Shel was already gathering the drawings, putting them in a stack. "Whatever it takes to make this happen and quickly."

Ten minutes later they'd loaded the car with supplies and were headed home. Addison was right, this much Shel knew. The risk was huge with no guarantee of payoff. The night ahead of them would be a long one.

CHAPTER TWENTY-EIGHT

"Harper's down for the count," Shel proudly announced when she reentered the living room of Addison's home. "It took three reads of *The Little Engine that Could*, but she's finally asleep."

Addison had abandoned the easel and was now seated, hunched over the tiny kitchen table. Shel was only just noticing how frustrated she looked.

"What's wrong? You need more coffee?" Shel started toward the kitchen counter which now held the coffee machine she'd robbed out of her own rental house. "I can get you anything you'd like."

"I must say, you're a lot more pleasant to forge for than my ex," Addison said, raising smiling eyes to her girlfriend.

Shel grimaced. "Please don't…" Her painful-sounding voice trailed off. She shook her head. "This is for a good cause—the very best. We'll never, ever do this again."

"I know." Addison's eyes returned to the paper laid out before her. "I'm struggling with some of the finer points. I think I'm just so tired."

"I know," Shel quickly acknowledged. She took a seat next to her, shrugged and quietly said, "If there was anything I could do to help, I would."

"I know you would." Addison grinned at her in the semi-dark house, another issue that wasn't positively contributing to the extensive process. "We're only on number three. I need a break."

"Take a break," Shel said, secretly hoping it wouldn't be a long one.

"Can you go over this plan of yours again?" Addison sounded less than hopeful and Shel wondered if it was just tiredness. She prayed it was. "I just need time to get used to it. The idea of seeing him again…"

"I know, honey," Shel said. She cupped her fingertips over her lips for several minutes, deep in thought. At last she spoke. "It depends upon what kind of cooperation Milford can get us, but you'll be wired when you pay him a surprise visit. You'll appeal to his ego, tell him you've had a taste of the real world and you realize how good you had it."

"He won't buy that."

"That's when you show him your bag of money."

"That I don't have," Addison quickly put in.

Shel half-heartedly nodded. "You'll have…something."

"It better be real money because Richard doesn't know much about detecting fake art, but he knows everything about real money."

"I can appreciate that, thank you," Shel quietly said. It had been on her mind constantly. She continued, "I have a little bit of money, not much, but it's in hundred-dollar bills in a backpack at home."

"Why?"

"I don't trust banks." She neglected to mention that the money also belonged to her ex. She continued, "I'm thinking we can band bundles of ones with hundred dollar-bills on the tops."

"He'll flip right through it," Addison quickly interjected.

"The stack you hand him will be solid hundreds. You'll give him a peek of the rest, but nothing more. You'll tell him the rest is somewhere else—the same place you're keeping Harper. That's your leverage."

"This is a long shot."

"This whole plan is built on long shots. Let's not focus on that aspect of things." Shel felt troubled, but continued. "You'll give him the money then you'll show him the drawings which won't speak to their value as much as it will to your willingness to keep up his ridiculous charade. Your drawings are nothing without his document skills and you'll tell him that you need him. That should appease his fucked-up ego."

"He does want me to need him," Addison quietly confessed. "I think if I'd have acted needier for him, I could have escaped some of his beatings."

Shel internally cringed, but tried not to let it sidetrack her from their plan.

"Hopefully, he'll buy the story, see the drawings and money— plus he's got his pretty wife back—maybe he'll see it as a winning package. You know Fortier better than I do."

Addison tipped her head slightly, a look of confusion coming to her face. "How do you know his last name?"

Shel's heart nearly stopped and she wondered if her luck had reached the end of the line. She blinked, smiled, stammered, "Y-you told me."

"I didn't."

"Honey, that first night with the wine…" Shel chuckled, more nervously than convincingly. "You told me a *lot*."

Addison seemed to consider this. She seemed to relax some. "Go on."

Still perturbed about her doubtful expression, Shel forged ahead with gusto. "If anything goes wrong, we'll be nearby."

"Who? Can we count on the cops or the FBI?"

"At very least you can count on Milford and you can definitely count on me." Shel leaned close to her, whispered, "Please know you can count on me."

"I do," she whispered back.

"Good," Shel said. She kissed her. "Good."

Their kissing escalated until they parted breathless. Shel collected the art tools with businesslike precision, neatly placing them on the kitchen countertop. She switched off the overhead light, leaving the room to the dim shadowy glow of the hallway nightlight. She patted the tabletop. "Come here."

Addison obediently did as she was told, gently perching her bottom on the wooden edge, waiting. Shel wrapped her arms around her, kissed her deeply. When their lips again parted, Shel sat down in the chair, quietly moving it close until she could nestle her face in her lover's bosom. She kissed her there, slowly unbuttoning the paint shirt and shoving it down Addison's bare shoulders. She gazed lovingly at the woman's beauty.

"Trust me," she whispered. Addison nodded. Shel gently lifted and placed the palms of Addison's hands on the tops of Shel's thighs. She parted her legs in order to pull her close as possible, kissing everything within her reach—breasts, neck, belly, breasts again. Shel slipped a hand under Addison's bottom and was pleased to find she was wet.

They kissed slowly, deeply, all the while with Shel flicking teasing circles with her fingertips, not fully entering her. Addison's movement against her grew more purposeful, leaning against the heel of Shel's steady hand.

"Come to me," Shel whispered. "Trust yourself to let go."

Addison's eyes closed, her rhythm slowed, her movement more thoughtful. Shel watched as each breath brought a sense of renewed trust, evidenced by the slow-growing intensity with every thrust. In moments she tensed and her stomach visibly quivered. Her breath caught, frozen until a small cry of release emerged from her lips until the last hard-earned orgasmic ripple passed through her. An invisible cloud of trust and love wound around them as Shel pulled her closer still. Addison's body pitched forward, softly collapsing. Weeping, she rested her cheek against Shel's shoulder.

"I've got you. I'm here," Shel whispered.

After several minutes, she clasped her hand and assisted her down from the table. Thoughts of artwork long forgotten, she led Addison to the couch and shook out two soft throws draped there.

"This will work. You'll be safe," she whispered. "I will keep you both safe. You'll see."

With Addison curled against her side, they fell asleep in a nest of blankets.

* * *

A pounding on the front door awakened them too early. Shel leapt up, realized she was only partially clothed, and scrambled to assemble her wardrobe. Addison did the same behind her as Shel opened the front door as much as the chain guard would allow. It was Milford.

"What time is it?" Shel asked.

"Early," Milford grunted. She glanced over her shoulder at the empty green house across the street. "Are we playing musical houses?"

Shel closed and unchained the door to let the cop inside, but she didn't leave the doorstep. In a gruff whisper, she said, "I need to talk to you. Pronto."

"Alone?" Shel was simultaneously surprised and concerned.

"I have to get back to the station for roll call. Meet me on the patio of the Palm Pub in half an hour."

"Palm Pub…" Shel looked confused as to why she was meeting her at a bar.

"Away from eyes and ears," Milford told her. She started away, but turned back and locked eyes with Shel. Her expression was deadly serious. "Those girls go nowhere today, you hear? Not school, not work."

Shel's stomach bottomed out as she heard herself say, "Understood."

She closed the door and turned to see Addison setting up her artwork at the table. Shel went to her, wrapped her in a surprisingly tight hug and whispered, "I have to go somewhere. Do something for me, no questions asked, promise?"

Addison drew back slightly to see her girlfriend's troubled expression. "Okay."

"Stay home today and don't take Harper to daycare." Shel touched her chin. "Work from home. Promise me?"

It appeared for a moment as though Addison had planned to protest, but the look on Shel's face instead had her agreeing. "Okay."

"That's my girl," Shel whispered, pressing a kiss on her forehead. She glanced at her watch. "I'll be back as soon as possible."

Shel hugged her tightly once more before heading to the door. She turned with one last plea. "Promise me?"

Addison nodded and watched her go.

* * *

Early as it was, the Palm Pub was still closed and Shel wondered why Milford would pick the place for their meeting. She selected a seat on the empty back patio and waited. Minutes later, Milford showed up bearing cups of coffee. She set one in front of Shel before taking a seat.

Shel's hands were unusually clammy and the coffee cup felt oddly hot against them. Milford peeled her plastic lid off and began dumping packets of sweetener in her cup. "We've got problems."

Shel didn't answer, only nodded for her to continue.

"I know you're having a good time across the street in la-la land and all, but your girl is in trouble. A BOLO came across my desk today for Kathleen Fortier out of Louisiana. Kidnapping and extortion, believed to have fled to Florida." She paused long enough to take a sip of coffee that was obviously too hot. She grimaced then continued. "Won't be long before somebody recognizes a pretty face like hers. Interstate, federal offense—this is big-time."

"I've got to get her out of here," Shel numbly said. She wiped the white out of the corners of her mouth. Her eyes darted from side to side. She wondered if they were truly alone.

"Kid, listen to me. She can change her name and address as many times as she wants, but she can't change a fingerprint. She'll never own anything—not a house or a car or—"

"I've thought of all that. I can find a way."

"Get real." Milford found herself glancing around the vacant patio as well, her paranoia a reaction to Shel's. "I hate to rain on your love parade, but what if she really is the nutjob her old man claims she is? Meanwhile, I find no real evidence against this Fortier guy. It's not looking good."

"What about the underground network. You said they could be subpoenaed."

"They can't offer a qualified opinion about her mental health." Milford squared with her, shrugged. "Reality is that anyone with a good enough sob story can get into one of those networks. We both know it."

"And the dead clerk?" Shel was grasping. "Coincidence?"

"Only he knows for sure, and he's obviously not going to corroborate her story."

"But the paintings and the anonymous money showing up—"

"Where's your proof? It's called anonymous for a reason. Now, you know how hard we've been trying to cobble a reasonable theory, but maybe there isn't one. I hate to be the one to spell it out, but mentally off folks are very manipulative." Milford's tone dropped and she refused to release Shel from her stare. "And before you cite her obvious change in income, know that crazy people need attention more than they need money."

Shel's gaze locked with hers. "What about my instincts."

"You sure your instincts aren't slightly tainted right now? It's an attractive package, I admit, but you're one of those types who want to swoop in and save the day, no offense."

She rubbed the creases in her forehead, felt a headache coming on. "You say her picture is circulating?"

Milford nodded. "I wasn't even looking for it."

"Anything else?"

"Isn't that enough?" Milford asked. She looked exasperated for her friend. "Look, kid, so you didn't get your payday and you didn't get your happy ending, but it's not all bad. You got the heck outta Shreveport. Get yourself a job, pay your taxes, start over on the up and up with the world. I'll handle Addison or Kathleen—whoever she is—from here. It's off you. This is a brand of distressed damsel you can do without, no offense."

"And if I choose not to?" Then, although a clarification was wholly unnecessary, she added, "I…like her."

It felt like the understatement of the year.

"Do we really need to have that conversation? All the like in the world can't change a person's guilt or innocence. It is what it is." Milford sat up straight. "Naturally I'm obligated to uphold the law, so call this a little courtesy between friends. I'm decent like that."

Shel hadn't touched her coffee, she felt dazed. "I need some time to think. Can you give me a couple of hours?"

"You're going to run for it, aren't you?" For the moment, Milford looked like she hated herself. Her internal conflict was obvious. "I'll give you until five. I'll stop by for your answer. If you're gone, I'll know what it is."

"I know this goes against everything you believe in, Milford," Shel muttered. She ran her hands through her hair. Her eyes were unfocused when she looked at the cop again. "I know that."

Milford spared her the lecture. She only nodded and stood, dropped her cup in a nearby garbage receptacle and left.

* * *

Shel steered her car into the circular driveway in front of her green rental house. During the short drive home, she'd considered a multitude of possibilities, from Fortier having cops in his pocket to the wealthy fraud pulling off a good sob story about his ex kidnapping their child. Or was the sob story hers, as Milford hinted it could be? Either way, there was no way getting around the fact that Addison had kidnapped Harper from her biological father. She mentally abandoned the plan to have Addison help her get a confession out of Fortier. Now that the cards were stacked in his favor, it seemed like an impossible idea.

With a head full of bad notions and worse options, she readied her house key, but the door was already slightly ajar. Shel toed it the rest of the way open and took a cautious step into the foyer.

"It's me." Addison's voice came from the vicinity of the living room. Shel's shoulders slumped with her deep sigh of relief as she rounded the corner. Addison was waiting for her return, sitting primly on the couch in her sweet knee-skimming sundress. At her feet was the original Kathleen Fortier painting that Shel had purchased from the Loyola art sale in New Orleans. Lying on her lap was Shel's Glock. Suddenly it seemed Shel had everything to worry about. Her eyes met Addison's.

"Welcome home, dear."

CHAPTER TWENTY-NINE

Shel made two strides toward the couch, but slowed dramatically when she saw Addison's hand move to the gun lying on her lap.

"This looks bad." Shel's preemptive effort sounded weak.

"It really does look bad." Addison nodded then went quiet. Her gaze alternated from the painting to the gun to Shel, and back to the painting again. Her voice was monotone. "I cannot argue that."

"Please let me explain." Shel took a smaller, more cautious step toward her. Addison seemed too preoccupied with her own thoughts to process Shel's words. "May I, please?"

"When you called him Fortier, that was my first clue. I knew I hadn't told you his last name, wine or no wine. You live the kind of life I have, and you keep very careful track of what you're saying." She looked contemplative. "Of course there was a possibility you'd done research, drawn your own conclusions, that sort of thing. I wanted so badly to believe you could be trusted."

Her words felt like physical pain. "Addison, please—"

"I told myself it would be okay to trust you. Never mind you'd moved across the street from us in the dead of summer or that you'd made radical efforts to insert yourself into our lives." She shrugged.

"I told myself you were nosy. Later I thought you liked me. How naïve of me."

"I do like you," Shel put in. "I *more* than like you."

"Stop insulting me, please." Addison raised her hand as if she could physically halt Shel's words. "I found the papers…" Her voice momentarily trailed off and when their eyes again met, Addison's were watery with tears. "I found everything."

"That is how it started out, I admit that—but it's not that way now, I swear." Shel's tone was pleading when she asked her, "I'm firmly on your side here. Can't you tell how I feel about you?"

"As I've already explained, I'm not real good at…people things." Addison swiped away a tear that rolled down her cheek. Though clearly rattled at the breadth of the deception, she was remarkably calm. "I was very honest with you and you neglected to mention that you'd been hired by my ex to find me and Harper. It's hard to let go of a thing like that."

"I've been trying to think of a way to tell you without scaring the hell out of you or causing you to run," Shel earnestly told her. "Everything I'd been told about you seemed wrong. It *felt* wrong. I decided to hang around and decide for myself. Then I met you and fell in love."

"You don't have to lie anymore."

Shel took a step closer, whispered, "I am in love with you, Addison. Put yourself in my situation—can you think of a good way I could have told you any of this?"

"Any way at all at any time, really," Addison flatly said. Her eyes looked hard like they had when Shel first met her. "I gave you my trust. It's the ultimate deception."

"I know that and I'm so, so sorry. I swear I only want to help you and Harper." Shel took another step, was almost standing directly in front of Addison. "I understand if you don't ever want to see me again, I do—but *please* let me help you."

Shel took another step, but that was as close as Addison wanted her, evidenced by the way her index finger began rapidly tracing the gun's trigger.

"What a mess," Addison quietly lamented. She appeared to consider everything with a calmness that was extraordinary considering what she'd been through. During the silence that followed, expressions that hinted self-doubt and indecisiveness crossed her features, creating an ebb and flow in the dark atmosphere. It was like watching clouds blowing in front of a bright moon. Shel willed herself to remain patient, tamping down the anxiety that was peaking and falling inside her in rhythm to Addison's changing expressions. She dared not move, ever aware of her finger on the gun and the consequences that would arise should one of those poor moods decide to carry her away.

At last she raised her gaze to meet Shel's.

"I worked hard to get us here and now look what you've done." She sounded unnervingly aloof, but not necessarily homicidal… "You've ruined everything."

"Baby, please don't do this," Shel quietly begged of her. "Please."

"I have no choice. We have to start all over again."

"He'll find you. He always does." Shel's chest felt like it would explode and she wondered if she was having a panic attack or heart attack. Without Addison in her life, she would prefer the latter; she knew that now. "Please, please let me help."

"You've done plenty." Addison lifted the gun and pointed it at Shel. "It's over."

CHAPTER THIRTY

Milford paced the semi-circular driveway in front of Shel's rental house. She would stop periodically to check her watch, sigh and curse under her breath. It was nearly five thirty and her guy with his warrant for Kathleen Fortier's arrest had yet to show. For the fourth time in twenty minutes, she pressed the button on her radio and didn't attempt to hide her aggravation.

"Six-oh-one, what's your twenty?" When no answer came, she tried elsewhere. "Dispatch, this is five-ten on location. You got a twenty on my paperwork?"

"En route."

"My ass. Rookie," Milford muttered off radio. The plan had been to meet Officer Jake Miller at the residence, and together they would take Kathleen into custody. He was late and she was impatient. She moved to pop the top button of her uniform blues. She'd sweated clear through in the past half hour waddling and swearing in the late afternoon Florida heat.

She'd already hammered at the door of the yellow house and peered under the shutters. The place looked abandoned. She'd crossed the street to Shel's rental, but again no answer. Disgusted, she guessed Shel had made her choice. For some reason, Milford had sincerely believed it would be the right one.

"Wrong again," Milford angrily chastised herself aloud. She returned to the front door and pounded on it again. She'd already tried the back entrance, and though she wasn't to enter the premises—especially without backup—she'd tried both locked doors just in case.

The window on the front door was too high for Milford to get a look and the overgrown shrubbery situated before the windows wouldn't make taking a peek inside easy.

"Damn you, girl," she said, as if Shel could possibly hear her. Milford took a heavy step down from the cement stoop and leaned her body against the closest shrub that turned out to be as thorny as it was dense. It dipped low with her weight, giving her a painful, albeit decent look into the living room. "Damn you anyway."

Milford's sleeve snagged on a thorny branch and she was struggling to get it free when she saw movement against the far wall. After much blinking to focus through the glare of the glass, she saw the cat perched on the arm of the couch. While Milford knew it was highly probable that Shel could run with Addison and the baby, she couldn't imagine the woman dragging the cat around the country only to abandon the animal in Naples.

She followed the cat's gaze downward and saw feet wearing shoes she recognized by now. Milford couldn't swallow.

The cop quickly back-pedaled her way out of the thick, thorny bush, nearly losing her balance. She caught herself, scraping her ankle against the rough cement stoop in the process.

"Code two!" Milford practically spat into the walkie. "Code two—did you copy? Possible ten-fifty-nine. Need backup, *now*."

She didn't have to list every code that could apply to this situation—hostage, ambulance, kidnapping—and she certainly didn't want to entertain the notion there could be victims. Waiting for dispatch had her itchy.

Fueled by the adrenaline rush sweeping through her, Milford threw open the flimsy screen door and made a quick evaluation of the older wooden door behind it. Squaring her wide hips, she solidly kicked the door beneath the knob until the frame splintered and separated. The door burst open, swung wide and struck the adjacent wall with enough velocity to send bits of plaster flying.

Leading with her gun, Milford quickly cleared the empty rooms before returning to the living room. She grimaced, her heart in her throat as she approached the base of the couch where Shel lay in a heap. Her hands and feet were tightly bound by leather belts, her mouth silenced by a knotted T-shirt, wide eyes straining to see the cop over an oversized makeshift gag.

Milford breathed an audible sigh of relief then dropped to her knees before Shel. She slid the soft, bulky gag roughly over Shel's head disregarding both her ears and the hair that was knotted into the tie. Shel winced in pain, but only coughed for several seconds. Milford next went to work unbuckling the woman's arms.

"Hold the hell still," Milford quietly reprimanded her.

When she was free, Shel leaned against the couch rubbing the welts on her wrists, still coughing.

"I thought you were dead," Milford told her.

"Disappointed?" Shel barely glanced at her before going to work at the buckle on the belt binding her ankles. "She's gone."

"I figured you were too," Milford said quietly. "Frankly, I'm proud of you."

"Well, I was tied up," Shel admitted. She unfastened the belt, threw it aside.

"Got sick of waiting for that nincompoop kid-cop to meet me at the station. I came ahead and he didn't even show with the warrant, dammit anyway. I had momentary visions of me trying to strap you across the seat of my bike to haul you off to the ER. I'll throttle that kid—I will." Flustered, Milford pressed the button on her radio, but only static sounded down the line. She glanced at Shel who was now rubbing sore, welted ankles. "I can't believe you let her tie you up like that. She stronger than she looks?"

"She had my gun."

"You weren't seriously worried she would actually hit you?" Milford didn't wait for her response. "When did she go?"

"Around noon." Shel slowly stood and took a few wobbly steps, cringing all the way. "I think she went to be reinserted back into the system. She mentioned starting over again. I've got to find her. I'm going to Winston's house. She was…rambling. She said that's where she was going. He must be the one on the Naples end of this operation."

"Wait—you can't do that," Milford firmly told her. "You can't storm some wealthy guy's castle and demand the whereabouts of one of the people his group won't even admit to harboring. Now you need to leave it to us."

"Milford, the cops haven't done right by her in the past. Why should things be any different now?" She limped toward her bedroom, but the cop was hot on her heels.

"Do you hear yourself? The woman tied you up…" She paused to glance at her watch, "nearly six hours ago and left you. What if I hadn't come along?"

"But she knew you would and so did I." Shel found her paperwork scattered all over her bed. She sighed. "God—it might not even be in here now. She took a lot of stuff. She found everything."

"Sounds like she had a busy morning." Milford dryly remarked. She folded her arms in front of her. "And so now you wanna just take off, like some kind of Lone Ranger, searching the countryside until you find her? Pray tell, who's financing this leg of the journey— Fortier?"

"Maybe I can stop her before she goes." Shel madly rifled through the paperwork, her frustration increasing at knowing that Addison had removed virtually every important piece of information she'd collected. She muttered, "I need Winston's address."

"I don't get it," Milford muttered. "Do you know how crazy this sounds?"

Shel angrily spun around to face the cop. "I love her. I love her and I trust her."

Caught off guard, Milford went silent.

She then snagged a familiar yellow note that had been floating in a chaotic sea of paperwork. It had Winston's address scribbled on it. "In my gut I know she's good. I can feel it." Shel crammed the note in her jeans pocket and turned to face the cop. "Now I'm going to find her with or without your help."

Milford reached around to her side and tugged something on her belt.

"Handcuffs?" Shel's tone was terse and her arms slapped down to her sides at the jangling noise. "If you're planning to arrest me, you should know I'm planning to resist."

Milford surprised her by unfastening and dropping a key on the bed in front of her. "My personal piece is under the seat."

"Milford…" Shel sputtered, shook her head. It was an unprecedented gesture.

"Get going, already. When the dust settles they'll remember I didn't have my bike and that will spell trouble for you." A siren could be heard in the distance, but Shel only stood staring at her. Milford raised her voice. "Get yourself in hot water and I'll swear you stole it all. Do *not* screw me over."

Shel didn't understand, but didn't ask questions. She snatched up the key and bolted for the door. She'd only barely gotten her bearings on the bike when a patrol car whizzed past her. In the side view mirror she watched it come in for a landing in the driveway of her rental house. She drove.

CHAPTER THIRTY-ONE

The old two-lane bridge leading to Pine Island was teeming with early evening anglers, sipping from brown paper bags, casting lines into the water below. A rustic sign posted on the roadside told her she was in Matlacha, which appeared to be an artsy little town, judging by the colorful cottage shops and tiny hotels overlooking the water.

Slowly, she steered the rumbling bike past fishermen lugging poles and gears, past meandering tourists in wide-brimmed hats. She passed old fishing shacks that had been revitalized into brightly painted art galleries, bars and tourist traps, each with a front yard boasting elaborate, vibrant artistic spectacle. One such display was a stunning glass bottle garden glinting in the remaining sunlight. Mesmerized, Shel looked away from the road too long, nearly colliding with a group of late day dog walkers suddenly in front of her. She hit the brake hard, hard killing the engine.

Shel nodded her apology toward the group, restarted the bike then checked the yellow note she'd tucked into her jeans pocket. Following the scribbled instructions, she turned sharply onto a dusty gravel path and aimed the bike toward the outskirts of Matlacha.

After a mile of nothing more than evenly dust-coated clumps of palms, the road narrowed precariously, almost disappearing under canopies of banyan trees with low, drooping branches. Only when she was about to turn around and go back to town for clarification did she spy a hint of a house through thick, tropical foliage. She continued along the winding trail that ended next to a two-story pale blue beach compound. Six security signs boldly posted around the driveway interrupted the otherwise natural environment. Shel parked, pulled the helmet off her sweaty head, and secured it on the bike seat. She headed up the path toward the house, knocked on the front door.

Balmy breezes smelling of salt and mildew tickled sweat-damp hair and cooled her head. She relished the modicum of relief until she heard the door unlocking. When it was open, Silvia Frances stood in the doorway.

Each woman simultaneously recognized the other; both were taken aback.

"Miss Frances?" It was a needless question. "I-I was under the impression that Steven Winston lives here."

"May I ask how you got this address?" Silvia's forced politeness hardly masked her chilly tone. Clearly she wasn't thrilled to see Shel—perhaps anyone—on her doorstep.

"Do you know Mr. Winston?" Sweat ran down the back of her neck and arms, stinging her abraded wrists. Shel was tired of the day and every surprise and antic that had come along with it. With more exasperation than curiosity, she asked, "Are you his tenant?"

A figure appeared at her side, a taller, considerably older, silver-haired gentleman with smiling eyes. His grin was cordial and his tone indicated his gentle demeanor. "I'm Mr. Winston. Is there a problem?"

"Steven, this is a woman I met at an art fair. She's about to tell us why she is here." Dressed as she was in evening pants and a thin jacket, her cocoa curls were still perfect no matter how casual her attire. Her posture remained defensive.

Steven Winston politely asked her, "How can we help you, Miss…"

"Shel Carson. I'm here about Kathleen Fortier, a woman in your network." She looked from Steven to Silvia. "Also known as Addison James, I believe you're familiar."

"I represent Ms. James's interests in the art world, not her private life." Silvia forced a phony smile designed to quickly appease then dismiss Shel. "And I'm not acquainted with the other woman you mentioned."

"Kathleen and Addison are the same person," Shel unnecessarily clarified. She shook her head. "Look, I just need to find her. She's in danger."

"If my wife says she doesn't know who this Kathleen woman is, then she does not."

"Your wife," Shel quietly repeated, digesting the information. "I appreciate your rules about confidentiality, but this is an emergency."

"I'm afraid we can't help you." Winston started to take a backward step, his hand on the doorknob.

"Wait." Shel abruptly stopped the door from closing with a stiff arm. Seeing their surprised expressions, she quickly removed her hand from the door. "I know you're running the program for abused women, and I know Kathleen—*Addison*—came to you today to be reinserted into the system."

"I have no idea what you're talking about." But it was apparent that he did. Suddenly, his smile was gone and so was his mood for conversation. He touched something on the foyer wall panel then placed a protective arm around Silvia's waist, shooting Shel a look of warning. "I've just alerted security. You should go."

"I need to know where she is." The desperation in Shel's voice was obvious. "Her ex has been tracking her—"

"Goodbye," Silvia firmly said.

"Richard Fortier wants his wife back and he won't let anyone get in his way! I can help her." Shel looked frantic as she reiterated, "I need to find her, *now*."

Husband and wife looked at each other for several seconds. It seemed they reached the same unspoken decision.

"We're done here," Winston calmly announced.

A familiar toddler's voice was heard coming from inside the house. Shel's pulse quickened, her eyes widened. "She's here?"

Shel's relief was erased before it could set in. Silvia looked troubled. For the second time that day, the sound of sirens could be heard in the distance.

"No," Silvia said at last, her eyes locking on Shel's. "I'm afraid she's not."

"But Harper—"

"The police are on their way," Winston said unnecessarily.

Silvia seemed to disregard his statement. Her eyes held a faraway look and when she spoke her voice was low, haunted. "It's always the same story. Nobody can believe that a wealthy, handsome, charismatic man could beat his family."

"Sweetheart—" Winston attempted to intervene.

Silvia touched his chest, dissuading his polite interruption. Two police cruisers came onto the property, stirring up a dust cloud as they sped toward the house. Silvia didn't seem to notice. She droned on in her sudden listless tone. "Salt of the earth pillar of the community are Teflon-coated. Nobody can touch them."

"Richard Fortier is looking for Addison." Shel turned compassionate. "I want to find her first."

"She went after him," Silvia confessed. "She left Harper—said to take care of her if she doesn't return."

"When did she go?"

The cops were now out of their cars and headed up the sidewalk toward them. Given their quick response Shel knew the child was in the safe hands of caring people. At the same time, she worried that any interference by cops could hold her up, causing her to lose even more precious time. As she was trying to figure a way out of her potential jam, Silvia made a cool halting motion toward the officers. They abruptly stopped, hands touching gun belts at the ready. Respectfully, they hung back.

Silvia spoke quickly, her voice low. "At noon she brought Harper to school. I brought the child straight home with me."

To be clear, Shel stated, "She went to New Orleans."

Silvia nodded. "She had a car."

"Thank you."

"These guys are as devious as they are rich and powerful." Silvia's eyes contained a hopeless look. "You don't know what you're up against."

Shel had started down the front steps, but turned to give her one last look. "I'm beginning to."

Shel pushed between the cops and headed for Milford's bike.

* * *

Shel drove back to the main road, pulled into the parking lot of the CVS. Ten minutes and twenty bucks later, Shel was the owner of a disposable phone. The kid at the counter had activated it for her. She checked the same slip of paper with the directions which also had Milford's number scribbled on it. The cop picked up within two rings.

"Milford, it's me."

"You find 'em?"

"Only Harper." Shel quieted some as several waves of fishermen walked toward the bridge toting Styrofoam coolers and poles. "Silvia Frances says Addison is headed for New Orleans by car."

"Silvia? The preschool—"

"Yes. She's married to Winston," Shel hurriedly filled in the blanks. "The kid is safe, but Addison's got a head start on me by at least…" Shel glanced at the clock on the chapel across the street, rubbed her eyes. "Six hours."

"You better fly."

"I could go a hundred and not catch up to her at this point."

"Not on my bike. You still on the Island?"

"Yes."

"Get back on the main road, drive deeper in for several miles. At Pine Island Center you'll hang a right. Follow the signs for the airport."

Shel squinted, glanced around. "This place has an airport?"

"More like an airstrip," Milford clarified. "Get yourself there. My friend Dina will be waiting for you. Don't dally—she doesn't see too well to fly at night."

Shel quickly processed her directions as she toed the bike toward the driveway.

"Stay under the radar, and I mean that," Milford went on, sounding as frustrated as Shel felt. "They swept your house. Everyone's looking for you. Word must not have reached the island or the cops wouldn't have let you go."

"Great."

"Also, they took your phone. You're officially popping up as a person of interest. We shouldn't even be having this conversation."

It didn't mean she was a suspect, but it wasn't good either. "Thanks for the heads-up."

"Fly there before you get caught in any number of nets, and be careful. If you get caught with my stuff—"

"Stolen. Gotcha." Shel flipped the bike's toggle. "I'll watch myself."

"Found Addison and her ex's picture in the society pages of an old *Times-Picayune* at the library. I've requested one of those fancy face matches. I hope Fortier is the only one I find in the system."

So did Shel.

"Leave my bike at Dina's." Milford was quiet for a second. "Be sure to come back in one piece."

"Thanks, Milford. For everything."

Shel ended the call and shoved the phone into her jeans pocket. She flipped the cover down on the helmet and pulled out of the CVS parking lot and drove deeper into the island.

CHAPTER THIRTY-TWO

Bucky couldn't believe his good luck.

Just when he'd figured Shel Carson had tossed that mobile phone into a Dumpster, it suddenly resurfaced. He stared at the screen on his laptop, watched its hidden GPS tracking app pinging away in Naples, Florida.

As he knew Carson had been spending a lot of Fortier's money in that general area of the state, he figured she'd zeroed in on Kathleen Fortier's location. Now it seemed Carson was on the fence about turning her in.

Finally he had her coordinates. He'd fueled up his vehicle and brought a duffel bag, not for toiletries and clothing, but for his money he intended to bring home with him.

It was a plus that a friend had successfully hacked the Naples Police computer and placed Mrs. Fortier's photo and information in a BOLO status. It was a risky move on his part, but now if the woman so much as went to the grocery store, a cop would recognize her. Having thoroughly papered the NOPD with mental health "documents" about her special case, she'd be handled with kid gloves, as society women often were. As her personal attorney,

Bucky would be notified the moment she was taken into custody. Pick up or delivery, either way, it was almost over for Kathleen Fortier. He was so close to his money, he could feel it.

There was a lot to be said for the power an attorney could wield. The respect—and women—they easily got was certainly another perk. Bucky was happier than ever that his first prison break visit had been paid to his own rotten attorney. Only a couple of years before, the loser of a lawyer had begrudgingly taken Bucky's case as a pro bono job. The sloppy drunk could hardly be called a coping alcoholic. He couldn't even hold his shit together for two measly jail visits paid to his client. Then came a lackluster trial and Bucky went away.

Then Bucky came back and his lawyer went away. Permanently.

To the outside world, it appeared the hermit-like drunk had cleaned up his act, got a personality, a new lease on life, a spring in his step…That he seemed like an entirely different person came down to one simple fact: he was. Over the course of a few months, after a visit to a world-class plastic surgeon, hair color and contacts, Bucky had become his own lawyer. His actual lawyer was in the ground, layers beneath a flower bed that was home to his prizewinning petunias. He delighted in showing them off to anyone who paid him a visit. To Bucky it seemed that the attorney had achieved more dead than he ever had alive.

Bucky had studied enough law—and had been in trouble often enough—that he had a real understanding of the system. He'd be the first to admit to his inner circle colleagues that he lent real truth to most of the jokes about dumb lawyers. The friends would laugh, tell him he was full of nonsense, and that he was quite brilliant and charming. Because he was. Considering his former roster of fellow travelers, Bucky had come a long way. Most of his old friend set were druggies, thugs and common hustlers who operated stupidly and carelessly, usually ending up in the pen or dead. Bucky was made for better than the likes of them and so was Richard Fortier. Together they'd risen from bottom feeder status to that of Carnival Kings in their New Orleans palaces. Their friendship had proven to be both long lasting and profitable.

Fortier had a good head on his shoulders and some mad forgery skills; he also had special problems that required careful handling. Bucky was the only one he trusted for all things lawyering and nonlawyering. He'd be lying if he didn't acknowledge that Kathleen had been an integral part of their mutual success, but even a useful partner becomes a dead one when she steals your loot. She was indeed a dead woman.

He couldn't wait to catch up with her and personally make good on that promise.

CHAPTER THIRTY-THREE

As Milford said she would be, Dina was waiting for Shel's arrival. The introductions were quick, then the reserved, gray-haired woman confidently piloted the small craft to a private landing strip in Hammond, Louisiana. From there, Shel called a cab for a ride into the city and waited for it to arrive.

It was almost ten. She'd calculated Addison's drive from Naples to New Orleans at around twelve hours given low traffic and optimum weather conditions. She figured Addison had been driving since noon. It would be a close race to see who'd arrive at the Fortier mansion first and Shel tried to ignore the multitude of what-ifs nagging at her. Particularly the biggest what-if of all: what if she was all wrong about the kind of person Addison really was?

She was restless as she waited inside an office that was actually a skeletal mobile home. She repeatedly checked her watch as Dina filled her travel mug with coffee and made small talk with the airport desk clerk.

Time and again, her thoughts went to Milford and the fact that she was running Fortier's picture through the system. That she hadn't heard anything from her friend had her wondering if the news was bad. Twice Shel had tried to call, but there was only a funny beeping sound and she wondered if she was out of tower range. Most of all, she hoped like hell that Addison's picture didn't hit a facial match in the criminal system. That would change everything.

A knock on the acrylic office window rattled the place and didn't do much for Shel's nerves. A cabbie was on the outside waving at her. Shel again thanked Dina before leaving the building and following the driver across the tarmac to his cab.

"French Quarter, right?" He saw her nod in his rearview mirror. "Any particular place?"

"I'll tell you when we get closer." She breathed a deep breath of night air. It was humid, like Naples, only heavier and fishier. She now found herself oddly longing to be safe in the little town she'd previously only considered to be a quick stop on her way to freedom. It was unsteadying how fast everything had changed in her world.

Her head ached and she closed her eyes, but only for a moment. She focused on the pain in her head if only to keep from thinking about her strained back and sore legs from having been tied up for so long. Add that to hunching over a bike then a flight in a plane so small her knees had felt like they were under her chin...

"You come in to party?" The cabbie glanced into his rearview mirror and noted her obviously distressed expression and tired-looking clothing. He didn't bother her again, only aimed the cab toward Ponchartrain Bridge and quietly drove.

The cabbie dropped her at Hotel Le Richelieu where Shel made a limping jog the remaining two blocks to the Fortier mansion. Dodging a few rambling revelers, she was out of breath by the time she arrived on the doorstep of the iconic building. Gas lamps uniformly dotting the slate gray exterior whirred and glowed completing the eerie atmosphere, making her feel as if she'd stepped back in time or off a postcard. Yellow light emanated from a row of windows, second story of the looming fortress.

The wrought ironwork gate designed to lend extra protection to the entrance was hanging ajar. She nudged through the gate and gingerly knocked on the massive door, surveying her surroundings as she waited. A tall cement planter situated at one side of the doorway nearly masked the modern key and touchscreen behind it.

Her gaze wandered upward, following the cement walls until they came together in an ornate archway of exquisitely detailed plaster rosettes, but to her surprise she saw no camera. Her heart pounded and her head prattled interminably as she clutched the heavy door handle. Thoughts of deadbolts and a blaring alarm system quickly dissipated when the door easily opened. Her stomach bottomed out as she considered the reasons the door would be unlocked and unarmed at this hour. Throwing a cautionary glance over her shoulder, she quietly slipped inside.

She stopped inside the foyer, acclimating herself to the dark interior. No blips or beeps sounded to show the place was alarmed, considerably different from the bells and whistles she'd witnessed during her first visit to the mansion, evidence beyond just her own jitters that something was wrong. That Addison could easily have the key and the codes told her the woman was already there.

Shel drew her borrowed gun. Guided by occasional flickering wall-mounted torch lights, she softly scooted along smooth floors, avoiding looking at Fortier's prized paintings, dreadful scenes that still haunted her memory. In such dim light they would surely appear even more horrific. She felt for her footing carefully as she took each step, determined to get to the floor with the lighted rooms. When she reached the second level she heard a pair of familiar voices. Shel readied her gun as she listened to their escalating conversation.

"I want out," Addison could be heard saying.

"Oh, you're out—out of your mind." It was Fortier's voice. "Kathleen, I gave you a nice life and home, and the opportunity to do the very work you love."

"I'll do whatever it takes to keep you away from us."

Shel intended only to gently nudge the door, but it creaked, loudly announcing her presence. Fortier, dressed in a silk robe and pants, was seated on the couch. Addison stood inches away, her trembling hands tightly gripping the hijacked gun. Given the woman's obvious agitated state and the fact that her rattled aim was trained directly on him, Fortier appeared remarkably calm. Both heads turned her direction as Shel stepped inside the room, Milford's gun in front of her.

"Addison, I've got this," she quietly said.

"Addison?" Fortier's slow-growing smile showed his amusement. He turned in his seat and extended his hand, mocking her in his intense southern drawl. "Why, I don't believe we've had the pleasure, Miss Addison."

She ignored his sarcasm. "It's over, Richard."

"I believe it is over, my lovely estranged—and apparently deranged—wife."

"Cut the act, Fortier," Shel warned. Her demeanor softened when she addressed Addison. "Give me the gun."

"Frankly, Ms. Carson, I have grave concerns regarding your loyalty."

It seemed an earnest statement. While it was clear he didn't believe Addison's threat that she would—or could—shoot him, he appeared on the fence about Shel's intentions. "You can clearly see that my wife isn't of sound mind, can't you?"

"I'm not your wife." Addison's eyes flicked toward Shel then quickly away. "You shouldn't have come here."

"I'm sorry I didn't tell you the truth." Shel took a cautious step toward them, kept her voice low. "I want to help."

"You don't understand—I have to do this."

Shel was nervous. Even a bad shooter could get lucky and Addison was standing perilously close to her target. The woman was tearful, but her resolve remained intact.

"Honey, this isn't the answer."

"She's unstable. I told you that when I hired you to find my daughter." Fortier played what he probably felt was his best card, and appeared disappointed that he didn't get a better reaction. "Remember? I told you she's mad out of her mind!"

Shel ignored him, focused solely on Addison. She took a closer step, held out her hand. "We'll find a different way."

"I'm sorry, no."

"Kathleen—or *Addison*—you need some help." Fortier softened his approach. "Let's get you some help, please darling."

"Stop," she said, tears freely flowing now. "Stop telling lies."

"Now be a good girl and put down the gun. It'll all work out, you'll see."

"Back off," Shel warned, shooting him a look. She studied the angle of Addison's drawn weapon, her mounting anxiety and twitchy fingertip on an already unsteady gun. Shel risked a closer step. "Focus on me, please."

Addison cast small glances her way giving Shel the smallest confirmation that she'd penetrated the woman's mania.

"Harper needs you," she gently prodded. "Think of her."

"Yes, please think of Harper," Fortier echoed her pleading tone.

"You are a thief and a liar," Addison retorted.

"Whatever you say, I forgive you."

"Forgive *me?*"

Shel watched their absurd play, the cynicism and accusations, and wondered what she'd gotten herself in the middle of. Was it possible Fortier cared for his daughter, or was he a mastermind wife-beater as Addison claimed? And was she truly desperate or truly a liar…? At the moment, both were putting on award worthy performances. Shel leaned with all her emotional might on her instincts, praying they would not fail her on this, but in the background, the pair's rapid-fire exchange needled at her self-doubt until she felt her head might burst.

"Both of you shut up!" Shel suddenly had their attention. She looked at Addison, said, "Give me the gun. *Now.*"

"No."

Fortier looked exasperated. "Call the authorities, for God's sake."

"Tell her about the art fraud and the money you stole," Addison squinted, clearly trying to better her aim. With growing conviction, she commanded, "Tell her."

"What are you talking about?" He looked genuinely befuddled. "Please, Kathleen—where is the baby?"

"Tell her about the buy offs and the loan sharks and the fake art—tell her every bit of it!"

He hesitated then calmly said, "I'll not ensnare myself in the trap of a madwoman."

"You son of a bitch," Addison muttered, looking exhausted.

"Addison, do the right thing," Shel sternly told her.

"Think of our daughter!" It was Fortier.

"I *am* thinking of my daughter."

"If you do this, Kathleen, they'll put you away for good," he stated. "You'll lose your freedom."

"You took my freedom long ago."

Shel took a closer step. "Addison—"

"Nothing you can say will stop me."

"Well then, Kathleen…" The last remnants of Fortier's pristine composure melted in front of them as did his thick put-on New Orleans accent as he leaned close, whispered, "Go fuck yourself."

Despite her trembling hands, Addison racked the Glock's slide like a pro and pressed the barrel against Fortier's temple. She sounded loose, airy. "Let's play your favorite game."

"No!" Shel trained her aim first on Addison, then Fortier, then back on Addison. She could take either one of them; she could kill the liar. She knew protocol: remove the threat. With Addison's flinching finger on the trigger of a gun pressed against his temple, he would die. She licked her lips, swallowed hard. Her hands were clammy on the grip. "Don't do this."

"Do you know he skates on everything?" Addison tapped the gun against the side of his head, emphasizing each word. "Everything! People think I'm crazy and he gets a pass."

"You are crazy." The line of perspiration over his lip glimmered in the low light as he taunted her. "Do it, Kathleen. Pull the trigger."

"Harper needs you, Addison," Shel asserted, her aim continuing to bounce between them in a hellish decision-making process. *Remove the threat.*

"This isn't an old-fashioned game of roulette, Kathleen." Fortier chuckled. "That Glock will put a hole in my head the size of a cannonball—spatter my brains everywhere. I hope you've got the stomach for that. This close up there's no room for error really, is there?"

"If anyone shoots the son of a bitch, it'll be me." Shel narrowed her gaze at him, once again retraining her aim. She repeated, "I'll do it."

"Well, Carson, you're as big a sucker as I was." He boldly grinned despite his present position. "She's setting you up for the fall. You'll sit in jail while she gallivants around the countryside looking for her next mark."

Addison shook her head, showing very real signs of losing it. "You're a liar."

"Women, Jesus Christ." Fortier now mocked them both. "Somebody fucking shoot me already."

Decision firmly made, Shel said, "Addison, step away. I'll handle him."

In a daring move, Fortier turned his head so that the barrel of Addison's gun pressed front and center to his glistening forehead. His gaze drifted upward as he commanded her, "I'd rather see you handle it. Go on, *Addison*. Fire away."

Addison squeezed the trigger, but lifted the gun at the last second, firing a shot into the far wall. It ricocheted off a ceiling beam and hit the crown molding causing plaster to rain and feather in the distance behind him. Whether the miss was intentional or not, it brought everyone to a flinching high alert.

Overcome that she'd been unable to do what she'd so badly wanted to, Addison fell to her knees. The gun clattered onto the floor in front of her.

Shel leapt to the sobbing woman, fished her mobile phone out of her pocket and dialed 911. An automated hold message came down the line, but her attention was captured by another sound. She slowly turned to see Fortier above them, her discarded gun now in his possession. She could no longer hear the words coming across the phone. Her head felt light, her feet and hands, tingly. The last time she'd let a gun get away from her, a woman and her child died. Hypnotized by her own catastrophic error, her focus slowly zoomed back in on the gun Fortier held.

"Gimme," he ordered, wagging his fingers to indicate her weapon. Disbelieving the very bad place she'd put them in, Shel had no choice but to give up her gun. He snatched it, stuck it in his robe pocket. The silk sagged under its weight. Addison had been stunned into silence, her teary eyes wide as she realized the breadth of their dire situation.

"Bet you wish you'd shot me."

Neither woman spoke or moved. He motioned for them to stand; they did.

"My little wife has no idea what happens when you fire a gun, do you, dear?"

Obviously intimidated as much by Fortier's words as the gun he held, Addison didn't budge.

"You get an invisible residue all over you—irrefutable evidence that you tried to shoot me." He cast a quick glance over his shoulder at the bits of plaster still falling. He grinned evilly. "A shitty shot for sure, but it works. Picture this—wealthy man, alone in his home, the estranged wife comes back around, firing wild shots—I did everything I could to calm you down. I had no choice but to kill. God bless the State of Louisiana and the Stand Your Ground law—amen!"

His expensive slippers scuffed through remnants of plaster as he sauntered toward them and leaned terrifyingly close to Addison. "What was it you said? I skate again. *Free pass.*"

"I already called the police." Shel tried to appear confident.

"You called nine-one-one on a disposable phone. That's a lot of towers pinging to pinpoint a single location." He tipped his head to one side, blinked. "And you were a *real* cop? Wow."

His focus came back around to Addison. "Let's get down to business. Where's my money?"

CHAPTER THIRTY-FOUR

"Well? I'm waiting." Fortier stood before them, gun pointed at Addison. "Where's the money, honey?"

"I don't have it," Addison numbly confessed.

"You don't? Well, then who does?" He walked a slow circle around the pair. "I know Bernard didn't have it. He told me before I killed him. The coach—oh, what's his name?" He paused, pretended to briefly ponder the puzzle. "Fattish guy, early 40s…?"

"Oh no…" Addison shook her head, looked at her feet. "No, no…"

"What was it he said after he came down off his tough-guy high horse?" His gazed bounced between the women. "They all say a bunch of gibberish in the end. Panic, I guess."

"He had a family!" Addison wailed.

"So did I, you rotten bitch." Fortier stepped close, his red face very near hers as he spat, "I had pretty little wife and child *and* money and you took it all!"

Addison started crying again, her chin dipped almost to her chest, her body heaving with her sobs.

"My associate tells me she's in Naples, Florida," he plainly announced. He looked at Shel, gave her a tight grin. "Thanks for that, by the way." He then looked back at Addison. "I'll get her and you can go to your grave knowing that full and well."

"No, no…" Addison quietly sobbed.

"You want to do something good for your child? What fate will you bequeath your precious Harper?" He tipped his head to one side. "Tell me where you put my money."

Shel was helpless before the sick game unfolding before her.

"I gave it away," she blurted through her tears. "I gave it back to the charity you stole it from."

Fortier took a half-step back, seemingly caught off guard. He blinked several times as the information sunk in. "The newspaper headlines. That big donation…?"

Sobbing, Addison nodded.

His snarky smile disintegrated before their eyes, giving way to an expression that rapidly cycled from disbelief to panic, then anger. He took a step back and fell into a harried pace in front of them. His angry tone rose concurrently with his volume. "*My money was their big-fat anonymous donation?*"

"Yes." Addison's own voice held a deep resignation that said the woman had quickly accepted her dark destiny. "P-please, I beg you to leave Harper alone."

Fortier ceased his pacing and spun to face her, his eyes glinting with steely hatred.

"Funny." The word seethed through his low, maniacal chuckle. "That's the last thing your godparents begged for *you*."

Shel felt her stomach bottom out as he marched toward them wielding the Glock, his purposeful eyes trained on Addison, his finger on the trigger. Behind him, the flurried fallout from the earlier misfired shot rapidly evolved into a full-fledged, vigorous snowstorm of plaster and wallpaper. At once, a symphony of creaking window casings and shattering glass hit a dreadful crescendo, showering them with a million tiny shards. The wall had exploded.

Chaos unfurled as SWAT members, their guns thrust out before them, infiltrated the library. Shouting incomprehensible commands, they encircled Shel, Addison and Fortier. Squinting against the cloudy debris, the women raised their hands in surrender as their knees hit the glass-covered floor. In seconds, Fortier also went down.

CHAPTER THIRTY-FIVE

"I got to hand it to you, that was quite a trick you pulled off."

Shel and the cop sipped beers, relaxing in the new chaises on the front porch of her little rental house. Soothing sounds of cicadas could be heard rising up in the background for their evening sonata in the otherwise quiet neighborhood.

"That's the best you got?" Milford's look bordered on insulted. "You're awfully selfish with your praise."

Shel rolled her eyes, but gave her what she had due. "You saved the day."

"For the love of Mike, don't sound so surprised. I'm not dead, I'm just in Naples." The cop took a sip of her beer, scoffed, "Think we don't ever see action in this sleepy little town? Please."

"Anyway, you saved us." Shel's gaze drifted to the house across the street, now shuttered and vacant, just as Addison had left it weeks ago. Her tone took a melancholy turn. "I'm not too sure I was all that deserving of your help, but you gave Addison a chance to start over. I'm forever grateful for that."

Milford glanced her way, then back toward the hazy orange sun dipping low in the sky over clusters of palms. Quietly she said, "Oh, you're worth it, hotshot."

As if to distract herself from all the things she didn't want to think about, Shel softly said, "Since I know you're dying to brag about it, tell me how it all went down."

"Took you long enough to ask." Milford brightened. She drained the last of her bottle, set it aside, leaned forward slightly in her chair and began to unwind her tale. "First, I found the sleazeball's picture and faxed it to Fort Myers."

"Cut to the chase, Milford," Shel interrupted her, rolling her hand with hopes of expediting the story she'd already heard in bits and pieces. "You're a super cop, you already told me."

"Sap the glory outta my story, why don't you?" Milford tried to look offended, but in truth, Shel knew she was anxious to get back to her tale. "Anyhow, a buddy of mine did an extensive computer search and bam—there's our big cheese New Orleans art honcho in prison garb, charged with theft, forgery and about half a dozen other things."

"He was in the system and nobody found him."

"He was in a system, just not ours." Milford shrugged her meaty shoulders. "He'd been flushed clean out of NCIC—Lord knows how he managed that. Fort Myers couldn't help. The savior of the hour is Lil, the Central Avenue librarian."

Shel sat up, gave Milford a good look. It was the first time she'd heard this part of the story. "Get serious."

"Yep. I'd had her look for his picture, the one I told you about in the *Picayune* society pages. Long after I was gone, she continued her search." Milford shook her head. "The woman is nothing if not persistent."

"Foiled by a librarian," Shel said, still stunned.

"And now let's get back to me," the cop said, shooting her a look. "By the time I got the word from Lil, you were already headed Fortier's way. I made a bunch of frantic calls to the Bureau who wasted more damn time cross-referencing every detail. I was sweating the time it took, I admit."

"I was sweating it," Shel admitted. "I should have known you'd have our backs."

"You had your own back. Every call that comes through nine-one-one is recorded." She made a low whistle. "Fortier was screwed in multiple ways that night. It's really over for him."

"I can't believe no one found him before now."

"Like many of 'em did, he made his escape during Katrina. Records either conveniently vanished in the flood or he persuaded them into vanishing—he's linked to a half-dozen other similar scammers. God only knows who—or what—is directly responsible."

"They just let him walk out of prison."

"Imagine the burden of the prison guards. Water's rising, the prisoners will die in cages, so the guards turn 'em loose. I don't blame 'em. I wouldn't want it on my conscience."

"I suppose." Shel was obsessed with conscience and choice of late. She finished her beer and set her empty bottle next to the cop's. "So Fortier walked, but stayed in New Orleans. That's a brass balls move right there."

"The guy turned himself into a local hero. Anyone who gave him the eye had their palms quickly greased, and in the end nobody was in a terrible rush to do anything about it. I supposed they reasoned it was forgery and theft, not murder." Milford paused, arched an eyebrow. "Well, not until now, anyway. That was a fortunate confession you got out of him, whether you intended to or not."

"I intended to try and stay alive," Shel confessed. She pictured Fortier with his gun trained on Addison. "I only hoped he'd kill me first."

"I know how badly that worked out for you the last time," Milford somberly said. "I'm glad you shared that story with me."

"Adrenaline makes me spill my guts." Shel referred to a conversation they'd had on the way back to Naples. Milford had come to retrieve her after days of lengthy interrogation by the Louisiana Bureau. "You seemed like a good person to tell."

"By the way, your lady—Silvia Frances—she was an abuse victim herself and the key witness in some big trial against her ex, kind of like your girl. When it was over the Fibbies plunked Ms. Frances in a protection program, which is the reason for the trouble I found myself in when I checked out her files. You should have heard the FBI apologizing for putting me through seven flavors of hell once they found out I was on a case."

Shel's amused eyes flicked in the cop's direction. She grinned big. "Oh, Officer Milford was on a *case*."

"That's exactly what I told them." Milford shrugged unapologetically. She softened some. "Course I also told them I couldn't have done it without your help."

"Don't do me any favors," Shel sarcastically told her, though she was secretly pleased to have her name mentioned alongside something good for a change. She again became serious. "I'm sure Addison already did, but I want to thank you."

"Sure, kid," Milford said. "You heard anything new about her?"

"Immunity in exchange for testimony," Shel told her. She tipped her head to one side, considered it. "No prior convictions and it worked in her favor that she'd given the money back to the charity."

"I'm sure." Milford went quiet for a moment. "I was sorry to hear about your Loyola coach. Guess we didn't win on that one."

"He and Bernard Smith went to great lengths to keep her safe." Shel shook her head still disbelieving she'd so badly misread them at the beginning. "These network people are good at what they do, Milford."

"God bless 'em for it."

The sun dipped at last, casting an ocean of orange and blue watercolors across the sky in its wake. Shel leaned back in her chair, clasped her hands over her chest. "So, what's all this mean for you, Milford?"

"Promotion and a big raise."

"You serious?"

"Hell, no, I'm not serious," Milford scoffed. "It's still government."

"Yeah."

"So, I retired."

Shel lurched forward in her lawn chair so quickly she was almost folded up inside the contraption. "What? You can't retire."

"I can and I did." Milford looked more relaxed than Shel had ever known her to be. "I'm getting old, kid. That's the simple truth of it."

Shel wrinkled her nose. "You're going to what—take up golfing or knitting?"

"I'm gonna do some independent work. Kind of like what you used to do, only on the up and up."

"You're kidding me."

"Not at all," Milford said. Shel could see a slow-growing smile on her friend's face. "I should tell you there's an open spot on the Naples PD. I could put in a good word for you, but naturally you're subject to a background check."

"That interview would be over before it got started." Shel practically cut her off.

"You don't have a bad record, only a reputation for a bad attitude." She glanced at Shel's surprised face. "I was bluffing you about the drug thing. There was only mention of you not following orders given by Internal Affairs. I saw the shooting and the hospitalization and connected the dots. It was a risk, I admit."

"A sneaky risk," Shel said, half-admiringly. She looked straight ahead, muttered, "Bitch."

"Yeah." Milford seemed to take proud ownership of the title.

"Maybe you'll be better at this sneaking around business than I thought." Shel leaned back in her chair. "Thanks for the heads up about the job, but I'll pass."

"You could always pitch in and help me now and again."

"Seriously?" Shel gave her another funny look.

"Playing by my rules, of course."

"You and your honor and integrity," Shel pretended to grumble. She then raised her voice, aiming her words in the direction of the screen door behind them. "She's not even my boss yet and she's already horrible to work for."

Addison toed open the flimsy door and stepped onto the narrow cement porch juggling three new beers. She set two on the space between them and clicked her tongue admonishingly. Shel grinned brightly at the sight of her, happy to have her firmly on board.

"She'll need a contract," Addison put in, not missing a beat. She plopped down on the cement slab next to Shel's chair and leaned her head against her shoulder. Her eyes flicked skyward as she contemplated. "And benefits and insurance."

"Benefits and insurance…?" Milford nearly choked on the first swig of her new beer. She wiped her damp lips on the back of her hand. "I'm puttin' no such thing in writing. I'm a small business owner, for Pete's sake!"

"You have a license for that sort of thing?" Shel mimicked a line from one of their first conversations.

Addison gave a casual shrug. "I could probably whip up something that looks as good as—"

"No." Shel and Milford firmly cut her off in unison.

Addison settled back again. "Touchy crowd."

"Actually, we're about to become small business operators ourselves," Shel announced. She gave Addison's arm a quick squeeze. "We're taking over the lease on the gallery. Old guy is retiring. There's a sweet little apartment over the place. It needs a lot of work, so we'll live here for another six months or so in the meantime."

"You're kidding me?" Milford was taken aback. She nodded toward the lime-green rental house. "Then why all the trouble of reroofing this one?"

"In the old guy's contract, just like the pool." Shel rolled her eyes. "Your damned integrity is rubbing off on me."

"I saw pallets of shingles around back." Milford scratched her head. "You know what you're doing?"

"There's a kid who helps me during the day, but I'm learning quickly."

"And you've got the clams to do all that?"

"Well, while Fortier's dough is permanently frozen, Miss Kathleen Fortier had a substantial chunk of change waiting for her at a variety of places where she'd consigned her work." Shel looked proudly at her girlfriend. "There was enough to keep us in rent and school payments for a couple of years."

"Sadly, Kathleen Fortier earned more money than Addison James probably ever will." Addison spoke about the personalities in third person, looking momentarily bummed. She suddenly turned it around, confidently proclaiming, "Still, I'll stick with Addison James."

"You'll be back on top in no time," Shel said, planting a kiss on the top of her head.

"Well, I'm glad you're hanging around." Milford rose up, adjusting the waistband on her pants.

"I'll play shop clerk for a while and if that drives me nuts, I can always pursue a job as a part-time, non-contracted, underpaid assistant private investigator."

"That's a hell of a lot to put on a license." Milford retrieved her helmet from the front step. "And yes, there will be proper licensure."

"So many rules—I'll go nuts, I swear." Shel also stood up and shook the cop's hand. "Thanks again, Milford."

"No big deal, hotshot." She shuffled down the steps and hopped on her bike. In seconds there was nothing left of her but the Harley's fading rumble.

Shel sat back down and scooted aside, making room for Addison on the same lounger. Above them, the sky had blurred and was beginning to sparkle with nighttime.

"You know, I'm actually going to miss this little house," Addison said. Shel cuddled her close, kissed her.

"Nah. We deserve a fresh start. All of us."

"How's your back?" Addison looked concerned. "You've been climbing around on that roof all day. We just got back, don't you want a day of rest?"

"I need to stay busy. It's sort of therapy for me, swinging that hatchet, stomping around, making noise." After a bit, Shel nudged her. "I've been meaning to give you something."

Addison followed her inside and to the bedroom. Shel disappeared inside the closet, her voice muffled as she rummaged through the suitcase there.

"I found this a while back. I think it belongs to you."

At last she reemerged with something shiny dangling from her fingertips. Addison carefully accepted the bracelet and held it up to the dim lamplight. Her lips parted in awe. "Where did you get this?"

"At the mansion the night Fortier hired me." Almost reluctantly, Shel confessed, "The palm tree charm is what had me looking for you in Florida."

"It's not a palm tree," Addison whispered. She took a backward step, sank onto the bed, her eyes glistening over her wide smile. "It's very old. See how it's worn around the edges?"

Shel sat next to her and took a closer look at the charm, nodded.

"It's the Tree of Life. My mother designed it for the charity." Addison moved her finger along the old, worn brass. Her attention then went to the next charm, a tiny frame that contained a baby picture. "And this is my baby picture."

Shel was just as surprised. "I thought it was baby Harper."

"I haven't seen this since I was a little girl." She put her arms around Shel and hugged her close. "This means so much to me."

Shel stroked her back. "You deserve to be happy."

They were quiet for a moment.

"You know what else would make me happy?" A playful mood suddenly came over Addison. She gently set the bracelet on the nightstand and lowered her chin, giving Shel the look she most loved. She wriggled one finger, motioning toward her, whispered, "Come here."

They kissed deeply, pausing after a moment only to hastily remove and toss aside their clothes, then slid between the sheets. Their fast-advancing passion was quickly halted by the sound of Harper's cry from the small bedroom. Both women sighed then softly chuckled.

"I got this," Addison said, reluctantly slipping out of bed and back into her pajama pants and T-shirt.

"I just want us to replace all those nightmares with good things." Shel gave her a sympathetic look. "It's been a while for her. I guess I was too hopeful, too fast."

"Stay hopeful. The therapist says it takes time." Addison leaned in, gave her a quick kiss, whispered, "Be back."

"Standing by."

When several minutes had passed, Shel wondered if Addison had fallen asleep in the child's bed. Feeling a warmth and almost smugness about her sweet family, she slipped out of bed, pulled on a shirt, and quietly slipped through the house to the smaller bedroom. When she reached the doorway she froze, her smile faded and her stomach lurched.

Quietly sitting in her bed, Harper's terrified eyes were fixed on her mother. Addison stood bedside, a man standing behind her, his gun pressed to her head. Shel's stomach bottomed out, her head felt light, her vision sparkling black. She knew the intruder. His disheveled hair, scruffy face, wrinkled clothing and body odor looked a far cry from his pristine image as Richard Fortier's attorney, but certainly matched the picture of the villain in her nightmares. Shel was looking at Bobby Buchanan, a.k.a. Bucky, the man who'd shot her.

He nodded to acknowledge Shel's long-ago memory. He took a coy tone, even chuckled. "Hello there. Remember me?"

She said nothing to the man whose eyes channeled coldness and determination for his mission. She'd seen him this way before. Now, his hand gripped the gun pressed to Addison's temple. The image of her lover's face seemed to transform to the one belonging to the young mother she'd tried to defend in a seedy undercover apartment years ago. She'd also cried; next could come the part where she begged for her child's life. It was the scene that played on a chronic loop in her nightmares and she knew its conclusion all too well: they died.

He seemed to sense Shel's mental fade. "Stay with me, sister. There's business to discuss. You've got my ten million dollars and I want it—*now*."

CHAPTER THIRTY-SIX

"I don't have it," Addison softly cried. She looked at her wide-eyed, obviously shell-shocked daughter. "Turn around, baby. Don't look. Don't look…"

Shel couldn't think clearly, and this time, she had no gun to lose. She heard someone begging for the life of the child, but this time it was coming from her own lips. He laughed and cut her off.

"A real mind-fuck, isn't it?"

It was. She knew him too well. Before her mind had been clouded with Oxy, she'd studied him and knew his MO by heart. When he'd been captured, she'd made herself available to the prosecution to make sure he'd go away for a very long time. Even during her subsequent addiction and work troubles, she'd continued to follow his case. By the time he'd gone to the pen, she'd lost everything important to her.

"Buchanan," she said at last, trying her best to remain focused. "Let's not repeat the past."

"No way!" He grinned. "At least not the part where I go to prison. I'll do better this time, I promise you that. Leave no witnesses—that's my new motto. I can't tell you how well it's working for me."

It was obvious they had history, but Shel prayed he wouldn't spell it out in front of Addison and her daughter. She swallowed hard, nearly choking air lodged in her throat that felt more like a golf ball.

"Calm down," she said more to herself than to Buchanan.

"I'm calm," he mocked her. "But you don't look so hot, I've gotta say."

Addison continued to sob. "I don't have the money—didn't you see—"

"We don't keep that kind of money. Not at the house—do we look crazy?" Shel loudly stomped all over Addison's intended confession, as it was clear Buchanan had no knowledge of the anonymous donation. As for news about Fortier, it hadn't yet hit the papers. She spoke before her girlfriend could jeopardize their precious position, running with a lie that she was creating on the spot. "It's in a building we rent."

He blinked several times, as if trying to decide whether or not she was lying to him. At last, he snarled, "I call bullshit."

"Really?" Shel made her best effort to appear confident, but not to the degree that he would harm his primary hostage. She refused to even allow her eyes to glance at Addison's face. She was in full-on negotiating mode. "You want to toss the place, be my guest. There's no money here."

More blinking and staring. "How about I shoot the kid and then you'll tell me?" He seemed nervous, spittle flying from his mouth with his rising anger. "Better yet—how about you choose who I shoot first. Will it be this one?" He shoved the gun hard against Addison's head causing her to cry out in pain. "—or this one?" Buchanan then pointed the gun at Harper. Both women reacted in a flurry of words and pleas that was clearly music to his ears. "Well then. I guess I know who to start with."

"You harm her and you'll not get a thing," Addison said, her fear having given way to anger. While Shel could appreciate the mother's willingness to protect her daughter, her eyes dispatched a desperate plea that Addison remain quiet.

"The money is in a safe, inside a building near the city dock," Shel said calmly, but firmly.

"How do I know you're serious?" His glistening forehead, coupled with the mounting stench emanating from him, said he was worried. He again jammed the gun hard into Addison's side. "Huh?"

"We leased a shop." She scrambled for bogus details. Details made the difference between a believable lie and a poor one. "You'll see the balance is down ten grand—that's first and last month plus deposit."

He appeared bewildered at the information. "If you're lying to me, I'll kill all of you."

"The key is in the other bedroom." She cast a quick glance over her shoulder. "Let's go."

"Uh-uh," he shook his head, made his point clear. "Everyone goes."

"That's unnecessary," Shel calmly insisted.

He again employed a mocking tone. "I'll tell you what—they can stay if I kill them. Since you've witnessed my work, I'll let you decide."

"Fine, fine," she hurriedly agreed.

He harshly pushed Addison down onto the bed. She quickly recovered, moving to comfort whimpering Harper.

"No time, Mama. Let's go." He waved his gun, earning a glare from her. She scooped the child into her arms and held tight to her and followed along as Shel led the group to the larger bedroom. "Get the key—what are you doing?"

"I'd like my pants," Shel told him, motioning toward her bare legs. "It'll raise a few eyebrows if we all march out of here looking this way."

He glared at her. "Hurry up."

Shel plucked a pair of jeans off the floor and gave him a look. When it was clear he wasn't planning to turn even slightly to offer her privacy, she hastily pulled on the jeans. Not moving quite as quickly due to the child she wore on her hip, Addison also followed suit, slipping into a pair of shorts she'd earlier discarded. She struggled to button them with her only available hand, speaking comforting words to the child all the while.

Shel went to the nightstand and pulled open the drawer. Her gun box was there, open and empty, her gun still in the custody of the Louisiana Bureau. He stood in the doorway, his gun trained on her, giving her no choice or time to think. She fished out the key and closed the drawer. Perhaps at the city dock they could manage to flag the attention of overnight security. It was highly doubtful they would be armed with anything more than mace. Perhaps she would think of a better plan on the ride, but that also seemed doubtful given the state of her nerves and the preciousness with which she regarded the lives presently on the line. There was no safe at the gallery, and that would make Buchanan plenty mad. Things would end quickly from there.

She raised the key to show him. He impatiently nodded and glanced over her shoulder at Addison whose quick movements were making him jumpy.

"Blondie—chill the fuck out."

"I'm getting my shoes," she mumbled.

"Where you're going they don't need shoes." He again motioned toward the doorway. "Let's move."

She stepped into one tennis shoe but clumsily kicked the other one under the bed. She got down on all fours and waved her hand beneath the dust ruffle, finally reemerging with the missing shoe. She stood and stared at them, still holding the shoe. Preoccupied by concerns Addison couldn't possibly fathom, Shel didn't even blink.

"Let's go already!" Buchanan shouted, clearly at the end of his patience. Shel started for the front door, but he crudely grabbed at her shoulder, digging his fingertips into her collarbone. "Back door. No need to draw attention."

He'd actually touched on Shel's deepest fear because she knew something he did not. They couldn't draw attention to themselves if they marched out the front door and sent up a flare. It was the off season and the neighborhood was empty.

He herded them out the back door and into the black night. While Shel's internal panic skyrocketed, Addison's tears had stopped and she now seemed extraordinarily calm. As she was still wearing only one shoe, Shel wondered if her girlfriend was in shock. It was when they were being roughly ushered down the few steps that Shel caught a glance inside the shoe and suddenly understood the reason for Addison's cool demeanor. It didn't do much to alleviate Shel's worry, in fact, her anxiety hit fever pitch.

In a seemingly flawless move, Addison dropped the shoe and pointed a tiny revolver at Buchanan. "Drop the gun, you son of a bitch."

Though clearly surprised, Buchanan snatched a hand out and roughly yanked Shel to him as he stumbled over the threshold of the door and into the backyard. Recovering his balance, he pressed his gun against Shel's temple and grinned.

"Drop it," Addison repeated, also stepping into the backyard. Even if there was a chance she'd never hit a thing she was aiming for, her look of intention was spot-on. Without removing her gaze from his, she allowed the toddler to slide off her hip and down her leg to the ground. In her most serious tone she said, "Baby, you go around to the front of the house. Mommy's going to make the bad man go away. Hurry. Run."

Shel watched the child scamper past a pallet piled with bundles of shingles. She then disappeared into the thick shrubbery that ran along the side of the house. She felt the gun jam harder against her temple. She swallowed hard and took shallow breaths.

"Ballsy move, I'll give you that," he said. In the night, his wide toothy grin made him look like the Cheshire Cat. He took a few steps backward, his feet sliding on discarded shingles, making for uneven footing. He'd put about five feet between them, still clutching tight to Shel. "You must really not give a shit about your girl here."

Addison behaved like it was business. "You shoot her, I kill you."

"Fortier was right—you are one stupid bitch."

"Now," she said, ignoring his jab. "Drop it."

"Stupid," he repeated, chuckling. "You really think you can hit me with a single shot from a snubby? Let me explain something to you, sister—that's a mere toy compared to what I'm holding. Inaccurate as hell even for a seasoned shooter." He momentarily lifted his gun away from Shel's temple, looked at it admiringly. "Now this here is a real gun. One shot, she's dead." He replaced the gun against Shel's temple, nodded at Addison. "How fast is your recovery? Mine is record breaking. Then my second shot is for *you*."

Addison still stared at him without budging. Close as they stood, her eyes showed clear signs of concern. It was all he needed to know he'd won. Buchanan quickly upped the ante by cocking his gun while it was still pressed against Shel's temple. It was the loudest, most dramatic sound she'd ever heard. She clenched her eyes shut and when she reopened them, Addison looked thoroughly rattled.

"Drop it, now," he demanded.

"Honey, listen to me," Shel quietly begged of her. Her voice cracked when she explained, "I've seen this before. He'll shoot me anyway. Don't put down the gun."

Addison's gun lowered a slight bit, but her confidence was rapidly disintegrating. She shook her head, tears sprang to her eyes. "No."

He seemed to be enjoying the exchange. "I would say do put down the gun, but that's just me."

His words caused Shel's head to buzz; she'd heard the same threat years ago, only there was a different hostage and it was she holding the gun.

"Don't listen to him—I'm telling you." Shel's words were firm as she earnestly looked into Addison's eyes, sending her an unspoken warning to hold tight to her gun. Her soft words sliced through the night. "He will kill me anyway. Just get out of here."

"All this talk about me—like I'm not here." Buchanan laughed and pulled Shel close, giving her arm a twist that caused her to flinch in pain. "Are you willing to find out? Are you willing to watch me put a bullet through your girl's head?"

Addison meekly raised her gun in surrender. Shel's legs suddenly felt too weak to hold her. It would be just as she said: he'd first kill her then Addison. It would be over with inside of two seconds, and who would protect Harper…?

"Drop your gun, dirtbag."

The familiar voice bore an unfamiliar intensity. Eyes wide, Shel scanned the dark backyard for its source. Officer Milford's short, shadowy form could be seen emerging from the side of the house, gun out in front of her.

Buchanan was as surprised as anyone. He thrust his gun out before them, nervously firing a round in the direction of her voice.

Milford wasted no time returning fire. He ducked, pulling Shel down to the ground with him. She landed hard. In her peripheral vision, she was aware that Addison was also on the ground, hands scanning the surface for her discarded weapon. Buchanan got off two more shots as he dragged his hostage with him behind a low pallet of shingles. He leaned out and fired again. Shingles exploded, raining asphalt dust onto them. With her face forcibly pressed against the ground, Shel's movement was restricted. She blindly reached out her arm, feeling the grass and crumbled shingles for anything that would help. She tasted the tarry dust in her mouth, felt dry crumbs in her eyes, but her focus was on something out of reach, gleaming in the light from either a sliver of moon or a distant streetlamp.

Another shot and she heard him grunt and she wondered if he'd been hit. His momentary release of her was all she needed. She rolled away from him, grabbed the handle of a rusted shingle hatchet and gracelessly scrambled to her feet.

"Milford!" she shouted, hoping not to be mistaken for Buchanan as she rounded the low piled pallet. In the darkness, she slipped on shingles, making very little progress toward safety. She didn't know where he was, could feel him everywhere…

At more gunfire she dropped into a squat. Her adrenaline had peaked and the sound of her heavy breathing filled her ears as she crawled toward the house. The sound was loud, and then she realized it wasn't entirely her own. Buchanan grabbed her foot, pulling her back toward him like the monster he was. She dug the hatchet into the ground, attempting to anchor herself. More shots said Milford was zeroing in on them. She hoped Addison had gone to Harper…

She attempted to get on her feet, but he pulled her back to him. In her awkward position, she put her full weight behind the effort, and jerked the hatchet from the ground as he pulled her upright. She spun in his hold, nailing him squarely in the forehead with the crude tool. His maniacal expression didn't alter right away, but his gaze somehow drifted upward toward the weapon lodged in his head. It was as if Buchanan himself couldn't believe he was dying.

He emitted a horrible gurgling death sound to the background of continued gunfire coming from both directions of the yard. Momentarily supercharged with adrenaline, she held tight to the hatchet handle, keeping his body in front of her as a shield against wildly flying bullets. His body flinched with the hits until she couldn't hold his weight any longer.

"Hold your fire!" Milford screamed.

As Shel released her grip on the handle, the heavy body fell against her, dropping them both into the pool with a splash that felt more like a tidal wave. Exhausted and with hurt emanating from everywhere, Shel heard faint sirens amidst frantic above-water screaming. She was helpless under the dead weight pushing her downward, dragging her like a stone to the pool's bottom. Her mouth tasted of blood, her eyes sparkled blackness and then nothing.

CHAPTER THIRTY-SEVEN

Shel drifted in and out of consciousness, aware that she'd been fished out of the dark pool, fretted over then transported to a hospital. She'd come around some when the doctor checked her over, moving limbs that didn't feel like they should be moving, causing her an unbearable amount of pain before they mercifully induced temporary sleep.

When she awoke again, she was groggy. Her arm had been immobilized in an elaborate sling, and she knew she'd been shot, but to her relief her body appeared to be otherwise intact. Her gaze roved the very limited view of the patient bay: dim lights, a clock illuminated with 4:42, a white board listing contents of her IV, and thankfully beneath the board, Addison, sleeping in a chair, Harper cradled in her arms.

Shel attempted to sit up, but fell back in pain. At this time of night, they didn't need to be awakened anyway. Behind them, a rotund outline could be seen through the milk-glass door. Milford entered the tiny room and quietly went to Shel's side.

"I'm awake," Shel told her in a low, grumpy tone.

"Just wanted to check on the patient." Milford's shock of red hair wildly bounced as she shook her head. She kept her voice low. "You look a sight. How bad is it?"

"Just a nick. I'll live."

"Scott Buchanan," Milford said. "I take it you're familiar."

Even nodding caused Shel pain.

"Must have surprised the heck out of you, given your history." Milford tipped her head slightly, looked contemplative. "Must say, he didn't look nearly as suave with a little hatchet sticking out about right here." She pointed to her forehead. "You got him, all right."

Shel was still struggling to connect the dots. "He was in prison. I saw him go with my own eyes."

"Sprung during Katrina, just like Fortier." Milford tossed a look over her shoulder at Addison and quieted her voice. "He tracked down his defender, took his life then assumed his whole identity. Fortier's former inmate became his lawyer and partner in crime."

"Nobody seemed to notice that the lawyer looked altogether different?"

"They didn't look all that different to begin with. Little work here and there made up small differences. Attorney Dubois wasn't married and had no family. Buchanan told everyone he'd been in a car wreck and had some short term memory problems."

"These guys had an answer for everything."

"Had is correct. It's over." Milford settled down, looked thoughtful. "I'm sorry it happened to you, but it's like I told you, nobody's bigger than the law."

Shel leaned forward and attempted to get her water cup. The pain in her shoulder stopped her short. Milford motioned for her to lay back and handed her the cup. Shel took careful sips before handing it back. "Where'd she get the gun, anyway?"

"Me—where else? I didn't think she'd actually use it. It was more for confidence." Milford smirked. "Twice in a week one of my personal pieces is in official custody. Now, how's that make me look?"

"Like someone dumb enough to loan out her gun."

"And just how was I to know you two were going to keep shootin' people with 'em?"

Shel's eyes flitted toward the chair where Addison slept. She touched her shoulder, whispered, "I'm lucky this is the only place she got me."

"About that part…" Milford replaced the cup on the rolling patient tray. She took a small backward step looking guilty as hell.

"What?" At first Shel didn't follow then at once her eyes went wide. "Wait—*you* shot me? Milford, did you shoot me?"

"I didn't do it on purpose, for the love of Mike." It was Milford's gruff attempt to calm her. "I was just trying to neutralize the situation. It was you who was swingin' a guy around on a stick."

Milford made a rough pantomime and beneath Shel's grim expression was laughter she could barely contain. "I will remember you shot me."

"What—you want to shoot me now?" Milford turned slightly more serious. "I've never seen anyone do that with a roofing tool."

Shel managed a tight grin. "Face it, Milford, I've made your life a hell of a lot more interesting."

"You picked up the pace around here, that's for sure." Milford stared at the bulging gauze wrap on Shel's shoulder. "They do a good fix-up job on you?"

"It'd be better with some real pain meds instead of whatever they've got me on." Shel winced. A new thought occurred to her. "Why'd you come back to the house?"

"Went to Stopwatch Diner for a bite and decided to take a spin down to the beach." She gave a nonchalant shrug. "Rode past your place, baby's in the front yard, I called for backup."

"Thank you," Shel told her. "I'm saying that a lot lately. I'm starting to feel indebted."

"Don't think of it that way. Think of it as being beholden."

Shel painfully shifted, drew in a sharp breath. "That means the same thing."

"Does it?" Milford brightened, heading for the door. "You're a pain in the ass, you know that, hotshot? See ya around."

At the sound of the door closing, Addison awakened. She rose and carefully placed the blanket-wrapped tot on the chair. Coming to Shel's bedside, she clasped her hand, smiled. "How do you feel?"

"Like I want to get out of here." Guarding her sore shoulder, Shel scooted over in the bed. Addison carefully lay down next to her. In seconds she was tearful against Shel's good shoulder. "It's okay. Everybody's all right."

After a bit Shel said, "Funny." Her lips flinched into a momentary smile as she looked for words. "All I wanted to do was save you. Get you away from that life and that terrible person. But it turned out to be you who saved me."

Addison was still tearful and her voice was tiny, childlike, "I heard you say you thought I shot you."

"No way," Shel quickly told her, patting her back. She reupholstered the statement. "Well, I thought you shot me a *little*."

Addison's mouth flinched into a quick smile and they shared a soft laugh. After the moment, she again turned serious.

"There's still so much to do. There will be hearings and testimony and the press will be a nightmare." Addison's sparkling eyes locked on hers. "Will it be too much for you? I wouldn't blame you if—"

"We'll do it." Shel clasped Addison's warm hand, raised it to her lips, and kissed it. "We'll do every bit of it together."

Bella Books, Inc.

Women. Books. Even Better Together.

P.O. Box 10543
Tallahassee, FL 32302

Phone: 800-729-4992
www.bellabooks.com